In the fourth millennium humans finally invent the warp-drive and set out to explore the Galaxy. The first mission is sent to our nearest star, Alpha Centauri, and the starship returns to a stormy acclaim.

It then comes as a shock when aliens visit earth and announce that the Galactic Federation intends to lift its quarantine around the Solar System. Since humans now have the warp drive, would they like to join the Galactic Federation?

This story brings humanity for the first time into contact with a variety of alien life-forms: elfin-like creatures, dinosauroids, insectoids, and many more when Embassies are sent to other worlds. As the humans fan out from their home world they encounter a number of adventures which shape humanities future for generations to come, like floating cities in the sky.

The story comes full circle when it culminates in another first contact, but this time from another galaxy making first contact with the Galactic Federation.

Worlds Beyond Ours

Sasha Garrydeb

London

2011

First published in Britain in 2010

by ABC Publishers

24 Treadgold Street London W11 4BP

e-mail: abcpublishers@ntlworld.com

Printed in GB by ABC Publishers

A CIP catalogue record for this book is available from the British Library.

ISBN 978-09548144-4-1

ABC Publishers,
Notting Dale,
London W11 4BP

Some contextual visuals illustrating the story's settings

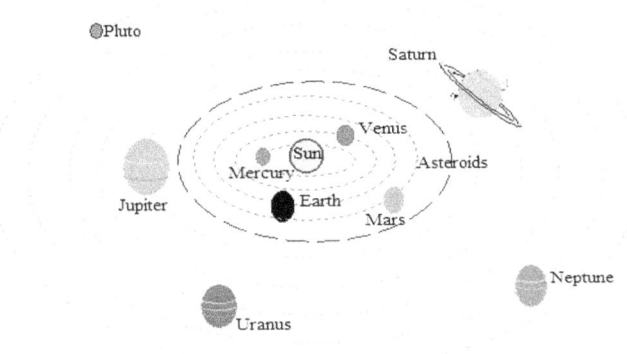

Our Solar System

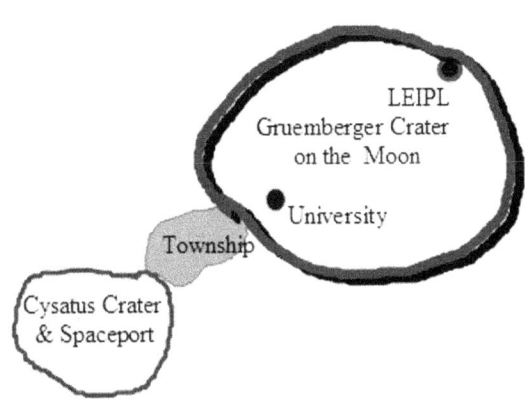

The Lunar Experimental Interstellar Propulsion Laboratory
at Gruemberger Crater on the Moon

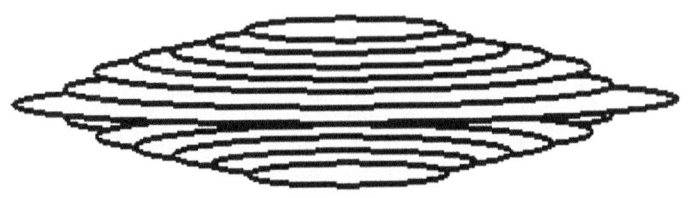

The Liquid Metal Starcruiser
of the Visitors

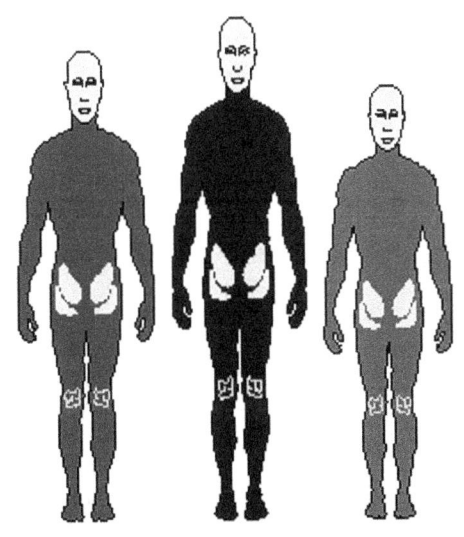

Ufi   Kileni   Velred

The Visitors from the
Galactic Federation

Centaurus Constellation

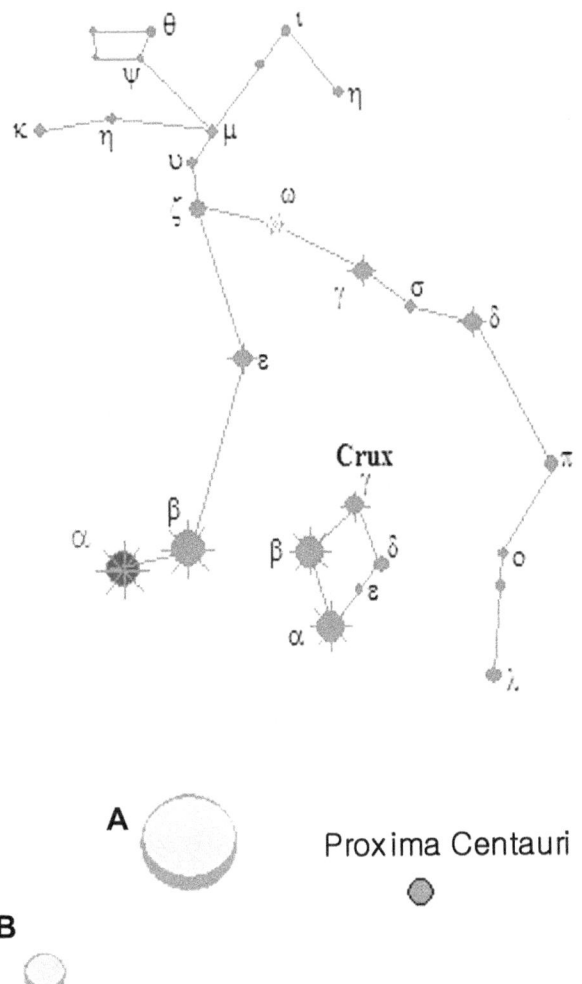

Alpha Centauri A is a yellow star similar to our Sun; Alpha Centauri B is a smaller and a more vividly orange sun; Proxima Centauri is a dim red star at a great distance from the planet.

The distance between Alpha Centauri A and B is 25 times the distance of the Earth from the Sun.

The Galactic Federation

The Milky Way

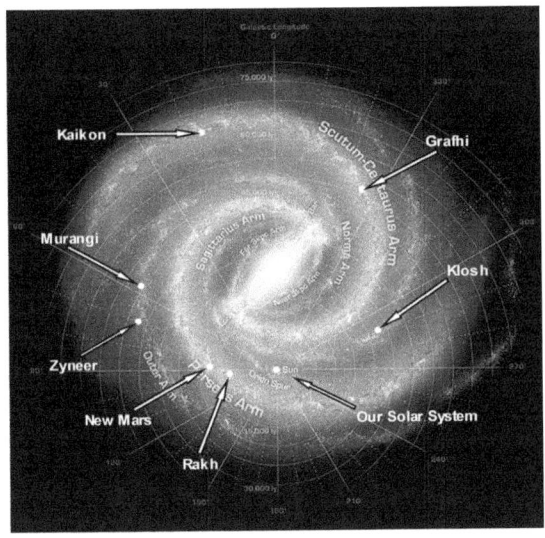

Galactic Quadrants

Kaikon	Grafhi
Zyneer	Rakh

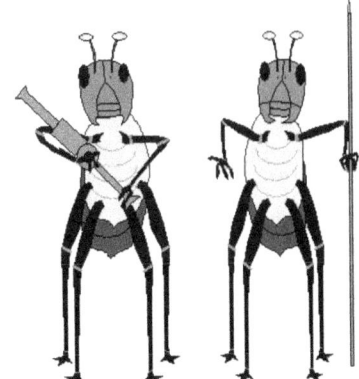

Sterile Female Warriors of
the Rogue Klitka Hive

Royal Palace Guards

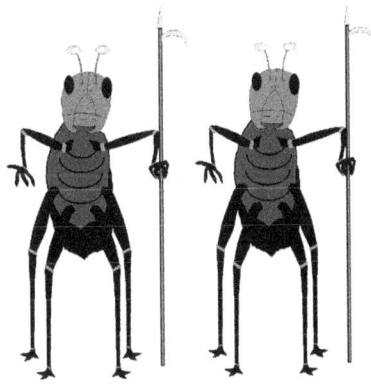

Zind Hive

Contents

Chapter One

A Meteor Too Far

'**H**ow the hell's it doing that?' Sven's voice was getting edgy with frustration. 'It's still accelerating...'

'You're asking *me*?' Gina said incredulously, eyelids rose in mock astonishment.

'I'm just talking out loud,' he tried to excuse his outburst.

'Are we close enough to get some readings?'

'Yes we are—well...it's not Taenite or Kamacite,' he was scratching his scalp through his blond hair.

'For the benefit of our viewers: can you be more explicit?'

Sven turned his Nordic features to the camera, 'Most meteorites are composed of alloys such as Taenite or Kamacite, generally made up of eight common minerals, usually involving combinations of iron, nickel, magnesium and some other elements. That thing—out there,' he waved at dark space, 'is something else. It's not anything I've come across. It's registering a light composition.'

'You mean it's alien?' Gina cajoled.

'You keep sticking this word "*alien*" in all the time. What *I'm* saying is, I don't know *what* that is...I want to make sure you're taking *in* what I'm saying.'

'Yes, thank you Sven. I do hear what you're saying.' She tried not to look disappointed. A frown expressed itself under the flat crew cut, all the rage with fashionable women that year.

'It looks hot; it looks like a meteor, but the instruments say otherwise. To top that, the speed...well it shouldn't be doing that. Frankly, I think we should turn back.'

'You were *chartered* to get to within five kilometres of that fireball. We're a good five *thousand* kilometres from it. Do you want to be known you're someone who couldn't keep to your side of the bargain?'

Sven acquired a pained expression at the gibe. 'All right...*all right*. Have it your way. I'll try to catch it...but be it on *your* head.'

She shot back with a smirk, 'It always is.' She swept her right hand through her short black stubbly hair in a show of assertion. Arizona dark features determined to dominate any situation.

After a few minutes, the Holo-camera captured the silent intensity of Sven's efforts in the cockpit to gain on the meteoroid. Ryan heard Sven cursing under his breath—in Swedish.

'It's no good,' Sven finally spat out. 'I can't catch it! It keeps accelerating. Every time I gain a little, that *thing* out there pulls away from me. It's playing cat-and-mouse.'

This looks like the beginnings of a good public squabble, Ryan thought, gazing at the Holocast. *Might even end up as one of those old "ambulance chasing soaps,"* he chuckled under his breath.

Captain Ryan was on a mission with orders to clear the path of the Conway meteor of all sightseers. Glued to the Holo-Vid, he tried to relax his muscle bound physique in a sturdy chair in his cabin, leaving his Number One to manoeuvre the SpaceCruiser *Nautilus* along the projected route. He ordered the Holo-Vid to tune into the next Holocast from Gina Young, the intrepid reporter on *Solar Challenger.*

A little while later, the holographic face of a woman exuding enthusiasm again appeared on the wall of the cabin, catching Ryan's attention.

'This is Gina Young live on board *Solar Challenger* bringing you an update on our exclusive story of the Conway meteor. We've almost caught up with the meteor as it speeds its way through our Solar System. Sven Tjockensen, the famous explorer and our intrepid pilot seems to think the meteor's somehow changed velocity, preventing us from getting close. Tell us Sven; you sure the meteoroid has altered pace?' The Holo-camera switched to Sven's rugged features.

'Yaah, I'm sure. When we set out to chase that fireball, I registered it at a constant 343,000 kph, or Mach 287. Now I'm registering 497,000 kph and escalating

'Sven—what's behind the speed increase?'

'I've *no* idea. I mean, how can an ordinary meteor increase speed?' His puzzled face told all.

'Good question Sven. How *can* an *ordinary* meteor change speed? So you're saying its *no* ordinary meteor?'

'Don't put words into my mouth. I'm not saying *anything*. I don't know. Let the scientists; the so called experts, sort it out.'

'Thank you Sven. We're going to accelerate, try and catch up; *that's right isn't it Sven?*'

'If you say so! It's *your* money.'

* * *

Sometime earlier, on Earth, the Holo-Vid in the corner of President Ying Li's large wood panelled office gave three loud bleeps and switched itself on. It was programmed to record news of the spectacular meteor heading through the Solar System.

'Please stand-by for an important news bulletin,' a male disembodied head announced. 'The Conway meteor this station has been following for the past week, has just sped past Pluto and entered our Solar System. We go over live to Gina Young, our Reporter in the Pluto Biosphere, watching the meteor go by. What can you tell us Gina?'

A woman's hard face replaced the disembodied head. She was trying to keep from shivering on camera, encircled by a freezing atmosphere and the immense dome structure in

3

the background. The five-kilometre dome sat on a plateau, framed by the unmistakable craggy cold blue-white scenery of Pluto, stretching to the dim distant horizon.

'This is Gina Young coming to you live from Pluto. I'm standing outside, having just watched the Conway meteor pass this planet,' the woman reporter was enthusing, 'and it's caused a furious uproar amongst the watching scientists. The vast majority are claiming whatever passed us here on Pluto, could *not* have been a meteor. They say the Conway meteor's profile is completely wrong—for a meteor, that is. It isn't heavy enough, or dense enough—for a meteor.

'Some go as far as to claim it's an alien ship. The one item they all agree on is the speed's *not* under gravitational control. But if it's not propelled by gravity, then one has to ask, what *is* it propelled by?' She paused for effect. The camera caught the frozen humidity of her breath drifting away. 'A number of scientists suggest that the meteor slowed down appreciably as it entered our Solar System, as if it were manoeuvring, trying to avoid hitting any of our planets.

'Others are calling that "fanciful" and "wishful thinking," questioning how a meteor could possibly slow to manoeuvring speed.' Again, she put in a pregnant pause. 'This reporter's about to board a chaser-craft to get to the bottom of this controversy. In half-an-hour I'm going to board the Space-yacht *Solar Challenger,* piloted by the famous explorer Sven Tjockensen. We're going to get close enough to the meteor to definitively answer the all important question of, "Is this a *bona fide* meteor—or not?" Please keep tuned to our exclusive gripping updates, to the dramatic twists in this exciting story. Only Holocast Earth Station-45 has this exclusive story. Stay tuned!' The Pluto Holocast ended and the original disembodied male head reappeared.

'Off Holo-Vid,' commanded President Ying Li. *These damn Holocasts get sillier and sillier*, he thought. *Aliens indeed! They'll do anything to stir up some sensational interest. Even now, at the beginning of the fourth millennium, they still hope we're as gullible as we used to be.*

On-board *Solar Challenger* the soap continued: 'Why aren't we gaining on it?' Gina was saying in a demanding high-pitched voice.

Sven's gruff response came back, 'Cos the damn thing's accelerated again.'

'Well, put some speed into it,' Gina shouted.

The tiny camera was faithfully recording the public *tête-à-tête* between the intrepid reporter and the gruff explorer.

'Did you hear that folks! This is Gina Young coming to you live from *Solar Challenger.* We've been pursuing the Conway meteor for the last half-hour. As you just heard, it seems to be pulling away from us.'

'*Captain*!' It was Ryan's Number One on the intercom. 'We've just received orders from Space Corps HQ to abort the *Solar Challenger*.'

Ryan answered in his flat Boston accent, 'Is that right? I'm watching it on Holo-Vid—right now.'

'Yes sir, but we've been ordered to abort.'

'How far are they?'

'They're just coming past Saturn's rings right now, following the meteoroid.'

'Right! Let's get to it.' If Ryan was to make headway up the ladder of the Space Corps, he learnt to be prompt in complying with orders from Corps HQ. 'Contact the *Solar Challenger,* give them the bad news.'

'Yes sir!' snapped his Number One.

Ryan's cavernous green-blue eyes watched the Holo-Vid as Sven received a call from the SpaceCruiser *Nautilus* advising it to break off pursuit.

'I'm on charter to Earth Station-45,' Sven told his caller, as if it was sufficient response to the request.

There was a pause on the Holo-Vid as Sven listened to Ryan's Number One ordering Sven to call off the chase.

Sven turned to Gina. 'I've *orders* from the SpaceCruiser *Nautilus* to abandon pursuit of the meteor,' Sven told the camera, and Gina.

'They can't do that. Ignore it,' she snapped.

'I can't. They tell me I'll lose my space pilot's licence if I don't obey immediately.'

Gina took the opportunity to perform on camera. 'Folks, we've just been ordered to abandon our attempt to verify the authenticity of the Conway meteor by the SpaceCruiser *Nautilus,* in violation of our human right to freely travel the space lanes. Our distinguished pilot, the famous explorer Sven Tjockensen's been blackmailed into complying, by threatening his licence. We've no choice but to abandon this mission, reluctantly and under protest. I'm handing you back to the Studio.'

The Holo-Vid returned to the disembodied male announcer. Ryan turned the Holocast off.

'Number One?' Ryan spoke into the intercom imbedded in his left shoulder epaulet.

'Yes sir!'

'This business of the meteor accelerating—I think we'd better investigate, don't you?'

'If you think it's necessary, Captain.'

'I think it might be wise. Set a course to intercept.'

'Aye aye, sir.'

The *Nautilus* came about, and headed for the looming bright red meteor. The aggregation of speeds, both of the meteor and SpaceCruiser produced in short, an encounter.

'Number One? Set a parallel course, keep her steady at a distance of fifty kilometres.'

'Aye Captain...*Sir*? We're losing it!'

'Say again?'

'The meteor sir, it's moving away from us.'

'Are you sure? Double check that!'

Try as they may, they couldn't keep up. Reluctantly, Ryan had to admit the meteor accelerated at a rate inconsistent with an inert body. At that point, the meteor displayed an extraordinary burst of speed, behaving as if it contained a powerful engine, an engine propelling it towards light speed. Ryan's on-board neuro-computer extrapolated the speed it would reach, if it maintained current acceleration. His red bushy eyebrows shot up as he heard the computer's predictions.

'It's not possible,' was his despondent, lame comment.

Boniface, the computer analyst who brought Ryan the news, shrugged, 'That's what the machine predicts, sir.'

'I'm not blaming you Mr Boniface. I just find it hard to swallow.'

*   *   *

It took the meteoroid another half a day to pass through the rest of the Solar System, accelerating inexplicably. By the time it left the Solar System, it reached a speed deemed impossible by current science; namely, it exceeded the speed of light. At least, the instruments recorded that, the ones trained on the weird object.

It caused uproar amongst the scientists, confusion held sway, one section insisting it was only a bizarre lump of rock, despite contradictory evidence. A larger section insisted the meteor was the long sought after evidence for extraterrestrial life.

But with nothing to show for the latter, except Holo-Vid footage and instrument recordings, it was neither here nor there whether there was life out there. If the fireball was some kind of spaceship, it didn't stop to say hallo, didn't change anything in the Solar System. Well, that's not entirely true; it generated a lot of heated arguments.

Since Earth Station-45's involvement was intended to grab people's attention. A lot more people were sucked into the argument than was sensible for any kind of informed discussion. Questions were asked at World Government HQ. Ying Li as President of the World Government received a lot of flack from people looking to exploit a controversial public episode for their own ends.

One more consequence of the object's swift visitation was that Sr. Perez, the World Government Commissioner for Science was asked to put more impetus into the faster-than-light research at LEIPL, the Lunar Experimental Interstellar Propulsion Laboratory on the Moon.

Chapter Two

Kiron

In the space of a few years, human history was to undergo profound upheavals. The interstellar Starship *Kiron* returned from Alpha Centauri, bearing news of a habitable planet. That prompted more belated millennium celebrations.

The festivities were promoted by the giant R-Tech Corporation
. Their androids built the Starship for the mission to Earth's neighbouring solar system 1.34 parsecs away. The year was 3003 AD.

It took nearly four weeks for the *Kiron* to get to Alpha Centauri. Two weeks of exploration and surveying, and four weeks to make the return journey. A mere astonishing ten weeks to complete a voyage humans could only have dreamt of in their thousands of years of serious stargazing and millions of years of evolution.

* * *

The human race roamed the Solar System for nigh on seven hundred years, always constrained within its boundaries by the photon drive, only able to explore their own lifeless planets. True, Europa, Jupiter's second moon, wasn't lifeless, but the life it contained was at a primitive stage of evolution. The huge thirteen meters long worms swimming in the waters below the thick ice derived their energy from chemosynthesis, swimming around thermal vents of Europa's crust.

Elsewhere, robot probes sent beyond the Solar System reached a certain point, then inexplicably failed. There was no way of determining why?

So, the development of the warp drive at LEIPL, was able to release the innermost desire of humans to explore the outer reaches of their Galaxy.

Up until the beginning of the twenty-third century, the principal interplanetary drive was based on a pulsed nuclear reaction engine propelling a spaceship by a series of nuclear fission explosions. At the end of the twenty-third century, it was replaced with pulsed fusion engines.

By the twenty-fifth century the photon drive was the norm, and until the invention of the warp engine, most of the interplanetary flights were based on improved variants of the photon drive. The photon drive worked by annihilating equal amounts of matter-antimatter, releasing nuclear gamma radiation directed in a collimated beam through a special thrust chamber at the rear of the ship. Since the photon drive was forced to carry all its matter-antimatter onboard the spaceship, realistically it was confined to travelling the Solar System.

It needed the impetus of the bizarre Conway meteor to suggest there must be some form of propulsion system able to break Einstein's impediment. There *was* Holo-Vid footage of something travelling *beyond* the light barrier. Much as the sound barrier had been broken in twentieth century, LEIPL was set up to break the light barrier; even before the Conway incident.

❊   ❊   ❊

The LEIPL laboratory went deep into the northern side of the imposing grey-black Gruemberger Crater. The Crater at the Moon's South Pole was eighty-seven kilometres wide, two kilometres deep, with a smooth floor.

It was chosen as the base since all the ice was gathered there at the Moon's South Pole, much needed for oxygen, hydrogen, and water. The Main Township and University burrowed deep into the looming south-western rim. The strengthened maze of tunnels and habitats went fifty kilometres into the direction of the neighbouring Cysatus Crater, connecting the township to the Space Port.

Everything was reinforced against continual moonquakes, a constant feature of peoples' lives. The less severe happened daily, whilst big crustal ones usually occurred monthly, more intensely during perigee. To add to the problem, incoming meteorites peppered the surface. Larger ones incoming roughly once a month, too small to cause craters visible from Earth, but severe enough to produce lingering reverberations. Taken together with the destructive solar winds, it compelled the original builders to fabricate down deep into the Moon, seeking some form of protection from the surface hazards.

LEIPL's Director, Patanjali, was a tall, wizened, cranky old genius with a thin brown parchment face, penetrating brown eyes, aquiline features, shaggy grey hair, and a white goatee beard. He was beginning his two hundred and forty-ninth year of longevity.

Born at Lucknow in Uttar Pradesh in 2754, he looked like the average person's perception of the serious minded Professor. Invited to live on the Moon over a hundred years ago, he still maintained a razor sharp mind, belying his appearance. He claimed the Moon's one-sixth gravity would enable him to live forever.

Professor Jawahal Patanjali spent a lengthy time as a leading academic at MIT, Massachusetts, lecturing on astromechanics and general astronautics to groups of young students, more eager than talented. He watched, dismayed, as all the brilliant astro-students fought for a chance to enrol at Gruemberger Astronautics University, at the Gruemberger Crater on the Moon.

When he reached a hundred and fifty, Patanjali decided a move. Conscious of the termination policy on Earth, he informed his wife and three sons of an offer of a Chair at the Gruemberger University. He firmly intended to take up the post.

His wife agreed without argument, but all his sons had wives, families with families, grown grandchildren; many held important positions on Earth. They declined to follow their patriarch. He pleaded for them not to break up their extended family, but to no avail. So in 2904 he moved to the University on the Moon; there for fifty years, Patanjali lectured to eager *talented* students, thoroughly contented with his lot.

His research produced some amazing innovations, for which the Nobel Committee honoured him, bestowing a second Nobel Physics prize in 2954, for inventing interfaces controlling the conversion of energy into mass, using Hermian crystals. Rich veins of Hermian crystals were discovered fifteen years back in the Caloris Mountains off the Plain of Odin, on Mercury.

As a direct result of his newly acquired second Nobel Prize, he was offered the prestigious post of Director of LEIPL by Rodrigo Perez, the World Government Commissioner for Science. Patanjali moved to LEIPL from the University, located on the other side of the craggy Gruemberger Crater. For the next forty-seven years, he worked all the hours he could squeeze from a day, trying to unravel the physical theories that would allow him to break through the light barrier.

Every novel approach he tried seemed to end in some obstruction. He concocted numerous experimental variations, using unique methods. His tests near lunar space gave many a fine firework display when they failed. Recently he settled on the potential of the Hermian crystals, fiddling with their matrices. Somehow, his instincts suggested *they* held the key. He tried to solve this prodigious problem, but each time failed to approach it from a satisfactory angle.

Patanjali added to Schadenglaube's theoretical research on faster-than-light propulsion of three centuries earlier, but converting the theory into a functional drive was proving a real stubborn challenge. Previous progress in that region was stalled for centuries; many a promising avenue of research ran into a *cul-de-sac*.

*   *   *

Following the Conway incident, Perez concluded it was time to bring some new blood into LEIPL, encouraging a re-focusing of the research under the irascible double Nobel Laureate.

The difference was finally made by the arrival of Leonard Hopkins. He was reassigned as a Research Assistant from Gruemberger University, by Perez. Hopkins was a *cum laude* student with a number of major prizes under his belt for his research in astronautics. Leonard was a physical contrast to the Director, slightly balding with a chiselled face, thick-bodied, medium height, and deep clear blue eyes. Perez's computer profiling suggested he might be just the fellow to revitalise Patanjali's efforts.

At first, the old man thought the young man pushy, and kept him busy with petty tasks. Hopkins was totally irrepressible, performing each given task with energy and distinction. Eventually Patanjali felt ashamed at having treated the young man in such a shabby manner.

One day, he took him into his confidence. 'Leonard, come over here. Look there,' he pointed to a lab top, 'that is the model I've devoted my recent energies on. This is the research you were sent to help me with.'

Leonard sauntered over to the Holographic model rotating on a square in the middle of the laboratory table.

Patanjali continued, 'I've unlocked all the relevant files...all the models on the neural computer. I want you to have a good look at them, and...I'm inviting your comments.'

The young man's face lit up and his eyes shone fiercely, staring into the Holographic model. 'Professor! I don't know what to say. I'll try not to let you down.'

Patanjali finally gave Hopkins the run of the project he'd sweated over in his recent years; the monumental work of his prodigious brow.

After a couple of weeks, the youth began to work far longer than Patanjali, way into the night. It became clear he was becoming obsessed with the problem. Two more weeks, then Patanjali began to worry over the young man's health. He resolved to have a friendly word with him.

Yet the old man let another couple of weeks slip by—then after a particularly tiring day; he approached Hopkins.

'Leonard—I don't want you to take this the wrong way, but I've been noticing all the late nights you've been putting into the lab.' He looked benign. 'I think you really ought to slow down a bit.'

'You don't know the half of it,' Hopkins said with a half smile, looking a little furtive. 'I think I've cracked it.'

'*What!*' exclaimed Patanjali. 'You mean....'.

Hopkins couldn't contain his excitement, 'It's all down to those crystals. I've reconfigured three of the matrices, added another couple of phases. The figures on the η-photons are beginning to reach 3×10^9 meters per second on the model, and that's just past the speed of light.'

'But I thought we agreed to use the τ-photons in the model?' queried Patanjali.

'It's all down to the extra phases,' went on Hopkins as if he hadn't heard the query. 'You were stuck on varying the matrices, but adding the phases and using the η-photons turned the tide. If we now substitute the tachyons in place of photons....,' he left the sentence hanging, so Patanjali could fill in "the eureka" moment for himself.

'*...we might have a drive capable of producing a varying thrust past the speed of light,*' Patanjali finished in an excited rush. More calmly, 'It'll give us the speed we need to create the rift into curvature.'

'Without your previous work Professor, I wouldn't have managed it,' said the young researcher, somewhat diffidently.

'Thank you kindly, but I must say the same for your work. Without your contribution and perseverance, I would still be stuck at the point where you found me when you joined me; remember that in the coming months.'

Patanjali sat down heavily, and in one-sixths gravity; it wasn't an easy accomplishment. As foreseen, the low gravity was kind to his human frame, but the years still had taken their toll. It would seem his life's work had come to a fitting conclusion by the serendipitous efforts of one Rodrigo Perez, who sent him this talented Research Assistant.

The rest of the week was spent re-calculating the model's figures; making sure the results they obtained, would stand up to scrutiny from their peers. Even when they satisfied themselves the theory was sound, and the results error-free; Patanjali would return to the neural computer and re-calculate the numbers again.

After all this time, all the effort expended, all the years he put in, he just couldn't believe the light barrier finally fell, and in such an unexpected manner. Once the rest of the community accepted their findings, Patanjali was certain; Hopkins would receive a Nobel for his work. He was going to push hard for it on Hopkins' behalf. Then there would be the next stage; building a Starship for the practical test-run of their invention, for a cruise around the galaxy.

It wasn't long before the grapevine informed Perez of the breakthrough, and Patanjali got a call from the World Government Commissioner for Science.

'Congratulations,' said the holo face of Perez, beaming with a self-satisfied smile.

'Commissioner!' exclaimed Patanjali in mock surprise, as he looked on his benefactor. 'To what do I owe the pleasure of your call?'

'Quit the sarcasm,' said Perez, face serious. 'Have you begun to develop the outline for test-running your invention?'

'In fact, I'm building the bicycle right now,' Patanjali responded straight-faced.

'What bicycle? What are you babbling about?'

'The one we're going to ride through the galaxy!'

'Metaphors—and at your time of life. So how long before we *really* start building?'

'It depends on not hitting any snags,' came the serious response.

'But you're the *astromechanics expert*, Professor.'

Came the dry reply, 'Yes, and I still have to produce the plans.'

'Well, all right. I'll let you get on, but I'm coming to visit you in two weeks; I'm warning—now. In advance.'

'Thanks for the warning—and... thanks for Hopkins,' he added more gently. Patanjali's voice took on a sincere tone.

* * *

The Lunar spaceport situated at the Moon's South Pole was inside the grey shallow forty-seven kilometres wide, high rimmed Cysatus Crater, linked to the Gruemberger Township. Before her momentous journey, for eighteen months, the Starship *Kiron* was readied beneath the floor of Cysatus Crater. The lab, backed by World Government, took on a large number of astromechanical engineers, all working overtime on a mass of plans, trying their utmost to speed the construction of the Starship. It seemed as if every member of the work force was staring at plans on their portable holoprojectors.

Perez's lightning visit came. He authorised the entire Moon's facilities be concentrated on the building of the *Kiron*, as the new Starship had been named. In tow, he had a number of his fellow Commissioners from the World Government who came to see what the fuss was all about—and what the trillions of credits were being spent on. As usual, reporters tagged along to record the event.

One pushy reporter managed to sidle up to Perez and pushed a mini-mike into his face. 'Commissioner Perez? Could you tell our viewers why the starship's named *Kiron*?'

Perez pinned the reporter with his gaze. 'And you're...?'

'Gina Young from Holocast Earth Station-45.'

'Well, Ms. Young.' Perez looked straight into the camera, 'If the destination of the first Starship is to be the Solar System's nearest neighbour, the Alpha Centauri triple system: then it's only appropriate that the name be associated with the Centaurs of ancient Greek mythology. Are you familiar with the mythology?' He paused, knowing full well she wasn't—and wouldn't contain herself.

'No, I'm not—and I'm sure most of our viewers are as ignorant. Maybe you would be kind enough to explain.'

Chalk one up for the reporter. She managed to turn that one nicely, thought Perez. 'Kiron of mythology was unlike the other Centaurs,' he began, 'He was descended from Kronos and Philyra; as wise and kind as the others were brutish. He was well versed in all the arts, in medicine, a friend of Apollo and tutor to many of the mythological heroes. It was Zeus, so the story goes, who sent him into the heavens as the Centaurus constellation, to perpetuate his immortality, and it seemed only fitting to bestow his name on a ship visiting his immortality.'

'Hmm. That's a pretty story. Thank you Commissioner.'

*   *   *

Within a year of the invention of the warp drive, the superstructure of the *Kiron* was finished; thanks largely to the androids leased by the R-Tech Corporation to the World Government. The warp drive was something else. Problems were being thrown up all the time, as they worked to the limits of materials technology. For a Starship to be able to travel through space at above light speed, it had to have a way of shielding itself from the interstellar molecules, dust particles, gas and other debris found in space.

* * *

Patanjali enjoyed showing off the project to visiting dignitaries. So much so, that the PR people scheduled regular promotional tours to encourage a positive image about the project to fellow scientists, politicos and the general public. It generated free media publicity, providing stories and holo images for the press.

One Senator from the European Federation politely asked Patanjali on one tour, 'How does this new warp engine work?' Not really expecting an answer was surprised when Patanjali launched into an explanation.

'The fuel for the ship comes from interstellar debris. The energies involving such collision are enormous, and have to be dealt with by shrouding the ship in a force field, capable of deflecting and absorbing the encountered energies.' Patanjali didn't really care if the Senator was listening or not; he continued. 'On the other hand, the ship requires energy to convert into matter, and one of my previous inventions, the "energy⇒matter" converter, was the obvious solution. The enormous energy encountered could be absorbed, then converted into the required tachyons.'

'Tachyons?' queried the bemused Senator.

'Faster-than-light particles detectable by Cerenkov radiation—given off like the shock wave from a sonic boom.' Momentarily, Patanjali felt he was talking to an idiot. The thought flitted through his mind, *fancy not knowing what a tachyon was.*

The Senator stared at Patanjali open mouthed. All he could mutter was, 'Oh!' He was a financial wizard sent to discern where the credits were vanishing—and listened to the explanation as to a foreign language. Through his mind went, *what the hell's he talking about?*

Patanjali blithely continued, 'It was clear a method needed to be found for storing the redirected energy from those interstellar collisions. For this we designed and built an exa-condenser sink surrounded by a containment field.'

The Senator realised Patanjali didn't care if his listeners understood him or not. He simply enjoyed talking—*at* people.

Patanjali addressed the rest of the party as though they were his students, 'When fine-tuned, the energy collected, fed into the "energy⇒matter" converter, producing tachyons. The tachyons fed into Hopkins' Hermian crystal configuration, and functioned in a manner similar to lasers being focused by diamonds in ruby crystals.' Patanjali took a pause, looked at his audience—smiled, and continued. 'The Hermian crystals had the property of refocusing and enhancing the tachyons discharged into the field-contained thrust chamber. This produced warp drive, far in excess of what was needed to break the light barrier. We added a photon drive for sub light travel, so in effect the *Kiron* has two types of engine.'

The Senator stopped—punched some keys on his wrist computer, then beamed a broad smile at Patanjali. The rest of the Senatorial party copied their leader—and all smiled.

Patanjali took this as a sign of approval—smiled back at them and launched into the rest of his speech. 'Finally, all the technicalities of the warp drive were resolved and the immense engine, yoked to the photon drive, was installed on the Starship. Earth weight, the ship weighed over 10,000 tonne but only 1,667 tonnes Luna weight. The $^1/_{20}$ th lift-off energy and the $\frac{1}{6}$ th moon weight was the prime reason the ship was constructed here on Luna, other than my presence of course. All the construction materials were either fabricated on Luna, or shipped from Earth.'

'And how many crew are there to be?' the Senator's young female aide queried

Patanjali frowned, 'The *Kiron* has a complement of 400 crew.' He thought, *What a mundane question.*

'And who's to be the Captain?' the female aide persisted.

'Ahh! That's still classified.' Patanjali wagged a finger at the aide. 'The Captain of the ten week mission was chosen from a large number of highly experienced space captains. There was a rush of applications for such a prestigious assignment, as you can imagine. Enormous kudos is going to surround the first Starship Captain. He'll climb rapidly through the ranks, making him comfortably off in the process. He's going to obtain any position he subsequently desires. When we inform the selected candidate, only then will we publish his name.'

'So it's a *he*—is it?' she smirked.

'The ship itself is equipped with unheard of luxury accommodation.' Patanjali pointedly ignored her gibe. 'The psychologists seem to think it's essential. It's been decided to set a new standard for this class of ship. The final design, the Ergonomic Psychologists insisted LVF be included or "long voyage factor," mitigating for an absence of years from the Solar System. It's supposed to give the crew a degree of comfort thought to be indispensable for their mental health. These new Starships are to be the precursor to a fleet of such star roaming vessels, sent out to the far reaches of the Galaxy, to explore and report their findings. The fleet is intended to transport colonists to new worlds, to expand human horizons from their humble Solar beginnings, out to the far reaches of the unknown.' Patanjali stopped, seemingly satisfied—turned to the Senator, smiled again, and walked off, leaving the party staring at his back.

The Senatorial party had expected a smooth-talking PR person; instead, it got this cranky old scientist talking techno-babble at them.

By early 3003, the Starship *Kiron* was ready for its maiden voyage. It was scheduled to depart Moon spaceport when commissioning and testing were completed.

* * *

Captain Patrick Ryan's earpiece informed him there was a message left for him at the Cape York Spaceport information desk, in Queens land, Australia. It was the news he'd been waiting for. Good or bad, finally he'd have a clear idea of where he stood.

He'd been travelling the Solar space lanes for over a hundred and twenty years, and was still hungry for adventure. When the grapevine told him the World Government was looking for a Starship Captain to command the first warp drive ship ever built; he didn't hesitate, and energetically applied for the job.

After an in-depth barrage of psychometric and academic tests they started on his experiences and knowledge base, putting everything through sequential modelling programmes. The results were extrapolated to determine whether he was able to handle the new ship and the simulated emergencies. His childhood, parenting, schooling and service record were taken apart, examined. His recent career, picked over and thoroughly scrutinised. In short, nothing was left untouched by the examining panel. One incident worked heavily in his favour; the recent encounter with the Conway meteor as the Captain of the SpaceCruiser *Nautilus*.

He was informed firstly; he was short-listed for the post. Now he was waiting to find out if he'd succeeded —or failed. When he got to the desk, he found two messages and a parcel.

They could have teleported this stuff to me, he muttered angrily.

His parcels caught up with him where and when they could. Sometimes by teleport, sometimes by post. The hundred and thirty year old middle-aged blonde at the information desk eyed Ryan appreciatively, playfully teasing him before giving him his mail. She looked at Ryan, a tall well-built man, with a shock of red hair, bushy red eyebrows, cavernous green-blue eyes, a strong nose, a square jaw to match the square shoulders—and fantasised. He was always given a favourable look by the ladies. He claimed it was his smart sky-blue Space Corps uniform, in which he radiating a hard competence.

The first message came from the Director of the interviewing panel, officially written on simul-paper, informing him he'd been given the job of captaining the *Kiron*. The second message was from President Ying of the World Government, wishing him success in his endeavours, also on simul-paper, which just added to the importance attached to his new position. There was a plasto-parcel containing a silk sky blue cravat from his woman friend in Brisbane. She saw him when she could; didn't complain—treating it as part of life for a spacefarer's lady.

Ryan's earpiece announced Rodrigo Perez, 'Hallo! Am I speaking to Captain Ryan?'

Ryan answered in his flat Boston accent, 'Yes.'

'I want a quick word with you. Firstly, may I add my congratulations on your new job, and your promotion to Commodore. Secondly, I want you on the Moon for simulator training as of yesterday.'

'Thank you for the first. As for the second,' Ryan objected, 'I had plans to do a little celebrating.'

Perez's voice hardened, 'There'll be plenty of time to celebrate when you get back; now is the time to knuckle down and get to work. I want you to catch the next Moon Shuttle and report to General Hoffmyer; he's in command of the Centauri project.'

'Yes Sir.' There was no arguing with that tone of voice.

*　　*　　*

The Moon Shuttle swung out of the hyperbolic orbit and entered the descent flight path for the Gruemberger Spaceport at the Moon's South Pole. Touchdown was smooth and the craft settled into the platform clamps. The platform descended into the space lounge, whilst the overhead outer doors slid closed. When the landing yawning closed, the lounge was re-pressurised. The Shuttle doors opened, and the passengers disembarked along the moving floor of the swinging flexi-tube, down to floor level.

'Will Commodore Ryan please report to room 5A on Level 7,' Ryan's earpiece ordered.

Ryan was familiar with the Spaceport, having often been there, and made his way to where he was instructed. He knocked, and entered the office of the Spaceport Administrator. Behind the desk sat, a middle aged lithe looking individual whom he knew to be the Administrator. On a sofa against the wall, sat a portly military gentleman whom Ryan assumed was General Hoffmyer.

Hoffmyer stood, extended his hand. 'Good day to you Commodore. I trust you had a smooth flight.'

'Yes, thank you,' responded Ryan, shaking the proffered hand.

'You may be familiar with Administrator Singh,' said the General, 'being an old spacefarer, you must have been here before.'

'Hi Ranjit! How's the wife?' Ryan offered in the direction of the Administrator.

'Oh! Very well, thank you Patrick.'

Hoffmyer continued, 'Well! Down to business. We've booked you into the Gruemberger Excelsior, and I want you to go down to the Programmed Learning Centre on Level 11, and get acquainted with the *Kiron;* look for the PLC sign. You'll find your crew members down there; they're being programmed as they land from all corners of the Solar System.'

'When do I meet the great man?'

'You mean Patanjali?'

'Yes, Sir.'

'Now all the senior members of the crew have arrived, we're having a little dinner party tonight. You'll meet him then: casual dress. Eight o'clock sharp in the Excelsior Dining Rooms.'

'One more thing, Sir! How close are we to lift-off?'

'All being well, two weeks from now.'

'*Yes, Sir,*' retorted Ryan, unable to suppress the excitement in his voice.

'Now, go along, and get settled in,' said the General, pleased with the look and enthusiasm of his fellow officer.

Ryan said goodbye to Ranjit and the General, and headed for the Hotel, intending to shower and change his uniform. After a meal in the Hotel restaurant, he wandered down in the direction of the PLC. He found the Centre where the General said. He already knew it from previous visits, and reported to reception.

The same nurse behind the counter, reminded him of Hospitals, stern white uniform. The Centre was anything *but* a Hospital. Programmed Learning was the normal way of cramming information, on any topic of choice. For this visit, it was solely devoted to all the technical requirements the new crew of the *Kiron* needed to acquire.

Ryan was taken to a small room, its only furniture a single robust reclining chair in the middle. The technician asked him to take a seat, then engaged a restraining field holding him immobile. He felt as if being restrained by a wad of cotton wool. The halter was essential to keep his head perfectly motionless, enabling the schema matrices in the brain to be replaced exactly in the identical position. A snug helmet transponder was lowered over his cranium and the technician proceeded to adjust his console.

Ryan felt drowsy, closing his eyes for a minute, only to hear a voice trying to awaken him, 'Commodore! We've finished. You're free to go.'

Ryan shuddered briefly, then sat bolt upright. He mumbled lamely, 'I keep forgetting how quick this procedure is.'

Searching his new memory implants, he realised he had all the technical specifications for the *Kiron*. Names and faces of the upper echelon of his new crew, their backgrounds, all there. He now contained the memories of all astronomical data for the route to Alpha Centauri, the triple star system in the Centaurus constellation.

There were no side effects to what he went through, if anything, he felt refreshed. He left PLC with a spring in his step, not a wise move in one-sixth gravity. He nearly lost his balance, but years in space taught him lightning reflexes, and he compensated. To someone watching, they would have noticed nothing more unusual than a wobble in a hurried walk.

*   *   *

The dinner party was a great success; the Commodore got on well with Patanjali. A bigger surprise was Hopkins and Ryan hit it off. For the next couple of weeks, they were completely inseparable. Both men respected each other's expertise. One, a boffin as near to being a prodigy in his chosen field, the other, an exceptional spacefarer who roamed the Solar System. Ryan experienced countless adventures, done all the things the boffin would have liked to. Both complemented each other, and they swapped stories and experiences.

At the last moment, Hoffmyer gave his consent to Hopkins joining the crew of the *Kiron.* This was mainly at the insistence of Patanjali, who in turn was being cajoled by Hopkins for him to be included on the expedition. From an emergency viewpoint, it made sense to include one of the designers of the warp engine as part of the crew.

Patanjali felt far too old to re-adjust his routine to such a journey; which left Hopkins. Neither previously had been included because PLC had done such an effective job on the on-board Engineers, who now knew nearly as much about the warp engine as either of the inventors. On the off chance something unforeseen occurred on the voyage, Hoffmyer relented and gave his permission for Hopkins to go.

The *Kiron* was readied for a test run, intended to metaphorically clear its throat and show up any problems before the actual voyage. The photon drive was old technology, in use for many centuries now, but the warp drive was unknown and needed a good test-run.

On the neuro-computer, the model worked perfectly, and if everything had been put together the way the plans indicated, then it should work first time. Ryan ordered the crew to embark; invited Hopkins to board, and took the ship out past Pluto, some 60 billion kilometres from its Moon base.

It was ten times further than any human travelled from the Solar System. It took them just over a couple of hours to make history. The Solar route was cleared of other spacecraft to avoid accidents.

The distance chosen allowed the photon drive to engage and take them the first 100,000 kilometres. Then the warp drive engaged only for a second, speeding them past Pluto at Warp 2, decelerating the last 100,000 kilometres.

The return trip took another two hours, frankly amazing everyone on board. Despite having the reality fixed in their long-term memories, the actual excursion itself was an unbelievable adventure. It was as if they wandered into a magical fantasy.

Some doubted they travelled that far, but the ship's log confirmed it. It left the crew astonished. The warp drive worked like a charm, making Patanjali and Hopkins overjoyed. Hoffmyer was ecstatic with the results, and the log was copied for posterity, to go into the space museum.

*   *   *

Three loud bleeps and a Holo-Vid switched itself on in the corner of President Ying Li's large wood panelled office. The President was elsewhere. It was pre-programmed to record the momentous news of the *Kiron's* lift-off.

A familiar male disembodied head announced, 'Please stand-by for a major news bulletin.' A pause. Then, 'Only Holocast Earth Station-45 has this exclusive story. We go over live to Gina Young on the Moon.' The story was in fact, exclusive to every Holocast station in the Solar System.

The well-known face of the intrepid reporter replaced the disembodied head. 'This is Gina Young coming to you live from the launch ceremony at Moon Base. We're just about to witness President Ying's wife; Madame Ying Ji, name the *Kiron* here at the Moon's South Pole, in the forty-seven kilometres wide, high rimmed Cysatus Crater.'

The Holo-camera swung onto Ying Ji, saying to a gathered crowd representing the World Government, 'At last, the moment has arrived for humans to leave their cradle, their evolutionary birthplace, to voyage to the neighbouring star system for the first time. It is a tremendous symbolic juncture in the history of the human race. A little like the grown child reaching maturity, leaving home, blessed and seen off by their parents.'

President Ying, flanked by Perez and Hoffmyer, with a group of hand picked eminent scientists and politicians were looking pleased with themselves, watching the *Kiron* officially named.

Gina Young enthused, 'Now comes the moment we've all been waiting for. Madame Ying Ji has finished speaking and is about to name the Starship.' Again the pause. 'For those of us privileged to be here in person, the atmosphere is electric,' Gina Young confessed. 'The hard holo image of an immensus of Champaign, that's ten times the standard bottle for those not acquainted with their jeroboams and rehoboams, is just about to hit the stern of the new Starship right...now— metaphorically, of course, smashing against the side. A real bottle is simply impracticable on the Moon.'

Ying Ji recited, 'I name this ship *Kiron*, and may fortune protect all those who travel in her.'

'The crew are saying their farewells and boarding the Starship now.' Gina Young was telling the viewers. 'Captain Ryan is shaking hands with President Ying, who, according to our pick-up, is wishing him "*bon voyage*." Now, at the bottom of the ramp, Captain Ryan is shaking the hands of all the other dignitaries—before embarking. That's it. They're all aboard.'

Chapter Three

New Earth

The *Kiron* lifted into the dark blue serenity of deep space, heading for the brightest star cluster in the Southern sky. Outward-bound on the adventure of all adventures. Commodore Ryan occupied the Captain's chair; his experience suppressed any outward signs of excitement coursing through every fibre of his body.

'Set navigation for the Centauri system,' Ryan commanded.

'*Aye, sir*,' responded Lieutenant Delgado, an old shipmate of Ryan's.

'Helm, when we're done with impulse, set speed at maximum, Warp 6.'

'*Aye, sir*,' came from Lieutenant Oblomov, 76 years young and ever eager to please.

'And Mr. Oblomov, kindly change out of those brothel creepers when you get a chance, it's not an example we need to set. This is a Space Corps crew, and discipline *will* be enforced.'

'Yes, sir,' Oblomov reddened; embarrassed.

'Number One! We're going into deep space. You're familiar with the law of imbuggerance—keep your eyes peeled. Stay alert. You'll take the first dog watch; I'm going to bunk down for a while.'

'Aye aye, Captain,' acknowledged Kochanowski, shortened to "coach" by the crew. The "coach" captained a spaceship for over twenty years, but eagerly took second fiddle to get on the *Kiron*. A typical Pole out of Gdansk, hard as nails, rugged 94 years old, medium height, blue eyes, dark tousled hair.

Two weeks out, Ryan thought the crew might appreciate a break. He ordered a half way *chéile*. A little folk music, dancing, and song. They rotated the partygoers, so the ship ran smoothly. It was a great success, much appreciated by the crew.

Outside, warp speed made observation impossible. All that could be seen were strings of elongated light beams confusing the senses. Light wasn't passing them, but streaming in the opposite direction, away from them. The contradiction didn't prevent the crew from spending endless hours watching the dizzy illuminations from the observation lounge.

Control of the voyage was under the latest navigational neural computer. Delgado kept a human eye on it—just in case; four other cross-control computers interrogated all five computers. The warp engine was linked to the main neural computer, and would decelerate the ship five billion kilometres from the Alpha Centauri system. They would then close under impulse power, easing them to their destination—the G2V main sequence star.

The crew carried on with their routine maintenance. Hopkins spent hours in the Engine Room, checking and rechecking the warp engine, having a great time with the crowd there. The rest of the ship was under the watchful eye of the Captain and his Number One. PLC oiled the crew into an unruffled well-disciplined bunch, making their performance seem as if they'd been doing this sort of thing all their lives.

*   *   *

Deceleration caused great excitement, as the *Kiron's* photon drive engaged, switching to impulse power. Their arrival provoked those not on duty, to rush towards the observation lounge. They gaped at the celestial marvel spread out before them: the first humans to see their neighbouring star at close quarters.

On a dais near the captain's chair, Ryan had the triple Alpha Centauri system on his holo viewer. He looked hard at Alpha Centauri B in its long procession. The real-time image was overlaid with the eighty-year cycle describing an elliptic around Alpha Centauri A. The latter, a bright yellow dwarf star not unlike our G2 Sun, burning just as hot—just as brightly. In the holo viewer it was framed against the deep blue of space, the data had it as the "primary," one half of a binary, magnitude 0.27.

Its travelling "companion," Alpha Centauri B, was a much smaller orangey sun, magnitude 1.17, circling Alpha Centauri A anticlockwise every 79.92 years. The orbits of A and B at minimum was 11.2 Astronomical Units, at maximum 35.2 AU. Currently, as Ryan stared at the holo image, B was at 11 o'clock in its procession around A. They calculated the distance between A and B at 25 AU, or 25 times the distance of the Earth from our Sun.

The Omega Centauri globular cluster insisted on distracting Ryan, sitting in the lower right quadrant, outshining their objective. The cluster gave the impression someone had splattered the area with a spoonful of rice, making each grain wink at him, a tight middle radiating outwards.

Ryan forced himself to ignore Omega, concentrating on his mission, the binary. He was looking for planets circling α Centauri A.

'*What's that!*' yelled Ryan, swiftly pointing at a receding light disappearing into the Omega cluster. 'Mr. Delgado, replay the last twenty frames.'

As the holo frames replayed, the first few frames held a shiny accelerating object; it didn't look like *any* shooting star.

'Didn't you notice this?' Ryan confronted Delgado.

'No sir. I was distracted by Alpha Centauri itself.'

'Right! Now you see it; what'd you think it is?'

'Could be a comet. Computer! What's that receding light?' Delgado tried to shift attention to the computer.

From the computer came, 'It would seem to be an artificial body.'

'What makes you say that?' Ryan queried, taking over the interrogation.

The computer replied, 'The acceleration wasn't constant. Only an artificial body travelling under its own power could vary its acceleration.'

Contempt in his voice, Ryan continued, 'You telling *us* it was travelling under its own impetus? A spaceship of some kind?'

'That's my conclusion on the available data,' the computer confirmed.

'That's *impossible!*' insisted Ryan. 'I mean....' he broke off; brow furrowed. 'It's not the first time we've had such anomalous sightings,' he muttered, speaking mostly to himself.

He could do little about it—so he dismissed the evidence. When the bridge silence became overbearing, Ryan told Delgado to log it as a UFO, and in future—to keep his attention on his job. He then returned to the problem at hand.

'Mr. Delgado! Monitor the computer's measurements of Centauri A. You know the score. Energy, mass, density, the works. Then the same for B.'

'Aye, Sir.'

'Above all, I want the planets; their data.'

The swift answer came back, 'Two, Sir.'

'Well, import them.'

Delgado busied about importing the planets.

As the planets appeared in the model, Ryan said, 'Good! There they are!' After a pause..., 'Mr. Oblomov, take us on a straight course for the planets.'

'Yes Sir.'

As ordered, Oblomov decreed the computer manoeuvre the *Kiron* to mid point between the two planets.

'Navigation! Which one?' Ryan tested Oblomov.

'Well Sir, the figures suggest we make for the one tinged with blue. The other seems dead.'

'Yes! That's my choice,' Ryan agreed. 'Helm! Set us in orbit round the blue planet.'

Oblomov swung the helm to follow the skipper's directions.

Ryan told the computer to map the planet's magnetosphere.

'Is there an atmosphere, Mr Delgado?'

'Sort of,' observed Delgado.

'*Yes....Lieutenant?*'

'Well, it's not breathable, but it's got potential. There's even water vapour,' Delgado qualified.

'What about life signs?'

'Some flora, no sign of fauna—on land or sea. The climate's unstable. All down to the binaries.'

'Mr. Kochanowski! Make ready the shuttle. Stand by with the landing party.'

'Aye, Captain.'

'I want the landing party in suits; you know the drill. Full reports, lots of visuals, lots of samples. I needn't tell you to screen the samples—*before* you bring them aboard!'

Irked, Kochanowski responded, '*No* Captain!'

'I'd like you all back in about eight hours, *and* I want a summary on the hour, every hour. I don't want you out of contact with the ship at any time. Carry on, Number One.'

Kochanowski took control of the shuttle, swinging out of the port dock as soon as the bay doors opened. The twenty strong landing party were apprehensive, chattering incessantly amongst themselves, easing their nerves. The shuttle entered the atmosphere, and began to glow red with friction—before the force-field dampeners cut in. There was little buffeting to speak of, and soon they were through the minimal cloud cover.

An alien beauty greeted them below. A landscape of red sandstone with patches of what looked like blue shallow seas. Earth was mostly covered with water; this panorama was the reverse, mostly land with patches of what appeared to be water.

They set down on flat ground, half a kilometre from a cliff overlooking a large body of water. To the right lay a sandy valley with a river roaring down to the sea. The landing party disembarked, all experiencing the heavier gravity of the planet.

Kochanowski gave orders for the geologists to scatter and start taking samples. Instead, they simply stood in their suits, staring at the two suns in the azure blue-sky, a third red dwarf clearly visible through their visors. The view of the orbiting Centauri A sun, from the ground—was breathtaking. They were on a planet in a system containing the three closest stars to Earth, some seven thousand solar-system-diameters from home.

Centauri A hung in the sky as large, as bright, as their own yellow Sun. To the left hung Centauri B, smaller and orangeier. To the right, Proxima Centauri, a dim reddish star 0.19 light years from where they stood.

'I share your awe, but there's work to be done,' intoned the "coach." 'Let's get those samples started; measurements taken, flora analysed. I want a sample of the sea and river water. *G-e-t   t-o   i-t!*' he yelled into their intercoms.

Reluctantly, the scientific crew dispersed, whilst six Space Marines erected a force field, a 100-meter *cordon sanitaire* around the shuttle. Standard procedure —just in case. Instruments from above reported no fauna. So far, all they'd seen were plants; dwarf palms and shrubs. The ground looked dead; no insects or anything else crawled on the red soil. The plants seemed familiar, needing nitrogen, phosphorus, and potassium— these were in plentiful supply. Sub-soil Geophysics Holo-Imaging suggested the flora propagated by root diffusion. That meant a shrub type or weed was really one big plant. The implications were mind-boggling.

The planet generated a magnetic field, trapping electrically charged particles, giving a sort of Van Allen zone protecting the flora from the sun's raw radiation. The skies were quiet—empty, unsettling some of the crew. Even in their pressure suits, the silence felt eerie.

Time went swiftly, uneventfully. The scientists concentrated on allotted tasks, collecting, measuring. Many felt they'd hardly begun, when the landing party had to return to the shuttle. Samples were quarantined. They made ready for the return to the *Kiron*. This time however, there seemed to be a storm brewing; clouds looked dark and heavy.

The land appeared parched, and frankly; the last they'd expected was a downpour. As the shuttle climbed inside the clouds, the buffeting intensified. Lightning flashed all around them. Kochanowski attacked a steeper angle into space trying to escape the lower layers, putting pressure on the engines. They groaned, but maintained thrust. Soon the shuttle achieved the upper layers of the atmosphere, punching through into the comforting darkness of space. The crew gave a collective sigh of relief. The "coach" sighted the *Kiron,* and headed for the port dock he'd left eight hours earlier.

*   *   *

Eight more times the shuttle was launched to different parts of the planet. Enthusiastically named New Earth, it previously had been named Rigel Kent and Al Rijil. The story was the same each landing; sparse flora, no fauna. The seas turned out to be ordinary water, with an unusually high mix of salts. The rivers contained fresh water coming from the inland mountains. Primitive plankton swam in the sea, but no sizeable life forms. The structural makeup of New Earth's flora was nothing unusual, and on Earth would have passed off merely as exotic. The plant cells contained no mitochondria, and had a number of variations in colour and cell structure to compensate for the commensurate loss of energy. One phenomenon the exo-biologists found astounding; according to computer simulated forward projections, the flora lay dormant deep in the soil for an estimated fifty years at a time—that applied to *all* the flora. It was another result of the vicious climatic swings effected by the binary set-up of the star system.

Ten days passed since the Starship from Earth arrived in the Centauri sector. Astronomers on board took a myriad of measurements, whilst from above the shuttle mapped and explored New Earth.

Ryan sat in his cabin, taking a breather, talking to Kochanowski.

'If we ever settle New Earth, the tidal waves and climate will have to be stabilised—controlled somehow,' Ryan shared with the "coach." 'When A and B are at their minimum, the heat bakes everything; at its maximum, it's glacial.'

'Yeah!' the "coach" nodded. 'I'd hate to think what the tectonics are like at minimum. I'm surprised there's any plant life down there at all.'

'That's why they hibernate during the extremes. Life's tenacious, wherever you find it.'

On another part of the ship, the astronomers inquired into the immediate sector of space they were in. They were now 4.3 light years further out from Earth; their remit; to verify a number of interesting objects nearby.

Barnard's star, a red dwarf spectral class M5 was only 2 light years away. It had a pronounced wobble. The wobble on Earth was *assumed* to be due to the presence of a number of Jupiter-sized planets orbiting the star. Would they please confirm the presence of these gas giants? The astronomers looked; yes, there were two planets in circular orbits round Barnard's star. One, the size of Jupiter with a period of 11S years whilst the other's mass was half of Jupiter and a period of 22S years.

*   *   *

According to the tight schedule, only four days were left before they were due to return to the Solar System. They still had to visit the second planet in the system they'd named Kiron, previously named Agena.

Ryan ordered the *Kiron* to make the small hop into orbit round Kiron, intending to stay there for the briefest time before leaving the Centauri constellation. Kiron was mapped and analysed. Ryan felt the need to stretch his legs on some solid ground, so he took the shuttle down to the planet himself.

Suits were essential. It had no atmosphere to speak of, and only had two-thirds earth's gravity. The planet was pockmarked with craters, completely lifeless. The only mitigating factor—it had a great deal of mineral resources. These could be mined by a future colony.

He stayed on the planet for five hours, using the shuttle to jump about, accompanied by geologists taking samples. He felt the need to do a thorough job of surveying the planet.

*   *   *

The return voyage began with a small celebration, rounding off the successful conclusion of a remarkable expedition. It may have been somewhat—premature, even rash, considered bad luck by some, to celebrate before they arrived back in their Solar System. Ryan thought the crew needed a morale booster— acknowledgement of a job well done; so he ordered the break. The excitement had been intense, and the crew needed to blow off steam. All Space Corps ships were "dry"; their normal recreation being the gym, holo-interactives, concerts, the extensive computer library, or games that didn't involve gambling. The crew were picked so their personal habits conformed to these criteria. So the ship's celebrations involved lots of special food, programmed into the "energy⇒matter" dispensers, lots of soft drinks, music and dancing. Even a concert or two by talented members.

The four-week journey homeward-bound passed without incident. Ryan stayed in his cabin for long stretches, writing his report on the expedition, reading, talking to Hopkins. He entrusted the running of the ship to his Number One. He would be recommending the "coach" as Captain of the next Starship.

Since everything worked smoothly, it seemed a prudent move, taking the pressure off the crew, always a little nervy when the skipper was around. After the four-week journey, the *Kiron* decelerated near Pluto into the

Solar System five billion kilometres from Earth. The rest of the way was on impulse power using the photon drive.

The *Kiron* slotted into Moon orbit mingling with an armada of space vessels, long distance liners, short haul tugs, Space Corps cruisers, Corporation cruisers, short hop shuttles. Anything that could get into space was in the armada. Sheer exuberance brought together this collection of assorted craft to escort the returning interstellar Starship; a space parade for the first human vessel ever to have left the Solar System.

Ryan requested a stay in Moon orbit for 24 hours. This gave the crew a chance to talk to their families, catch-up with their solar-com-mail, rest for a day. It allowed them to download all the data gathered by the expedition to the appropriate academic and governmental neural computers. They would enter Earth's orbit the following day.

*   *   *

In New Caledonia, the World Government prepared a suitable homecoming for the heroes, another way politicians had of usurping the glory, ever mindful of the coming elections. The General Assembly of the World Government went into full session. Momentous speeches were written, delivered, and self-applauded.

'We are gathered here in this magnificent auditorium of the General Assembly following yesterday's triumphant return of the Starship *Kiron* from Alpha Centauri.' Pause. 'This is Gina Young from Holocast Earth Station-45, live—bringing you these historic moments—from World Government HQ in New Caledonia. We hand you over to President Ying addressing the General Assembly.'

President Ying, relaxed, spoke at length....'These are portentous times we live in. I take this opportunity to thank the scientific community, in particular Professors Patanjali and Hopkins of LEIPL. Without their Warp drive, none of this would have been possible. The courageous efforts of Rear Admiral Ryan—and all four hundred members of his crew, will go down into the annals of exploration history with Columbus (1492), Cook (1771), Gagarin (1961), Seleni (2468), and Retegen (2654).'

Ryan's eyebrows shot up. That was the first he'd heard of his promotion to Rear Admiral.

'This momentous heroic first voyage to another star system....' Ying continued—with speaker after speaker joining in, praising the nobility of the crew, their bravery, their inclusion onto the long list of explorers who had opened new worlds.

In the meantime Gina Young was telling the viewers, 'Reports are being received of a new planet discovered by the expedition. Provisionally named "New Earth" by World Government—it's likely to make way for a significant outburst of human colonisation.'

Kiron's crew were presented with the Space Corps Exploration Medal; followed by the World Government Medal; then more medals from various governments. That was how the politicians hogged humanity's first voyage to the stars.

Global celebrations included a dazzling computer controlled firework display set-off by the space stations in near-Earth orbit. The display lit up the night sky around Earth with a multitude of stunning fractal designs, through the various time zones, following the setting Sun.

In contrast, Ryan underwent a gruelling global holo-news conference, hosted by the pushy Gina Young, designed to pacify the hungry newshounds. He concluded by repeatedly retelling the story of their journey on numerous host-shows, and how they landed on New Earth.

Chapter Four

Visitors

The World Government General Assembly in New Caledonia was in danger of turning into uproar when the President announced, to an astounded audience, he'd personally been contacted by aliens. They'd projected themselves into his office, announcing they were representatives of "The Galactic Federation," whatever that was.

Looking at the three holo forms standing by President Ying's side, various delegates demanded to know if these "aliens" came in peace?...and—what did they want?...what did it mean for the people of earth?...and—why didn't our Solar Defence Force out on Pluto pick them up *before* they entered the Solar System?

But above all, standing there like that—were they infectious?

The hall bioacoustics made it seem each delegate was standing next to the President's ear. The excellent bioacoustics, essential during normal business; now produced the impression of an obstreperous crowd, surrounding the President, about to attack.

None of the delegates needed to be physically present; holo conferencing was the accepted norm. It gave the same sensory information as their presence, but many delegates simply liked to be there—physically. Anyway, old habits died hard. The old system of "virtual conferencing" was still quite popular; it didn't require any room space, was mostly for those who couldn't afford the holographic version.

*   *   *

'These are all good questions and deserve considered answers' replied President Ying, somewhat less calm. 'It would seem this visit,' he continued above the noise, 'resulted from our Warp Probe to α Centauri A, and since we're able to go there, we've been invited to join this "Galactic Federation". They say it was the invention of the warp drive engine that *forced* this "Federation" to initiate first contact'.

The President was beginning to perspire, although the large rotunda was well ventilated from the New Caledonian heat.

*   *   *

The French had been cajoled, then obliged to relinquish New Caledonia in 2445 to the World Government, to mark the 500th year of the World Government's foundation. The long mountainous island 1,500 kilometres east of Australia in the western Pacific was not ideal, but the Melanesian Kanak population made numerous requests to the World Government to take them over, make the island a World Government Trust Territory. The innumerable referenda finally clinched the island's fate. Ultimately, it simply became the Sovereign Planetary Territory housing the World Government. Mont Panié in the northern part of the island was flattened for a massive redevelopment and the rubble transported for use as landfill to extend the landmass way out into the Pacific between Noumea the capital, and Mont Doré. It added a fifth to the island's habitable flat land. Mont Humboldt, near Noumea, was built into a mountain resort where the diplomats could retreat from the heat. The population prospered with rich pickings from the World Governments presence.

*   *   *

'I'm informed,' Ying continued, 'this Federation of theirs kept a close eye on our progress for well over ten millennia, adhering to a strict policy of non interference'.

The assembly ruckus persisted and Ying had to call for order several times before he could proceed. The aliens stood impassively amongst the rambunctious democratic exhibition.

'The Federation insisted', Ying persevered, 'each planet be allowed to develop to warp level technology by its own efforts, before contact became inevitable. It's the warp drive that makes further concealment of the Federation impossible'.

There was a further outbreak of shouting from a number of delegates, forcing Ying to call for quiet, before he could go any further.

'Gentlemen, *p-l-e-a-s-e,* be calm, there really is no need for all this commotion. If you just give me a chance to explain, all will become clear. *Firstly,* there's absolutely no danger of cross infection from their species; what you see here, he pointed at the aliens, are holo images, projected in a friendly human form. We're all familiar with that. The real aliens are still in their cloaked starcruiser circling the Earth.'

'Starships?' someone shouted, 'how many?'

'Cloaked? Are we being invaded?' yelled another furious delegate.

'I'm sorry,' said President Ying, 'but your conduct gives me no choice. I invoke a closed session of the Security Council's permanent members.'

Further uproar.

'I'd hoped to explore our momentous deliberations *in* the General Assembly, but this commotion is leading us nowhere.' Ying began pounding his gavel, ending the open session.

'We'll report back to the General Assembly on the progress of our meeting with the aliens. In the meantime —Marshals, please clear the Assembly.' Ying then pronounced more formally, 'Will the five permanent members from Asia, America, Europe, Africa, and Australasia please remain for the closed session.'

* * *

Ying Li exuded a typical Mandarin courtesy. Punctilious when it came to protocol and diplomacy. Everything about him declared he was a venerable Oriental scholar. Medium build, 176 years old, neat in appearance, jet black hair parted to the sides; thin dark penetrating eyes set in sallow flat features. He oozed charm, had a permanent smile above an evenly curved chin. Educated at Beijing and Harvard, with a PhD in Administration from Cambridge, marking him a brilliant technocrat. Originally, from Hong Kong, he spoke the local Yüeh dialect at home with his wife, Ying Ji, and spoke forty-three other languages like a native.

He scrupulously rose early each dawn, performing his T'ai Chi Ch'uan routine in the peaceful morning dew of his oriental garden. Chosen to head the World Government for the thirteenth term; such was the measure of respect and esteem he commanded on the international stage. It was difficult to dislike the man who exuded grace and charm, while he mentally picked your pockets.

* * *

As the closed session of the permanent members of the Security Council got under way, Ying introduced the aliens to the chief delegates.

'This is Kileni, the head of the Federation delegation. He tells me his home-world is Klosh.' Kilcni was seemingly dressed in a violet jump suit—everyone wore some kind of jump suit on Earth. That being the fashion at the time. 'The one in the green jump-suit is Ufi, from Ufass.' The second tallest of the three. 'The last is Velred; the one dressed in a blue-grey jump suit. He's from Velhrud.' This individual was the shortest of all.

Each wore similar poker faces and looked like any normal human; at least their holo projections did. From the people present, it was clear no one had any idea where the named alien home-worlds were located on the star charts.

Ying next introduced the human chief delegates to the aliens. 'This is Mme Kamala Peshwa from India, head of the Asian delegation. Standing next to her is Frau Gehilde Schröder from Germany, head of the European delegation. Then Sr. Rodrigo Perez from Mexico, head of the American delegation. Chief Seswe Akuffo from Ghana, head of the African delegation, and finally Kamisese Rabuka from Fiji, head of the Australasian delegation.'

The three aliens joined the other five delegates at the permanent member's table in the middle of the hall. President Ying took the Chair; a hush descended as the Earth delegation waited for the remarkable proposals the Galactic Federation intended to put.

'I suggest we begin by asking the delegates of the GF to place before us their official proposals,' Ying said quietly.

Kileni muttered something incomprehensible. He fiddled with something on his wrist, then began again, in an almost refined accent, 'We bring you sincerest greetings from Grand Custodian K'Rel and the Grand Council of the Galactic Federation of Systems. We offer you a seat on the Federation Council as the newest, and most honoured addition to our Federation....'

Ufi then went on without a break in a gurgled singsong, '...it is not often we are able to invite a new member onto the Council; the last initiates were the Barog four and a half of your centuries ago....'

Velred took over seamlessly as in a well-rehearsed act, in a deep baritone, '...and *if* you feel ready, and *if* you agree...you will need to choose two hundred diplomats to send to Federation Quadrant HQ, to install a permanent Embassy on Rakh. You will need to sign the accession *on* Rakh, roughly one thousand and eighty of your light years from this planet. You will, of course, need to take this matter to all your peoples for a comprehensive discussion....'

Kileni took over again, '...we will offer you transport to Rakh until you're able to build your own new starcruisers. This will be with the technology we'll transfer to you in due time as part of the benefits of accession. We've been monitoring your progress in what you call the Centauri system, and it's to be commended.'

That part regarding "technology transfer" brought a visible gasp from the human delegates; it also initiated almost-visible mental saliva wetting. But "a thousand light years?" "Monitoring us?" Alarming questions began to form in the delegates' minds.

The technology transfer was going to be *the* incentive, and certainly a massive selling point to the scientific community. It would encourage them to push in favour of joining the Federation. But the aliens must have known this when they offered this appetiser. So what else?

'We had a report from Admiral Ryan; he'd sighted a UFO in the Centauri system. Was that you?' Ying queried.

'Most probably,' Kileni responded offhandedly.

'And the strange Conway meteor rampaging through our Solar System?' Perez inquired, feeling the need to order past events in his mind.

Perez considered himself the spokesman for *all* scientists of the Universe, blunt to the point of rudeness —and somewhat conceited.

'That's another story.' Kileni left the answer hanging.

'You may decide to delay your accession for years, or even decide not to join at all,' Ufi, his mouth was opening and closing. For some reason the mouth motions and the words were out of synch. He continued in his gurgled singsong, 'but that's a decision only you and your planet can make. We of course urge you to accede and participate in the grand decision making process that orders relations in our galaxy'.

'Of course,' Velred intoned in his baritone, 'if you decide against joining the Federation, then you will have to trade for any new technology in the normal manner.'

The aliens looked at the bemused, dumbfounded faces of the Earth delegation, as it sunk home they could actually decline the invitation to join this Galactic Federation. They would also get a chance to *reject* acquiring a brand new technology.

'We'll need a copy of this protocol we're to accede to, so we can have an informed discussion,' Ying told them in his best mandarin manner.

'Naturally,' Kileni said smoothly. 'It's being downloaded as we speak, translated into the language of World Government. You will see the protocol consists of 201,500 of your standard A4 pages. We recommend you convene your best lawyers and begin to determine whether it's acceptable to you. We're forced to point out; the document is unalterable and has been signed by all the Federation members. As such, we cannot make any specific changes to the protocol. It has been in this form for some five thousand of your earth years and you sign it as it stands.'

'Frau Schröder!' said Ying, pointing at the raised hand of the European delegate.

'I would like to ask—how long it would take for our delegation to reach Rakh?' She bore the poker face of a life-long diplomat, and said this without a hint of interest, trying to calculate the aliens' gullibility. Schröder was a tall blonde blue-eyed German Frau, lean and hungry, forever pulling her left earlobe in an unconscious slow movement. She wasn't aware she was doing it.

'I am able to fathom the reason behind your question,' Kileni replied quietly. 'It is a journey of about one earth hour. Most of the time is wasted at either end.'

This information produced open stupefaction. One delegate spluttered; another's intake of breath could easily be heard, whilst Chief Akuffo exclaimed, 'What did he say?' Akuffo always pretended he was hard of hearing, forcing people to repeat what they said. It gave him that extra time to think of a response.

'How?' Came a joint cry from America and Asia. 'It took us four weeks at warp to travel 4.23 light years to the Centauri system,' exclaimed Sr. Perez in exasperation, 'and you say only one hour to travel one thousand light years?' He had overseen the Centauri project for the World Government and somehow felt cheated by the aliens' information, as if somehow he was personally responsible for not being able to match that speed.

'I can tell you—we use—portals—instead of warp,' all three aliens said in unison, looking pointedly at Perez. 'You'll see this in action when we go to Rakh, at which time we'll explain the workings.'

President Ying, still perspiring, looked at the cool holographic images of the aliens. At the back of his mind, he wondered what they really looked like. He asked, 'Apart from the protocols, is there anything else you want to tell us?'

'Not at the moment,' remarked Kileni in his near refined accent. 'We will have much time to discuss matters of mutual interest, once we have come to an understanding over the protocols. This first contact is a delicate matter and we need to proceed according to strict procedures laid down by the Federation.'

'As you wish. My Holo-Vid tells me we have received all of your protocol,' said Ying, 'and if there's nothing else, then I propose we adjourn the meeting for deliberations. I see we've received your communication frequency and the encryption matrix for further contact', Ying said, looking at the Holo-Vid again. 'We'll be in touch; you may be sure of that.'

'One more point,' said Kileni hesitantly.

'Yes?' Ying said with interest.

'We need a little feedback on our translators. We feel we might be coming across somewhat mechanically. Is that how you perceive our voices?'

'They're coming across just fine,' offered Ying.

'Thank you for being honest.' Kileni said in departure.

The holo aliens vanished, and the human meeting was adjourned for a short break. Fermi's Paradox had finally been answered. Humanity's lonely existence had come to an end. From this point on, the Universe would seem a little more crowded—and a lot more exciting.

Chapter Five

Referendum

Ying recommenced the adjourned meeting with, 'Now our visitors have gone we need to have a look at this protocol.' He added, 'We need to get our lawyers onto it.'

'Maybe we should proceed to a smaller room,' said Frau Schröder, rubbing her left ear. 'We can examine the protocol there in a more friendly atmosphere.' She didn't wait, but led the way out of the Assembly Hall. She always assumed people would follow her.

The entourage arrived at the wooden doorway leading into a medium sized circular room. A sizeable round mahogany table stood in the middle. The various delegates began occupying seats in preparation for serious haggling. That being the nature of World Government.

'Who's in the Legal Department right now?' Rabuka said to empty air. A tall muscular Fijian and a snappy dresser. He wore a light beige jump suit like a halo.

There was a communicator lodged behind his right ear. Everybody had one; it was this millennium's version of the ancient mobile phone; a personal intercom all rolled into one. Vibrations from the voice box passed through the skull and were picked up by a sensitive biochip half a millimetre square, housed in a convenient container attached to the skin of the squama near the right temporal bone. It wasn't implanted, so people could remove it when they needed to.

'This is Goldman Sir,' a voice came back.

'If you look at your Holo-Vid, Goldman, you'll find a two-hundred thousand page legal document,' Rabuka told Goldman in his booming voice. 'I want the whole department to drop everything and start analysing this protocol. I want a detailed report on your findings within six hours. Get as much outside help as you need to complete the job in the specified time. This must be meticulous; it's a first for us humans. I want you to be absolutely clear on this—do you understand?'

'Yes *Sir*,' Goldman responded.

Rabuka, in the past a high-flying lawyer, was currently in charge of the World Government Legal Department and intent on getting this right. Then Rabuka turned to Mme Peshwa and said in a lowered tone, 'I know the legal computer will give us a summary right now, but I'm taking no chances with something this serious.' It was one lawyer confiding with another.

He was right as to the legal computer; the Holo-Vid began producing a summary of the document as he spoke, listing the main clauses.

'The first Article concerns non-interference in others affairs,' commented Mme Peshwa in her high off-key drone. She also a lawyer by profession, listened to a computer summary of the document in her earpiece whilst the rest were talking. She continued, 'It's really detailed as to what we should and shouldn't do when we come across another planet, or another sentient species.'

'What of our in-house lawyers?' Akuffo demanded. He hadn't heard Rabuka's interchange with Goldman. 'Aren't they supposed to produce a summary for us.'

Rabuka looked exasperated and boomed, 'That's what they're doing: going through the alien contract with a fine toothcomb.'

Akuffo, a former journalist, persisted. 'What are we going to do about the media?'

'We should agree on a formal statement, then get our Press Department to release it with a dampener,' Ying suggested. 'Something that outlines the facts with scant detail, asking for patience due to ongoing discussions—including a promise of further details as the information become clearer'.

Mme Peshwa remarked, 'A shame we can't keep it quiet altogether.' The secretive mentality of lawyers everywhere, had risen in her. 'Pity the open General Assembly meeting made that impossible'.

Rabuka added, 'We should issue instructions to all the national delegation heads requesting them to do their utmost to keep their media in check regarding this alien contact.' More lawyer paranoia. 'The last thing we want is a world wide panic,' he added.

Both lawyers sat next to each other and immediately began to put together a draft outline of what they had in mind. Akuffo, the journalist, endorsed the wording of the final draft for "grab" impact. Its purpose was to overpower and direct the real news.

The intention was to show a Holocast of the aliens, in their reassuring human holo forms, standing on the World Government podium, benignly offering the invitation to the Solar System to join the Galactic Federation. No mention to be made of cloaked starcruisers or near-by Portals. Long media discussions or in-depth analysis was going to be discouraged. The emphasis was on keeping it short and simple. Sound bites still reigned supremely.

'What do you think?' Mme Peshwa finally asked.

'About what?' said Ying, spiralling out of deep thought.

She droned irritably, 'The media handout!'

'If you will all please look at your Holo-Vids, we can take a swift vote on whether to approve this handout,' her high key drone came out more loudly than intended. Looking at the heads nodding, 'I take it we are in accord on this?' Further head nodding concluded the matter. She routed the screen handout to the Press Department marked "urgent."

'Now back to the matter in hand; the protocol,' Rabuka said.

Mme Peshwa emphasised, 'We really need to see how the main points of this document analyse, the tone, the trend it takes.'

President Ying put in, 'We ought to determine whether it's favourable towards us or predatory, that ought to be quite straightforward.' He looked around, 'I suggest the two lawyers present give us a summation.' Everybody nodded.

The two lawyers agreed.

Mme Peshwa began, 'If we take the main stipulations the computer indicated, we can stop at the Articles that need closer scrutiny.'

Rabuka took over, 'As we mentioned previously, the first Article has a great number of clauses dealing with non-interference in other's affairs. It goes into quite a lot of detail on things we "must not do", including restrictions on aggressive behaviour and claims on others' territory.

'Wait...other clauses infer if there's the slightest sign of life on another planet, however minute, microbes, bacteria, or the like, we must not interfere or colonise the planet. There, evolution *must* be allowed to follow its course.'

Mme Peshwa's drone took over, 'The larger the life diversity in the Galaxy, so it seems to suggest, the richer the mix to the Federation over time. They want to allow an appropriate gestation time for the eggs to hatch, so to speak. They intend to supply us with a list of planets and Systems that are off limits when we get to Rakh. There's a large number of clauses defining how we ought to behave as civilised members of the Federation.'

Frau Schröder still rubbing her left earlobe put in, 'We'd have objected strongly had someone interfered in our evolution millions of years ago!'

'I suppose so,' Perez conceded half-heartedly. His European ancestors had been brutal colonisers of others' lands, all but eradicating the American natives. His pioneering instinct had manoeuvred him to be put in charge of the Centauri programme. He was going to find it difficult to swallow some of the prohibiting clauses.

Perez continued, 'Anyway, it's plain we've had the benefit of this policy; the Earth and our Solar System was quarantined until now. No wonder we never got an answer to our attempts to contact other worlds with the Search for Extraterrestrial Intelligence programme; you probably know it better as SETI. This is true of all the successive programmes.' It was frustration talking. His voice rose, 'How could Fermi's Paradox "Where are they?", be answered when we were so effectively isolated.'

There followed a short silence after the last outburst.

Akuffo broke the silence, 'It's going to make our attempts to find other planets to colonise, somewhat difficult—if not impossible.'

'Surely, the existence of the Galactic Federation's done that already,' Ying said bluntly.

'Yes, I'm sure you're right,' Rabuka agreed. 'If you recall, we have Europa; Jupiter's second moon isolated for the same reason. Ever since we found primitive life below the ice sheets on Europa, we've insisted those creatures be allowed to evolve as far as they're able to, in isolation. Nobody's been allowed near Europa for over five hundred years for fear of contaminating it.'

As an afterthought, Frau Schröder asked, 'What's this "Fermi Paradox" Sr. Perez mentioned?'

Perez was only too happy to succumb to his role as a lecturer. This was right up his professional boulevard.

'Enrico Fermi was an Italian-American physicist in the twentieth century.' A beam spread on Perez's rugged face as he entered his role. 'Fermi insisted, as there were roughly 100 billion stars in our Milky Way galaxy, the mathematical probability of there being other life was extremely high. We should be in the middle of a lot of galactic interstellar traffic, and he then asked the simple question, "Where are they?" meaning the aliens. It became known as the Fermi Paradox.'

'Thank you,' responded Frau Schröder. 'You're a mine of information Sr. Perez, shall we continue now,' she added, peeved at the simplicity of the explanation.

'The second Article...is devoted to diplomatic behaviour amongst the Federation Systems,' continued Mme Peshwa. 'Apart from detailing the diplomatic protocol for member Systems to follow in the method of establishing resident Embassies, other clauses seem to expand the concept of continuous mobile equilibrium.

'This allocates a role to each member of the Federation, a sort of anti-hegemonial clause promoting a balance of power. The crux of the latter, from what I understand, is to force all the Federation member's affairs to intertwine so they all hang in a complex balance.

'There's large tracts in the protocol on conflict resolution. It refers to the settlement of disputes, levels of arbitration, focused on resolution without conflict. The initial arbiter being the Quadrant Galactic Court based on Rakh. The final arbiter is the Galactic Court on the Grand Custodian's home-world.' Mme Peshwa called for a glass of water, which rose nearby, as if by magic, on a small platform from a hole in the table; she took a sip and continued.

'The third Article...is fair trade provisions—the theoretical position dealing with restricted trade items, prohibited merchandise. It defines and gives a brief outline of each member's laws on what is a proscribed item. For some, this may be an innocuous substance such as sulphur, or a synthodrug—depending on the life form's metabolic processes.

'Other members of the Federation are expected to restrict trade in that merchandise with the life forms that prohibit that trade. Again, they intend to supply us with a list of items prohibited, associated with the various life forms, when we reach Rakh. Other clauses forbid trade in armaments, great emphasis is laid on its proscription in any shape or form. Inter Governmental arms dealing only.'

'Thus far, all indications point to a thorough document, the tone seemingly benign. Would the lawyers present—agree?' asked Ying.

'So far, yes. It's a foregone conclusion the scientists are going to push vigorously for us to sign this protocol,' said Rabuka.

'Well, the inclination and manner of the protocol seems to be something I can accept, but then I'm only a lowly scientist,' remarked Perez, giving no sign of being lowly.

'I've just had a thought,' said Ying. 'We're being urged to sign on behalf of humanity, but we only represent Earth. What of Mars? Not to mention our colonies on the Moon, on Ganymede, in the biospheres around Io, Titan and Triton. We'll have to contact the Mars Embassy. You know how touchy they get if we take them for granted.'

'There are two options with Mars,' said Frau Schröder, a career diplomat. 'Offer them a niche within our delegation, say fifty of their people, or—they put forward a complete separate delegation of their own, *and* shoulder the accompanying cost of maintaining it.'

'It's something we're going to have to discuss with them. I'm sure they'll want to sign this document; they'll want the new technology,' said Perez. 'Mars is the only other independent player in the Solar System. We represent all the other colonies and we'll sign *on their behalf*.' He emphasised the latter.

'I'm glad President Ying brought this matter up,' said Frau Schröder. 'It could have been embarrassing if we'd signed for Mars, and then they disclaimed the agreement.'

At that point the document on their Holo-Vids disappeared, replaced by the crew-cut head of Gina Young, as ruthless a news-hound as they come in the Solar System. Powerful people cringed at the sight of her, dreading her questions, primarily because she had a knack of finding things out which people really wanted to keep hidden.

'President Ying,' said Gina, almost politely, 'it's impossible to get hold of you any other way.' She put in quickly, 'My professional dictates force me to ask you about the aliens, it's too big a story to keep quiet.'

'Stop this!' insisted Ying to the Holo-Vid. 'Hacking into our computer network is *criminal*, and I was assured—quiet impossible.'

Gina opened her mouth to say something else, but Ying switched her off, and the Holo-Vids went blank.

'This is intolerable,' asserted Ying, 'we must be allowed to deliberate this matter in peace, and *without* interruptions. The neural guardian is supposed to protect against this sort of thing. How in the name of Meng Zi, did she manage to bypass the neural guardian? I mean; the World Government network is off the global link, on an autonomous network.' He looked at Perez, as the technical expert, who ought to know. It was as if he were to blame for the disgraceful interference in their deliberations. 'Now, where was I before I was so rudely interrupted?'

'You were remarking on the tone of the protocol, and on this first perusal, it seemed benign,' Rabuka reminded him.

'That's right! In fact, I was asking whether all of you thought it was benign,' Ying resumed.

They had been working on the document for well over two and a half hours, and were beginning to need a break. At the moment when they most needed to pause, Goldman's face filled the Holo-Vid.

'President Ying? We've finished analysing the protocol,' he said smugly.

'Well done!' Ying said—then added impatiently, 'And...?'

'There seems to be no hidden small print; all the wording is unusually straightforward for a legal document, and the pros seem to outweigh the cons by a long haul,' replied Goldman.

'But can we propose the signing of the protocol to the General Assembly, as it stands, without being duped?'

'I'm certain of it,' responded the permanent head of the World Government Legal Department. 'At least from the legal point of view it's OK, however, there are other considerations.'

'That's our department,' responded Ying stiffly. 'Do we need to continue with our formal discussion of the protocol?'

Ying looked around the table, searching faces for dissent. All around him, he saw tired features. He saw they all wanted to close the session, which really hadn't been lengthy by World Government standards

'Let me sum up the position as I see it; then we'll take a formal vote,' Ying continued. 'We can't play the ostrich and pretend the Federation doesn't exist. Now we know they're there, it's impossible to delude ourselves we're alone. Furthermore, I feel we would be neglecting our duty of leadership if we didn't propose signing the document, and somehow attempted to remain outside the Federation.' He paused to let that sink in.

'How in the name of the Universe can we simply continue as before? I would have to resign if the General Assembly voted against signing the protocol. This is a momentous point in the history of humanity, I'd claim as significant as the first words ever uttered in the development of language, more than two million years ago. What we decide today, will dictate the future of the human race for a long time to come.' Ying paused.

It sounded as if Ying was rehearsing his coming speech to the General Assembly.

'There's all the new technology offered by the Federation. How can we explain turning it down? *No!* There's only one answer I must give the representatives of the Galactic Federation. We *must* sign their protocol.' Ying looked at their faces again, 'Well? What do you say?'

'As nominated head of the American delegation, I formally *urge* the World Government to sign,' said Sr. Perez, mindful of the technology waiting to be acquired.

Rubbing her left earlobe, 'The European delegation also recommends the World Government sign,' joined in Frau Schröder.

In her high voice, 'Asia has never stood in the way of progress. Let it be recorded Asia *insists* the World Government sign,' came from Mme Peshwa without any hesitancy.

'Australasia joins Asia in counselling the World Government to sign,' retorted Kamisese Rabuka in his deep Melanesian baritone.

Everybody turned to the delegate representing the African continent, Chief Seswe Akuffo. He began to get uncomfortable as the people round the table noted his uneasy silence. Breathing in a big sigh, he said, 'I'm not certain! This is all so sudden. The people of Africa do a lot of talking before making such an enormous decision. It gives us time to mull over the implications, and President Ying is quite right; things will never be the same whatever we decide. I suppose hearing my own voice is helping a little, giving me time to digest the ramifications.... All right. On behalf of Africa, I agree to support the signing, but with reservations. I would prefer to see a Solar-wide referendum, and let the people take the responsibility for their own future.'

'Then we're agreed,' said Ying. 'Computer! Did you register the outcome of the members' vote?'

'Yes!' came the neutral response from his earpiece.

'This idea for a Solar wide referendum Chief Akuffo would be happier with; I see absolutely no reason why we shouldn't try to accommodate him. It would give us a wider mandate to sign the protocol,' remarked Ying with a whiff of political insight.

'We'd have to organise the discussion, lift the media gag, but it would take the burden from us.' Ying turned to the surprised faces of the other members, seeking an indication of how they viewed the suggestion.

'Can I have a quick show of hands, if you favour such a proposal?'

All astute hands were raised.

'Good! Then, "computer?", can you begin the referendum procedures. You know—notifying all the various space colonies, the separate national governments. Oh! And schedule a Holocast for me for this evening at prime time, staggered over the time zones.'

'Yes Sir,' responded the computer into his earpiece.

'Thank you for your diligence and patience. If there is no other business?' Ying asked of those present.

Silence.

'Then I adjourn this closed session of the Permanent Members of the Security Council.' Ying paused to catch his breath, then continued, 'If we're to sell this referendum, then everybody had better return to their countries and grab some media time. We need to push the benefits of the new technology on offer; you know the sort of thing.'

Ying continued to speak as they rose from their chairs. 'I'll get our Press Department to download an outline before you start your journeys, and I'm going to invite the General Assembly to vote for the referendum idea. I'll phrase it as if it were their idea: I'm sure they'll pass it.'

Ying leaned towards his console, 'Computer? Will you inform all heads of the national delegations an extra-ordinary formal session of the General Assembly will be held in two hours.'

'Yes, President,' came back from his earpiece.

Chapter Six

Alien Documents

Three plenipotentiary Ambassadors relaxed on the cloaked alien starcruiser orbiting Earth. They watched one of those interminable Holocast documentaries on the new millennium. It was another crass attempt to encapsulate a thousand years in thirty minutes using sound bites. The aliens avidly absorbed everything put out by Earth's media.

The Holo-Vid commentary was saying, '...and so the tantalising offer of a mature new technology will prove irresistible to our scientific community. Let us remind ourselves; the third millennium had begun by making technology friendly and safe, making it accountable, cleaning it up from the previous millennium's ecological disasters.

'It was only in the twenty-second century, that global economic sustainable development had allowed our environment to recover. Now the Earth has clean fresh air, and a climate that is finally under our control. Energy production and transport no longer cause the previous chaos and pollution.

'Technology has made it possible for the entire human population to be totally enfranchised. It's put voting power into everyone's' home. Referenda are now frequent, causing headaches for the politicos, but it forces them to supply the best education so that people are able to make informed decisions.

'All our buildings and construction materials are either covered with solar collectors, or they self-photosynthesise. This provides free energy to the vestigial grid. Hard holo images have made travelling virtually unnecessary, providing the same sensory experiences as their owner's presence. Travelling off-planet is still a grimy proposition, but the new alien technology ought to change that.'

The voice-over was accompanied by appropriate visual archive material. The speaker's commentary was being translated for the alien viewers.

'Matter transfers, more popularly referred to as teleportation, has allowed goods to be moved around. However, it's unreliable for live transport due to energy seepage and particle interference. If one electron is lost in the process, or a neurone's electrical charge is changed, then reassembly is destructively altered.

'The current neural computer's power to handle the matter transfer has increased by 50%; unfortunately their circuitry isn't one hundred per cent stable. The recent biological memory is still as unstable as the old optical memory for that purpose. Transference of live human matrices to another location is tricky. All it takes to cause mayhem in the matrix is for some external particle to interact with the transfer beam, and the matrix would be scrambled. On our Holocast films' people teleport all over the place, but in reality it's far more complicated. We can't use matter transfer for humans; not until those problems are resolved.'

Parts of the documentary caused a heated debate amongst the aliens. Alien sounds were being bandied back and forth whilst the documentary was still in progress.

'...The storing and reprogramming,' the Holocast went on, 'of the brain's neural schemata using PLC, has become an accomplished fact. However, it requires an enormous amount of processing power that has to be isolated from the general network on a standalone computer. It needs at least five redundancy backups, where three have to agree with a decision before it is implemented. The process is costly and complex because it has to be 100% fail-proof. Lives are at stake.

'At the beginning of this millennium most people consider technology useful, friendly and indispensable. So much so, femto-robot repair systems are implanted in the majority of humans in place of their appendix. They clear the arteries, repair those organs needing repair, provide overall aid to the immune system, and prevent ageing. They're the natural successors to the nano and pico robots of the past.'

The commentator paused to catch his breath before continuing. 'People have the option at reaching maturity, age 18, when the body reaches its natural peak, to have the appendix modified to house these minuscule femto-robots, or to let nature take its course. All but a few choose to play host to the robots, whilst an insignificant group of fundamentalists opt for nature's way. Part of the social contract is, if the robots are implanted, then the host will live a healthy active life until they are two hundred years old. Then if they insist on living longer, they have to move off Earth to one of the colonies. If they stay on Earth, they are deemed to have volunteered to be terminated.'

More heated alien exchanges went back and forth.

'...By the twenty-fourth century, human ageing had been defeated. The chromosomal telomeres are now being prevented from fraying and shortening at the ends each time they divide. This is accomplished by the femto-robots adding the enzyme *telomerase* to the telomeres where and when needed, preventing the cells from ageing when they divide. The tiny automatons also switch the ageing genes off.

'Amazingly, many of us feel two hundred years of life is sufficient for one lifetime. However, if people want to live longer, they have to colonise, and Mars is always interested in receiving colonists.

'The resultant benefit of this policy is Earth's population has been stable for centuries. This cosy stability is about to explode, thanks to the arrival of the aliens. Many Social Psychologists insist this will reintroduce a much needed unpredictability factor back into Earth society.

'The internal bodily modifications have been accompanied by changes to the clothing people wear. The clothes now report on the state of the wearer's health, are IT storage devices, communicators and much more. These clothes are linked to slim ubiquitous PCs worn round peoples' waists, which in turn are linked to the general global communication network.

'Furthermore, life in this millennium is a matter of informed choices; nobody's life style is coerced into embracing any of the advances and changes in technology. It's often argued, by "resistants," there is little or no option, social pressures forcing people into following the norms. They mean of course the norms of the majority: but those pressures have *always* existed. The simple fact that the "resistants" exist at all, suggests the minority have been given room to express themselves. But as we know, it's in the resistant's nature to moan and complain.

'This "brave new world" of the fourth millennium is a multiplicity of choices, as it always has been. People work, or they don't, their decision. The androids do all the dirty heavy work, and being androids, don't object. If some people insist on not working, then a number of benefits of working are lost; not everything's available to the economically inactive. However, everybody is comfortably housed and well fed, but various advantages such as trips off planet are not available to the idle. It's what would be expected from any reasonably robust society.'

More furious alien exchanges. Tentacles were pointed and a lot of air jabbing took place.

'...The brain functions have been mapped for many centuries, and it's clear each person needs to be mapped individually. Peoples' schemas are organised as uniquely as their fingerprints, or their DNA. Memory is organised into a network of schemas, which manifest themselves physically in the brain as *bunches* of interconnecting neurones.

'There has been a profound knock-on effect in mental health, inasmuch that non-organic psychotics have the choice of living with their psychosis, or of having their schemas' adjusted. Their neural circuitry has to be downloaded, then untangled from their psychosis by a number of minor neural adjustments, or it could be a neurotic compulsive obsession. The repaired schema is then uploaded back into its place in the brain, in exactly the same position from where it was abstracted. This is by way of some sophisticated neural computer controlled scanning technology. All the other schemas are then updated with the new information; the interconnections appended, or removed. The organic psychotic has to be genetically adjusted to rebalance the system, to eliminate the psychosis.

'The long completed Genome Project has provided us with the tools to eliminate all inherited diseases, somatic as well as cerebral. Ectogenesis, now the norm, has liberated women from the vagaries of a nine-month incapacitation. The synthetic ectowomb is definitely here to stay by overwhelming demand. Yet, some women still insist on giving natural birth—and that's as it should be. It's their right.

The outmoded notion of cloning by way of stem cells and organ growth has been made unnecessary by the introduction of femto-robot technology. They prime natural stem cells to re-grow by epimorphosis, any accidentally severed parts.

'The overabundance of Genetically Manipulated food within the pristine environments of the high-rise factories has been a prodigious human achievement. After extensive research and testing, only those GM foods found to be safe over a hundred year trial period are produced for human consumption. The protein and carbohydrate production lines of those high-rise factories have eliminated all human and animal hunger. The strict ban on releasing any GM strains into nature has been in practice for many centuries and seems to be permanent. All is contained in the high-rise factories.

'No animals are now killed for food, on land or sea —this being replaced by textured proteins, simulating any meat or sea products, or otherwise killed for sport. Poverty has been eliminated, primarily by removing the obstacles leading to poverty. It isn't uniformity and mediocrity that has descended on our planet; simply all encumbrances to psychosocial normality have been removed.

'The substantial lunar colony is thriving and is home to many of the scientific institutes and all benefit from the one-sixth gravity. One of those institutes was recently responsible for developing the successful Warp drive.

'In the twenty-seventh century Mars demanded, and obtained independence from Earth. They have transformed the red planet into a habitable home by seeding both the atmosphere and the land, eventually allowing some sixty million people to live there—and it's still expanding.

'Sizeable colonies have been established on a number of moons around the major planets of the Solar System. Other colonies have been established in biospheres when the moons were too hostile, even on far off places such as Pluto

'This is the state of our Solar System at the start of the fourth millennium. Now we have been contacted by aliens who have invited us to join their Galactic Federation.'

At this point, the holographic image of the three alien Ambassadors was shown to the viewers.

'It is without doubt; the next millennium promises to be far more significant for the human race than any previous period in our long history. May increasing enlightenment be our guide. The future's in our hands. Good night and thank you for staying with us.'

The alien image hung in mid air on the Holocast for what seemed an unnecessarily long time: probably for the viewers to become used to the notion of aliens.

The aliens stirred themselves and switched the Holocast off, then they got down to some serious discussions—which an Earth fly sitting on their weightless wall, would have been fascinated and astonished by.

Chapter Seven

"Antis"

For the human race, it came as something of a shock to realise it wasn't their galaxy that they had to share *their* galaxy with other sentient cultures. Intuitively, humans had known there must be other life forms in the Universe; indeed they'd searched the heavens for other intelligences ever since the first SETI programme. They pursued the searches at the start of the third millennium, and yet for the following nine hundred years there was only silence from the dark reaches of space.

The scientific community concluded with no results to confirm or deny the existence of another species; humanity was the only intelligent life form in the ever-expanding Universe. Although to suggest we were alone—went against all mathematical probability—the Fermi Paradox.

They were now disabused of their insular theory with the visit from the "Galactic Federation." The quarantined Solar System—with its quarantine lifted—was invited to join—what—? The GF? An unknown quantity! But one thing was certain—the novel situation would inevitably produce unsettling times for the humans in their Solar System, whatever the politicians decided.

To add to the problems, the news of the newcomers' arrival had been carefully leaked to the Holo broadcasters. Accordingly, all the media had gone out of their way to report the "aliens'" arrival in as sensational a manner as they could. In this case, it tended to stir-up a panic reaction from a sizeable minority.

The World President had to go onto the HoloVid, in an attempt to allay people's fears, to explain the extraterrestrials' intentions. It was up to the World Government, in the form of Ying Li, to try and calm things down.

But at the beginning of the fourth millennium, the majority of peoples' increasingly mature reaction to the antics of the news gathering media, produced less panic than might have been expected in an earlier era. It resulted from folks thinking themselves sophisticated, having travelled extensively around their Solar System.

Programmed Learning played a great part in promoting this evolution of attitude, by reducing ignorance. Large parts of the population considered themselves up to the educational standards of the old twentieth century Masters degrees. That's how far worldwide knowledge had advanced. The wise application of such learning was still down to each individual.

The strangers' arrival provoked a lot discussion and excitement solar-wide. Quite naturally, there was an immense interest in the future of the Solar System within any Galactic Federation—whatever that meant.

*   *   *

It seems the aliens had been in touch with Mars, at about the same time they contacted the World Government. They understood the delicate dilemma of dealing with Mars, and their need to be treated as a separate entity for the purpose of negotiations in signing the proffered GF protocol.

The aliens' appearance on Mars had caused the same uproar as on Earth. So by the time President Ying informed the Martian Embassy of the aliens' proposed accession treaty, they weren't in the least surprised.

They later made the decision to accept Earth's offer of a combined delegation to send to Rakh; that is if they decided to sign. However, Mars insisted they would sign separately. There was to be no referendum on Mars. They would sign; they had already indicated as much. For the Earth not to sign, and have humanity represented by a former colony, was an insufferable possibility.

World Government agreed on an impartial Solar referendum, but as usual, now made strenuous efforts to bias the vote. It engaged the services of the most effective Marketing Agencies on Earth—to develop a campaign for the signing of the alien contract. The culmination of this campaign was to be a sky filled with holo images and slogans, inviting people to cast their ballot in favour of sending a delegation to Rakh. The visuals were especially effective at night.

Holo adverts insisted nothing but good could come of the signing, and lauded the amazing benefits bound to come out of the new contact. The claims were diverse and frankly; most tended to be outlandish. Technology made it possible to dispense with population sampling— and an accurate Solar-wide opinion poll of just under six billion, suggested there was a strong majority in favour of signing the alien accession treaty. However, there was also a substantial cautious minority who would abstain. A vociferous minority set against any contact in principle, and thought humanity should go it alone!

World Government had scientists, and spin-doctors on all Holocast channels, hailing the future advantages of signing such a benevolent document; predicting dire consequences for the future of humanity of *not* signing.

Tame Futurologists were invited to forecast the direction humanity would take, with aid from the newcomers, and alternatively, without such aid. These same Futurologists played up the fact Mars was intending to sign, irrespective of what Earth did. A ploy most people found transparently offensive, and beneath the dignity of those playing that card.

*　　*　　*

Ying's earpiece sprang to life, saying something—startling the head of the World Government. He recognised the mechanical voice of Kileni of Klosh. Kileni was requesting a meeting. Ying agreed, and it hauled Ying out of an unaccustomed period of daydreaming.

Kileni's holo image appeared in his office. 'I'm sorry; did I startle you?' intoned the alien.

'Well just a little,' responded Ying. 'What can I do for you?'

'I could have called on the Holo-Vid, but it's just as quick this way, and certainly far more friendly. We're most pleased by the World Government's campaign to persuade your population of the need to enter the Galactic Federation.' Kileni was making small talk, which didn't bode well. 'My main reason for this visit, is to ask World Government to begin setting up the initial Galactic University. It will be the first of many. We'll download a paradigm for you to follow: topics, syllabuses, and provide the holo tutors where necessary. You'll need to supply the best brains capable of accepting the new information and technology.'

Kileni paused as he saw Ying fiddling with an electronic pad on his desk. He waited until he had Ying's full attention, then continued. 'We have tutorials in exobiology; your intended Embassy delegation for Rakh will need to study the various life forms they will encounter. There are the Diplomatic protocols for the various life forms, their customs and taboos. We'll provide a whole new re-statement of astronautics, as *we* know it; a whole new interpretation of advanced physics your scientists will need to absorb, both theoretical and practical. New interstellar charts for the galaxy, and much more.'

'Would this not be more appropriate *after* we've signed,' suggested Ying.

'Our stochastic projection suggest—you *will* sign. It's essential we move forward, there is much work to be done before we leave for Rakh, for the official signing ceremony. At the point of departure, we'll download plans for building Earth's first starcruiser, as we promised. We'll also supply you with plans for some radical enhancements to your planet's transportation system, energy productions, and the like. I understand you'll need to move at a measured pace in reforming your society, but I'm here to urge you to make a swift start. Your Programmed Learning system will facilitate matters, but I caution you; PLC is a short term solution.'

That brought a frown to Ying's forehead.

Kileni continued quickly, not giving Ying time to interrupt. 'The new life forms you'll encounter will take some readjusting to, and you may want to slow the PL down a little. At least you ought to spread each enhancement over a longer period, bearing in mind the updates are so radical.'

Ying said firmly, 'There will have to be an official signing ceremony *here*, on Earth, to satisfy *our* population, *our* politicians, and *our* media.'

'Yes, of course!' Kileni agreed. 'We always intended that,' he said reassuringly. 'But, you understand we deem the main formality to be on Rakh. We're inviting you to join, but *you're* the one that's joining a large number of other systems in the Federation. Convention has it—the moment of formal accession is marked on the Quadrant HQ, in this case Rakh.'

'So be it,' uttered Ying solemnly. He knew he'd be able to carry this with his fellow members in the World Government, and so was comfortable speaking for the whole human race. 'As for the Universities, we'd already decided to upgrade our PLC's with the new information you pledged to provide, and we intended to broach you on the matter. It's most fortunate you brought the subject up. By the way, what did you mean PLC is a short term solution?'

'I think that's a delicate matter and ought to be dealt with by a Council of experts.' Kileni had become extra serious. 'I'd like to leave the subject for the moment, if you don't mind.'

'As you wish. One more item from my side...we request a media unit accompany our delegation to Rakh, to cover the signing ceremony. Probably Holocast Earth Station-45.'

'That will be acceptable,' replied Kileni.

'Any further problems you wish to discuss?'

'Yes! I regret to inform you the Federation wishes you to refrain from any more visits to the planet you've named New Earth. We feel you've done no damage to the ecosystem there, and it should be allowed to develop in its own unique way—through time. Can I rely on you to enforce this difficult task?'

'Yes, your right. That *is* going to be one of the more contentious tasks. It will be difficult to quarantine that planet, but we *will* comply.' Controlling his anger, he asked, 'Anything else?' in a suppressed polite undertone.

'No. The Universities happened to be the main point.' This was said with no hint of falsehood. 'The paradigms and syllabuses were downloaded as we spoke. You now have all the new information in you data banks. It would be wise if the "antis" didn't get hold of these files.'

'Antis?' queried Ying, feigning ignorance.

'The minority opposed to the signing of the treaty,' said Kileni pointedly. 'From our past experience, the "antis" will contest our contact vigorously, you may be sure of that,' even mechanically, his voice had a tinge of resignation in it.

'We're used to democracy, *and* attempts to abuse it,' said Ying somewhat indignantly.

'Yes—I'm sure you are!' Kileni paused, then— 'May I raise an old point from my previous visit. It's not a formal thing. How is the voice intonation now? We've adjusted the programme for emotionality.'

'Seems just fine,' responded Ying, bemused by Kileni's concern to get the translator's intonations as human as possible. However, he didn't mention there was no discernible improvement.

'Thank you for your patience,' said the alien, and the holo image disappeared.

*   *   *

Ying Li sat in deep thought for a while, pondering the turn of events, in particularly with Kileni. The meeting had been unnecessary, and it was more likely the alien was letting him know they were monitoring the progress of the "pros" and the "antis." Deep down, he knew the real point of the visit concerned New Earth— yet, that planet was lost, and that was that. It would be a difficult battle to prevent the would-be colonisers—the big corporations gearing up for new business—but that was left for another day. It felt strange to have all Earth's communications monitored by extraterrestrials, representing a strange Federation, sitting unseen in their cloaked spaceship. The Space Corps had attempted to find the alien starcruiser, but without success.

He cleared his throat, and spoke. 'Computer! I want you to trawl through your memory and abstract the names of all scientists who are good diplomats. Any diplomats who were scientists—include any scientists with law degrees. Then fine tune in diminishing steps, for negotiating skills, for tenacity, for affiliation to Earth, for reflective calmness, for affability and interpersonal skills. Continue for excellent reporting skills, for independence and ability to survive in hostile environments. Naturally, I intend you exclude any unstable personality types.'

'Yes, President,' replied the computer in his earpiece.

It was clear to Ying that a totally new breed of diplomat was going to be needed to represent the Solar System. He'd better start selecting and building this new team. As with all diplomats, priority had to be given to the interests of those sending the diplomat. Diplomats had to be able to appreciate the host's culture, and in this case particularly, as it was an advanced technical society, they couldn't be fazed by it; hence the scientists.

He wondered the criteria Mars might use for their representatives. His mind was skipping around, tending to indicate nagging worries were probably trying to attract his conscious attention. The excitement of recent days triggered his memory of the story of the bust up with Mars three hundred years back. It demanding independence, and the Security Council demanding the then World President's head on a platter. In the end, sanity prevailed—lest belligerence turn to war. Then, spilt blood would be the final arbiter. Yes, those were trying times, times when great changes had overtaken

Earth. If they weren't careful to steer this new situation —things could go sour.

With the latter in mind, he'd set up think tanks to brainstorm a) the aliens' intentions, b) to plan what Earth needed to stay ahead, and c) to counteract any problems they might encounter from their population. To supplement the think-tanks, neural computer modelling would be used to explore all the possibilities, lay out all the problems the brainstorming would throw up, giving projected time lines and suggested solutions.

The technological material downloaded earlier by Kileni was being analysed, by machines and humans. Some of the results, even after only five hours, were raising eyebrows. Extraordinary mind boggling Chemistry and biology was only to be expected. But the Physics?

They'd have to re-evaluate the results of human research, scrap much of the astrophysics, take on concepts some thought, to say the least, were a bit outlandish. The aliens had travelled to Earth through a Wormhole, creating and controlling Black and White Holes. The terminology was familiar, but using them as tools for travel?

'President Ying!' said his earpiece, demanding attention. 'President Ghali wishes to speak to you on a scrambled line. Are you available?'

Now what in the name of K'ung Fu Zi did the President of Mars want with him? Ying racked his brains and didn't manage to come up with anything. It's not his usual style to make social calls, so he must be after something.

'Put him through.'

'President Ying,' said the holo image affably, on his table.

'Mr. President. To what do I owe the pleasure of your call.'

'I would have thought you'd have guessed. The aliens!' voiced Ghali quietly.

'Yes....?' Ying raised his eyebrows.

'Have you heard how they travelled here?' whispered Ghali.

'You mean through a Black Hole,' Ying's face was impassive.

'I mean just *that*,' Ghali muttered. He seemed to be worried about being overheard. 'We're backward compared to them,' he moaned. His face, still youthful with its dark Coptic features, the result of Mars' one-third gravity. Although older than Ying, he didn't show his 193 years.

'Steady on there,' encouraged Ying. He'd never seen the despondent side of the Martian President. The man was losing his self-esteem. He couldn't afford to do that, *and* be effective.

'I'm sorry, Ying,' Ghali said with a little more composure.

'Look—' Ying said. 'I know we've a lot of catching up to do, but we've nothing to be ashamed of. This is as far as our evolution has taken us, that's all. They've been at it a lot longer, and it's not surprising their technology's ahead of ours. It would be surprising if it weren't, *n'est-ce pas?*' consoled Ying.

'I know you're right, but it's still like going cap in hand.'

'It would be if we were begging, but we're not. Who came to whom? They sought us out, not the other way round. Why? Because we succeeded in inventing the warp drive. They didn't have a choice. We're going to Rakh; heads held high. We earned the right to sit on equal terms, with the other races. Remember, they had us in quarantine, until we broke through with the warp drive. It's our endeavours that have got us this far; lets push on the way humanity has always done. Stay alert, be flexible, and learn; but above all, be inquisitive.'

'It's a tonic listening to you Ying. Thanks. I really needed that. My advisers are too sycophantic.'

'My pleasure. Now, that's not why you called!'

'No. We've picked our fifty people to join your delegation.'

'What? Already?'

'When can your group meet with our bunch?'

'What criteria did you use to pick them?'

'They're our best brains, all scientists. My son is to lead them.' The latter was said with deserved pride. The President's son, Dr. Theodore Ghali, was a brilliant renowned biochemist.

'We've not chosen ours yet,' muttered Ying. 'I guess we're being slow, but I was moving forward cautiously. Sometimes this business has me spooked. I'm worried I may have missed something, and we'll end up paying the price.'

'Hold on there. You're beginning to go down my *cul-de-sac,*' put in Ghali with a smile.

'The detour's infectious,' replied Ying. 'I'll speed up the selection process, and we'll bring them together on the Moon in a week's time. That suit you?'

'Fine by me,' Ghali responded. 'Thanks for the pep talk Ying, and say hallo to Jiang for me. Bye.' The holo image faded, and Ying was left alone with his thoughts again.

'Computer! What's the result on your trawl?'

'There are some 125,000 personnel on the list,' it came back smoothly.

'We need around 2,000 for the first intake.'

'That would be my estimate as well,' impassively.

'What happens to the list if one of the criteria is possessing a hard science degree?'

'54,000.'

'Do that, then make it 2,000 from that. Make sure they understand; the incentive is three times their current salary. They're to drop everything; this is far more important. Have them report to New Caledonia by noon tomorrow. Book rooms for them in the conference Hotels. I want to see the most senior personally; should be around two hundred. Make room in my diary; let's say a combined dinner for us in the World Government Banqueting Hall.'

'Yes President Ying,' then his earpiece went quiet.

Ying looked out of his window into a brilliant vivid-blue Pacific sky. There was not a cloud in sight, apart from a small glint of reflected sunlight travelling from his left to right, in the far distance. As he watched, the speck grew larger, and he began to make out a Hover at around 300 meters above the ground. It seemed to have something in tow.

How quaint, thought Ying. *A Hover towing a message banner. Most likely someone was trying to impress their girlfriend.*

As the Hover towing the banner closed, he began to make out the message. Shock spread across his face. It said in large bold letters:-

Ying was aghast. Who on Earth could be behind this violation of the World Government Sovereign Territory? Not any of his personnel—surely? Who wrote that rubbish, anyway? The New Caledonians were a peaceable bunch; keen to be a part of World Government.

'Security!' Ying called to the air.

'Yes Sir, we see it,' came from his earpiece.

'I want to know who's behind that, names and location,' barked Ying, working up into a minor rage.

'We're onto it,' came from Ka-ula, head of security.

Ying watched six fast World Government police Hovers hem in the rogue Hover, top and bottom, front and back, and both sides, escorting it to the landing stage on the roof. *Smart move*, thought Ying. Preventing it from landing at ground level, would put it out of sight of prying eyes. This sort of thing could produce a lot of adverse publicity.

'I want a full report within the hour,' Ying said to the air.

'Yes Sir,' said Ka-ula.

'While you're at it, I want you to contact Interpol; find out if any more of this sort of thing is going on anywhere else. Who's doing it and how big it is.' He regained his composure quickly, was again soft spoken.

Chapter Eight

Rakhian Embassy

Nearly a week went by without further incident from the "antis." The banquet for the new rank of diplomats had been highly rewarding for Ying. The high flyers were keen and eager to begin. The two hundred plus were senior personnel, ranked by position and age. Some were Nobel Laureates, an honour highly gratifying for Ying.

After the formal introductory dinner, the following day, Ying appointed Professor Claude Joubert from the Sorbonne and Max Planck Institute, as head of Earth's proposed delegation. The Ambassador to be was a tall Provençal native, swarthy and built like a professional swimmer; habitually wearing a serious demeanour. An eminent diplomat in his own right *and* a Nobel physicist. Ying had been biased in his choice, since he knew Claude Joubert from a time when he headed the European delegation at World Government, twenty-four years previously.

*   *   *

Ying had been in touch with President Ghali again, catching him at home in Ares, the windswept capital of Mars sitting in the Chasma Borealis. The capital was near Mars' North Pole, where the only water on the planet was retained as an ice cap.

"Old Ghali," Ghali's grandfather had led all the Copts out of Egypt, some three quarters of a million in all, and settled with them on Mars. Its familiar arid deserts were reminiscent of Egypt's harsh wilderness. "Old Ghali" had wanted to perpetuate the pre-Arab Egyptian civilisation in the deserts of Mars, setting up Coptic Monasteries out in the desolate wastelands. All that was missing was the heart of Egypt, the Nile.

Ying needed to know if Ghali was coming across any opposition from his population, to signing the treaty. Ghali told him, a few hundred disgruntled resistants who had avoided PLC, who lived on the margins of society, were making trouble. Nothing to be concerned over, not in a population of some sixty million. It was good news to Ying, non too happy with the Hover incident.

*   *   *

It turned out the Hover pilot was a discontented former World Government employee, who held a grudge against his boss. The boss had caught him unawares in *flagrante delicto* with a colleague that day, and had fired them both on the spot. The man set out to embarrass his boss, *and* the World Government, by informing the media he was going to pull the stunt.

He'd arranged for a media unit to be waiting on the ground, expecting a payment from them. The media in question, was a minor Holo Station who were in a ratings battle, and desperate for a scoop. Luckily, Ka-ula had the prescience to force the Hover to the roof. The ex-employee had been put on the next Hover Shuttle back to Venezuela, and declared *persona non grata* in New Caledonia.

*   *   *

Some time later, Ying's earpiece chimed, 'Joubert here, we're ready to go to the Moon.' At the same instant, a holo image appeared near his desk.

'Good, I'm coming with you,' Ying asserted.

'May I remind you; you have a session of the General Assembly scheduled for tomorrow,' his secretarial computer informed him.

'Damn! Your right! I'd forgotten! Well, you'll just have to do without me,' he said to the Holo image. 'You've got your briefing Claude, and all your personnel have been updated with the new information by PLC. I'm informed; Simeon Ghali has chosen his son to lead the Mars delegation. Try to deal with the nepotism gently,' Ying urged. 'I really don't want any discord with Mars. Humanity ought to try and put forward a united front; don't you think? *Bon Voyage*, and I'll talk to you again Claude, before you depart for Rakh.'

'Mr. President! Just before I go—I called to tell you Kileni has established our link with Rakh by way of a relay-transmitter near Pluto, a million kilometres out in clear space. The relay activates a 60-terrawatt micro wormhole allowing a compressed data-stream to be sent. There's another relay-transmitter near the connecting White Hole linking it to Rakh, which means a virtually instant voice link. I'm still bowled over by being able to communicate over one thousand and eighty light years, practically without delay.'

'Why don't you call me Ying? We've known each other long enough! About Kileni's relay—that's good of him! As for the Diplomatic Bags, I've ordered our tightest encoding to carry the diplomatic signals to you. It's probably pointless. If they wanted to break the code, they could probably do it as soon as we send, but I'm going to follow diplomatic tradition.'

'Doubtlessly you're right; I do appreciate all this support. Talk to you soon. Bye Ying,' and the holo image faded.

* * *

On the Moon, Earth and Mars diplomats were mixing congenially at a cocktail gathering in the Excelsior Dining Rooms, as Ying and Ghali had arranged. Some gentle chamber music was being floated in the artificial air to add to the uplifting selenial ambience. People were merrily clinking glasses containing Martian Zald, a low alcohol wine made from a light grape grown in the one third Martian gravity.

Claude Joubert was in deep conversation with Theodore Ghali, son of the Martian President, whose dark swarthy complexion would have fitted well on the wall of any ancient Egyptian tomb, except for a few special features that had evolved over a thousand years on Mars. He was two meters tall, resulting from the low gravity, had large ears for amplifying sound in the thinner atmosphere, and a large chest for the lower oxygen content of the Martian atmosphere. He was only 184 years young, extremely composed and distinguished looking.

Both were engrossed on the united strategy they ought to adopt in their diplomatic dealings on Rakh. They knew each other well from scientific conferences, and had a healthy respect for each other's intellectual prowess. They had decided to do their utmost to bury their political differences and present a united front in their dealings with the Galactic Federation. United they stood, but divided they would surely fail their respective populations, and fall foul of any devious dealings. Divided they would be prone to be played off, one against the other. The stakes were too high for petty squabbles and past antagonisms to get in the way of their coming endeavours.

These new precursor diplomats were to represent humanity before the Galactic Federation.

Chapter Nine

Prejudice

'To understand the "antis" who are coming up with these objections,' Professor Maskalik was saying to Ying, 'it may help to understand the nature of prejudice itself— put in some kind of a historical context.'

'I've only got a few minutes,' Ying said, 'but go ahead anyway,' feeling he'd opened a can of worms.

He'd called the Clinical Psychologist in for a chat, before sending him to Earth's Rakhian Embassy to look after the staff's mental health.

'Historically,' Maskalik plodded on, 'the family unit preceded the tribal unit, and parents protected this unit from outsiders. Tribal units defended members and their territories from interlopers; calling such newcomers foreigners—implying they didn't conform to their belief system.

'During Earth's Dark Ages, one village would call neighbouring villagers, foreigners. Towns fought towns, illustrated by Italy's Middle Ages. When towns and cities unified, countries fought countries. Later, groupings of countries fought other groupings of countries, marching behind the cross of the Crusades. The protestations of the Jacobites, the Axis of the Fascists, the pretence of the Communists and Trotskyites, Jewish Zealots counter pointed by the fundamental crescent of Islam, or even the anti-religious fervour of some atheists—all righteously killed with lust.'

'Can you get to the point,' interrupted Ying.

'I'm coming to it. Those groupings claimed to uphold righteous common values, following a conformity rejected by their opponents. This demanding prejudice had a hand in all Earth's wars, reaching back to the Sumerians—until the lasting peace of the twenty first century.' Maskalik, an old hand at lecturing, was getting into his stride.

'Part of the problem lay in *how* history was taught, in primitive chauvinistic forms, such as king lists, victories over others, superior achievements, such as "best in the world", "Übermenschen", and "chosen people"—supposing a superiority of culture.

'This self-suggested superiority impelled them to impose their own law and order on other cultures, which were deemed to need ordering. In fact, it was used as a pretext to conquer and plunder. This self-professed superiority was passed down the generations, reinforcing prejudices.'

'Is there much more of this?' Ying again interrupted.

'I'm almost done,' Maskalik replied. 'I'm trying to give you an insight into the nature of prejudice, and into the "antis". Let there be no mistake,' he went on, 'the prejudices and the self-selected *Übermenschen* of the twentieth century had their beginnings in the Stone Age, and were not subdued until the dawn of World Government.

'To cap it all, in the twenty first century, continents were ready to fight continents, until the much maligned United Nations got in the way. Then, in the twenty-fifth century, planet was pitted against planet, Mars versus Earth, again the renamed World Government stepped in, but it was regarded as biased towards Earth. Being the government *of* Earth, it had the moral sense to back down, and Mars became an independent Planetary Republic.

'Authoritarian parenting styles laid down the framework for prejudice, producing poor decision processing, imbuing people with a lack of confidence and self esteem. An authoritative parenting style, on the other hand, had the opposite effect, developing good decision processing, a lack of prejudice, lots of confidence, good coping skills and enhanced self-esteem. It turned out parenting was the ultimate culprit as to how a child would turn out. With the aid of PLC, current parenting in the fourth millennium was always authoritative.

'Social and Group Identity was deemed to lie behind much of the prejudice, where conformity to a group's ideals made intolerance to anyone outside that group, a prerequisite to belonging to the group. Even in a classical music club, Beethoven fans have been known to exchange blows with Mozart fans, and Wagner fans with Verdi fans.

'Negative stereotyping produced learned helplessness, which encouraged an *Übermenschen* outlook in others. Frog, Kraut, paddy, wetback, honky, Paki, goi. If those derogatory epithets didn't encourage a dismissive and negative attitude to all those mentioned, then what was their purpose? Why compose all these disparaging names for other people?

'It was these sorts of problems the PLC addressed, facilitating further evolvement from our primitive selves, eliminating those insecurities and enhancing the populations' confidence and self esteem. Overall, PLC did a good job, but it could not force rational people to attend modification sessions. Some people simply refused to have anything to do with the tampering of the internal structures of the brain; little appreciating the nurturing they went through, had already done that.

By this time, Ying was seated with his head in his hands. 'I thought you were finishing?' he sighed.

'I am. I'm just rounding off,' claimed the Psychologist.

Oblivious, Maskalik continued, 'The psychologists proposed a number of ways to alleviate the problem of prejudice. Role Reversal, Intergroup Contact, Invoking the Law, Cognitive Reflection, and these were only a sample of some of the adjustment methods employed.' Maskalik sat back and looked at Ying.

'*That*, Professor,' Ying told him, 'was possibly more useful for an undergraduate student—but for our "antis," the *Abnormal* Psychological modality is presumably far more effective,' Ying speculated—a glint gleaming in his eyes. 'Well thank you for stopping by. May I wish you success and as little work as possible on Rakh.'

*   *   *

Out in the Solar society, the resistants had begun to make themselves felt by hacking into computer networks considered safe, making themselves a bit of a nuisance with various other pinpricks. For Ying it was all too familiar. The dilemma of the right to protest clashing with the timing of the protests. Ying was a democrat at heart, and a technocrat by profession.

The mandarin technocrat wanted the signing of the accession document to go without a hitch, whilst the democrat wanted to be out there with them, asserting their right to be heard. The simple fact was, the tiny group of resistants posed no threat to the accession whatsoever, they merely reminded all authority they governed by the consent of their populations, not despite them.

Ying knew the rulers only retained their legitimacy, if they acknowledged that—the people had elected them to be in their exalted positions. The enshrined principle long supported by K'ung Fu Zi (Confucius (551-479 BC)), was based on the Chinese feudal ethic that expected the ruler to act with benevolence and sincerity, so justice could be enjoyed by all his subjects. Meng Zi (Mencius (372-289 BC)) contended "man was naturally good" and insisted whenever a ruler lost the goodwill of his subjects and resorted to oppression, then the Mandate of Heaven was said to be withdrawn and rebellion became justified. This theory was derived from Meng Zi's belief that ultimate sovereignty lay with the people. Heaven may have granted the throne, but succession depended on the people's voluntary acceptance of the ruler. For the Europeans, this was enshrined in the first version of the basic rights of the eighteenth century French Republic and the *droit de vie*, incorporated into the World Government Charter a millennia ago.

Despite this intellectual tussle in his psyche, Ying decided to play it safe. He had already been given a detailed report on the breakdown of the resistants by Ka-ula. He knew who the "antis" were, their numbers and locations, and that they didn't pose a threat, but terrorism could raise its ugly head again, even after all these centuries.

Ka-ula had particularly underlined the name Rosa Steinberg. Ostensibly, desperation was the motive force that caused law-abiding citizens to turn to *other* means to try and attain that which they couldn't achieve through the democratic process. Ying was overstating the problem in his mind, and by doing so, assessing the worst-case scenarios.

*   *   *

In a mining colony on Mercury, deep into the Caloris Mountains, Kim Pak Kwon was sweating in his air-conditioned mining suit, trying to prise a large

Hermian crystal from its surroundings with a laser probe. As he cursed and swore at the reluctant crystal, his laser probe swung a little more violently and slipped out of his hands. Before the automatic breaker switched the laser off, the beam just grazed his lower left legging, puncturing the suit. As the air escaped, so the automatic repair system kicked in, and the suit sealed itself. He sat down with a thump. He looked at his left leg somewhat shocked for a few moments, then climbed back to his feet, picked up the probe and continued. It was part of the hazards of mining anywhere.

Back in the Mining Canteen, Kim sat sipping a mug of hot syntho-coffee and complained bitterly to his companion, Uri Rabbinowitz. 'This is a hell of a job!'

'Tell me about it,' agreed Uri.

'I nearly fried myself out there.'

'Pay's not bad, though.'

'Heard any more about us pulling out?'

'They're keeping *stumm*,' Uri said.

'Damned aliens; I thought we were on a good earner when they started building the Starships. The crystals were the most precious commodity anywhere. Busted my gut to get this job. *Now....!* Damned aliens!'

'We shouldn't have invented the warp drive, then the aliens would have left us alone,' suggested Uri.

'But then we wouldn't have needed the crystals and—' he broke off as he saw the smile spread on Uri's face. 'Fuu—nny!'

'We're gonna need the crystals anyway, come what may. They're needed for the "energy$\Rightarrow$matter" converter. They're just not going to be as precious as we thought.'

'Suppose your right, but I'd still like to see the back of those aliens. They give me the creeps.'

Chapter Ten

The Chase

The sun scorched the surrounding landscape as Rosa piloted the Hover, skimming over the bushy ground in the outback, trying to stay off the traffic radar. The overhead satellites were probably tracking her craft, but it added to the drama if she tried to avoid them.

All that could be seen in any direction was a light coloured brown arid earth; the colour burnt into the psyche of every Australian. Rosa's companion in the machine was a youth of forty, blond bleached hair, muscular yet lithe, wearing a slouch hat and, like Rosa, faded khaki.

Rosa Steinberg had grown up at the end of the third millennium, in the back streets of Shanghai. It was a well laid out prosperous city of skyscrapers with some thirty million inhabitants. Numerous slum infestations shamed the city fathers. Rosa was from one of those slums, and consequently grew up tough. She avoided the Programmed Learning Centres by not having her birth registered, and avoided all schooling, barring one: the messy rough and tumble school of life.

She obtained her education from a back street bootleg PL peddler, and considered herself extremely bright. Forever living at the fringes of society made her immensely resentful, but she wore it like a devious badge, using it when it suited her. Some of the bootleg PL programming had bizarre elements of a defunct pseudo religion incorporated, by those who still tried to push that sort of thing in the black economy.

There was something called "communaism" that held a pentagram of saints to worship: St. Marx, St. Lenin, St. Stalin, St. Trotsky, and St. Mao. Despite her natural intelligence, it was only to be expected such mental programming would leave her misguided.

The Hover was heading for a cave system at the foot of Mount Woodroffe, a hundred and seventy kilometres southeast of Ayers Rock, north of the Victoria desert. Their hideout was in some of the most inhospitable barren landscape on Earth, well away from prying eyes.

Rosa landed the Hover under a bluff, got out and helped Vinnie unload the goods onto a hover sleigh that had been secreted under the cliff. Then she set up the holo camouflage for the parked vehicle. It now looked like a boulder, unless of course someone walked right into the rock. Rosa then manipulated more buttons on the hand held holo generator, and the cliff face disappeared, revealing an entrance to a cave.

Both looked furtively around before dragging the hover sleigh in behind them into the cave. She reset the exterior holo cliff face, obliterating the mouth of the cave, and headed for the door of an instant long 'spring-up' shack standing 30 meters inside the cavern, sleigh in tow. Rosa deactivated the booby-trapped force field and entered the shack. Lights came on automatically, and they made themselves at home.

In one corner was a communications table. In another, stood a microwave and sink for their food. Another corner contained a lot of military hardware, laser rifles, and laser guns. There were even photon grenades, the pre-programmed anti-personnel type which when thrown in the air, hung for a second, orientating itself. Then split into eight or more individual missiles, latching onto human targets, zapping them with a stun beam, or splatting them out of existence.

In the fourth corner stood her *piece de résistance*, a real menacing device. Hanging in a small anti-gravity cradle on a table, was a half assembled Neutron bomb. By the standards of the day, quite a primitive device, but atrociously effective. The device was so small, once assembled it could easily fit into a small suitcase. It was intended to take out all the population of New Caledonia, the island containing the building of the World Government Assembly.

The inventors of the Neutron bomb in the twentieth century intended it should eliminate all life, whilst leaving the buildings intact. It had been outlawed by the politicians, and had been illegal for over a millennium. The present technology was vastly superior from when first invented, and it was a ridiculously easy device to put together, if the person was psychotic enough.

*   *   *

Rosa had met Vinnie some years ago, whilst tramping around Siberia. He had been working on one of those old fashioned *Raketa* boats on the Lena River as a seaman, and bored out of his 'tiny'. He'd never aspired to anything much except body-building and martial arts, which left him somewhat vacuous.

He'd been plainly scared of having his mind tampered with and had declined PL enhancement. That was his human right. Many had tried to convince him of the benevolent aspect of the PLC, that it would reduce his fear, merely enhance his intellectual capacities, but he wasn't considered paranoid *enough* to be forcibly reprogrammed.

For Rosa, he had all the qualities she liked in a man. He wasn't too bright, was well built, was easily led, and above all, was easily controlled. They had spent a couple of years in Asia, moved on to America, then back to Asia, finally settling in Australia.

In the intervening years, the resentment grew until it threatened to consume her. She, followed by Vinnie, had infiltrated a small group of malcontents, calling themselves "AA1" (Aussie Antidotes 1). Australia somehow had a knack of breeding such types. They were protesting against the Programmed Learning Centres; insisting it was against nature to tamper with someone's memories.

At the outset, she simply seemed to aspire to follow the group leader, who succumbed to her sexual charms, and made her his deputy. Finally, her malevolent nature came to the fore, and the group's leader found himself in custody, for criminal damage to a local PLC. The real culprit was Vinnie of course, made up to resemble the group leader. With the group leader safely out of the way and reprogrammed, she took over and started to transform the group. Slowly, she transformed them from a peaceful band of protesters, to what they later became: an assorted collection of terrorists.

She moved the group out to the outback, where they were more isolated; then began to work on them. Some left in disgust, but those who stayed, six not including Vinnie, became dedicated. They were currently out on various minor errands at her behest. They had nicknamed her "the Vixen" for her cunning and sheer beastliness.

The arrival on Earth of aliens suddenly gave Rosa a *raison d'être* for all her past preparations. She decided, single-handedly to destroy the World Government, so the aliens couldn't negotiate with anyone—and then they would go away. Thus, she would save the Earth, and people would recognise her, would eventually see the selfless act for what it was: an act of courage on behalf of her fellow human beings.

As with all delusions, Rosa had lost her perspective on reality, and retreated into fantasy. Vinnie was no reality check, and the rest of the group feared her obsessional behaviour.

*   *   *

On a couch in Mullhagen's office, sat Fräulein Heidi Frisch, a Colonel from the European/World Government Security Bureaux. She had an air of composure and confidence about her. Standing at his window, Inspector Mullhagen of the Australian section of Interpol, looked out on Brisbane Avenue, located in the Borton District of the capital. He was deep in thought, looking at a wide thoroughfare leading off the State Circle, down to the eastern end of Lake Burley Griffin. Canberra was a cool green city standing on the artificial lake, and Mullhagen was loathe to leave it for the sticky hot climate of the western coast.

He straightened his shoulders. 'There's no alternative but to head for Perth,' he turned and looked at the self-assured blonde Colonel.

'World Government Security is grateful you alerted them about these "antis". I feel I *need* to emphasise, I'm here purely as an observer,' she was trying to placate him for intruding on his patch.

He'd been alerted that a couple of people from the Steinberg cell had come in voluntarily, in a sort of self righteous "disgust", to inform on their former cell leader. Putting on his jacket, he invited the blond Colonel to join him, and called for a Hover to take them to Perth.

In downtown Perth, at Police headquarters, Mullhagen peered at the faded khaki, and thought the four individuals seated before him, must have escaped from the set of a Holo Film production. He turned his nose away from the sorry looking individuals; dishevelled, unshaven, and frankly a little high in the heat.

'Well, I'm waiting,' he demanded.

'We're a peaceable lot, at least we were until that Vixen joined us,' said the only woman amongst the four.

'We managed to get away from her, and that doting thug she has in tow, and came straight here.' The woman was fully scared at what she'd gotten involved with.

'We didn't mean any harm,' piped in a rough male voice. It came from a roguish looking person sitting to Mullhagen's left.

'So what did you get yourself into?' insisted Mullhagen.

'She's gonna start a war, what with all the arms she's stockpiled.'

'What arms? Come on, out with it.' Mullhagen was starting to lose patience.

'Out at Mount Woodroffe,' prattled the third male member of the group.

'Look, one of you; start at the beginning and bring me up to speed, before I lose my patience with the lot of you, and throw the blooming book at you.' Mullhagen looked at the woman, then at Heidi, standing in the corner listening.

'Well, a couple of years ago,' tears were beginning to roll down the woman's face, 'we had a group against PLC. Then this bitch turned up at a meeting, and flaunted before Judd, he was our leader then, and he took a shine to her.' Sobbing, she continued, 'Next thing you know, she joins the group and Judd makes her his deputy. Then Judd got done for wrecking a PL place; only he hadn't done it. He gets put away, and this Rosa takes over. She starts throwing her weight around, and this Vinnie of hers, makes sure nobody objects. Then she moves the group from Perth out to a bleeding cave, out at Mount Woodroffe, and starts building this bleeding bomb.' Tears were freely flowing now.

'*Hold it*. What bomb?'

'Well, I think she called it a "nutron bomb," or something like that.'

'Are you *sure*? It's important. Try to be more precise. Was it really a Neutron bomb?'

'Yes, I'm sure that's what she called it.'

'How big was this bomb?'

'Not big,' she was getting agitated.

'How big? This big,' Mullhagen pressed her, describing a wide circle with his arms.

'No. Much smaller! You could put it in a small suitcase. That's what she was gonna do.'

'And where was she going with this bomb?'

'To the World Government, you know, in New Caledonia.'

'You being *straight* with me?' Mullhagen leaned over towards her, a definite menace in his tone.

'I *swear* to you, on my mother's ashes,' she whimpered.

'OK. You say she's at Mount Woodroffe?'

'She was expecting us back there. She sent us out to stock-up on food. That's when we decided enough was enough.'

'How do we find this cave of hers?'

'We know the frequency of the camouflage field,' she offered hopefully.

'You're gonna take us there,' he pointed at her. 'Sergeant, lock these three up tight,' he pointed at her male companions. 'And get the Special Squad ready. Fully armed.'

'*Yes sir!*' responded the Sergeant.

'One more thing, there's two or three more members of this group running around, get their names from these three, and round them up.'

'Yes sir.'

'Colonel Frisch! Anything to add to the proceedings?'

Heidi smiled at Mullhagen, and shook her head.

'Well, let's get going then,' and Mullhagen led the party out to the Hovers.

The woman was pleading all the way to the Hover, 'You don't need me along—surely. I'll only get in the way—'

'That's *enough*! You're coming and that's *final*,' he said gruffly.

*　　*　　*

The Police Hovers descended on Mount Woodroffe at dawn the following day. The exact spot was pointed out by the frightened woman, who led them to where the mouth of the cave should have been. The Special Squad led by a Major, had all sorts of sophisticated equipment that quickly determined the existence of a holo camouflage field, determined its frequency, and neutralised it.

Mullhagen and Heidi stayed in their Hovers and let the heavy Squad do their job. They led the woman into the cave towards the shack. She was pulling back, not wanting to go with them. Her reluctance made them suspect something wasn't quite right. A scan located a booby-trapped force field, soon deactivated. A further scan showed no life-signs, suggesting the place was empty. The Major entered the shack and reported to Mullhagen the fugitives had recently fled, taking the bomb with them.

The Hover, with Rosa on board, was identified by satellite pictures, despite the rotating camouflage, heading towards the Antarctic. Traffic was warned to stay clear of her as she was armed and dangerous, and the Antarctic authorities were informed a pursuit was in progress. Any assistance would be most welcome.

*   *   *

Rosa had managed to hack into the police communication traffic with all the equipment in the corner of the shack, and had been well forewarned of the arrival of the armed apprehension squad. She had grabbed the suitcase with the bomb in it, and had fled in their Hover with Vinnie.

She'd rigged up a rotating frequency multiple camouflage field for their Hover, which blended the vehicle in with the terrain as it travelled over it. She headed south towards the coast, and left the Australian landmass at Cape Adieu, heading over the Indian Ocean towards the Antarctic, recklessly skimming over the waves, in a mad dash to outwit her pursuers.

As Rosa's Hover approached Wilkes Land on the Antarctic continent, she forced it even lower, some ten meters off ground level. She had expected to be chased by the authorities at some time in her undertaking, and had made extensive getaway plans. The plans included just this sort of scenario, with her heading for South America across the Antarctic, to Punta Arenas.

She followed a straight line to the 4,528 meters high Mount Kirkpatrick, near the Ross Ice Shelf, intending to circumvent Amundsen City on its larboard side. As she approached the Thorvald Nilsen Mountains, a number of Hovers from the City intercepted her, and forced her down onto the Amundsen Glacier.

Rosa jumped out of the Hover, trying to make a run for it, was brought down by a glue gun. The sticky mess encircled her from the neck down, holding her firm, whilst the outer skin hardened. It made it easier to transport the prisoner, and she would remain like that for the journey back to Amundsen City, at the South Pole, and then back to Perth.

Vinnie hadn't been so lucky. He'd jumped out, but being faster, he'd raced, slid, and finally fallen down a deep ravine in the Glacier. By the time he'd reached the bottom, bouncing off the sides, he'd broken his neck. They retrieved the body, and took it back to Amundsen City. The suitcase with the neutron bomb was salvaged. Disarmed by experts, who were amazed at the simplicity and ingenuity of its construction.

Back in Perth, the Police Commissioner congratulated Mullhagen on his success in getting this terrorist business sorted. Colonel Heidi Frisch added her good wishes from the European/World Government Security Bureaux. However, they discovered Rosa Steinberg was well into a full-blown psychosis. It made it impossible for her to be tried in any court of law.

She was quietly taken to PLC and given a happy authoritative childhood, reprogrammed with a normal education, and given "specialist programming" in security work. She was mockingly assigned to the Security Department at the World Government—to protect that which she'd tried so hard to blow up.

Thus ended the episode of the only known terrorist cell on Earth in centuries, and Rosa lived a more tranquil life until her subsequent termination at age two hundred.

Chapter Eleven

Against the Aliens

Accounts of the discovery of New Earth, with a climate not too difficult to transform to sustain human life, had got a lot of business people excited. There were the potential colonists, the businesses that would supply the colonists, and businesses that would build the ships supplying the colonists.

The big transport corporations already sounded out the feasibility of buying a Starship, so they could sell tickets to New Earth. The opening of a new world was hell of a big business, and when the aliens appeared, corporations saw all that potential business slipping away. Somehow, the aliens' request to quarantine New Earth had leaked, and Ying had to admit it was true.

The problem for the aliens, lay in that there was life already on New Earth. True, the life wasn't sentient, merely vegetable, but the aliens had been specific, in one of their Holocast interviews. Even planets that held only bacteria were off limits for colonisation. This prompted an outcry, mostly from the same business community that stood to gain from colonisation. Humans never had taken much notice of other life forms when they colonised. Why should they start now?

The aliens assured the interviewer, and viewers, there were a lot of planets able to be colonised by humans, and they would provide the terraforming technology when Earth signed the protocol. Somehow, the protesters didn't hear that—or simply didn't *want* to hear it. They went right on protesting.

Holo-Ads began to appear against the signing of the protocol. Why should humanity rely on aliens for their technology? Surely, we could get along without interference from outside. Why allow aliens to tell us what to do? It kept going on in this negative vein.

Then upbeat counter Ads appeared to disparage the negativity, lauding all the benefits that would amass from outside contact. Were humans a group of ostriches? How could they simply ignore the Galactic civilisation out there? We'd searched for life on other planets for millennia, and now we've found it; were we going to pretend they're not there? What kind of maturity does that demonstrate?

A real humdinger of an advertisement battle began to develop between the "pros" and the "antis." The "antis" money came from businesses ready and geared to colonise New Earth, whilst the World Government orchestrated the "pros."

The "antis" didn't stand a chance changing the "pros" minds, and they were keenly aware of that. What the ads were intended to accomplish, was to harass the World Government, sufficiently to extract some form of indemnity for the loss of business they *claimed* they'd suffered.

It was—a form of blackmail, and the preliminary round, by the business community, in trying to squeeze a negotiated recompense out of World Government. They were demanding they get first bite at any new technology transferred from the aliens, and any new contracts to build whatever was to be built. There was a fleet of star cruisers scheduled, if Earth joined the Federation.

R-Tech Corporation was angling to be nominated for the latter contract. They were keenly aware of the tremendous looming changes, and wanted to be, more than that, *needed* to be at the forefront of that change—

for the opportunities. R-Tech invested large sums in producing the antis Holo-Ads; a tactic they were convinced would pay healthy dividends.

* * *

The evening breeze was a welcoming change from the heat of the perpetual sun beating down on New Caledonia. Ying rested his tired brain in a spacious alcove reserved especially for the President of the World Government, high on the balcony restaurant, fifty storeys above street level. At the press of a button, a cup of Mocha materialised on the table in front of him, a spin off from the "energy⇒matter" converter Patanjali had invented.

His mood still perturbed by the Holo-Ads battle unfolding on worldwide Holocast. The matter of Rosa resolved itself satisfactorily, but this new turn of events with the Holocast PR war, although not serious, was bothersome to say the least. To plan a campaign, he'd invited his chief Economist to join him at table, but something kept him, and he was late.

Ying finally spotted him, weaving in and out of the tables, in the distance. He waved at the tall dark Qechua Indian coming towards him in a smart white tropical suit.

'*Hola!* Huáscar,' Ying called as he approached.

'*Hola! Sr. Ying,*' responded Huáscar, sitting down at the table.

Ying got down to business. 'Have you seen the Holo-Ads R-Tech's promoting?'

'Yes! They *must* be piqued,' Huáscar responded.

'I want us to find a way to stop them. It's utter blackmail.'

'What did you have in mind?'

'Well, you're the economic genius. I want to hit them in a way they'll understand. After all, these ads are designed to force financial concessions from us. They'd soon stop if instead of gain; it caused them financial pain. I want you to come up with a way of causing that financial pain.'

'Legal, or otherwise?'

'Both! I want to send a strong message to the whole financial community. They *can't* blackmail the World Government, and hope to get away with it.'

'We could try undermining their derivatives hedging. If it worked, it would scare them out of their wits. We could get into deep waters if the Global Financial Watchdog traced it back to us. It's your call.'

'What other options are there?'

'Get a Corporation friendly to us, to put in a hostile bid. They'd hit the Global Stock market buying up R-Tech equity. That simply takes money, lots of it.'

'Yes, I could use the emergency fund to finance it. We don't lose if we buy low and sell high. What else?'

'We could covertly inform R-Tech shareholders what they're up to, get them to call an emergency GM and censure the Board. It might also give us the wrong result. The shareholders may well back the Board.'

'OK...That's out then.'

'Put our peepers on Tamaguchi and his crew. Let them dig up all the rotten dirt there is on the R-Tech Board.'

'Might work.'

'See if we could influence their suppliers, and any contracts.'

'Right. I think we'll go with the derivatives, if that proves too difficult, then abandon that line. But we might as well go with the peepers simultaneously.'

'I'll get right on it, Sr. Ying.'

'Keep me up to speed, Huáscar!'

Huáscar got up from the table and left the restaurant. Ying sat relaxing for some minutes—before deciding to call it a day. He beckoned his private Hover, and ordered it to head for home, to his family.

*   *   *

Marcus Tamaguchi, Chief Executive of R-Tech was furious. The grim gathering around the polished silver table in the Board Room was dumbfounded and fuming. Zvi Mendelbaum, the Finance Director and Company Secretary, looked simply sheepish, whilst Paul Hogarth-Svensen, the venerable founder and Chairman of R-Tech was shouting.

'That sneaky son of a bitch,' yelled Hogarth-Svensen.

'Look here Paul; I warned you those ads were sledgehammers to crack a small nut. We'd been better off taking the direct approach,' Marcus was trying to quieten the old man.

'That underhanded lowlife, that blackguard, … lousy shyster,' Hogarth-Svensen was getting into the superlatives.

He had been raging like that for well over half an hour. He started when Zvi brought him news that someone had been trying to manipulate their derivatives portfolio. Those Futures Contracts were off limits—used only as a hedge against global price rises. Marcus told him there were also snoopers digging around in their personal lives, looking for any dirt they could use.

R-Tech Corporation was housed in an "Intelligent" hi-tech building serviced by the most sophisticated androids—it had its own security. They were alerted by their confidence IT gate-devices when hackers went after private files in the Personnel Department.

Then, their Futures Contracts started going the wrong way, price wise. At that point, their security Model alerted the human interface; the company was under siege from outside elements.

At first, Marcus thought it was a hostile take-over bid. A feedback trace located one of the sources to an Industrial Detective Agency normally employed by World Government. Then it clicked—they realised their Holo-Ads had triggered this antagonistic reaction from the World Government Secretariat. It had to be at Li's doing, so all the invectives Hogarth-Svensen was mouthing, were aimed at Ying.

'We're going to have to pull the ads,' declared Marcus.

'I want him put down,' retorted Hogarth-Svensen.

'Talk sense, Paul,' Marcus pleaded. 'You want to have the World President killed? He's outwitted us! That sly fox has got us by the shorts.'

'Two can play at low down ploys.'

'Paul, you're talking about *the President of the World Government*,' Marcus mouthed emphatically, hoarse desperation edging his voice.

'They can't get away with stunts like this,' Hogarth-Svensen yelled back.

'I said it was risky.' Marcus was back to a strong even boardroom voice. 'No! You overruled me. Now— will you please listen to me.'

'All right! All right! So what do you suggest?'

'I've just told you. We've got to pull the ads. It's that, or else we'll get more of these probes, and they're just warning shots across our bows. If they really become serious, we could be in for a lot of trouble.'

'*Hell!* I hate having to retreat. OK! Get in touch with the Ads Agency. Tell them to pull them. Then send an apology to Ying, personally. That lets him know, we know.'

Four days after the first Holo-Ads appeared on behalf of the antis, Ying received a confidential cryptic apology from Marcus Tamaguchi, CE of R-Tech. It was a holo message—simply saying sorry, in big flowery letters, signed by Marcus in person.

No explanation was needed. The Holo-Ads battle had been short and dirty, and Ying had accepted victory. He intended to invite R-Tech to submit a sealed tender for the starcruiser contract. It wouldn't do to ignore one of the leading hi-tech corporations on the planet.

Chapter Twelve

Black Hole

As Ying had anticipated, the Solar wide referendum went smoothly; endorsing World Government's view that humanity should sign the Solar System's accession to the Galactic Federation. Following the referendum, steps were taken to select and send a diplomatic delegation to Rakh, one thousand and eighty light years away.

The massive predicted majority in favour of the accession was heartening, but the tangible minority that had abstained—needed wooing. The tiny minority still wholly against any dealings with those loathsome aliens were being treated as merely an inconvenience—and that was frankly, a mistake.

Ying intended, subsequent to the referendum, there should be a grand signing ceremony held in the exalted auditorium of the World Government General Assembly in New Caledonia. It was agreed each President of every member nation of the World Government would attend the General Assembly personally, signing in the interests of their country. It would scupper the chances of any country later rejecting the treaty. Member countries could not later claim they had not personally signed.

*   *   *

When the time came for the ceremony at the General Assembly in New Caledonia, there were still a few minutes of consternation. The appointed time arrived for the aliens to appear. They didn't. That caused more than a little panic. After a while, of some serious head scratching, the holo images of Kileni accompanied by Ufi and Velred appeared, bearing profuse apologies. They had been in live communication with Rakh, and needed to finish the transmission. The excuses were accepted and Ying began the ceremony.

A thirty-minute speech in praise of "our new found friends" from Ying, "on this momentous occasion," was succeeded by a short but delightful speech from President Ghali. Then Kileni had his say, producing a much-appreciated speech. However, at the same time, he reminded people the *official* signing ceremony was to be on Rakh in a few days time.

Each of the permanent members of the Security Council then followed with short speeches; this ended the preliminary speechifying on Earth.

Ying proceeded to sign, on behalf of Earth and its colonies, followed by President Simeon Boutros Ghali for Mars. Kileni was next to sign, on behalf of the Galactic Federation.

This was succeeded by a procession of signatories starting with Mme Kamala Peshwa of India, for the Asian delegation.

'My goodness,' she inhaled. 'This is indeed momentous.' Then she quickly signed.

Frau Gehilde Schröder of Germany was standing behind her and said simply, 'Yah!' in agreement, and signed for the European delegation.

Sr. Rodrigo Perez of Mexico puffed himself up, took the pen with a Latin flourish, then signed for the American delegation; replacing the pen as if he'd just skewered a bull with it.

Chief Seswe Akuffo of Ghana was portly and regal. He approached solemnly, signed quietly for the

African delegation, then turned and retreated in good order.

Finally came Kamisese Rabuka of Fiji, for the Australasian delegation. There was a measured gait to his movements, as if each step mattered. He even signed as though the gods of Fiji were at his elbow.

Then came all the Presidents of the member countries of the World Government. The ensuing document was lodged in the official archives, whilst a copy was to be displayed in the entrance lobby, in a glass case for the benefit of visitors.

Then came an official reception, and a worldwide grand fireworks' display staged high above in the stratosphere, orchestrated by the Space Corps from space ships. The fiery patterns lit up Earth's night sky with an exuberance befitting the beginning of a new chapter in human history. The planet's population were invited to monumental street parties, organised and paid for by World Government.

On New Caledonia, a concert of classical music from all continents took place in the Assembly auditorium. For the first time on Earth, Kileni was invited to contribute some of his choice of music. The spectators was titillated by a short concert of extraterrestrial music. The audience bodily felt the alien music. It was played by Kileni on an extraordinary instrument; not just heard, but felt physically. The resonating frequency of the alien music somehow managed to match the frequency of the fibres in human body. Not aggressively, but stroking gently, flooding through the listener's fibres, in a soothing harmonizing fashion. Some claimed, "It tickled."

The military minded in the audience immediately grasped an alternate use for such an instrument. They felt uneasy at the thought. There are always those, fortunately a minority, who could only perceive a flower as the sum of its chemicals. They wondered if there was an alkaloid in there which might be useful in concocting a novel poison.

After the concert, Kileni took Ying aside. 'Are your Embassy people ready for Rakh? We depart soon, as you well know.'

'They're eager and waiting,' Ying told him.

Satisfied, Kileni thanked them for their hospitality, and vanished back to his ship.

*   *   *

The Hotel Excelsior on the Moon, served as the mixing point for the two delegations. Earth and Mars were intent they should establish a close rapport. Claude Joubert and Theodore Ghali spent a lot of time huddled together, working out the strategy and tactics they proposed to employ on Rakh.

Both human delegations had spent most of the week in hectic brain storming, at the command of their respective chiefs. The point was to evolve a coherent game plan, using some of the most sophisticated computer modelling techniques.

Their problem was lack of any previous paradigm dealings with alien races. All their much-vaunted modelling techniques relied on gathering all the *previous facts* and extrapolating a possible future mode of behaviour. Unfortunately, in this case there were no *past* to programme into the model regarding alien races. Predicting encounters and outcomes according to previous modelling proved theoretically interesting, but ultimately futile.

True to his word, immediately after the signing ceremony, Kileni downloaded a mass of information into the World Government computers regarding the component races in the Galactic Federation. To this end, each human member of the diplomatic delegation going to Rakh had been to the World Government Medical Facility. They were all to be inoculated against the various Rakhian bacteria and viruses their separate evolutionary paths had produced. They were screened at the same time against bringing in any earthly toxic fauna onto Rakh as carriers.

Cold and smallpox viruses had devastated the American Indian population, whose immune system had no protection against the incoming European diseases. With that lesson in mind, everyone was on alert when humans were to encounter a different race.

The human medical institutes were in contact with the Rakhian medical institutes, and between them came up with the necessary screening procedures and vaccines. The humans in their turn were obliged to take suppressants preventing them from contaminating the Rakhian population.

Following the medical check-up, member delegates visited the PLC to have the new information programmed into them. From data supplied; they discovered Rakh, the HQ of the Galactic Federation for this quadrant, was in the Zodiacal Constellation of Aquarius; lying along the ecliptic. It was along the yearly path of the Sun as seen from Earth, on a star known to them as α Aquarius, sometimes referred to as Sadalmedik. It had an absolute magnitude of 2.96 classified as a G2 star, similar to our Sun. They were able to confirm it was 1,080 light years from Earth.

Kileni offered to download the entire alien ship's database; for the Earth scientists to analyse, but it was soon evident it would overload Earth's computers. The aliens were using bio-computers and gluon-computers, far beyond the scope of current Earth technology.

Earth would have a great deal of catching up to do. It had just begun to employ biological systems for computing purposes; but compared to the bio-computers on Kileni's ship, it would seem there were many more steps along that road.

In due time, Claude and Theo came up with a *modus operandi* of how to proceed. They gathered their waiting Embassy people for a final pep talk. This was to be the last conference in their Solar System, away from snoopers. It was made crystal clear, their sole purpose in their diplomatic duties on Rakh, was to serve the interests of humanity. That meant, the folks back in their Solar System, above and beyond any other considerations, personal or otherwise.

All major, and initially, minor decisions, were to go through Joubert or Ghali *without exception*. Later they would be given more leeway and scope to act on their own initiative.

* * *

Joubert was informed Kileni's starcruiser had taken up position in standard lunar orbit, and they were requesting permission to land at Cysatus Spaceport.

'Their vessel is four hundred meters long and a hundred meters wide. They want to land out in the open, on the crater floor,' reported the agitated Lunar Traffic Controller to Ranjit Singh.

'Did they give you their tonnage?' He needed to know the impact the ship would make in the crater.

'Yes sir, five hundred metric tonnes.'

'That *can't* be right, not for a vessel of that size. Confirm it!'

'They confirm at five hundred.'

'*Well I'll be...,*' broke off Ranjit. He scratched his head and then continued, 'This stuff is going to take some time to get used to. Tell them to go ahead.'

'Yes sir.' The Controller passed on the permission. 'Sir! They're asking if the ambassadorial *entourage* is ready to embark.'

'Well, don't just stand there—ask Ambassador Joubert if he's ready to go.'

'Right away!' The Controller spoke into his personal mike, and got confirmation Joubert's party was ready. 'He's waiting at the airlock. The Hover shuttle is just connecting to their side of the airlock.'

'Good! Inform Ambassador Kileni the party will be with them in ten minutes.'

'Yes sir.'

In short order, the human party was invited to enter the alien starcruiser. Ufi was waiting to escort them to their quarters for the journey, but the internal scenery distracted the humans. What looked like a shiny metallic oblong from outside the ship, became a shiny metallic interior, but malleable to the touch.

Theo poked the wall of the corridor with his finger, and the wall gave, burying his finger to the first knuckle. He drew it back sharply. Shocked, amazed. He examined his finger for any sign of damage. Finding it intact, he rubbed it with his other hand for reassurance.

Human space vessels were brightly coloured, neat and spacious, with chic interiors. It was axiomatic the best designs were used for space—to boost morale and impart a psychological calm. Here, they were faced with one colour—shiny metallic silver, which seemed to be soft to the touch. Ufi led the way to a large number of adjoining cabins along one side of a corridor, deep in the heart of the starcruiser.

'We hope you will make yourselves comfortable,' Ufi sing-songed to Claude and Theo, leaving them standing at their adjoining entrances.

Ufi had each of the hundred and ninety-eight remaining diplomats individually escorted, by a crewmember, to their quarters. First time aboard such a ship, he thought it safer.

'When you've settled in, Ambassador Kileni would regard it a kindness if Ambassador Joubert and Ambassador Ghali would join him in the ship's lounge,' Claude and Theo heard their ear mikes tell them. 'You will notice the atmosphere has been modified to accommodate human breathing.'

'I'm getting a little irritated by their Holo images constant vanishing. I hope we're to meet the real Kileni,' Theo said to Joubert.

'You've seen their Holo images. I mean the true ones. You know what they look like,' retorted Joubert.

'It's not the same. I'd like to meet Kileni in the flesh, so to speak,' persisted Theo.

'Don't rush things. We'll have plenty of time to get to meet all sorts of races. As for Kileni, and the others, they'll appear in their own good time,' Joubert waxed sagely.

'I suppose you're right. Well, see you in ten minutes.' Theo went into own his cabin.

Joubert's cabin was sparse. An easy chair stood against the wall to his right, made of the same metallic substance; that was the entire visible furniture. Joubert was normally a calm person, an eminent man of science, a diplomat, yet here in his cabin, on this alien vessel, he was excited as a schoolboy with his first successful science experiment. He relied on familiar things to orientate himself, as do all humans; instead of the familiar, his surroundings could not be more strange. He felt everything was in the realm of the unknown, needing exploration.

Gingerly, he perched on the edge of the easy chair; finding it surprisingly soft—impelling him to sit back, get comfortable. A pleasant tinkling sound brought him out of his reflections. It came from the curved metallic wall to his left, where a small screen had suddenly appeared. He was certain it hadn't been there earlier, when he looked around the cabin. He climbed out of his chair and stood before the screen, which read in simple English "How to," followed by a list. The list had sub headings such as toilet, shower, storage, calling for assistance. It was the standard type of stuff one found in an unfamiliar Hotel room.

In order to obtain a sink, all one had to do was say the word, and it would appear. He tried it. Lo and behold, a familiar sink unit appeared against the wall, complete with an ultrasonic cleaning unit. It had emerged out of the liquid metal from the wall. "Shower" produced an ultrasonic shower unit. "Toilet" produced the same. Storage of his clothes was accomplished by saying "cupboard." Bemused, he unpacked and spruced up. Although the journey was to be relatively short, the discipline of tidiness was deeply inbred. He changed into a clean suit, then went to the ellipsoid outline of a doorway in the wall of his cabin; it was the way he entered. Sensing his presence, immediately a yawning appeared without a sound as a metallic portion retracted, vanishing into the wall, revealing the exit to the corridor.

Stepping into the corridor, he met Theo coming out of his cabin. A floating sign materialised out of thin air before them, announcing, "lounge," accompanied by directional arrows. They had little choice but to fall in behind the sign, which floated a meter before them, taking them along the corridor to the lounge.

The corridor seemed ubiquitous, giving the impression all parts of the ship were accessible from this one passage. A little way along, a cavity appeared in the wall to their right, revealing Kileni, seated on a massive cushion.

He was adorned by a transparent suit, present in the flesh, not the neutral holo image. This was their first encounter with him as he really was. He squatted on four flexible feet on the couch. He looked bulky, like a beige beanbag with feet and two pairs of manipulative prehensile tendrils extending from shoulder height. He had a head of sorts, a beaked mouth and two enormous bulbous yellow eyes, now focused on the humans.

From a human perspective, Kileni was not at all like his neat human holo form. The suit he wore was really to keep his skin moist, and he needed a rich oxygen atmosphere. However, any critique of Kileni's visual aspect could only come from a biased non-Kloshi viewpoint. Kileni was probably a handsome life form on Klosh.

'Greeting Ambassadors,' Kileni's invisible translator announced.

'Ambassador!' Joubert bowed just a little in Kileni's direction. Theo responded in a similar fashion.

'Chairs!' commanded Kileni. They appeared from the floor, opposite the alien. 'Please be seated,' he waved a tentacle.

Claude said, 'Thank you,' as he sat down.

'Are you experiencing any difficulties settling in?'

'No, err, just the unusual..., err, surroundings, and especially this fluid substance everything is made of,' reported Theo.

'Yes! We thought you might find that disconcerting. The metal is not known to your technology. It is fluid and rigid according to the pulses controlling it, which are finely modulated. It is of one colour to accommodate the myriad of races that use these starcruisers. You could call it a general purpose colour irritating no one.'

'That seems to make sense. And the whole vessel is constructed from it?' asked Theo.

'Yes. Now, let me invite you to take a tour of the ship, inside and outside.' Kileni passed his tendril over another tendril, which emitted a dull light from a strap. 'We've been under way for ten of your minutes now, and we're approaching your outer planet, Pluto.'

A meter wide circular screen appeared in the air before them showing the empty space outside. No! It wasn't empty. There before them hung Pluto, with a faint dot on its surface, probably the biosphere containing the Space Corps outpost. The spaceship was passing a relay-transmitter buoy, stationed near Pluto. Their ship came to an abrupt halt half a million kilometres out in space past Pluto.

'We're about to kick in the largest piece of equipment this ship carries, which simulates a collapsing star to generate a Black Hole,' Kileni motioned to the screen with a suited tendril.

As they watched the screen, there appeared a faint emission from their ship, out forwards into space. The emission began to form a small halo out there in clear space.

'In your terms, the ship has to generate a solar mass of 0.3125 to open a Schwarzschild radius of 937.5 meters, giving us a Black Hole sufficiently wide enough for the ship to enter,' Kileni informed them.

The halo began to increase, revealing a cavernous black yawning, drawing Joubert's eyes right into its depths. The halo was the edge of the event horizon, the Schwarzschild radius, where the powerful gravitational field bordered space, which if transgressed, sucked in everything, mass, bosons, leptons, quarks, photons, and gluons. At least, that was the current wisdom on Earth.

Here, on the edge of the event horizon, the ship hung, waiting for the generated Black Hole to stabilise at just under a kilometre-wide, rotating at an enormous speed.

Their vessel plunged into its darkness, and the screen in the lounge showed a series of multi-coloured lights flashing forwards, heading before them, not past, as one might expect. The ship was heavier than the neutrinos streaming before them. They had entered a wormhole human physicists had only theorised about, such as the hypothetical gravity tunnel through the fabric of space-time, but here, this alien technology had presented them with tangible reality.

'What stops us being spaghettified?' asked Theo.

'I'm sorry. I don't understand.' Kileni's blubber like features almost looked puzzled.

'When we cross the event horizon—what prevents us from being stretched to infinity?' Claude explained.

'Oh! Yes, I see. Well, this is a tame black hole—we have a special force field protecting us. We've engineered space-time, generating sufficient gravimetric energy until it's bent space-time into a black hole—but not so much that it becomes a singularity. Then the two bottoms of the entry and exit holes are joined in hyperspace to form a wormhole gravity tunnel.'

'This implies you can position these black holes *exactly* where you want them.'

'That's true. One here in your Solar System—the other comes out near Rakh.'

It was a form of cosmic subway, giving them a short cut generated by the Black Hole in their part of space, through to the connecting White Hole exit, over one thousand light years away in another part of space.

As the spaceship entered the third minute of its time in the wormhole tunnel, the external lights began to change direction; the ship was now seemingly moving much faster and passing those streams of light. The light outside—dazzling bright, and the screen automatically dimmed to enable the watchers to tolerate the brilliance.

Then as suddenly as they had entered the tunnel, they were quickly evicted into open space.

Looking at the screens rear view of the White Hole from which they had exited, they could see a continuous stream of light in its interior, with the occasional space flotsam. The spaceship halted by the second relay-transmitter buoy near Rakh.

Joubert and Ghali set their eyes on a view never before beheld by other human beings. The screen showed the darkness of deep blue space, but a space that was over one thousand light years from their Solar System, and both felt infinitely alone—far from home. It wasn't so much *what* they were seeing, but the point from *where* they were seeing it that was breathtaking—a soaring of the imagination.

Kileni interrupted their reflections, 'Now I want to show you something of the ship itself.'

Joubert sighed, 'I'm at a loss for words.'

Theo responded similarly, 'My mind is finding it hard to take in all this...this....' A faraway look transfixed his face. 'I knew when I awoke this morning, my senses would be bombarded with incredible data, but it's even more astonishing than I foresaw.'

The screen changed from the outside view to show the bridge.

'You will note,' Kileni continued, 'the screen in front of you now shows the bridge of the ship: or would you rather do a physical inspection?' he inquired through his translator.

'I think the exercise would do us good,' responded Claude.

'Well, good,' and Kileni floated up from his cushion in his suit, a few centimetres off the deck of the ship.

He turned, leading the way out into the corridor. As Claude's and Theo's feet achieved the corridor, so the floor started to move in the direction Kileni was floating. They simply maintained their balance, trying to stand still. The floor did the travelling. The corridor floor began to elevate gently, and small ridges appeared, allowing their feet to get a grip. They stopped in front of what initially appeared to be a dead end. A door unexpectedly opened, revealing the bridge of the ship.

On the previous screen, as they viewed the ship's bridge, they'd seen an alien without a suit. Now, two were busily staring into space, all suited up. One individual looked a burly stocky bipedal, but with three upper appendages; the second was a tall slim individual, a quadruped with two snake-like arms.

The bridge was even more alien, having no visible instruments, all command functions operating by voice. The bridge was a medium sized room with a couple of seats for the crew, otherwise there was little else for the humans to see.

The efficiency and reliability of their computer systems had to be excellent, and above all reliable, since the whole ship was hooked into it. The lack of instrument panels was the biggest difference between a human spaceship, and this alien vessel.

'Are there any questions you care to ask?' Kileni offered.

'To do that, we would need to have some common reference points. I'm presuming it's all voice controlled? Incidentally, which one is the Captain?' asked Joubert.

'Yes, your right to the first part—as to the second part—it's the tall one,' Kileni answered.

'I'm somewhat bemused your crew doesn't have a visual crosscheck on your computers—with consoles, I mean,' Theo put in. Then changing tack, he asked, 'Could we see the Engine Room now.'

'Of course! Please follow me.'

The party went out into the corridor, and the floor began to move again in a gentle downward direction. Kileni floated above the floor whilst the floor carried the rest down to the requested destination.

'What is with this floor? I've never heard of a ship's floor taking anyone for a ride.'

'I'm sorry. If you'd rather walk, I can tell it to cease moving,' Kileni offered.

'No. It's Okay. I just find it a little disconcerting, that's all. How do you control it?' Claude was starting to feel a bit tired. His nerves were a fraction on edge.

'By voice! Well, here we are.'

The corridor flattened out and a door appeared on their left. Claude hadn't heard any commands from Kileni; he was sure of that. Was he holding back?

They entered a room containing a large forty-meter doughnut-shaped structure in the middle of the massive chamber, again shrouded in ubiquitous metallic silver. Three aliens wearing, what looked like energy suits, scurried around the base of the toroidal structure. From that immense solid closed curve, they felt a power being generated unlike anything they'd come across on the vessel. The whole ship was silent, but here, this doughnut generated an imperceptible sacrilegious hum.

'There's a force field between the gravimetric generator, and us so we're quite safe. I would like to explain the workings of the engine, and the gravimetric black hole generator you see before you, but as I understand it, you yet don't have any reference points to comprehend the theoretical notations. Am I correct?' It was a question directed at the Nobel Laureate, Claude Joubert.

'I thought *I* just said that—earlier?' offered Claude.

'I think we've just been called stupid,' Theo whispered to Claude.

'No. He's right. We probably wouldn't understand it,' Claude whispered back. 'You're doubtlessly right,' he said loudly to Kileni.

'Don't feel offended, Ambassador; all new members go through a little inferiority phase at the beginning. It's only to be expected.' Kileni was being soothing, diplomatic, and relentless.

'Let me try to put it into perspective. Here, before your eyes is a technology dating back over a million years. That compares with *your* planet's first use of metal, cold hammered copper, only around eleven thousand in your past. When you agreed to join the Federation, you jumped technologically, forward a million years. It would have been criminal of you to turn down the offer to join the Federation. But it had to be your choice.' Kileni was being blunt, but effective. The two humans were suitably abashed. Claude gave Theo an embarrassed look.

Kileni continued, 'as we speak, you best scientists are tussling with the intricacies of replicating this engine in building a starcruiser like this. To accomplish that task, they have to restructure all of their metallurgical scholarship, much of their Chemistry and Physics, and above all, their astro-engineering.

'That painful task will take them at least two of your years before they're ready to build. Even using your PLC. Be patient with us; but above all, be patient with yourselves. Your species are used to running everywhere; it has moved you far and fast from your origins. For a few years, you need to relearn the art of walking.'

The two humans felt even more self-conscious of the superior technology displayed before them. In the meantime, as Kileni's speech was being given, the starcruiser had arrived at Rakh.

Chapter Thirteen

Rakh

'We've arrived in standard orbit around Rakh the Federation HQ for the quadrant. Would you like to see the scenery?' Kileni asked.

'Yes indeed,' declared Claude.

The circular screen reappeared, bearing a view of the planet below. Clouds shrouded the planet much like Earth, but whereas Earth was mostly blue from space, this planet was a majestic yellow, complementing the light emanating from its Sun.

'Could we see the star system?' Theo requested.

The screen displayed a yellow sun, they were informed, a G2 main sequence star. Simultaneously, the entire star system appeared below the screen as a holo projection, showing three more large planets of the size of Jupiter. Rakh was the nearest to this sun, around one and a half astronomical units away from it.

'We are ready to teleport down. As you know, the Rakhian atmosphere is 28% oxygen, compared to your 21%, so be careful at first, and a gravity 1.8 of Earth's,' was Kileni's announcement.

'We knew this would come, but I'm still apprehensive,' Theo declared.

'Trust us; we haven't had a teleportation accident for a thousand years,' Kileni reassured.

'Well, that's heartening, but all our experiments with teleportation have always ended in disaster,' lamented Theo in a lowered voice, embarrassed by his trepidation.

'Come on,' Claude asserted, 'lets start as we mean to go on. We *have* to be able to trust them.'

Kileni spoke to the air, 'Three to teleport to the Solar Embassy then wait a cental and convey a hundred and ninety-eight more to the same location.'

'What of our luggage...?' were the last words uttered by Theo on the ship as he dematerialised.

The next moment he felt a tingling sensation, and discovered he was standing, feeling a bit giddy from the rich air, in a resplendent low-ceilinged hall. His companions stood milling around him, steadying each other. The hall gave off the impression of being formed of living nature.

Ahead, a parabolic arch led to another hall. All around, there seemed to be a structural flexibility, an undulation, as though the walls were live and listening. Everything was gnarled and curved, as if a vision of Antoni Gaudí's work had resurrected from the ground.

The famous classical twentieth century Catalan architect had used the aesthetics of Pau Milá y Fontanals, resulting in buildings imbued with mystery and esotericism, all based on imitating lines of nature.

'We knew of your *penchant* for the Catalan architect, Ambassador Joubert, and it fitted perfectly with the Rakhian naturalistic ethos; so we had your Embassy built in the classical Gaudían style.' Kileni still in his suit, informed Joubert.

'It's beautiful,' effused Claude. 'I'm overwhelmed, and — just stunned! What do you think, Theo?'

'It's interesting,' Theo had been searching for a diplomatic phrase. He was more used to Martian architecture. Grit blasted plastic domes, adobe-like structures, where the sand storms smoothed out any gnarled organic effects.

'Is that *all* you can say. "Interesting?" I've never taken you for a provincial Theo.'

'I'm sure I'll get used to it,' parried Theo lamely.

'This is going to make me feel completely at home,' continued Claude disregarding Theo's lack of enthusiasm, 'and I can't thank you enough, Ambassador Kileni. This is really appreciated.'

'Think nothing of it. We hope you'll settle in. The signing ceremony is scheduled for tomorrow morning at ten, in the Amphitheatre, with Quadrant Custodian Thesor in attendance. You are both to present your credentials then.'

'*Ubongo!* Where are you?' shouted Claude. Adama Ubongo was Joubert's Ugandan Chief of Staff (CoS).

'Here Ambassador,' came a response from across the hall. Adama came hurrying to Joubert's side.

'Make a note. We're presenting credential at ten tomorrow. Get everybody organised. Unpack and allocate rooms. Offices downstairs, accommodation upstairs. Make sure the Martian delegation is abstracted from the Earth people, we want them to feel they have an identity of their own, and oh, make sure you apportion Ambassador Ghali equal due. Liaise with his CoS to sort things out. Well, you know the sort of thing. Get to it.'

'Yes, Ambassador.'

'You heard that Theo. Is it acceptable to you?'

'Perfectly acceptable.'

'Thank you Kileni; for all you have done.'

'We shall see each other tomorrow. One to teleport up,' Kileni spoke to the air again, and dematerialised.

'Well Theo, let's see to our staff. I'm dying to take a tour of the house and grounds.'

'Ambassador!' called Adama.

'Well?'

'The Embassy is upside down. I mean; there's one level higher, but five levels beneath us, *underground*. And they all have windows, and have the *sun* shining in them,' Ubongo was puzzled by the miraculous arrangement.

'Lead on! I want to see the house. This is an opportune moment. Coming Theo?'

The small group, Adama in the lead, sauntered off towards the stone sculptured stairwell leading to the lower levels. As they stepped on the stairs, the stairs began to move, descending at a leisurely speed, only this was a circular stair well and no joins could be discerned in the steps.

The group visited all the levels; Adama was right. Each room they visited had glorious sunshine streaming through their windows. The view out of the windows was of a luscious yellow valley, whilst the sun was in the afternoon, facing the windows, hence the lighting effect. If it was a holo image, then there shouldn't have been sun streaming in. It must be an atrium type of cavern, but how did the valley come to be there; they couldn't figure out how it was achieved.

The underground section was enormous and could fit four times their party. 'Adama! Don't skimp on space,' Claude ordered.

In spite of its size, the overall effect was of a soothing comforting cave in a cool summer's forest; even the aroma suggested the season was mid-summer— apart from the blue foliage. The Rakhians had indeed out-Gaudíd Gaudí; at least Claude Joubert thought so.

'Well, my injunction to you still stands, Adama. Put the sleeping quarters upstairs leave the ground level for reception, all the offices go downstairs. With this much room, we can afford to spread.'

'Yes your Excellency. The matter of the Martian Embassy has been raised by Faisal al-Rhumi; Ambassador Ghali's CoS. He's requested the Martians take the whole level beneath this one, if that's all right with us. Their fifty people will have a lot of space. I've agreed to their request subject to your approval; it will make the Martian Embassy distinct, and I've asked it to be treated with respect by our people. Do you concur?'

'Absolutely, Adama!' Claude changed subjects, 'Ask all the staff to assemble in the main dining hall in an hour after they've settled into quarters. I just want to see if there are any complaints.'

'Yes your Excellency.'

Some time later, after Joubert had left the extraordinary long dining hall with its two hundred seater table, having dealt with a few minor gripes, he decided to see the outside of the Embassy. Did it have a garden? What was the flora like? Was it as yellow as it looked from space? He approached the front door; the thick gnarled oak-like doors opened smoothly and silently revealing a noonday. The oxygen rich atmosphere invigorated but made him heady. He felt more energetic than usual, compensating for the heavier gravity.

He began down the steps, but the heavier gravity gave him more momentum, leading him to stumble. He cursed and steadied against the stone rail to the right. Turning, he looked back and saw a plaque on the jamb, each side of the door, with what looked like the Solar System Coat-of-Arms.

This was something he, Ying and Ghali had cooked up to identify their home world. The Solar System was on the Orion Spur of the Carina-Cygnus Arm of the Milky Way and so they had sketched the cross-section of a ships keel, a swan sitting in the middle and a hunter standing in front. Carina (Keel)-Cygnus (Swan), Orion (Hunter). It was all very logical. They had a plaque ready to go up but...it seems they'd been pre-empted. It gave him a momentary feeling of helplessness to see such competence by the Rakhians.

Slowly, the dizziness passed, and at the bottom of the stone stairs, to the right, he walked to a small tree at the edge of the blue lawn. The long winding driveway was in front. The panorama was of trees, and more trees, not entirely unlike the trees on Earth, except they looked a little bit shorter and had more foliage; all blue. Back on Luna he'd been told instead of chlorophyll the foliage contained galazophyll, hence blue.

The driveway was marble covered, or it appeared marble; was smooth and tinted orangey-yellow. All the trees were evenly spaced with neat circular patches of clear brown earth around them, or was he supposed to call it clear brown rakh.

Claude moved a little away from the building, out onto the driveway and turned. The Embassy edifice, a rhythm of undulating horizontally curved edges illuminated with flamboyant trimmings, suggesting bones, muscles, wings, petals, caves, clouds and even stars. It was truly poetical, not a straight line in sight— which brought to mind an ancient saying—"nature abhors a straight line." These twists and gnarls somehow brought the building alive. The granite facade was a rock-face covered with organically shaped growths. The roof was a long low parabolic flourish capping the whole magnificent manor. He breathed a sigh of delight.

Claude stared, unable to take his eyes off the enchantment flowing into his senses. He was a scientist, but over the years had become a poet, an emotional Gallic articulator, *and* a painter of some renown. Extending his life span had allowed him to achieve a breadth of artistic attainment a twentieth century person could only envy. Since longevity was the norm, the inhabitants of Earth were able to master many professions. Each enriched the other, until they achieved a spiritual all-inclusive contentment.

* * *

Early the following day, Ambassador Claude Joubert, accompanied by his Chief of Staff, Adama Ubongo, were ready in the embassy reception hall, waiting for Ambassador Theodore Ghali and his CoS, Faisal al-Rhumi. It was half past nine in the Rakhian morning, with half an hour to go to the official signing of the protocol and the presentation of their credentials to Quadrant Custodian Thesor of the Galactic Federation.

Down the stairs came hurrying Ambassador Ghali, followed by al-Rhumi, full of contrition for delaying the other's departure.

'I'm terribly sorry to have kept you all waiting,' Theo exclaimed, looking abashed.

Both Earth and Mars would join in the signing of the accession treaty to the Galactic Federation, and then present their credentials to the Quadrant Custodian. This would be done on the podium of the Great Amphitheatre of Rakh according to protocol. The Amphitheatre was their eight hundred thousand year old Holy of Holies.

They had learnt from Kileni, Grand Custodian K'Rel had arrived in person on Rakh for the signing ceremony. This greatly enhanced the importance of the gathering, and the infrequency of the occasion.

Kileni materialised in the hall in his suit, just to the right. 'I trust you rested well,' was his opening remark.

'Thank you, yes we did,' Joubert responded.

'Then I assume you're ready for the days main event.'

'We were just waiting for you,' said Theo.

'We'll teleport after I remind you of the formal etiquette we're to follow. We'll rematerialise in the centre of a clearly marked golden ring on the podium of the Amphitheatre. Whatever you do, do *not* step outside the ring before you sign the protocol. It would give grave offence—a lasting embarrassment for both sides. The inside of the ring is non-Federation territory, for ceremonial purposes. The ceremony will be conducted in Rakhian, by the Grand Mehir of Rakh, who will firstly welcome the Grand Custodian to Rakh. The Grand Custodian will then thank the Grand Mehir, followed by a speech of welcome to the human representatives of Earth and Mars. The Grand Custodian will then invite both you and Theo to step outside the golden circle to sign the protocol. Only the two Ambassadors will approach the dais before the Grand Custodian, where you may both make a brief speech. Then the formal signing procedure of three copies will take place, the documents will be received by the two of you, and the third will go to Kaikon, home world of the Grand Custodian.

'In the closing remarks you will both be presented with a symbolic *shantun*. The real *shantun* is a larger recognition apparatus announcing the end of your Solar System's quarantine; you are no longer off limits to Federation starcruisers, since you have now joined the Federation. As we speak, the real *shantun* is on its way back to your Solar System. It will transmit a signal out to the relay-transmitter past Pluto, which will be boosted five billion kilometres further out. Have you any questions?'

'No. We've acquainted ourselves with what you've just said, from the clip you left in our machine last night. I think we're ready to go,' was Claude's contention.

'Five to teleport to the Amphitheatre ring,' Kileni commanded.

'Six,' corrected Claude, 'our media reporter from Earth is due to accompany us—for the Earth Holocasts. Remember, you agreed.'

'So I did,' Kileni corrected.

To Adama, Claude whispered, 'Where is that damned woman?'

'Here she is now.'

Gina Young came swishing down the steps—knowing full well, she was now the centre of attention. She joined them, seemingly apologetic—yet Claude knew better.

'Sorry everyone,' she threw at them gaily.

'Six to teleport to the Amphitheatre ring.'

They rematerialised in a shimmering circle of golden luminescence, surrounded by a vast Amphitheatre. It was open to the glorious yellow-blue sky, and a warming glow of sunshine radiated on the gathered crowd.

Without waiting, Gina Young rushed to record the location. 'This is Gina Young reporting live for Holocast Earth Station-45, bringing you an update on our exclusive historic story from the famous Amphitheatre. We're on Rakh, standing in an ellipsoid shaped arena, able to seat *a hundred and fifty thousand*. The raised dais and podium occupies one subsidiary vertex of the ellipse. The gently sloping area has beautifully inlaid curved walls, making the rising tiers seem to hang in the open space, *and it is full to the brim.*'

Gina Young never rambled, but she went on-and-on reporting all the way through the ceremony, quietly buzzing in the background. All those around her tried to ignore the moderate prattle emanating from the insistent newscaster.

Claude and Theo, conscious of representing the whole race of humans, stood shoulders back, head erect, resplendent in their Ambassadorial uniforms. The formalities were all too brief, and the protocol of accession was signed, with all due pomp and circumstance. Gina Young reported for Earth's media using her Holo-recorder to document the whole ceremony for the folks back home. She would splice herself in when she got back to the studio.

The Grand Custodian wore an atmospheric suit, clearly uncomfortable with the rich oxygen content of the Rakhian atmosphere. He was a small individual only a meter high, a large head, imposing big black eyes. He levitated throughout the ceremony using an anti-gravity belt, probably finding the Rakhian gravity too uncomfortable. At the conclusion of the speeches and the exchange of documents, the Grand Custodian handed Claude the ceremonial *shantun*, and in a surprise unscheduled gesture, gave him a neatly wrapped mystery package.

The Custodian then lifted his arms into the air, and an almighty roar went reverberating around the Amphitheatre, followed by a gentle tingling sound. The sound touched the inner essence of the humans present, seeming to gently dance along their nerve fibres. They didn't just hear the tingle; the felt it, and were comforted by it. It was at that moment, Claude later commented, he thought the Earth had finally grown up, and become adult, joining the rest of the sentient life in their Galaxy.

Chapter Fourteen

The Mehir

The ancient Rakhian civilisation had flourished for just over a million years, imbued with a million years of glorious Rakhian history. A million years of Art, Philosophy, and Science, deeply and earnestly penetrating their contemplative psyches.

Over many millennia, through the quagmire of evolution, they had hauled themselves into civilisation, establishing themselves as the dominant species on their planet. The first Mehir had helped them negotiate the difficult period of the early warring city-states. He had unified the warring factions with an iron fist and had wisely concluded that settling conflicts through force was a mug's game. In that single flash of outstanding inspiration, he had built a planet-wide cradle in which the future Rakhian civilisation could progress.

The Mehir had outlawed the use of violence, and set in place a rigid hierarchical succession. It enabled his lineage to entrench and enforce his eternal peace. It was only made possible by bringing all the planetary factions under his autocratic rule.

The foundations of Rakhian society embodied in their revered constitution was that disagreements were to be resolved peacefully. This allowed them to embark on constructing the foundations of their peaceful social, cultural, political, economic, and technical development.

From that moment, Rakhian society had progressed in a linear fashion, instead of the lengthy alternating ups-and-downs that punctuated human history. Over time, the Mehir's function had become ceremonial, and the society developed democratically with an extravagance about reaching a consensus, the purpose of the cherished old Amphitheatre.

To record his thoughts at this solemn occasion, Claude talked quietly into his personal databank. 'Standing on this ancient alien planet, I feel a sense of awe. By comparison, we humans have just stepped onto the first rungs of the ladder leading to true civilisation. This is my assessment of the gulf that separates our myriad of hosts from human thinking. How is it going to be possible to close such a chasm? Yet, I have arrived at a remarkably simple conclusion. We must conduct ourselves not as the *devious* human selves we are capable of, but the open honest human selves the situation requires us to be. Anything else will be exposed as sham, and harm any future relations. That is not to say, we ought to be innocent, simple or gullible.'

These recorded thoughts had a relevance to the official invitation he and Theo had received from the Grand Mehir, to later attend a reception, in their honour at the Mehir's estate. In attendance would be Grand Custodian K'Rel, Quadrant Custodian Thesor, Grand Mehir Nathur, and Primearch Reithur, accompanied by many other prominent members of Rakhian society. It would be an opportune moment for Joubert to thank the Grand Custodian for the small package he had received at the signing ceremony.

It contained a crystal recording cube, with a number of long symphony like pieces involving tingling music, together with holo images of the players in performance. One of the pieces was the tingling composition they'd heard in the Amphitheatre at the signing ceremony. The significance of the gift was a cultural exchange, and at that level, it was much appreciated by Claude. It all seemed to bode well for the future.

The four humans were teleported to the Mehir's estate dressed in their ambassadorial finery. They were met by a short slim powerful Rakhian, who reminded Claude and Theo of a benevolent elfin-like person from Earth's Teutonic mythology.

'Ambassador Joubert? I'm your guide and elucidator. My appellation is Rothan,' said the splendidly attired Rakhian.

'Pleased to meet you,' said Claude.

Both sides talked in their own language, and were interpreted by a small green circular brooch on their lapels.

'May I introduce my party,' offered Claude. 'His Excellency, Theodore Ghali, Ambassador for Mars. My Deputy and Chief of Staff, Adama Ubongo. His Excellency's Deputy and Chief of Staff, Faisal al-Rhumi.'

'In a little while, I would like you to meet the Ambassador for Barog, the last planet to enter the Federation before Earth, around four hundred of your years ago. I venture to suggest that you would have matters in common, as the latest two new members of the Federation.'

'That's kind of you,' responded Claude.

'I'm afraid I find this a little trite,' complained Theo into Claude's ear.

'Patience my dear Theo, patience,' Claude whispered back.

They were introduced to the Ambassador for Barog, His Excellency Portuk, and a two-meter tall, muscular dinosauroid, whose translator invited them round to his Embassy for a chat. They left Adama chatting with the tall Barogian, making future arrangements. Claude managed to thank the Grand

Custodian for his kind reception of Earth's representatives, and for that extra little present.

The Quadrant Custodian invited them to attend the first meeting of the Grand Council, at which they were to discuss the problem of "New Earth" and human history. "New Earth" referred to the planet in the Centauri system that had been scheduled for human colonisation, now deferred. His office would let the Embassy know of the time and date. That sounded ominous.

The Grand Mehir insisted they join him for a tour of Rakh in the following week. The Primearch scheduled an official meeting with both Ambassadors for two weeks.

The whole evening continued in the same vein, with polite chitchat, curious stares at the new human species, from amongst an immense range of sentient species. Quite a number were in suits against the horrendous oxygen gas in the atmosphere. The same gas that the human party found so invigorating.

Diplomatic functions whatever the country, whatever the continent, whatever the planet, seemed to pursue a networking format. To the average outsider it might be deemed as attractive, abounding with intrigue and spies, but to others simply excruciatingly boring. However, that was the sparkling life of a diplomat.

* * *

The week went by. The Embassy was rapidly put to order, and began functioning. At the subsequent weekend, Claude and Theo began looking forward, and made ready to tour Rakh at the invitation of the Mehir.

The Mehir's aerohopper arrived, waiting outside in the driveway. Rather than teleport, the Mehir thoughtfully provided a more refreshing start to the trip by allowing them to view the scenery from a primitive form of transport.

Teleporting around was all well and good, but the sense of having travelled from A to B was missing. One moment a person was standing in one room—the next moment they were standing in another. Claude certainly appreciated the Mehir's gesture in sending the anti-gravity aerohopper.

They climbed aboard and lifted gently off the ground, then hovered for a second before whooshing off left. They hadn't orientated themselves yet as to the points of the Rakhian compass.

From their vantage point, they could see that the land was covered in a vast forest. Trees stretched out to the far horizon with building evenly spaced in amongst them, below the canopy. Many of the buildings were constructed below ground as needed, with only one floor ever protruding above ground level. With no tall structures littering the landscape, it gave the impression of one vast garden.

The sun shone overhead, but in the distance appeared a towering haze. Nearing, they could see a looming glistening sculpture rising high above the tree line. As they paralleled the sculpture, it dawned on them; they were looking at a clear liquid, which may have been water. The sculpture described splendid spirals, some naturalistic branching, and a central stalk that looked like a flower of some kind, all with a hint of colour. The image *hung* there, with just an inkling of movement.

Momentarily mesmerised, they stared at it transfixed by the thought the water molecules were being individually controlled. Somewhere an artist was able to create and control a water sculpture. Smaller similar sculptures were arranged in a line near the large one, with some form of holo plaque in Rakhian, presumably the sculptor's name.

Children played on antigravity sleds in a clearing near them, cavorting in the air, being exuberant, boisterous and young. Since the aerohopper was automatic, there was no one with them they could quiz on the sculptures, and Claude made a mental note to ask someone if the sculpture was really made out of water. They passed close to three more different water forms, representing a wide variety of aqueous enigmas.

As they neared the Mehir's palace they came on another sculpture, but this was created out of a colonnade of pure light, rising over three hundred meters into the sky. It may have been produced holographically, but they could see no source. Claude suspected the individual photons were being controlled somehow to capture the outline. The semblance was of a virtual rainbow spiralling ever upwards.

The aerohopper alighted on a circular designated pad, and the two Earthmen got out, walked up the stairs towards a Rakhian guard, in full uniform. It would seem the Mehir was old-fashioned enough to retain the ancient ceremonial trappings of his ancestral position. A doorway appeared in front, and another Rakhian, probably the chamberlain to the Mehir, greeted them with a slight bow of the head.

'You are most welcome. If you would care to follow me, I will take you to the Mehir.'

'Thank you,' offered Claude, with little enthusiasm for the regal trappings. He was a staunch Republican of the old French mould, and had a natural distaste for royal pomp. 'I must say I'm surprised to see this regal display in such an ancient culture,' he whispered to Theo.

'The French have their *chasseurs* at the Palais de l'Elysée, guarding the French President, even now,'

Theo whispered back. 'A little theatre adds to the notion of romanticism in a culture, be it palace, church, temple or mosque. The signing of the protocol the other day was pomp and ceremony. Did you object?' There was no escaping the logic. Claude had not only accepted the ritual, but had thoroughly enjoyed it.

'Touché,' Claude whispered, 'Point, set and match to you.'

They approached a couch containing the outlines of the Mehir, seemingly engrossed in a manuscript. The chamberlain coughed gently, and the Mehir put the manuscript aside and rose to his feet; arms outstretched. He was light featured, slight with a narrow chest, and stood one and a half meters tall.

'I'm so pleased you could make it,' the Mehir exuded charm. He looked puzzled at Claude's proffered hand.

'Sir, I was honoured by your kind invitation. I've already experienced some delightful sights enroute to you, and am looking forward to the trip,' he said loquaciously looking down at the Mehir. This was Joubert at his most diplomatic.

The Mehir looked at Theo next, who quickly withdrew his proffered hand.

'We needn't stand on ceremony, call me Nathur.' The sudden informality startled them.

'I'm Claude and this is Theo,' responded Claude.

'Shall we make a move?'

'By all means.' The Mehir said something incomprehensible to his chamberlain, who rushed off immediately.

'We'll take my Hopper; it's somewhat more generous.'

The party moved outside to a large Hopper with a fair sized lounge in the midsection. All boarded, and it lifted off veering right. The forest canopy flooded their eyes with luscious blue foliage. On Earth, chlorophyll painted everything green, but here on Rakh, galazophyll, serving the same purpose, coloured all the foliage blue.

The azure landscape suggested the society had sufficient maturity, had become confident enough to clear the skies of phallic symbols puncturing the heavens with false supremacy. There were none of the ugly skyscrapers still scarring Earth. Instead, they built a garden, and lived surrounded by beauty and tranquillity.

Yet, there was no doubting their advanced technology, which had a laid back quality to it. It wasn't pushy, it wasn't showy, and it didn't need to say "*Hey! Here I am, aren't I flashy?*" It was subtle, calm, and efficient. At least—it was the impression Joubert was left with when he looked at the alien canopy.

The Hopper climbed, approaching a sizeable patch of blue-green water that reminded Claude of the question he had.

'May I pose a question, err...Nathur?'

'By all means Claude,' answered the Mehir casually.

'There were some fluid sculptures we passed on the way to your residence. Is the suspension "*water*," and how are they assembled?'

'The liquid is ionised water, shaped by a gluon-computer controlled model, fixing the sculptured matrix atom by atom into a layered force-field.'

'There, you see Theo; I was right.' Claude was delighted.

'Did you like them?' the Mehir asked.

'On Earth we make a great deal out of fountains, but I concede we have nothing like those sculptures. The laser image outside your palace was another delight,' more diplomacy.

'The sculptured lights were computer-controlled photons; we'll see some more later. If you wish, I could introduce you to the artist who created them?'

'That would be most generous of you.'

The Mehir pointed out of the window—downwards at the ocean, 'If you observe, below...there, where the circle is, a similar sculpture is being assembled.'

Claude and Theo looked where he pointed—and could see nothing.

'It's important I point out the flora and fauna of the habitat around the sculpture,' he kept pointing, 'is not damaged by the process. They're well segregated.'

The Hopper was passing over a sea, and below in the water; a fifty-meter circle had been defined, with a twenty-meter wide hole in the middle. Now, Claude and Theo discerned something happening. Into the new hole, water fell as in a natural waterfall, more water appeared at the defining rim of the circle, and fell into the hole.

It was a weird creation, not a whirlpool, but a true waterfall in the middle of the sea. It was something easy to achieve with a holo image, the Red Sea parting, but outrageous to actually construct in the middle of the sea. The Rakhians were an extraordinary species, and this bent for artistry seemed to express their character uncommonly well.

All Claude could say was, 'Most extraordinary.'

'Bizarre to say the least,' came from Theo.

'You don't approve?'

'No..., I mean *yes*. It's simply so *eccentric*, building waterfalls in the middle of the ocean.'

'Someone in the palace must have given the artist our itinerary. It is playful art; it does no damage, and is visually stimulating. It would seem he's trying to get our attention.'

A light began flashing on the dashboard. Calmly, the Mehir spoke to the Hopper in Rakhian. The craft swung sharply to the left and dove downwards heading for the distant landmass.

'Anything wrong?' asked Claude.

'A minor problem,' the Mehir told them. 'A fine meteor shower has evaded our space defences and is heading for this area. We are simply taking evasive precautions and heading for cover. Our nearest protection will be in the fluorescent tunnels on the seashore over there,' he pointed towards the looming land.

The Hopper skimmed the shoreline until it was directed into an entrance yawning that unexpectedly appeared out of nowhere. Down the Hopper went into the far end of the tunnel and settled on the landing pad.

'Please follow me,' said the Mehir as he hurriedly opened the hatch and jumped out.

Claude and Theo didn't wait to be asked twice. They were on the Mehir's heels. The Mehir hastened them into a glittering fluorescent tunnel—then relaxed his gait to a walk. Having got his guests to safety, he stopped and beamed at Claude and Theo.

'We're safe now!' he declared.

'That can't be usual,' Theo burst out.

'No! Your right. I didn't want to alarm you, but the meteor shower was not a natural phenomenon. Someone hurled them at Rakh. My communicator tells me we're under attack from space pirates. A hit and run assault.'

'*Space pirates?* You're joking, right?' Claude's voice raised a tone.

'I'm afraid it's their response to our crackdown. We've been trying to eradicate them, but as you can see, they're refusing to go quietly.'

'But how did they get past your outer-perimeter defences?' queried Theo.

'Most of our military and civilian ships are assisting in a massive evacuation of a failing Dyson planet. These opportunists have got to know of that; the relocation is a massive operation. But we'll be safe down here until our forces drive off the pirates.'

'What is this place?' asked Theo.

'It's another one of our sculptures—the famous fluorescent sculptured tunnels beneath Rakh.' He said it in a manner suggesting they should be familiar with this famous landmark.

The Mehir noted the blank stares of both Claude and Theo and seemed disappointed.

'The walls of the tunnels are an indeterminate fluorescence changing from one abstract shape to another,' he tried to explain. 'To add to the visitor's fun, the tunnels act as a complex labyrinth going on for kilometres, zigzagging between the underground buildings. All visitors here, are monitored by a central control and if a visitor feels they've had enough or can't find the exit, then all they had to do is call Central Control. They will guide them out with directional arrows—the artist intends to stimulate the visual senses and tickle the spatial grey matter. It's what you call a "maze".'

Claude simply said, 'I see.' Then continued, 'May I ask you another question?'

'Yes, of course.'

'How long has the title of Mehir been simply ceremonial?'

'Oh, for around half a million years. As you're aware, we have a functioning Government. You're scheduled to meet Primearch Reithur next week aren't you? He's the elected head of the Government; elections are every ten years. The Primearch has a group of Councillors, and to ensure there is accountability; there's Convocation of elected regional representatives. I believe it's much the same where you come from.

'The only anomaly for you, may be the incongruity of the function of the Mehir in a million year old civilisation. You see I've been investigating you and your society. You're what they call on your planet,' he turned to Claude with a wry smile, '"an out-and-out Republican," am I not right?'

Claude's cautious response was, 'Yes Sir,' but he felt pride in the assertion.

'History may have taken a differing route here, but to me, there seems to be a clear historical convergence. The results appear to have turned out similar on Earth, as here on Rakh—don't you think?'

'Yes, it seems so,' responded Claude. 'By the way, are your compass points similar to ours? You seem to have studied Earth somewhat.'

'Exactly the same orientation. The sun rises in the east and sets in the west, placing north and south accordingly.'

'Thank you. That makes my life a little easier.'

'Let's take a walk through the tunnels while we wait for the all clear. Is that all right by you?'

'Fine.' Claude looked at the abstract patterns on the tunnel walls.

After near half an hour of wandering through the passageways, Claude exclaimed, 'Enthralling! What do you think Theo?'

'Breathtaking! I've never seen anything like it.'

At last the Mehir proclaimed, 'I'm informed the pirates have been dealt with. I'll have us teleported back onto the Hopper.'

'I'm ready to go. I'm getting a little dizzy from all these lights,' Claude agreed.

Soon they were back in the air and continued with their tour. The Hopper approached a group of mountains, which in outline appeared circular. From within the middle, there emanated more of the spectacular light sculptures, as promised by the Mehir.

The Hopper climbed ever higher, giving a better view of the mountains and the surrounding countryside below, *and* the emanating lights. The more they saw of Rakh, the more they realised it was a land with an entirely constructed environment. An ancient garden planet in love with the curves of nature, abhorring straight lines; a land of immense lakes and a controlled climate. In short, a land that had been elaborately groomed.

'There is a call from the Barog Embassy. Do you wish to take it?'

'I had better. There's no knowing otherwise.'

'Is that Ambassador Joubert?' his earpiece asked.

'Yes.'

'Ambassador Portuk would like you to call on him, at your earliest convenience.'

'Nathur! May I be permitted to terminate this trip, and may I employ your teleport to transport us to the Barogian Embassy?'

'But of course—business is business. You will find the Embassy bathed in a 26% oxygen atmosphere. If you teleport to the external main entrance, you'll find oxygen masks with your 21% mixture hanging there, if you consider the Barogian atmosphere's too rich for you.'

'Thank you for inviting us, and for your hospitality. It's been an enjoyable and eventful journey. We hope to be able to return the compliment at some time in the future. Could you set the teleport in motion?'

'It has been a pleasure, and—well, good bye,' sighed Nathur.

The Mehir then punched some coloured circles on a panel on his right side, and both Claude and Theo found themselves teleported to the outside of a sizeable dome, with a circular doorway just in front.

Chapter Fifteen

Dyson Planet

They stood facing the dome, admiring the geometric iridescent shape. Abruptly, a floating screen appeared framing a talking head. It suggested they would find oxygen masks to the left, on pegs in the entranceway.

Claude and Theo entered the portal, found the masks and put them under their arms, just in case. They continued forward to what seemed to be the reception, a little giddy from the rich oxygen, to find the rest of the talking head. She hissed and whistled, which translated as:

'The Ambassador is on the floor below, waiting for you.'

Heading for the stairwell, they looked around the subdued greenery of the atrium before descending to the lower floor. They stopped at a door at the bottom of the stairs. Theo knocked—and they both entered. Seated at a circular green glass desk was Ambassador Portuk, still seemingly tall and muscular, even behind his desk. They observed large yellow forward-facing dinosaurian eyes scrutinising them; black intelligent pupils slanting vertically sat in a rounded head. A protruding enlarged torso completed what they could see. His skin was smooth but had a somewhat greenish pigmentation. His hands rested on the desk; each had three long fingers and an opposing thumb. Dressed in a deep green diplomatic uniform, this was an imposing representative of his planet—depicting strength.

'Ambassadors Joubert and Ghali! Thank you for coming at such short notice. There are two items of importance I would like to discuss with you.'

'The request sounded intriguing, and almost urgent,' Joubert remarked.

'Already the Grand Mehir has pre-empted my proposition somewhat.'

'How so?'

'By obtaining from Kileni, parts of your Earth's history.'

'Curiouser and curiouser,' Theo muttered under his breath.

'This may sound unusual to you, but I am authorised to make a bid for your Solar System's history, and separately, for a complete set of your human emotiograms. We are a society that enjoys experiencing virtual emotions, and I'm informed humans are extraordinarily well endowed—with emotions.'

'*I beg your pardon*? Let me understand this. You wish to bid for Earth's *history*? What do you propose to do with such a purchase,' Claude was flabbergasted.

'The history will be placed into carefully selected periods and episodes, more familiar to our audience, then reproduced and put out on the Pragmacasts.'

'*Pragmacasts*?' queried Theo.

'It's experience orientated entertainment where the recipient is "involved" in the story. It's a little like your Virtual Reality. We badly need something *new* for our population to experience.'

'And the emotiograms, where do they come in?' Claude asked.

'It's all tied in. The participants wear a transponder band around their temples that accesses all the relevant sensory parts of the brain, such as the visual cortex, auditory, olfactory, tactile, and gustatory. Integrated into the transmitter are emotional stresses so if, say, a talker is angry or sad, then the participants can feel the anger or sadness. Pragmacasting is a far-reaching business on Barog, and I'm authorised to offer a reasonable fee for the products in question.'

'This is the most fascinating, and most astounding proposition I've ever encountered in my whole life,' blurted out Claude. 'I really need more time to respond to such a proposal properly. I'm sure we can do business; well I think I'm sure, but I need to examine how this "product" is to be packaged. We need to be certain the sale of such a commodity doesn't damage Earth's reputation or credibility. And we need to put a realistic value on the items. I would also need to consult with my planetary government back home, as will Ambassador Ghali. Let me get back to you.'

'But of course. Because others will come forward with a similar offer, I thought we ought to have this earnest meeting. I hope you will give our submission priority—and serious thought.'

'You can *count* on it.'

'I have another proposition for you. There is what we call a Fargo planet, in serious trouble with its sun—a sun that is failing. Let me see, I think in your language you refer to it as a "Dyson Planet." Are you familiar with the type?'

Gently, Claude rubbed his chin. 'Isn't that where all the planets in a solar system are assembled together and the material used to build an enormous hollow sphere. Then the people live on the *inside* with the sun at the centre. Seas, Oceans and continents are built artificially on the inside of the sphere—giving it a larger area than all the previous planets collectively. Is that what you mean?'

'Precisely! I'm on my way with our contingent of starcruisers to join the evacuation fleet. I was wondering whether you would like to accompany me today, to observe the Federations rescue operation to save the entire inhabitants of that planet.'

'This day?'

'Yes.'

'Is it far from here?'

'About twelve and a half thousand light years away. Why?'

'I and Theo have a meeting in a week with Primearch Reithur, head of the Rakhian government, and as *our* host, we—the Ambassadors—must keep the appointment. However, this would be a spectacular chance to see the might of the Galactic Federation in action. It would be a pity to miss it. Would you allow my Deputy to go in my place?'

'Of course. What's his name?'

'Adama Ubongo. He will be my eyes and ears in this matter.'

'I will expect him within two hours, and then we really *must* leave. It has been a pleasure meeting you both. I look forward to doing business with you.'

'If we *do* decide to do business, how would you like the material transferred?'

'A straight forward data cube will hold all the information.'

'Right! Can we teleport from here, or do we have to go upstairs?'

'You can go from here.'

'From here then. Nice to have met you Ambassador. Goodbye.'

'Goodbye.' Portuk spoke into his communicator. The next moment they were in the gnarled hall of their own Embassy.

'Adama!'

'Yes your Excellency,' replied Claude's earpiece.

'A moment of your time. Pack for a week's journey. You're going with the Barogian Ambassador to a Dyson Planet.'

'*Right away*?'

'In two hours. Take recording equipment. I want a full report when you return. The Barogians will fill you in.'

'Yes, sir.'

'*Theo*! Do you want to send Faisal with Adama?'

'No. Adama's report should do it.'

Both Ambassadors retire to their quarters to freshen up after their eventful trip with the Mehir. An hour later, Adama announced he was packed—and ready to travel. They met on the ground floor for a final briefing.

'Adama! Are you familiar with the Dyson Planet concept?'

'The theoretical concept is familiar to the average schoolchild back on Earth.'

'Well it seems it's a commonplace tactic in the Federation. To prolong the life-giving rays of a planet's sun, a shield is built around the depleting sun at the planetary distance. The shield is set rotating to induce gravity, then the interior of the shield is terraformed using the other planets of that solar system, and the population dwells inside. It's like inhabiting the inner skin of a football. It is such a massive undertaking, it must be the ultimate solution before evacuation is compulsory.'

'Why go to all the trouble? Why not just evacuate immediately?'

'There is an enormous emotional investment in a home planet. A species will make a tremendous effort to delay moving. Would you leave Earth? The stress of moving home is ranked number 32 on the Social Readjustment Rating Scale, which includes death and divorce. Moving planets must be number one in terms of stress, equal to the death of a spouse. We're talking major stress; it's the death of *a sun*. Before the Federation, it would possibly have meant the extinction of the species.'

'Put like that, I see what you mean.'

'So I want a comprehensive report.'

'Yes sir.'

'Have you worked out how to use the teleport yet?'

'Apparently, you give the destination aloud, and the command is accepted by their computer system, no matter where you are. The key word is teleport, plus the destination.'

'Right! Look after yourself. Give the command.'

Adama gave the teleport destination, and was promptly disassembled. He reappeared inside the dome of the Barog Embassy, to be welcomed by the receptionist.

The receptionist hissed—which translated as, 'The Ambassador is expecting you, please go down.'

Adama fought the fainting fit from the rich oxygen. 'Thank you,' he muttered and set off for the stairs.

He met Portuk coming up the stairs.

'You must be Adama Ubongo,' Portuk quipped.

'Yes sir.'

'We are a little behind the fleet's schedule. I see you've brought a travel holdall. Are you ready to board the ship?'

'Yes, ready to go.'

'We'll up-relay right away then.'

Portuk gave the co-ordinates and they rematerialised on board the Barog starcruiser. The vessel was made of the same fluid pulsed metal; only here it had a greenish tinge to it. Adama had noticed earlier Portuk had a greenish skin, and he presumed there was a ubiquitous natural trait for the Barogians to see everything through a green tinted dinosaurian perspective.

They settled in the lounge of the ship and Portuk called for a screen, which materialised before them. Adama expected to see the darkness of outer space, yet outside was a sea of flickering lights, thousands.

'You see before you an armada few have ever witnessed. For this effort, the Federation fleet has assembled near Rakh—this being the Quadrant HQ. We'll go to the rescue from here.'

'So many ships—the fleet's *enormous*,' stuttered Adama. 'I've never seen such an impressive sight. Can I record this for my report?'

'Of course you may. There'll be an official record for our archives—you may have a copy if you wish.'

'Yes, thank you. That's most generous of you. What is the planet's name and distance?'

'It is called Iruam by the inhabitants, and is twelve and a half thousand light years from here.'

'How long has it been since they transformed it into a Dyson Planet?'

'Some twenty thousand of your years ago. They first dismantled all the other planets in their solar system, and then they took their planet to pieces, and reassembled the whole mass into a Dyson ball. The solar mass remained the same, so no major gravity shifts occurred in their solar system.'

'I don't know if you're aware of it Ambassador, but Iruam has been Dyson for a lot longer than the existence of human civilisation.'

'Call me Portuk, we're going to be together for a while, and Ambassador is so formal. Yes, I was aware of it. You will adjust in time to the incongruity. We Barogians, have only been with the Federation around two hundred years, and the adjustments we've made have been incredible, but we've managed them.'

'I'm sure you're right. I can see it will take time.'

'You're a vigorous bunch—you humans, and you've come a long way, quickly. If you adjust as speedily as your Embassy staff seem to have, you really have little to worry about.'

'Thanks! I *think* that was a compliment?'

'It was! The fleet seems to be ready to get under way.'

'Twelve and a half thousand light years in which direction, I mean towards our Solar System, or away?'

'Away, I'm afraid. In any event, the way we travel would make no difference, surely?'

'I suppose not. It's just; I'm getting a little home sick.'

'How do you mean? Sick of your *home*?'

'No. I mean I miss my family.'

'You have a spouse and children?'

'I do. I mean we do, a little girl.'

'How quaint.'

'Aren't you married, Portuk?'

'I have a mate, but our offspring are a clutch of eggs centrally nurtured. It optimises their mental health.'

'*Chacun à son goût*, as Ambassador Joubert might say.'

'I beg your pardon?' Portuk looked at Adama quizzically.

'Each to his own taste. It's a human expression, in this context it means each culture has its own way of doing things.'

'Oh! I seeeee—ssss.' Portuk gave a wry grimace, which Adama took for a dinosaurian smile.

Portuk continued, 'Anyway—back to the business at hand. The Barog contingent is made up of fifty starcruisers, which will evacuate around a thousand of Iruam's people. Since they have a population of around four billion, it means either four million ships or a hundred trips with forty thousand ships.

'If each planet supplied fifty ships, then it would need eight hundred planets to evacuate Iruam. As you are aware, the Federation consists of well in excess of a thousand planets, so we have ten thousand ships in reserve, should some other emergency arise. You're witness to a flotilla—out there—of forty thousand spaceships. Each will make a hundred trips, to the new home world for the Iruamians, which will take around sixty Earth days, at two trips per day around the clock. The reserve ships will spell the tired, and replace any malfunctioning vessels. After the population has moved, their baggage and equipment goes next. That's the extra ten days.'

'This is the most inspiring operation I've ever had the privilege of witnessing!'

'I must admit—it is for me as well. Any questions?'

'Is their new planet far from the old one?'

'Four hundred light years.'

'There weren't any closer?'

'Their High Council opted for distance—to make a fresh start.'

'That's probably wise. Looking back—can cause much heart break.'

'You sound as if you talk from experience?'

'I do.'

The combined task force began to move off in staggered lines five abreast, making five long lines. It fanned out across a wide five million-kilometre front. Each lead ship was to open up a jump point—a Black Hole—thus the reason for the immense distances separating the lines.

Once the Holes were open, it would take little time for the whole line of eight thousand vessels to proceed through the wormhole tunnel, emerging in the system around Iruam. If each ship took a second to transit the Wormhole, then the whole eight thousand would take just over two hours, a respectable movement in anyone's language.

The re-emergence of some forty thousand space ships around Iruam, although expected, nevertheless left little leeway for any unexpected manoeuvres. Every ship of the flotilla was tied in to the Mother StarCarrier, whose immense computers controlled the whole operation. The StarCarrier was the most enormous spaceship Adama had ever imagined. Only a few of these vessels existed and it carried a complement of over five thousand. Its purpose was to act as the logistics HQ, and it had arrived earlier, acting as a beacon for the other ships.

The Barogian vessels under Portuk were stationed on the rim of the vast fleet, which gave Adama a vantage point to observe the proceedings. He saw the large Dyson Planet at the centre of the fleet. *It* was *huge;* a gigantic sphere with beacons of lights saturating the space around it. However, even at that distance, Adama could see the massive space doors, an open shaft of sunlight exuding from the open portal.

Slowly, ship after ship went through the massive doors in the top lane, coming out again in the bottom lane, laden with the evacuees. Some inhabitants were teleporting up from the outer skin of the planet, the outside open to space, as if from the surface of a normal planet.

In their urgency, every method was being employed to speed up the process. Although, in reality, there was no *immediate* hurry—the sun inside still had a couple of years before it became dangerous, the inhabitants had dithered and waited till almost the last moment. As things stood, they had vacillated and left it late—ignoring beseeching advice.

After a few hours of idle chatter with Portuk, during which time Adama learnt more about Barog's dinosaurian society, their turn came to enter the space doors. Adama was using his Holorecorder, aiming it at the screen in the lounge of the ship. It was the best he could do, shoot the screen or insist a shuttle be provided especially for him. That would have created more traffic, and probably interfered with the evacuation operation.

Thus it was, Adama recorded their ship's entry through the gigantic space doors. The traffic flow had been streamed top half in, and bottom half out, so some semblance of order could be maintained. As the vessel entered inside Iruam, the light became dazzling. They entered what should have been effectively a paradise. All around, yet—above and below, as far as the eye could see—were fertile fields, villages, mountains, rivers and seas.

Once their eyes adjusted to daylight, they could see—ahead, the deep yellow sun already exhibiting patches of orange. It revealed the core was running out of hydrogen fuel, and its time was ending. An inside out world, whose time had come—to die. The sun would go on like this, in its death dance, for thousands of years more, first shrinking—becoming hotter. Then when its core was burned up, it would swell into an ever-expanding red giant, shattering the Dyson sphere.

It certainly couldn't sustain life any longer. The Dyson world would turn to cinders, before being gobbled up as the sun expanded into a red giant. Eventually, it would turn into a planetary nebula, then into a white dwarf, and finally into a cold black dwarf.

Their ship headed to the left of the dying sun, joining a queue of waiting ships, where they were to pick up passengers. Everything looked—so picturesque —so beautiful, yet it was a prelude to a tragedy for the inhabitants. They were leaving their home planet—for good.

Adama, already homesick, was holding back tears of empathy with these unfortunate people. Yet, they were privileged in a different way, in that they had joined the Federation, which enabled them to avoid extinction, a Federation that had found them another home. That was a true galactic munificence.

'When we get out into open space, would it be possible for you to let me return to Rakh?'

'But you haven't yet seen the new home for these people,' Portuk seemed to have taken the request as a minor slur, 'this business has only just got under way.'

'I mean no offence Ambassador, but I feel I have enough material without going any further. I'm also feeling a little *down* at the moment; this tragedy reminds me how much I miss my wife and child. I really would be bad company. Better if I return to Rakh. Will there still be the official record of the operation for us?'

'But of course! I simply regret you will miss such an unrepeatable experience.'

'I regret that also, but this calamity is exacerbating my depression.'

'Well, if you must, then you must. I will give the order.'

'I *am* sorry,' Adama tried to excuse himself.

When they had cleared the Dyson Planet, Adama was transferred to a smaller Barogian vessel, returning to Quadrant HQ with an interim report on the course of the evacuation.

After Adama had time to meditate on what he had done, he felt a little ashamed at his weak behaviour. It wasn't like him to let his feelings get in the way of work, especially in such a retiring manner. He still felt overwhelmed by the memory of the sight of forty thousand spaceships, enacting their precise ballet in space. The thought of such an advanced concept as the Dyson Planet failing after only twenty thousand years took his depression down another notch. His mind fed his depression, reaching overload, and he sought something familiar, something from his own world to latch onto, to comfort him. He *needed* human company.

Chapter Sixteen

Space Pirates

Adama realised something was wrong when the small Barog ship lurched to a halt. The vessel had been enroute to open a transit Black Hole; instead, it had come to an abrupt stop. As a precaution, he donned his atmosphere suit, then called for a view screen, which materialised before him at eye level.

He demanded the screen give him an exterior view. This showed a series of large interconnected shining boxes. The same boxes were suspended around the vessel, as if a net had been cast, and his vessel was trapped inside. How this could have occurred, was beyond his scope. He had little idea what was happening, apart from the atypical frantic bustling of the crew inside the ship, signifying something had gone seriously wrong.

A few minutes went by—an eternity, then he heard noises out in the corridor; high pitched squeaking, clicking and rasping. The cabin door retracted smoothly, revealing, what looked like two medium-sized insect-like apparitions. Both were suited, holding objects in their raptorial forelegs, which could only have been some sort of weapons. They looked at the suited figure of Adama—then at each other, and without saying a word, nodded at Adama. Promptly, the teleporter engaged.

*　　*　　*

Adama rematerialised in a darkened cramped room, just making out a yellowish haze inside. Dazed, he shook his head. What the *hell's going on*? He felt for his inbuilt communicator on his shoulder, but was surprised to find it missing. Fearful, he inched into a corner, sliding down the wall, squatting.

He'd already been in a reverie of self-doubt back on the ship, sinking into self-pity, when this calamity struck out of black space. It was a disaster, he was certain. He'd been snatched by god knows what, and now the *moirai* diced with his fate. *What in this miserable sector of space, did these apparitions want with him?*

*   *   *

Some time went by, he'd no idea how much. Then, he was visited by a screen, simply appearing out of thin air in the middle of his cell. He jumped to his feet. There, framed in the screen, was the unsuited form of one of his abductors.

It had two short vestigial antennae protruding from its head; each topped by a luminous bulb. It had two large black composite eyes, below them, what may have been a mouth, all resting on a yellow thorax. The luminous bulbs were flashing furiously, and to his amazement; he understood what they flashed. The apparition was using some form of translator.

'Welcome to ourrr home, huuman.'

'You...you...you've no right to kidnap me. Why did you do it? Are you going to release me?'

'Noo!'

'Wha...wha...what do you want from me?'

'We arre going to keep you as a pet.'

'*What*.....? You can't *do* that! You've no right! A pet? You're mad! What the hell for?'

'Amuusement.'

'Are you...completely out of your *mind*?' He realised they were toying with him.

'No. We are in your mind!'

'*Please...*tell me, what it is you *want* from me,' his voice began to plead.

'From *you*? From you we want nothing.'

'Then from whom?'

'You may be set free *after* they—pay, but if not, you will be—ourrr food.' The screen went blank.

Adama's thoughts spun in turmoil; he felt panic settling on him. *Stay calm,* he told himself; if he wanted to survive this ordeal, he would *have* to stay calm. There was no sense of motion in his cell. If he was off the Barog ship and on their home planet, he must have been held in teleport stasis all the way from where he was grabbed. He felt his hands and knees begin to tremble, prompting him back into the corner, where he slid down into a foetal position, onto his haunches against the wall of the cell.

Stress was inching along every fibre of his body, cramping his reason, forcing it into a peculiar narrow form of tunnel thinking. The corticosteroids were rioting in his body. From the PsyCorps lectures, he recalled some of the horrors the mind could unleash when stressed beyond its limit. Adama was a diplomat, a scientist, not some hardened combatant, and just before his kidnapping, he'd begun to feel depressed and homesick. If he was to survive, he knew he had to get a firm grip.

These could be the last hours of his life; for all he knew. He was to be their "food"; those were the creature last words. *Now stop it,* he said to himself. *I must find a way of avoiding random thought: try focusing on something familiar. Hey*! Was it his imagination or had the light dimmed further. *Yes, they'd dimmed.* He was sure of it. He began to hear a strange faint noise; nothing he could make out clearly, a bit like a tinkering sound.

He was sure *something* watched him; he could feel it on the nape of his neck. He forced his thoughts back to the bush landscape of Uganda, to his wife and little girl. He closed his eyes and tried to ignore the darkness and strange noises, by recalling the comforting memories of his youth.

Adama Ubongo was from the Bantu speaking Ganda people, who inhabited the south of Uganda, all around the western shores of Lake Victoria. His face was oval with large dark eyes. He was tall—muscular, with a dark complexion, and short curly hair. His hometown Masaka, was a hundred kilometres inland from the lake.

The countryside around Masaka was lush green, unlike some parts of Africa that looked brown and scorched. He'd gone into the bush as a youth, hiding, stalking, pretending to hunt, and roaming the coffee plantations with his friends. He recalled the smell of heat coming from the ground. He pictured his friends, their welcoming faces, their individual features, examining each expression carefully, noting minute details. He followed this, by bringing up the face of his wife Rutha, and his little ten-year-old girl, named Ruth after her mother. The mental exercise was calming him; after a while, he closed his eyes, and tried to doze a little.

A merciless clanging jerked Adama from his fitful napping. The cell was pitch black, and the clanging continued incessantly. Sometimes it would get louder, then just as suddenly, it would fade to a background tinkering noise. This random racket went on...and on, seemingly hour after hour, until Adama thought he'd lost his reason; his mind beginning to turn in on itself for safety.

Again, he went back to his memories, to the first year at the University of Kampala, where he first met Rutha. He went through each year of his studies in detail, each part of his Physics course. He recited every physical law he'd ever been taught. It helped, but the clanging *still* penetrated the essence that was Adama.

He was nominally a Roman Catholic, but after University, he'd let it lapse, as the inherent contradictions piled up. In an attempt to revive his belief, for Rutha's sake, he'd read all of Cardinal Newman's *Apologia Pro Vita Sua.* It didn't work. He then read Newman's *History of My Religious Opinions* —followed by *The Idea of a University;* his local priest had advised he should read the latter two. Neither of the tomes worked for him. Maybe the problem lay in the ancient setting, thousands of years of a long vanished period. For Adama, it had nothing to say to the African in him.

He thought reciting the Catechism might help, taught so strictly, learnt so laboriously, so long ago at school. Adama followed that by trying to remember the many stories from the Bible; still the clanging penetrated deep into his psyche.

He went on desperately trying to remember as much of the Bible as he could: he got to the Gospel according to St John, the fourth book of the New Testament—then as suddenly as it began, the clanging stopped. The silence was deafening.

At first slowly, the floor began to move—upwards, against the ceiling—then a little faster.

'*Stop it!*' Yelled Adama. '*P-l-e-a-s-e stop it!*' The floor slowed down. '*Just stop it!*' He yelled again. Half a meter separated the floor from the ceiling, and Adama was wedged in between.

Finally, the floor halted. For a moment, he lost his marbles, and just yelled and screamed in rage and fear. He let his pent-up frustrations—go, in some of the most terrible primeval human screams any alien could have heard in that part of the Galaxy. He screamed until he was hoarse. It was this heart-rending screaming that saved his sanity. Without the liberating screaming, in all probability, he would have turned in on himself, become catatonic. He'd travelled a fine line between neurotic, and ending psychotic.

Unfortunately for Adama, his tormentors hadn't finished with him yet. One instant he was squashed between floor and ceiling, the next, he found he was outside, out in the open without his suit. He took a breath of *air* and promptly choked; it was acrid, poisonous. He tried to hold his breath until his eyes began to bulge. He gazed in horror at his own peeling skin, seeing the red flesh underneath; flesh that ought to be skin covered.

It seemed his predicament lasted a period where time seemed suspended. He lungs were bursting from his chest, and he realised he'd maybe a second left. In resignation, he let out his breath—closing his eyes.

Amazed—he opened them. He was lying on the floor in the same cell. The cell had resumed its normal size. It was all an elaborate sadistic illusion—they had tampered with his brain. Being dumped outside was all deception, implanted by his callous torturers. Although the last episode was delusion, he felt an urgent need to know how long he'd been held captive. He stared at the oxygen indicator—the suit was good for *only* twenty-four hours—then the pellets depleted. The indicator showed he'd barely six more hours of air. *Why oh why pick on me?* He moaned in self-pity.

Chapter Seventeen

The Rescue

Claude Joubert was informed the small Barog spaceship was missing, and Adama Ubongo was a day overdue.

The Solar System Ambassador to the Galactic Federation on Rakh was going frantic. Professor Claude Joubert, late of the Sorbonne and Max Planck Institute, was a tall Provençal, built like a professional swimmer. An eminent Nobel physicist turned diplomat. A wife waited for him in the Camargue, and at only 150 years, he was fit as a fiddle.

The authorities on Rakh and Barog had mobilised their emergency procedures in an effort to determine what happened, but to no avail. The small ship was nowhere to be found.

Then someone thought of contacting the StarCarrier, directing the evacuation of Iruam. It controlled the region of space where the Barog spaceship was last seen. *Yes*, their computer had automatically monitored the small ship. It had been recorded as heading for open space, to open a Black Hole for its return journey to Rakh.

They had a computerised record of the ship being caught in a rigged force field meganet; only everyone had been too busy to take any notice. It was a million kilometres away from their zone of operations, and well away from the fleet—out in open space. No one looked closely, or thought to question the unusual activity. They were apologetic about not preventing the piracy, promising all their data regarding the event, and any further assistance that might be required.

Forensic examination of the area, and the StarCarrier's computer records, showed what seemed to be the space pirates. They had thrown the meganet, abducted the crew and beat a hasty retreat in a direction away from Iruam. These hoodlums had used the cover that a large part of the Galaxy was busy with the evacuation—to embark on a crime spree. Nobody believed the pirates maintained their direction for long. The vessel had opened a Black Hole, and disappeared. It could be anywhere in the Galaxy.

Claude contacted the Barog Embassy on Rakh, and found a distraught Ambassador Portuk; profusely regretful such a misfortune had befallen them both. He had some news—could he come over right away. The news might allay their worst fears.

Portuk teleported to Claude, rematerialising in the hall of the Solar Embassy. Encased in a green diplomatic uniform, Portuk's protruding enlarged chest heaved in the lowered oxygen level of Earth's atmosphere.

'I *am* sorry this catastrophe has struck us both.' He looked genuinely distressed.

'Yes—it certainly is a *catastrophe*. Please, let's go down to my office,' said Claude. 'You say you have some news?'

'Yes! We've received a ransom demand for the Barog crew members.'

'Any mention of Adama?'

'I'm afraid not. But if they're asking for a ransom for our crew, then they'll be in touch with you regarding Adama.'

'I hope you're right. Who *are* these people? I was under the impression the Galactic Federation was advanced, orderly, and without crime. Yet here we are! My Chief of Staff has been abducted, and for all I know, murdered. What is the Federation doing about it? *I'm sorry*! I should be saying that to the Quadrant Custodian, not to a fellow *victim*.'

'I'll try to answer your questions.'

'The space pirates are a curse who have plagued us for as many years as I care to remember. They're a collection of rabble from many races, groupings that have chosen to become outcasts. You must have them on Earth? They're the scum of the Federation, giving allegiance to none but themselves. To search them out would mean mounting an operation that would require sweeping the whole Galaxy. There is no gain to us in the cost-benefit analysis, of curbing these pinpricks we occasionally have to suffer. It's as usual, no consolation to the victims. So you see, we do have crime, and the Federation isn't by any means a perfect community. True, we haven't any crime on the planets of the Federation, but on the outskirts of all societies....'

'And do you know this group of pirates?'

'We're pursuing forensic computer scents, picked up from previous similar raids. This lot might be a group of sentient insectoids, whose home world is Murangi. The Murangi have an arrest warrant out on them for various crimes, and they're co-operating with the Federation authorities to help locate them.'

'Thanks. That's a damn sight more than we knew a moment ago.'

They'd been chatting in Claude's office, when his earpiece informed him a peculiar looking plastic canister had materialised in the middle of the upstairs hall. He ordered it scanned for booby-traps—made safe, then brought down to his office.

'I think we've just been contacted,' he told Portuk.

'This group has a prankster in it; so please be careful,' Portuk responded.

'I've taken precautions,' said Claude.

The canister contents arrived by way of the dark, swarthy Martian Ambassador, Theo Ghali. He placed an optical data cube on the table and sat down. Dr. Theodore Ghali, son of the Martian President, was distinguished and composed, with a complexion that would have fitted well on the wall of any ancient Egyptian tomb.

'When we scanned the strange canister, a concealed hatch flipped open and dumped this on the table,' he pointed at the cube, 'then the canister vanished.'

'They're being extra careful,' observed Portuk.

'Well? Let's see what they have to say,' quipped Theo impatiently.

The data cube was inserted into playback, and immediately a small screen popped up, suspended in mid air. It showed a darkened cell. In the corner sat Adama, still wearing his suit, resting on his haunches. The next view was of the floor ascending, and descending, showed Adama being squashed, then lying on the floor choking for no reason they could see. Behind his suit visor, they witnessed the heart-rending screaming, but no sound track accompanied the grisly spectacle.

'This is intolerable. Why are they torturing him?' shouted Claude, switching the player off.

'It's their twisted way of telling us to hurry,' remarked Portuk.

'The sick depravity of it. It's turning my stomach,' commented Theo, his face visibly upset.

'We need to see the rest of the recording,' insisted Portuk.

'Yes. I suppose you're right.' Claude switched the player back on.

Theo pointed, 'Look, here's the vicious tyke,' at the image of an insectoid who made no attempt to hide its features. 'Looks positively boastful, as if enjoying its work,' Theo said angrily.

'Only till we catch it,' put in Portuk.

"...we urge you to comply quickly," the screen told them, then went dark.

'Hey! What did it want? Wind it back a bit,' snapped Theo.

'Yes, I missed that,' added Portuk.

Claude wound it back, and they heard...*"We will release the human when we obtain the ransom from the Barog. If not, he dies. We urge you to put pressure on them immediately."*

'I'm *not* going to submit,' shouted Claude. 'We've had a long standing policy of not giving in to terrorism on Earth, and I'm not going to start now.'

'What about Adama?' insisted Theo.

'*You* or *I* could be next. It's a chain reaction. Give in once, and like an addict, they'll go after us again,' shot back Claude. 'If they can't succeed by this abduction, they'll leave us alone. It's simple psychological *operant conditioning*. I'm thinking of all the rest of the Embassy staff.'

'Yes I know,' muttered Theo, grudgingly resigning himself to Claude's logic. 'If we give them an *operant response* by rewarding them, then they will throw a *stimulus* at us again, by abducting someone else.'

'That's it. We can't let this chain of events get started. Nip it in the bud *now*, while we can.'

'It's your decision Claude,' said Portuk. He was listening intently to the flow of the human reasoning.

'I need to know what the Federation is able to do. More to the point, what *have* they done in the past, and what was the outcome?'

'To date, they've always pursued the culprits, with extreme sanctions,' Portuk explained.

'And the victims?'

'Sometimes the victims are rescued, and sometimes not. The policy of "root out the cancer" was laid down long ago by the Grand Convention, headed by the then Grand Custodian.'

'We seem to agree. Adama will have to take his chances,' said Claude.

'The policy may be right, but the sentiment is all wrong,' bemoaned Theo.

'Why haven't I heard from the Quadrant Custodian?' Claude wanted to know.

'They're embarrassed,' Portuk explained. 'So far, they've nothing to report, so they're keeping silent.'

'Theo! Can you get Faisal on it as a matter of urgency? We need to establish a line of communication with whoever's in charge of the rescue. Let's get started with the Custodians office. Find out what they're doing. As for this piece of blackmail,' he pointed at the cube, 'let's leave it for the time being.'

'Right! I'll get Faisal going.' Theo walked away into a corner, and began talking to his aide through the ear-com.

'May I ask, what you're doing about your crew?' Claude turned to Portuk.

'We have a task force enroute, with specialist equipment and an élite unit, deliberately assigned to this type of emergency.'

'A while ago, you asked me to join you on your expedition to Iruam. Does the invitation still hold for this expedition?'

'Of course! However, I'm required to formally warn you—this may be dangerous.'

'Understood! I'll log your warning. I know you've got to cover yourself in the event of something going wrong.'

'In that case, the task force is due in a couple of hours; I need to get back to my Embassy to prepare. We need to assemble *all* the information that's been gathered to date.'

'Right. I'll come to you in one and a half hours, agreed?'

'Agreed!'

Claude had the impression Portuk was giving him a consoling smile, but he couldn't be certain. The dinosaurian pressed on his wristband, and with that, the Ambassador for Barog teleported back to his own Embassy. The next one and a half hours dragged for Claude.

Faisal was told by the Custodian's PA the authorities were doing everything possible to obtain the release of Adama. The line they took, suggested, things were furiously in motion, but another call to Portuk proved to contradict that impression: they hadn't a clue where the pirates were. They were bluffing and blustering to save face.

Another message arrived from the kidnappers, but this time they were prepared, and able to track it. Portuk's people had teleported to Claude a Co-ordinates Trace Analyser, for just such an eventuality.

It dispatched a discreet trace; piggyback on the original beam, carrying it to the source, then recorded the co-ordinates of the source. They didn't know if that was going to be the hideout, but someone from the kidnappers was likely to be there. The co-ordinates were verified as being a small barren planetoid, just at the extreme reach of teleporting technology, on the edge of the Rakhian system.

Claude teleported to the Barog Embassy at the time agreed, where he met an unexpected bustle in the hall. A group of dinosaurian military were taking inventory of their equipment. Portuk stood talking to a huddle of officers, and it looked to Claude as if he was laying down the law. Portuk turned, saw Claude, appeared to frown, and hurried over. The dinosaurian facial appearances were still a mystery to Claude, as was the body language.

Portuk said brusquely, 'Good! Now you've arrived; we can make a move.' With one of his fingers, Portuk made a high circle to one of the officers.

'I'm placing myself under your command,' Claude said dramatically.

Portuk composed himself, 'I appreciate that, but it's quiet unnecessary,' and his face seemed to imitate a smile of reassurance. At least that's how Claude read the expression.

'Well, anyway, I'll try not to get in your way.'

It was time for the troops, assembled in the hall, to teleport to the Barog military vessel waiting in Rakh's orbit. The vessel looked menacing, externally and internally, more in keeping with its military role, but still in the pervasive green liquid metal. The cabin was filled with tall Barog military types in dark grey uniforms. They sat silently, concentrating on one of their number, explaining with hisses and snarls some part of the coming operation.

The ship cloaked, moving off in the direction of the co-ordinates Claude got from the trace device. Within thirty minutes, they arrived at the planetoid, and were just in time to see another vessel lift, heading out into dark space. The chase was short, with the Barog hot on the trail of the fleeing ship. The escaping vessel was no match for the pursuing military spaceship.

Portuk's vessel came abreast, just as the other ship tried to open a Black Hole. The Barog ship de-cloaked, and the Captain sent an interference beam, collapsing the Black Hole, cancelling the escape. The Barog Captain ordered the pirates teleported to his vessel's brig. Now they had someone to work on.

'Would you care to see our prisoners?' asked Portuk.

'I wouldn't miss this for anything,' Claude replied with enthusiasm.

'This way.' Portuk led the way down to the brig.

They came on a Barog officer trying to question three prisoners. He was holding a small device, aiming it at the weakest looking prisoner.

'Now don't think of where you're holding your captives,' they heard the officer encourage.

'What's he doing?' Claude asked Portuk.

'Calibrating the cephalocorder to the individual's neural circuits.'

Claude looked puzzled.

'He's zooming in on the memory of their captives, stored in this prisoners brain,' Portuk patiently explained. 'If we know the species, then we know roughly where to probe their brain for the information. We need to suggest to this prisoner not to access the memory holding the captive's location, so the autosuggestion prompts that memory into activity. At that point, we zoom in on the activity, recording the memory with the cephalocorder. Is that clear?'

'Crystal.'

'Well?' Portuk was asking the officer.

'Yes, I think we have it; look.'

He held out the small screen of the cephalocorder. There were various faces.

'Wait! I'll have him enlarge it,' Portuk said something in Barogian.

A screen projected on the brig wall; then another screen appeared in the enlarged screen, showing a large room with dejected Barog milling around the room. There was no doubting; this was the missing crew of the lost ship. Then the screen moved to a table with a 3-D map of the pirate's location.

'Freeze!' yelled Portuk. 'Put *that* through the computer,' he commanded. Turning to the insectoids, he said sarcastically, 'Thanks for your help.'

The pirates stood dejected, knowing they'd been powerless to resist giving the information. It would almost certainly kill their associates.

Portuk led the way back to the cabin, where they were already examining the co-ordinates sent from the brig. The location of the pirates' hideout was a barren planet twenty-five thousand light years towards the centre of the Galaxy, in a part of space sparsely inhabited.

Portuk heard the Commander of the élite group call a tactical conference of his senior officers, to discuss the best way of handling the rescue operation. They were the experts at this sort of thing, and frankly, he wanted to let them get on with it. Portuk walked over to talk to Claude, and both went to a corner and sat down, leaving the conference to the professionals.

'Are you impressed by what you've seen so far?' asked Portuk.

'That bit with the cephalocorder was most impressive.' Praised Claude.

'Yes. I thought you took special notice when they were using it. Would you like one?' Portuk looked closely at his human guest.

'*Would I?* Are you serious?'

'When we get back, I'll arrange it.'

'That's most agreeable of you.' Claude ogled Portuk with one eye—but with typical human suspicion, he thought, *What's the catch?*

Portuk went on, 'For the waiting families, I need all the captives safe. It won't be long before we know the outcome of this enterprise.'

'I hope you can find a way of *preventing* them from murdering Adama.' Said Claude with heavy emphasis, making certain Portuk believed him.

'We'll do our utmost; you can be sure of that. I've given careful instructions to the effect.'

The Captain of their military vessel opened a Black Hole and entered the wormhole tunnel. They came out in the proximity of the planet the insectoids were using as their piratical home base. The Captain was aware, if the exit White Hole was too close to the pirate's planet, it would alert the pirates. To prevent such an occurrence, they'd exited some ten billion kilometres from their destination, out in the vast uninhabited cosmos.

The Captain cloaked their spaceship, proceeding in a gigantic circle that would place them, eventually, coming in from the opposite direction. The enemy would not expect that. Any subterfuge that would increase the surprise, would add to the survival chances of the hostages.

'This is where we're proceeding with some cunning,' Portuk confided to Claude. They sat at the rear of the cabin, watching the troops prepare. 'The ship is going to approach the hideout from the wrong side, so to speak, coming in slowly, being careful not to cause the slightest ripple in the fabric of space. The kidnappers have entrenched themselves in a series of caverns roughly a kilometre under the planet's surface. Our sensors have detected a number of force fields sealing the caverns off from the exterior.'

Claude was riveted by the description.

'They've even made themselves comfortable, generating an atmosphere suitable for their species—at least that's what the sensors indicate,' Portuk said with disgust.

The ship had scanned for the hostages, finding them half a kilometre from the entrance, at the back, deep inside the caverns, located in a series of special holding cells.

After a moments silence, Portuk resumed the commentary, 'We can't teleport in because the cavern's rock profile is too dense for teleports. They must have picked the hideout deliberately to pose such a problem.'

The Commander of the Special Forces was being compelled to go through the entrance with the thinner rock. That meant they'd have to fight their way through to the hostages, putting them in prolonged danger of being slaughtered.

The Chief of the élite group stood and readied his people for the encounter. Claude steeled himself for a disaster. How was he going to explain Adama's death to his wife? There was no question of Claude joining the affray; the Barog would not risk it. So, he gritted his teeth and watched the coming battle on the ship's screen, together with Portuk.

They watched the troops rematerialise near the entrance of the caverns, catching the pirates off guard. The light gravity made movement difficult. Atmosphere suits added to the clumsiness. As the pirates realised they were being attacked; they initiated a ferocious fight. The élite group fought its way through the caverns to mid point. They were then pinned down by a furious barrage of energy weapons. Despite the élite group being cloaked, suited, and each member having a sheathing force field, when the insectoid energy weapon hit one of the élite group, they momentarily lit up like a neon sign.

The insectoids' energy weapons were set to kill, but the rescuing troops had strict orders to take the pirates alive. Their weaponry was directed lasers, acting as a carrier wave for neuro-stunner chemicals, tailored to the insectoid neurotransmitters, paralysing them on proximity contact.

There was such a lot of dust and debris intermixed with chemical residue in the atmosphere; the screen in front of Claude began to fog up. As the firing died down, so the fog cleared somewhat.

Both watching Ambassadors saw the two sides had reached an impasse, neither able to dislodge the other. The insectoids unexpectedly donned atmosphere suits, so the paralysing chemical worked only if the pirate's suit was penetrated. Even with directed beams, the hit rate was appallingly low, due mainly to the many intervening boulders and rocks.

Then, additional troops materialised, using strengthened personal shielding, preventing the insectoid weapons from having any effect. A new bout of furious firing broke out, and again the view was obscured by dust and debris. The watchers heard an extra loud blast, followed by another—then a third.

There were a lot of exasperated *clicking* and *rasping* coming from the tannoy system, as the insectoids attempted to beat back the assault. Two more blasts in quick succession—still the damn dust obscured the onlooker's vision. Then—a sudden hush descended, and the dust began to settle, allowing the screen to clear.

Before Claude's eyes, there appeared the suited apparition of Adama, seemingly in one piece. The relief on Claude's face was almost tangible.

Tears streamed down Claude's cheeks, and he put his face in his hands murmuring, *'Thank god, thank god,'* over and over.

Portuk came, and put his arm around Claude's suited shoulders saying gently, 'Adama is safe,' and, 'It's been a successful mission'.

They discovered later, at the debriefing, the extra reserves with their reinforced shielding, had turned the tide of the battle. The space pirates concluded they would get better treatment, if they hadn't harmed the hostages, which proved the case. The troops rounded up the villains and put them in the ship's brig; where Portuk fiercely maintained, they belonged all the time.

Adama was battered, mentally and physically, but alive. He couldn't thank his rescuers enough, going round hugging every Barog in sight. As a matter of urgency, they put him in a cabin with an Earth atmosphere, so he could rest without his suit on.

Adama insisted on thanking Portuk personally, and profusely—with emphasis and enthusiasm. Portuk became a little embarrassed, until Claude stepped in and gently led the Barogian away, leaving Adama to be examined by medical staff.

Claude explained to Portuk, 'He's feeling the strain of it all.'

'Yes, I can see that. Our medical staff have familiarised themselves with your human medicine, just for this eventuality. I think they will sedate him for the return journey. But in the mean time, as promised, here is a personal gift from me to you; a cephalocorder. Remember! You expressed an interest in its workings,' Portuk held out the compact brain scanner.

'Why, that's generous of you. Thank you,' Claude was flattered by the gesture—suspicion at bay, for the moment.

The ship's photon weaponry was ordered to destroy the pirate's complex, so no one else could make further use of it. Then they opened a Black Hole and returned to Rakh.

Once in Rakhian orbit, the Barogian hostages were transferred to another larger ship, where they were given a thorough physical, and sent on their journey to Barog, back to their families.

Claude and Adama teleported back to their Embassy, to a rapturous welcome from all the diplomatic staff. They lined the gnarled hall and hugged the tearful Adama, handing him small gifts they had prepared beforehand. Quadrant Custodian Thesor, Primearch Reithur and Grand Mehir Nathur, all sent their best wishes, and lots more presents to Adama on his safe return.

Adama insisted the kidnappers hadn't been such a bad bunch after all. This was an indicator of future trouble. According to their resident Psychologist, Professor Maskalik, Adama was exhibiting classical *association* symptoms for his captors, long ago called the Stockholm Syndrome. Compounding the trauma, Adama insisted his wife, back on Earth, never be informed of the kidnapping, or of his ordeal. All this suggested; he might be trying to suppress the experience, denying it ever happened.

Adama returned to being his quiet efficient self, except for reports from his neighbouring roommates, who told of screaming coming from his room at night. The Clinical Psychologist reported Adama had cancelled his appointments with him, despite orders from Claude for him to continue the consultations.

One morning, Claude decided to take the bull by the horns and confronted Adama as he arrived to discuss the Ambassadorial appointments for the week.

'Adama! Please sit down. I need an explanation as to why you've stopped seeing Professor Maskalik?'

'Sir, can't we leave this till some other time?'

'No Adama. The longer we leave this, the worse it'll get.'

'But *sir....*'

'You're having nightmares, and they must be confronted. Look, Maskalik has clearly indicated you're suffering from a classical case of Post Traumatic Stress Disorder.'

'But I'm all right sir.'

'You're having flashbacks. Am I right—or are you going to deny that? I'm only thinking of your welfare, Adama.'

'It's just some bad dreams, sir.'

'And what about during waking hours?'

'Well...there was...' Adama hesitated, eyes in a far away stare.

'Yes, go on,' Claude encouraged gently.

'...the occasional insectoid face flashing in and out.'

'And the cell where you were held?'

'I su...suppose. Yes sir.'

'Come on man; admit it. Those are flashbacks.'

'They might be...' he said reluctantly.

'And I've noticed you're somewhat distant. More self absorbed.'

'It'll pass. I just need to get on with my work.'

'*Adama*! You know your avoiding dealing with this, and that's not like you.'

'I'm *okay—really,* I am!'

'I've been told of a holiday planet some fifty light years away. I'm asking Theo to investigate its condition for our Embassy staff. He's going tomorrow, and if he reports the planet is suitable, then I'm sending you on a well-earned vacation there. I'm not asking you to go. I'm *ordering* you.'

'Yes sir.' A look of resignation showed on his face.

'You can make it an ordeal, but I'd rather you enjoyed yourself.'

'If that's your wish.'

'*It is!* I'm willing to send for your family, Adama, so you can enjoy this holiday together. Would you like that?'

'More than anything, sir.'

'Consider it done. *Now*—we can get back to the Appointments Diary.'

'Yes sir.'

Somewhere deep down in Adama, the healing process began, and his manner seemed a little more at ease.

Chapter Eighteen

Marooned

Theo, impatient to teleport onto the small spaceship, was grinding his teeth. He was embarked on a mission to the beautiful holiday planet both Claude and he agreed needed a personal visit. They had the use of the Pragmacasts of course, and with it, they were able to experience the atmosphere and the weather system. Still, being human, they both decided, one would have to make a visit—in person.

A sector on that planet would be modified for humans; the atmosphere suitably customized with climate controls. Theo insisted the only way to test the veracity of the Pragmacasts was with his five senses. The Pragmacasts even had emotional input, but reality would only satisfy Theo when picking a spot for a vacation.

Claude thought Theo needed a break, almost as bad as himself, so he let Theo talk him into going on a personal inspection.

Once aboard the spaceship, Theo settled into the spacious lounge with the rest of the passengers. The spaceship went far outside the Rakhian solar system to open up a Black Hole, and as the halo began to appear, a tremendous tremor occurred throughout the ship. That was the first he'd experienced anything of the sort, and he knew something was wrong.

The lounge in the ship lurched, throwing him off the couch. A second crawled by, and he felt the enormous g-forces pushing him. He was pressed against the floor for at least ten long minutes, and then whatever was causing the g-forces stopped. He heard a lot of Rakhian high-pitched whistle gibbering, some alien shouting, and then a screen appeared mid-air in the lounge.

Theo got to his knees and climbed back on the couch. The screen informed him, "The ship has suffered a minor setback" then more waffle followed, ending with, "the Captain is dealing with it." A little later his brooch translator continued, "You will remain calm and stay in the lounge." Shortly after, more messages followed. "You will be kept informed on the progress of repairs." and "you will be told when we get under way again." Theo thought *that's a fat lot of comfort*. What he really wanted to know—how *serious* the problem was.

A Rakhian fellow passenger he'd been chatting to earlier, told him they had been thrown quiet a long distance off-course, something about a force-field backlash from the Black Hole Generator. That's what the Rakhian understood from the shouting coming from the crewmembers.

The short slim elfin like Rakhian, accustomed to twice Earth's gravity, was calm and composed in his explanation.

Theo asked his acquaintance, 'So—do you know where we are?'

'Not a clue,' came back the nonchalant response.

'You don't seem worried?' Theo inquired.

'Not in the least. We haven't had an accident in a long time; at least not a serious one.'

'That's reassuring.'

'Our technology's safe,' insisted the Rakhian.

'It's just all so new to me, and I'm having to take your word for it. I'm not really doubting you.'

'You're in competent hands, stop worrying,' the Rakhian continued.

'Why don't they say something?' demanded Theo.

'They just did.'

'I know, but....'

The ship screeched and grated with loud jarrings reverberating throughout the structure. The lights dimmed, then went out, and for a second, pitch darkness lasted for what seemed an eternity. Then the lights came back on, and so did the screen. It showed a view of the bridge with a huge piece of rock occupying most of the space. The liquid metal was creeping over the rock towards a point in the centre to seal the breach. Unfortunately, the rock was too deeply wedged inside for the metal to eject it from the bridge.

At first glance, Theo guessed a meteor hit the nose and penetrated the bridge deck. There was no sign of life there. Pandemonium erupted in the lounge. What had been a calm assumption based on earlier assurances, was realised now as a serious situation.

The Rakhian acquaintance stood transfixed in horror, staring at the screen in disbelief. His mouth was moving, but no sound came, griped by a speechless hysteria. Theo leaned over to the dumbfounded Rakhian and took him by the shoulders, gently shaking him. That produced the required effect; he closed his mouth and hung his head. Taking him by the arm, Theo led him back to the couch and sat him gently down. He put his arm around the hapless Rakhian's shoulders, engulfing the small individual in his armpit.

His first priority was to get a pressure suit on both himself and the Rakhian, just in case.

'Wait here!' He instructed the little alien, taking upon himself his welfare.

He went over to the near empty suit rack by the door, and picked up the nearest, then looked for an extra large one for himself, finding one with his name on it at the very end. Luckily, the lounge hadn't been full, or there wouldn't have been a single suit left.

He returned to the Rakhian. 'Put this on...hurry man! What's your name?' Theo asked the Rakhian.

'Thaner...' the Rakhian responded dejectedly.

Another ominous shudder went through the ship— at that point, Theo hurriedly donned his suit and insisted the Rakhian do the same.

Thaner submissively got into the proffered suit, and the action itself calmed him.

Theo needed information. 'Do you think the ship might explode?'

Thaner looked glum, then took a deep breath. 'No. It won't explode. I don't think so anyway. We simply could end up just floating in space.' He shook his elfin head and tried to be more positive. Picking out a small device from a pocket at the side of the couch, he began to talk rapidly into it. Thaner was firing questions in Rakhian, getting lengthy answers.

After a little while he put the device down and looked at Theo. 'We have problems.'

'You're not joking!' Theo's tone was highly facetious.

Thaner ignored it, or more likely, the translator ignored it. 'I mean serious problems.'

'Go on; either the suspense—or this ship, is going to kill me.' Theo couldn't help it.

'The ship *is* dead in space, but the worst part is the auxiliary engines have surged, blown themselves out, and are now useless. They tell me we were thrown a light-year out by the first accident—that burned out our shields.'

'Just hold it there a minute...it can't be right. *A light-year?*' interrupted Theo. 'That's around nine and a half thousand billion kilometres. You *must* be wrong?' Theo's voice raised a tone.

'I'm afraid not. The Black Hole generator is the pinnacle of Federation "power" technology. The energy required to open a Black Hole is tremendous. We're lucky it was only a light-year...not a lot further, and that we're still in one piece.

'Anyway, let me continue. Due to the lack of shields we got hit by a meteor, well you saw that. That's pushed us even further away. Then the auxiliary engines surged, and we got thrust towards our neighbouring Solar System.

'Now we're drifting. The projections indicate, in half an hour we'll be caught by the weak gravity of a barren planet in our neighbouring solar system, and it's pulling us slowly towards it.'

'Any good news? Don't be shy; let me have it.' More sarcasm, that's how Theo dealt with fear.

'What do you mean?' There was puzzlement on his elfin face.

'Sorry Thaner. A failed attempt at human humour.'

'Oh...., I see.' But he didn't.

'What are the chances of us going down?'

'You mean crashing on the planet?' Thaner's face contorted with the uncomfortable prospect.

'Yes!' Theo relentlessly insisted.

'That's the projection—if they can't get some power back on.'

'Well, let's go and search the ship, see what we might need if we end up on the planet.'

'It'll keep us doing something—and occupy my mind. We'll need suits. Extra oxygen pellets. Water. Food. Communications. Signalling beacon,' Thaner paused.

'That'll do for starters,' chipped in Theo. 'Where shall we look?'

'Let me try the "inquisitor,"' and Thaner picked up the device he'd used before, talking into it. A minute went by. 'Quick, follow me,' Thaner said, as he got up and headed for the doorway; Theo wasn't far behind.

'Do you know where to get the stuff on the list—the things we might need?' Theo wanted to hear his own voice.

'I think so.'

'You know... *Hey Thaner!* Wait for me!' The little Rakhian was darting along the corridor at a fast pace. 'We can't be far from Rakh. They must know we're in trouble.' Theo was grasping at straws.

'Maybe. Maybe not.'

'Look Thaner, I don't know how your systems work yet. I mean for all I know, you could be part of a culture that simply abandons any spaceship that's in trouble. I know that's not true, but you see what I mean.'

'Yes.'

'Well? Do you think Rakh knows we're in trouble?'

'Same answer as before,' the little alien was exasperating.

They arrived at an open doorway, and Thaner dashed in. Theo followed him and closed the door tight behind him. They were looking at a jumble on the floor; half-open cupboards, half empty shelves. Someone had already sacked the emergency storeroom.

Thaner began a methodical search for the items on their list, and managed to come up with extra oxygen pellets; some emergency dehydrated food rations, and a couple of short range communicators. No extra suits. No water! And most importantly, no signalling beacon.

To make matters worse, there was a persistent drone from the ship, getting louder by the minute. Then the lights went. There was a sudden increase in gravity and the ship tilted, throwing them off balance. They fell into a corner of the storeroom in a heap, yet still the liquid metal walls felt soft and yielding.

When the crash finally came, the compliant liquid metal cushioned the impact. It moderated the shock of the ship's collision with the planet. They both found themselves imbedded half way into the adjacent walls of the corner they'd tumbled into.

A hush descended on the ship, an eerie silence so sudden that in itself it created fear. No engine sounds, no thuds or shudders—most of all, no people sound. Both wore sealed pressure suits and had activated their oxygen pellets.

A few moments later, they eased themselves out of the walls embrace and opened the doorway into the corridor. Facing them was a brown sandstone facade where the other side of the ship should have been. No corridor. Whatever sliced the ship in half had done it neatly down the middle. The other side of the ship was missing.

They looked down into a gap between the earthen wall and what was left of the corridor, and saw a chink of sunlight illuminating light sandstone coloured soil five meters below. Theo looked at Thaner, then at the clay opposite, then again at his companion. They were astonished to be alive, astounded at the turn of events, and frankly just shocked at it all. One moment they were on their way to a holiday planet, now they were barely alive on a wrecked spaceship on what they believed was a barren planet. Both went back into the storeroom and Theo closed the door. They felt the need for safety to review the crisis facing them.

'Any danger of the ship blowing?' Theo asked quietly, as if the sound of his voice might set something off.

'Whistle...gibber...gibber...whistle.' Thaner was saying something but it was all coming out in Rakhian. Theo tapped the green translator brooch on his suit.

'I don't think so; there's nothing flammable on board.' The tap had worked.

'Are you sure? In a spaceship?'

'Pretty sure. I'm no expert, but we Rakhians have a fairly good technical background, and although I can't build you another spaceship, I've a shrewd idea of its construction.'

'You don't know how reassuring that sounds. Can you rig a signal for any rescue ship from this junk here?'

'I'll have to have a good look at what we've got,' Thaner pointed at the scattered items in the storeroom— in reality he implied the whole vessel.

'We've got to look for survivors in the rest of the ship.'

'It's be a squeeze along that non-existent corridor.'

'You're smaller than me; it makes sense if you go and look.'

'We ought to try calling for the screen; maybe it'll work.' Thaner knew it was desperation talking.

'Go ahead.' Theo crossed his fingers.

Thaner called quietly, then louder, and then bellowed. No screen.

'I'd better go and search. I'll hurry back. If there's any survivors, I might have to stay and help. If I'm not back in fifteen minutes, come and looking for me. Agreed?'

'Agreed.'

With that, Thaner opened the door and inched his way to the left, twisting, squeezing between the ship's corridor wall and the sandstone surface. After what seemed an eternity of wedging and pinching, checking every compartment along the way for signs of life, Thaner reached the remnants of the bridge.

Not a hint of anybody being alive on board. *Maybe they've all got off; maybe they assumed we were dead,* thought Thaner. He kept a sharp lookout for useful items, and made mental notes of where they were located—then headed back in the direction of Theo.

When he reached Theo he reported, 'I can't find anybody.'

'What.... *nobody*?'

'Not a single soul,' Thaner emphasised.

'Could they have abandoned ship—maybe they're on the surface?'

'That had crossed my mind.'

'In that case, we'd better grab some gear and do the same.'

'We've got to stay near the ship. That's the first rule of rescue; it's the first place rescuers will look.'

'Yes, I agree. But we've got to see if we can find the others.'

'I'll grab what I think might be useful and throw it down the gap.'

'At the risk of repeating myself, Rakh must know we've gone down.'

'It's still prudent to act as if we're here for a lengthy time; it'll increase our survival capabilities,' Thaner was being deadly serious.

'Did you come across any water on your travels?'

'I've made a mental note of where in the ship we need to go back to. I mean there must be shelter material in the ship. There has to be a food generator somewhere, which would give us the water we need. We also need a power source.'

'Good! Lets find a spot outside, away from the ship, where we can make camp, then foray back into it for things we need. By the way, what was the complement of the ship's crew?'

'It's a small cruiser, can't be more than ten. I see what you're getting at. There weren't many passengers; say fifty. There's a regular Spaceliner servicing the holiday planet; most people would have used the spaceliner.'

Theo wasn't entirely reassured about the ship being safe, not exploding. After a slippery climb down, they were standing outside, and then they saw what had happened. Their ship had hit the sharp end of an inselberg; a wedge shaped wind eroded rock, eight hundred meters long, a hundred meters high. It consisted of a tabular mass of resistant hard rock resting on an undercut pillar of softer material, the sharp end facing the wind. The other half of the ship was on the far side of the inselberg.

The impact had cleaved through the ship lengthways as if hit by an axe. The massive isolated wedge of hard rock put paid to any vacation hopes. Had the ship been intact, it might have carried them back into space, but now that was out of the question.

They rounded the inselberg and checked the other section of the ship, and found some bodies embedded in the corridor's liquid skin. They hadn't died from impact, but from asphyxiation. The poor fools hadn't suited up. Theo counted some seventeen alien passengers, all with hideously distorted features, and bulging eyes. Their own criminal negligence cost them their lives.

In the lounge, he found more. Some still clung to pressure suits, as if trying to put them on, when death overtook them. Others had their suits on, but hadn't activated the oxygen pellets, probably a panic reaction. Theo found himself getting angry.

Finally, Theo and Thaner accounted for most of the passengers, but could find no sign of the crew anywhere. They searched both sides of the ship thoroughly. They could have been sucked out by the vacuum of space when the meteor hit, but they couldn't all have been on the bridge at the same time.

Maybe some managed to get to escape pods. When they checked, some of the escape pods had been activated. That was the first hopeful sign, since each pod had a distress beacon built in, able to transmit their co-ordinates. Hope turned to outrage as they realised the crew had abandoned the passengers.

*   *   *

The planet they'd crashed on was nothing special. An atmosphere of sorts; its composition registered on the suit visor as 94% CO_2, 3.9% Nitrogen, 1.3% argon, and 0.07% oxygen, with smaller amounts of krypton and xenon. Planet rotation made for a sixteen-hour day. The shape of the rocks suggested fierce windstorms raged at some time in the season.

They hurriedly hauled survival items out of both sections of the ship. This took till sunset. All went smoothly and Thaner inflated a low profile survival dome for the night, nestling it beneath a firm overhang under the inselberg.

The following morning the pink sky looked ominous. The terrain insisted there could be no deluge from the sky. It implied there had never been any other climate. Thaner found some kind of power tool and recommended burrowing into the blunt end of the hill, the other end to the sharp edge where the two halves of the ship sat.

The aim was to carve out a small cavern, a shelter to get out of the freezing cold of the previous night. It would position them a long distance from the ship, but since the pointed end of the inselberg took the force of the wind, the blunt end would give protection.

Leaving Thaner to dig the cavern, Theo determined to climb a jutting hill in the distant landscape, rising out of the plain. It rested on a broad gently sloping surface of bedrock situated at the base of a steeper slope some two hundred meters away. The height would give a clearer idea of what lay around. The steep-sided round-topped mound had a crag and tail on one side, making the climb relatively easy. After some puffing and huffing in his suit, Theo reached the top, and looked down onto an arid land that had been forever scoured by wind. In the distance, as far as the eye could perceive, was a flat tawny desert littered with rocky scree.

Further, away on the distant skyline, mountains reached skywards, looking as if they might contain snow, but it was probably wishful thinking. He desired to get higher to get a proper view of the surrounding terrain—but would have to settle for this.

A distant rumble joined the darkening sky, warning of a storm brewing on a gigantic scale. Theo hurried back to Thaner to see how things were coming along with the cavern—and found him finishing up. The entrance was sealed and secured with a couple of sheets of the liquid metal from the ship. Somehow, he'd cut out and dragged the sheets some five hundred meters. Thaner held some device to control the metal, making it do his bidding.

Theo inquired, 'Well, how are you coming along? Have you seen that sky?'

Thaner stopped for a moment. 'Almost finished.'

'Not before time.' Theo indicated at the sky nervously.

'Yes, I've been noticing that. There's some kind of windstorm brewing.'

'We haven't the slightest idea what the weather does on this planet. I'm grateful you came up with the cavern idea.' Theo was feeling edgy.

'Give me a hand to shift the gear inside,' Thaner nodded at a sizeable hoard of equipment piled near the entrance.

'How are you moving that?'

From his pocket, Thaner handed Theo a flat disc. 'Try this.'

'What do I do?'

'Just point at the cargo, and move the emitting beam into the cavern.'

He held down the button in the centre, 'What, like this?' at which split second the load lifted, and he pulled it along, walking backwards into the cave, leading the cargo with a mini tractor beam.

'That's it. You've got it.'

Theo was back out, gazing upwards. 'The wind's picking up. It's time we sealed ourselves inside.'

'Can't think of any reason why we shouldn't.'

Both went inside and Thaner hermetically sealed the entrance. Thaner sat down near the salvaged ship's replicator, scooping sand into a funnel on top. 'I'm adding matter into the replicator so it has something to convert,' Thaner explained.

In a few minutes, he'd created an oxygen environment. 'I've sealed the porosity so the oxygen can't escape. I'm telling you this so you know I'm thorough.' It seemed Thaner needed to explain his moves, as if to compensate for dismissing the accident right at the beginning.

'I trust you, I really do,' Theo reassured.

With a great sense of relief, the atmospheric conditions created in the cavern allowed them to remove their suits.

The storm was truly beginning to rage. Although shut in, they heard the din and racket vibrating the cave all around, hammering away at the sealed entrance. The clamour lasted for the rest of the day and all night, sometimes abating, then after a lull, picking up even stronger. They told stories, played a few simple games, and organised their equipment.

Thaner had acquired some useful gadgets from the ship, some damaged, which now he attempted to repair while the storm lasted. They stayed cooped up in the cavern for some sixteen hours, during a lull, trying to establish if it had diminished; thus, a whole planetary cycle went by.

On the second day, they couldn't hear any more wind, and the vibrations ceased, so they waited a few more hours, then donned their suits and ventured outside.

There's was an arc of relatively clear ground before the entrance of the cavern, but the sand built up away from the entrance in the direction the wind had blown. The reason for building the cavern into the blunt end of the steep-sided hill was vindicated. The wind hit the sharp end of the resistant solid rock, carried sand over the top and deposited a huge quantity in an arc away from the entrance.

Thaner observed: 'This is going to make moving around a lot more difficult.'

'I know this isn't the time, but this scenery makes me wistful—can't help thinking of home.'

Thaner looked shocked. 'I was under the impression *your* planet looked more like Rakh, not this dreary wasteland.'

'I'm not from Earth. I was born on Mars, and it looks pretty much like this, at least most of it still does.'

'I'm longing for the lush yellow of Rakh—that's what I miss.'

'The surroundings giving one comfort, are the ones we grow up in,' observed Theo.

'Quite possibly. Look, I still need a little more time to put together the uplink communicator and repair the distress beacon from the damaged lifepod. Why don't you scout around, see what the storm's done.'

'You sure? If you need me, use the communicator. I won't go far. See you in half an hour.'

With that, Theo filled up the water flask in his suit, checked he had enough oxygen pellets—then went outwards. He climbed over the arc surrounding the entrance, and viewed the sea of sand before him. It had engulfed everything, turning a barren rocky landscape into undulating dunes. Walking further out from their temporary shelter, he turned the corner of the hill in the direction of what was left of the ship.

The wreckage was only supposed to be four hundred meters away, but nothing could be seen except sand. At the sharp end of the hill was a huge mound. In past storms the sand would have slid by the frame, but the ship had acted as a barricade and the sand accumulated around it. Theo blinked a number of times, not able to believe the evidence of his eyes. Instinctively he raised his hands to rub his eyes, and hit the visor with his clenched gloves. That brought a smile of absurdity to his face. He stood dumfounded. *Where's the bloody ship gone?*

Somewhere, beneath five or ten meters of shifting gravel, lay the broken half of the vessel. It must be the same on the other side. Their predicament on the planet was not improving. *Bloody storm,* he cursed in his head. *Bloody planet.* If they wanted to salvage anything else, they would have to do a lot of digging, and he knew it was virtually impossible to dig an alleyway in sand. Maybe the device Thaner had for digging out the cavern would move the stuff. It was a question needing an answer.

Gazing at all the sand, Theo became sentimental, remembering his early years zooting around on the sand zippers, racing others, then vanishing like a willow-the-wisp behind some dune. He haunched down in his pressure suit by the mound encasing the ship, mulling over his memories. To his right lay isolated crescent shaped dunes slowly migrating down-wind, horns forward.

To Thaner it had been inexplicable so much sand could suddenly appear from nowhere. Theo on the other hand, coming from Mars, knew how these sandstorms could blow up and move billions of tonnes around the planet. Dust, gravel, lifted thousands of meters into the atmosphere, carried many hundreds of kilometres before being dumped temporarily. With each passing storm, one moment scree, then sand appeared covering all, and then scree reappeared.

He peered into the day's heat, watching a strong wind lift the sand grains, moving them in a series of bounces above the fiery landscape. In a dune to the left, the wind had blown the sand up the gently sloping windward side. When the grains reached the top, they rolled down the steeper leeward side.

Enthralled, contemplating nature all around, glimpsing the solitary landscape performing a stark wonderful ballet—Theo felt glad to be alive. Sitting there, he felt relief for the first time since the accident. His mind blocked out his predicament; the fact of being stranded on an uninhabitable planet, waiting and hoping to be rescued. Not knowing whether the Federation Rescue Services were even aware they needed rescuing. Then like a dark cloud—worry reasserted itself. *What in the Solar winds am I doing on this alien planet, so far from home? A few years ago, I hadn't met an alien; now I'm on a planet full of the blighters. It's one hell of an upheaval, enough to boggle my poor mind.*

*   *   *

Thaner's shouting from the communicator roused him from his reverie. He turned to see him yelling and gesturing at the sky. In utter astonishment, he glimpsed a craft approaching from the same direction his ship had come down when it crashed.

As the craft neared he recognised a Rakhian shuttle, and his feelings surge inside as he expelled a sigh of relief.

Thaner arrived, puffing and panting in his suit, hugging him round the waist. He kept shouting, 'My communicator worked!' then repeating, 'My beacon worked!' They both began singing and dancing around excitedly in the sand, pent-up tension oozing out.

The shuttle landed well distant from the steep sided hill, stirring up clouds of sand, which took a while to subside. When all settled, the teleporter relayed them inside, into the lounge, where Theo found Claude and Faisal waiting.

'What a blessed relief,' murmured Claude as he hugged Theo.

'Let me introduce you to my saviour,' Theo said turning to Thaner. 'Thaner, this is Ambassador Claude Joubert from Earth, you remember, I told you about him in the cave, and you heard me mention my Deputy, Faisal al-Rhumi. This is he, in the flesh. It was his beacon you picked up.'

'We're grateful to you Thaner, for saving the Martian Ambassador. We were closing in on this planet, but your beacon pinpointed the exact position, and let us know someone was alive down there.'

'Pleased to meet you Ambassador,' Thaner extended both his palms face upward, in the Rakhian manner of greeting.

Almost formally, Claude said, 'If there is anything in my power I can do to help, you may name it.'

'I've heard so much about Mars and Earth from Theo, I feel I would like to visit your Solar System,' Thaner looked a little embarrassed at responding so quickly to the offer.

'That would be our great pleasure to arrange, and of course you will be our honoured guest,' responded Claude.

The shuttle personnel had the unpleasant task of retrieving the dead passengers from the crashed ship. They needed to secure computer records of the wreck so the Disaster Analysers could ascertain the causes of the accident.

They then lifted off and headed back to the mother ship in orbit around the planet. The docking of the shuttle and subsequent journey back to Rakh was essentially uneventful, especially when compared to the escapade Theo and Thaner had just survived.

'I must ask this question,' Thaner said quietly to the Captain. 'What happened to the crew of our ship?'

'We picked up nine dead bodies floating in space, and a further three lifepods with the rest of the crew alive. They are to face criminal negligence charges for abandoning the ship before seeing to the passengers' safety.' The Captain's stern features were set in a manner that indicated he meant business.

'I see—that clears that up,' groaned Thaner.

'Don't let their plight worry you. You survived, that's all that matters.'

Some hours later, they reached Rakh and teleported down to the Earth-Mars Embassy, where the Martian contingent insisted on holding a celebration, overjoyed at seeing their Ambassador safe and sound. The Earth contingent was no less happy to see Theo back, since they had a great fondness for his easy and pleasant manner.

The Rakhian authorities asked for a report from Theo as to his experiences in the doomed vessel, the behaviour of the crew, and his survival tactics with Thaner, on the desert planet. Quadrant Custodian Thesor sent his congratulations on Theo's remarkable survival, and looked forward to personally hearing Theo's account of the story.

'Claude! The more I think of the planet I was marooned on, the more an idea keeps bouncing around in my mind.'

'I've a different problem I want your help with,' Claude replied.

'All right, you go first.'

'To alert the duty officer at the Embassy to the precise whereabouts of our people outside the Embassy, I want us to establish an automated IN/OUT notice board on the computer. Not the usual type, but who's going where, when they're expected to arrive at their destination, and when they're due back. Each person having to register as they come and go. It's to prevent people going missing. What do you think?'

'I'm game. But would it have helped me?'

'I'm not certain. I still want to try this for a while. I can't do it without your help.'

'Go ahead. I'll back you all the way.'

'What was your idea?'

'Well, it's this. The Federation has prevented us from colonising "New Earth" in the Centauri constellation, right? Why can't we terraform the desert planet I crashed on, and colonise that instead? It's in the next solar system, only a light year from here. Or is that somehow Rakhian property?'

'Theo, sometimes you amaze me. That's brilliant. I like it. I'll immediately find out if anybody claims the planet. Would the Rakhians object to having human company in this sector of space?'

Theo sat in the armchair, dialled a soft drink, and watched Claude talking to someone.

Claude made several calls, was given the run around, before the answer came back the Rakhians were prepared to negotiate in good faith. That meant they were claiming the neighbouring solar system and its planet, but were willing to bargain over the price. Claude would have to get ready for lengthy and tough negotiations.

'By the way Theo, did you know Adama's wife and child arrived? They left yesterday for the vacation planet you were supposed to check out.'

'Uh? Oh yeh, I'm glad. That fellow needed a good holiday.'

'You're welcome to go and finish checking the planet.'

'No thanks. Not just now. I'll wait for Adama's report on it.'

Chapter Nineteen

Maiden Voyage

Ryan had been tossing and turning, struggling pillow, struggling with the controls of the ship. The pillow was tightly gripped, the controls of the ship were held tight, but he woke with a start. There *were* no controls on the new ship. Dream and reality were incompatible; his mind had woken him to resolve the contradiction.

On the Moon, the new style Federation starcruiser was almost ready: the first in her class. She was due for her trial calibration run. The builders on Earth had mastered the novel metallurgy in half the time estimated. They managed to get to grips with fabricating the fluid metal, then setting up the manufacturing line in just over six months. The liquid metal was controlled at the miniscule level, atom by atom, which required more sophisticated gluon-computers that had to be built before the metallurgy could begin.

To help with the transfer of technology, a sizeable group of Rakhians had arrived on Earth, the species chosen because they could survive Earth's atmosphere without pressure suits. There was somewhat less oxygen in Earth's atmosphere than on Rakh, but with a little augmentation from portable masks, they adjusted. They were vaccinated and forced to take suppressants to prevent bacterial and viral cross contamination, but stoically put up with the medical assault.

It was a novel experience for humans to be instructed in advanced techniques by little elfin like individuals, who had a million year old civilisation behind them. However, both species integrated satisfactorily, worked well together, and respected each other's particular traits. It boded well for future relations.

The humans were a young race, pushy, brash, adventurous, but willing to learn, whilst the Rakhians were gifted in science, reserved but vigorous, gentle, confident, and even complacent. They had made themselves comfortable on their garden planet to the extent their sense of adventure had almost disappeared. The two races complemented each other.

The final assembly of the SpaceCruiser was done on the Moon. All the components were shipped there as soon as they came out of the manufacturing process. This was partly for gravitational reasons, partly for security. The Moon's facilities had been vastly improved and the whole of the Gruemberger Crater had been converted for production of the vessel.

Expert personnel had transferred to the enlarged habitats constructed alongside the old ones, giving the Gruemberger Township a real Argonaut feel. The earlier Starship, the *Kiron,* had been assembled on the Moon, and all the facilities were enhanced for the coming build, being transformed to accommodate the smaller alien ships. Whereas the *Kiron* had weighed 1,667 tonnes on the Moon (10,000 earth tonnes), carried four hundred crew. The new ship would be half the size, weigh one third and have a crew of only fifty.

They had installed the new cloaking system using "fuzzy" technology, involving the distorting of the photon's pathways so they circumvented the cloaked object. To another ship's instrumentation, it was rendered invisible. The biggest challenge to Earth's sciences however, was the Black Hole Generator. It required an assimilation of completely new concepts and principles for Earth's physicists, laying down radical new manufacturing processes, and developing new ways of handling powerful tools. This was where the Rakhian advisors helped the most. The alien technology was transforming the Earth beyond recognition.

The natural choice for Captain for the new starcruiser had to be the only member of the Space Corps who had captained a Starship before. Patrick Ryan was given first refusal; only he didn't refuse. He grabbed the appointment with both hands. It needed the approval not only of Ying but also of Ghali on Mars. In another momentous *volte-face*, the Space Corps had been amalgamated with the Martian Space Corps. It was a magnanimous gesture of reconciliation of the only two independent planetary bodies in the solar system.

PLC had been refined and redefined, to provide more sophisticated, subtle and powerful interventions, if and when required. Ryan had gone to the newly reformed PLC to acquire the technical knowledge for the new starcruiser, so he got to know the ship. When he'd completed the assimilation, he was informed his crew had already been through PLC and were waiting for him at the Excelsior Hotel.

He arrived at the Hotel and was greeted by a group of familiar faces waiting in the lobby.

'General Hoffmyer! How nice to see you again,' he shook hands. Ryan had been informed he'd taken charge of the new vessel's programme.

'Congratulations on your promotion, Vice Admiral Ryan,' Hoffmyer said guardedly, seeming to hint at a touch of jealousy in the rapid rise of this relatively young man. At a hundred and seventeen, he'd made Vice Admiral. It was previously unheard of.

'Professor Hopkins! What a pleasure. Glad you could make it.' Patanjali's young assistant had matured visibly, thought Ryan.

'Kochanowski! I see they bumped you up the ladder as well, congratulations Captain.'

'Thank you Admiral.'

'Mr. Delgado! Mr. Oblomov!' Ryan looked at Oblomov's shoes, which made the young man blush at the memory of their first encounter. 'You two must be the youngest Lieutenant-Commanders in the Space Corps,' Ryan mused in a friendly manner.

'We hope so Admiral, we've worked hard for it,' was Delgado's response.

'It's a pleasure to see your friendly mugs again. You may be aware; they're going to hold the launching ceremony for the SpaceCruiser tomorrow. It's no secret they're naming it after the President of the World Government. After all, he started all this alien business. He and his wife arrived on the Moon, and they're with the Governor right now. She will name the ship at eight hundred sharp. We'll board and take her for a trial run at twelve hundred hours. Any questions? No! Good. Now lets go through and have some chow.'

The following morning, the newest addition to the Space Corps, the *Ying Li* was named by his wife, Ying Ji, who gave a short speech, concluding with, 'may space protect all who sail in her'. That over with, the President followed by wishing this new era in humanity's journey out into space, prosperity and peaceful contacts with other species. He hoped Hopkins Technologies Inc. would next begin building SpaceCruisers for the private sector, after the initial five for the Space Corps. Then humans could really begin to explore the Galaxy peacefully and make contact with all the other sentient races of the Federation. He concluded by wishing *bon voyage* to the newly promoted crew.

By then, it was time for the crew to board, and make ready for the trial run. Hoffmyer insisted three Rakhian engineers go with them in the Engine Room, to ensure things ran smoothly. They would only butt in, in the event they were asked to by the humans.

*   *   *

It was late in 3005 when the *Ying Li* finally lifted off from Gruemberger Spaceport, steering a course far beyond Pluto. The ship was voice controlled by the new gluon-computer. Ryan said what he wanted, and "old glue" made the ship carry it out. Helm was automatic, navigation was automatic, the human equivalents were there only as a backup, just as there was another computer backup, in case.

In reality, only Ryan needed be on board; "old glue" could perform the rest of the functions. On the passenger runs, when those vessels were built, the crews' main function was as service providers. They were the human face of the ship, or the face of whichever species operated it. Having crew added extra personal value to the journey. The passenger could ask their screens, but it's friendlier to have a real person deal with your request.

On the other hand, the *Ying Li* was a military vessel; part of the Space Corps, and the crew were there for military reasons. Ryan took the ship out as far as the relay-transmitter near Pluto, where he intended to activate his first Black Hole, half a million kilometres outwards into clear space. A Black Hole needed clear space; otherwise, it would suck in anything within the event horizon. He had done it many times in the simulator, but this time was for real.

'Computer! Set a Black Hole course for New Earth in Centauri,' Ryan commanded.

'Yes, Captain,' the computer responded.

Ryan stroked his chin, then instructed firmly, 'Activate the "excavator".'

The computer replied just as firmly, 'Yes, Captain. At once.'

Kochanowski, Delgado, and Oblomov were all on the bridge, seated at their stations, idle but alert, following the computer's operations. Other more experienced races such as the Barog operated from a bare bridge, no consoles, no furniture of any kind. The humans still had an obsession about controlling technology, making sure they were seen to be in charge. Sitting down and shouting at the machines put them in charge, so they thought.

The crew looked appreciatively at Ryan for choosing to go back to Centauri on a nostalgia trip. They could no longer land, since the Federation prohibition; still, the trip was appreciated. The Black Hole opened and the *Ying Li* went down the wormhole tunnel, through to the White Hole at the other end, into open space.

A few seconds following their exit, Ryan looked, and then looked puzzled.

'Computer! Where are we? This isn't Centauri.'

'No Captain, it isn't.'

'Then where are we?'

'I have checked my charts sir; they're muddled. But extrapolating on bare minimum information, which means I'm guessing. I believe we are near Laineren 5.'

'And pray tell, where the hell is Laineren 5.'

'The databank says it's thirty-nine thousand light years from the Carina-Cygnus arm.'

'*What*!' exploded Ryan.

'Are you telling me a four-light-year trip is thirty-five thousand light years *astray*?'

'That's what I'm extrapolating.'

'Mr. Delgado. Will you please confirm this imbecile computer's assertions.'

'Sir, I've been following the plotted course. Up to the point the Black Hole opened, everything was fine. Either there's a fault in navigation, or we hit an unknown phenomenon in the wormhole tunnel.'

'I want to know which it is, Mr. Delgado. Get right on it.'

'*Yes Sir*!'

'Mr. Oblomov! Get the senior Rakhian up here on the double.'

'Aye aye Sir.'

'Computer! Options?'

'My appraisal is, certain deliberate errors have been carefully input into my navigational maps. It would seem a large number of digits have been transposed, and unfortunately without being able to cross reference, I can't tell which are false and which are correct.'

'Be Certain. Please recheck your assertion.'

'I have, Captain. Several times. The answer comes out the same.'

'Let's be clear. You're suggesting sabotage. Is that correct?'

'Yes Captain.'

'And what of the backup computer!'

'I'm afraid they've been most thorough.'

'Also sabotaged?'

'Yes Captain.'

'Sir,' Oblomov had returned with a Rakhian in tow. 'This is Naroth, their senior engineer.'

'Has Oblomov explained our problem?'

'Yes my Captain.' The Rakhian wore a puzzled expression.

'I'm unable to help you with correcting the charts.'

'Have you any ideas. We can't just randomly open Black Holes and hope we reach a safe haven.'

'No my Captain, we can't. I'm going to suggest you activate your main distress beacon. Then put your people onto every piece of transmission equipment you carry, sending the Federation's version of "Mayday," and hope someone picks it up.'

'If that's your advice, we'll get to it. Number One, you heard Naroth?'

'Yes, Captain. I'm on it.' Kochanowski started to give orders to the crew.

Ryan continued to quiz the Rakhian Engineer. 'Naroth! Do you know? Is there anybody on Laineren 5?'

'I'm sorry my Captain; I haven't the slightest idea. It's out of our territory.'

'Computer! Is Laineren 5 inhabited?'

'According to the databank, no, Captain. The nearest Federation outpost is nine light years away. If I were to open a Hole for nine light years, we could possibly end up in the Galactic centre, and there's a super massive Black Hole there, well beyond our meagre engine's control.'

'It looks as if we're stranded for the moment. I want people to keep thinking of ways of getting us out of here. Naroth! I thought the Federation supplied the Galactic Charts.'

'They did my Captain. Somebody in your Solar System tampered with them. It could have been done before they were loaded into the computer, which would mean on Earth, or afterwards, which would mean on the Moon.'

'Stupid, and dangerous.' Ryan vented his frustration.

'I believe whoever was responsible, never intended you to return,' offered Naroth.

Ryan spat out, 'I'm going to do my damnedest to disappoint them. The culprit *must* be found.'

The SpaceCruiser floated in the darkness of space, with nowhere to go. The most advanced spaceship, vandalised by some petty Luddite. They had plenty of food, lots of air, and were in no immediate danger; just frustrated. Ryan also asked the crew to come up with ways of preventing the same thing happening again, to be suggested for implementation to Hoffmyer, *when* they got back.

A sleep period went by, without any response to their Galactic "Mayday." The morning following, anxiety began to manifest itself when an argument ended in a fight between two of the crew. The frustration and fear of not knowing how they were going to get home was causing discipline to fall apart.

It was a blessing when at the end of the second calendar day, they had visitors. An unknown ship appeared and stationed itself parallel with the *Ying Li*, making the Rakhians somewhat nervous. That made the humans even more nervous. If these experienced spacefarers were worried, then the humans really ought to be.

Over the intercom came a shrill voice. 'This is Captain S'pon of the Synoin cruiser *Var'n*. Can we be of any assistance?'

They had announced themselves as Synoins. Naroth told Ryan they were a race that had been invited to join the Federation some three hundred and fifty years back, but refused. They became a legend amongst the Federation. No one had ever refused to join the Galactic Federation before. Their technology had been forging ahead, even then, but from the look of their ship; it had substantially improved. Ryan thought it best if he let the Rakhians negotiate with the Synoins, and he suggested this to Naroth.

The Rakhians thanked the Synoins for their interest, and the Synoins explained they had heard the distress beacon and the Federation "Mayday" from the *Ying Li*.

Naroth cleared his throat, 'Well, in fact, yes, you could help. Would it be possible for you to download a copy of the Galactic charts from your ship. The current navigational charts over here are corrupted beyond retrieval.'

A shrill response came back from Captain S'pon. 'But of course, we Synoins would only be too happy to help our good friends the Rakhians.'

With that, the corrupted charts were put into back up storage, for forensics, and a frequency connection initiated. The Synoins charts were transferred to the *Ying Li* database. From there, the onboard computer used the new charts. As simple as that.

If one small word was written wrongly in a line of computer programming, the whole programme was rendered useless. The same applied to navigational charts that relied on correct co-ordinates being present. If the wrong co-ordinates were programmed, the charts were useless.

The Synoins wanted to know if the Rakhians required any *further* help. The embarrassed Rakhians thanked them profusely, but no further help was needed. The *Ying Li* was now back in full operation. Ryan was anxious to get under way. The Synoins departed and so did the *Ying Li*. Ryan decreed the computer set co-ordinates for home, and ordered the "excavator" activated. This time the *Ying Li* came out near Pluto, and everyone breathed an audible sigh of relief. An extremely angry Ryan fumed silently. And vowed vengeance.

Chapter Twenty

Sabotage

It was late in the day Ryan docked the *Ying Li* back on Moon base—the crew were in a foul mood. Everyone, apart from *someone* on Moon Base, was delighted to have them back. Ryan grounded the ship gently at Gruemberger Spaceport, then as a matter of priority arranged to see Hoffmyer.

'Number One, secure the ship; I mean tight. Nobody gets on board. ' Ryan was taking no more chances.

'Aye aye, skipper,' Kochanowski snapped back.

'Debrief the crew. See if they came up with any ideas on preventing a recurrence of sabotage.'

'Aye Captain.'

'All being well, I want to take her out again tomorrow at ten hundred hours. We still haven't done our shake down run.'

He sought out Naroth. 'Thanks for your help with the Synoins, and for the invaluable advice. I appreciated your presence on the ship. Could you possibly be ready for another run in the morning?'

Naroth calmly told him, 'That's what we're here for my Captain.'

The meeting with Hoffmyer was friendly but strained, and it seemed to Ryan as if he was feigning sincerity at their safe return.

'General, we are lucky to have got back,' Ryan was in an ugly mood.

'We'll get to the bottom of this,' protested Hoffmyer.

'It needs swift action. The saboteur must be caught instanter.'

'Yes, yes...I informed Space Corps Internal Audit as soon as you transmitted your sabotage suspicion.'

'It's more than suspicion, General.'

'We've notified Interpol on Earth, to get them started on the trail of whoever's responsible.'

'If those Synoins hadn't appeared, we might still be stuck thirty-five thousand light years from home.'

'Admiral Ryan! We *will* find who's responsible.'

'The computer on the ship is under guard. Forensics might want to perform diagnostics on the pathways. It replicated the new charts, leaving the old ones intact.'

Ryan left Hoffmyer and returned to his Hotel for a shower and a meal. Throughout dinner, a nagging thought kept running through the back of his mind. It couldn't have been Hoffmyer—surely. After dinner, he went to the foyer and watched the Holocast News for a while.

Three officers, a tall blonde and two lanky males approached his chair.

The blonde began, 'Admiral! We're from Internal Audit. I'm Leyland, this here is Colonel Frisch, and that's Pringle. May we have a moment of your time.'

'Won't you sit down,' Ryan pointed at seats.

'We're investigating the sabotage—trying to follow the route of the charts since they arrived in the Solar System. We've traced the maps to the Rakhian ship delivering them. We then trailed them being transferred to the secure Space Corps facility at Vandenberg. They were kept there until they were needed on the Moon a month ago. That's when they were loaded into the space vessel. That was under tight guard during its final preparation. We'd like to ask you about a fellow officer of you acquaintance, a Captain Scott.'

'You don't mean Jeremiah Scott. What's he got to do with this? We were at the Academy together. Class of 2900.'

'We *do* mean that Scott. Have you kept in touch?'

'Not really. An occasional reunion. Last one was five years ago. Why?'

'He was Captain of the ship delivering the charts to the Moon.'

'You're keeping something back. Out with it.'

'We think he's our man, but we can't find a motive. We don't want to use the PL without his consent. We want *you* to ask for him as a replacement for Kochanowski, who has been badly injured.'

'*What!* When! He was okay when we got in a couple of hours ago,' Ryan looked stunned.

'No Admiral. Captain Kochanowski is all right. *That's* the story we want *you* to sell to Scott. He's been ordered to report to you on the Moon.'

'Ahh, I see...I'll go along with whatever you have in mind, if it catches the saboteur. I must say: I hate intrigue. The idea of an injury isn't sustainable; our internal femto-robot repair systems would repair any injury in no time.'

'Can we leave the excuse to you? When he reports, he is to be sent to the PLC for upgrading. We'll then check what he's got in his memory banks. We want him to give us the motive. He could have been exceptionally clever and gone to a bootleg PLC and had those memories erased. I'm betting he's too cocksure, and hasn't bothered.'

'I'm told, since we've installed the gluon-computers, the improved version of PLC now shows up bootlegging. An immediate analysis throws up the incongruities. I suppose that's beside the point. When am I to expect him?'

'In three and a half hours.'

'Fine! Leave it to me then. I'll send him to PLC, and...I presume you'll be waiting for him there?'

'Yes, Admiral. We'll take it from there.'

'Keep me posted.'

'We will. Thank you for your assistance sir.' All three got up and left.

Ryan's eyes followed the blonde.

* * *

Captain Scott arrived on schedule, and they greeted each other as old friends from the Academy might be expected to. Ryan explained it was only going to be a temporary assignment for Scott, due to Kochanowski's mother being killed in an accident. He chatted with Scott for half an hour, then sent him down to PLC to be programmed with the technical aspects of the *Ying Li;* that's what he told *him.*

The same IA officers later informed Ryan, they'd found the motive. It was simple jealousy of Ryan's rapid promotion, his successful journey to Centauri, and his triumphant return. The main gripe Scott harboured was Ryan currently being given command of the most advanced ship in the Space Corps.

Captain Scott was running around, according to the version they discovered in his head, in an old broken down tub of a spaceship. Whilst others were prancing around with a silver spoon stuck in their mouths.

Scott simply could not understand—refused to understand. A new Space Corps was being built, and a new vigorous command structure was needed to run it. In spite of all the early PL screening used on cadets, people were still slipping through the selection process.

When he came out from PL, Scott was confronted with his memories, and then charged with the sabotage of the *Ying Li*. His sentence was to be totally reprogrammed by the PLC, then moved away from any space duties. Quietly in his head, Ryan apologised to Hoffmyer for having ever suspected him.

Next day at ten hundred hours, with Hoffmyer's blessings, the *Ying Li* lifted off once more on their original course for Centauri. They reached Pluto, went through the wormhole tunnel, and came out without any mishap on the fringes of Centauri space.

Ryan and the crew looked at New Earth, and a deep sadness engulfed them. Ryan proposed renaming the planet back to the original Rigel Kent, to lessen their feelings of a setback in not being able to colonise it.

True, it was the Federation that put the prohibition on, not the planet, but they felt if the planet could have made its desires known, it probably would have asked them to keep off. Somehow, nature needed to take its evolutionary course. Humans had the habit of grabbing and thinking later, often when it was to late. That would have to change, and the human race to mature.

The return voyage was speedy, peaceful and uneventful. The *Ying Li* returned to the Gruemberger Spaceport, then was officially commissioned into the Space Corps. The Solar System had a new class of transgalactic SpaceCruiser.

*   *   *

At Ying's urging, Hopkins Technologies Inc. were put in charge of producing the plans for a fleet of the new vessels. In addition, the World Government asked for Spacefrigates and Spacecarriers to be included. They might not be built, but they wanted the plans ready to go, if there ever was a need.

Hopkins Technologies had grown rapidly and had a vested interest in the manufacture and assembly of the new ships. Almost overnight, Leonard had set up a network of companies bidding for a big slice of the contracts involving the applied sciences.

It surprised Patanjali; his assistant was becoming a business tycoon on the back of imported alien technology. Becoming a joint Nobel Laureate for his warp drive had somehow jolted to life an entrepreneurial spirit in Leonard. He and Ryan were often in each other's company, and ever since the Centauri voyage, managed to get on extremely well.

Everything was moving well for Leonard, he even invited Admiral Ryan onto the Board of Hopkins Technologies as special advisor. An exceptional dispensation was needed, and obtained from Ying, for a serving military man like Ryan, to join the Board of a private corporation. What Leonard was doing, like any good business mogul, was planning ahead. He needed Ryan's growing influence in the new version of the Space Corps.

*   *   *

Since the Solar System now had its own Federation style Cruiser, there was an urgent need to make a trip to Rakh, to rotate and relieve the staff at the Earth-Mars Embassy. However, Ryan and his crew were ordered to take four days shore leave, then report to Admiral Petrusconi.

Petrusconi was his new superior under whom Ryan and his ship were placed in the new Space Corps. Ryan's provisional duties were to act as logistics and liaison for the Embassy on Rakh, putting him and Petrusconi under the direct control of the Diplomatic Corps, and as he had planned—Ying.

For his shore leave, Ryan went back to Brisbane, and tried to rekindle the flame of his lady friend. He hadn't properly thanked her for the silk cravat. He intended to thank her—many times over, and stay there for the duration of his leave, then report to Petrusconi on New Caledonia.

Space Corps HQ was situated on New Caledonia so it kept close contact with the World Government, responsible for its funding.

Petrusconi was expecting Ryan. After their initial handshake, his new boss asked him to be seated.

'I'm glad to finally meet you Ryan,' opened Petrusconi.

'Likewise Admiral.' beamed Ryan.

'Your exploits precede you. I hear you took the *Ying Li* back to New Earth for your shake-down run.'

'Yes sir. I just wanted to see the place for the last time, before we quarantine it for ever.'

'A lot of people aren't too happy on that score,' scowled Petrusconi.

'The Federation have a point, Admiral. *We* wouldn't be here if someone had stomped all over *our* planet when only our plants had evolved.'

'Well, put like that; it may make sense. Did you enjoy your leave?'

'The weather was perfect; it's the height of summer in Queensland right now. Luscious and thoroughly relaxing.'

'It's good you're relaxed. I suspect you're going to be kept busy from now on, for a while at least. You're to pick up a hundred diplomats from the Moon, and bring back the same number from Rakh. They've been there a year now. You'll be taking the new Earth Ambassador, Taras Fisenko, and his deputy, Chandragupta Vivekananda. Try to roll out the carpet, although it's a simple rotation of diplomatic personnel. You'll be carrying diplomatic mail, and some fresh supplies. You take your orders from Ambassador Joubert, when you get to Rakh. The rest of your orders are in this datacube. You leave for the Moon tomorrow, and Rakh the day after. If we have all the business out of the way, then you're invited to dinner. I won't hear of a refusal; my wife is expecting us. She makes a mean New Caledonian Salad.'

'I need to make a couple of calls, and then I'm yours for the evening.'

Ryan made sure the Moon put out a recall reminder to all the crew, and told them when he wanted the *Ying Li* to be ready to go first thing in the morning. He let Petrusconi take him home to meet his wife, let his wife give him an excellent meal, then his hosts insisted he listen to some Bach and Mozart to round off the evening.

Next day, Ryan caught a shuttle back to the Moon where he met with the new waiting Ambassador and the rotating diplomats he was to ferry. His crew were expecting him, relaxing at the Hotel.

'Admiral, have you heard about Scott?' All listened to Kochanowski's opening remark.

'Yes, I've been informed.' Ryan was reluctant to be associated with the despicable man.

'What in space got into him?'

'An aberration, no doubt.'

Oblomov chipped in, 'Why? I mean he had a good command.'

'Even with PL some people go rotten,' Delgado suggested.

'Number One, are we ready for tomorrow?' Ryan interrupted.

'Aye, skipper. We're loaded now; should be no hold up.'

'Good! Coach, please inform the waiting diplomats we depart ten hundred hours sharp, so I suggest they board nine hundred.'

'Aye Admiral.'

* * *

In due course, humanity's first ever independent trip to the Quadrant HQ of the Galactic Federation, Rakh, lifted off according to schedule. The *Ying Li* had a number of homeward bound Rakhians on board, technical advisors mingling with the rotating diplomats. They went past the planet of the Greek god of wealth, Pluto, and in no time had passed the Kuiper Belt ringing the Solar System. The ship went through the wormhole tunnel and exited near Rakhian space, to be met by the sight of the lush yellow planet.

The *Ying Li* entered standard orbit round Rakh and logged into Rakhian Space Control Centre. Although expected, it came as a pleasant surprise to the Earth-Mars Embassy to have a Solar System SpaceCruiser finally on their doorstep. There was a flurry of activity with the onboard teleporter as the Rakhian passengers relayed downwards to their homes. The replacement diplomats and the supplies were dispatched to the human Embassy.

Ryan, along with all of his crew, was invited to the combined Embassy to meet both Ambassadors and their staff. That was impossible of course, since someone had to stay on board the *Ying Li*. The Coach remained behind with a skeleton crew, with a promise to be relieved the next day. Ryan relayed down into a hall full of rapturous people waiting to greet him.

'Admiral Ryan, it's a pleasure—and a comfort to see you,' enthused Claude. 'You've no idea how reassuring it is to have our own transgalactic SpaceCruiser visit us like this.'

'Ambassador Joubert; the pleasure is all mine. You have become a legend back on Earth.'

'Ambassador Fisenko, Admiral Ryan. May I introduce Ambassador Theodore Ghali from Mars; my Deputy Adama Ubongo, Ambassador Ghali's Deputy, Faisal al-Rhumi, myself and Adama will join you Admiral, on the return trip.'

Fisenko shook hands with the outgoing diplomats.

'Pleased to meet you all,' Ryan enthused. 'By the way, this *is* a magnificent hall. Is it typical of Rakhian architecture?'

'No, I'm afraid not. They built this building especially for us, in the style of one of our great classical architects. Perhaps you've heard of Gaudí?'

'The Barcelona cathedral?'

'The "Sagrada Familia", that's the one. Finished in the twenty first century, and now a classic of its kind. We'll talk later. Adama, please show the new Ambassador and the Admiral to their quarters. They must be tired after their voyage.'

'That's good of you,' both replied in unison, and then smiled embarrassedly.

'We'll see you Admiral, in shall we say, an hour?'

'Yes. That'll suite me fine.'

'By the way, Admiral. How long can you stay?'

'We're here for two days, then we go back.'

To Ryan, Rakh seemed to be one giant park, and the Rakhians were extremely proud of their achievements. The planet had been transformed over time, into a true garden, a playground for nature lovers. It made the Embassy staff comfortable, and in turn, they tried to make the visiting crew feel at home. The crew were made a fuss of, being wined and dined that evening.

*   *   *

Taras Fisenko, Claude's replacement as Earth Ambassador on Rakh was aged 155, a tall swarthy Ukrainian, from L'viv. A distinguished Professor of Zoology at L'viv and Kyiv Universities, a visiting Professor at Sorbonne, and Heidelberg. Taras was handsome, blue eyed, and sure of himself. He had a wife back in L'viv called Vera, and two grown sons; Hryhori and Bohdan.

The new Ambassador insisted on going straight into conference with Claude so he could be brought up to speed on matters in hand, including the various negotiations. At dinner that evening, he seemed perfectly relaxed and at home in his new position.

*   *   *

Next day Adama took the crew for a Hopper ride to see the water sculptures of Rakh.

Later in the afternoon, Claude joined them and took Taras, Gupta, and Ryan to meet the Mehir, who requested any new human arrivals should regard his "humble" home as open to them.

The Mehir put an exhibition on of the ancient Rakhian art of *thowering,* a form of lassoing from the back of a *thergoard.* It was a small hoofed ungulate quadruped that looked like a cross between an armadillo and a reindeer. He also laid on a large spread from the food generator, programmed for the human palate.

Mehir Nathur invited anyone who wished, to have a go at riding the *thergoard.* Ryan couldn't resist the taunt, and with a little help, mounted the great beast. It may have been the heavier weight, or the strange smell of the new rider, but the *thergoard* gave an ear shattering bawl and stampeded into the yellow woods. It crashed into trees, breaking branches, finally unseating Ryan with a heavy thud. Ryan hit the ground and heard a loud crack in his leg. When the others arrived, he lay groaning, his leg twisted beneath him at a peculiar angle. The Mehir's face went ashen, that his gesture had misfired so badly. He yelled for a Physician, and in a few minutes, one materialised.

Immediately, the Physician ran a gadget over the leg, numbing it completely so Ryan couldn't feel the pain. Then he straightened the leg and changed the settings on the instrument—stopped, looked closely at the instrument, then at the leg.

'I don't quite understand this,' he said stroking his chin. 'The leg seems to be mending itself...rapidly.'

'It's Ryan's femto-robots at work,' Claude told the puzzled Doctor.

'You mean he has robots inside him? How charmingly old-fashioned.'

'They went to work when you straightened the leg,' Claude explained. 'The break will heal rapidly.'

The bemused Rakhian Doctor aimed the gadget at the break for a couple of minutes. When the Physician finished, Ryan was invited to stand, to put some weight on it. This he did, confident his leg was good as new. He thanked the Mehir and the Doctor, and they went back to the palace.

By the time the visit came to a close, the crew had been made most welcome and comfortable, despite Ryan's little mishap; they had no desire to leave. However, Space Corps orders placed a tight time frame on them, and all the returning diplomats were teleported on board the *Ying Li*.

A number of Rakhians were to go to Earth to replace the advisory mission there. Rotating Galactic diplomats for the Federation Embassy on the Moon were also beamed on board.

Ryan was sorry to leave, and made a point of letting his Number One take the ship back on the return journey. Ryan preferred to spend his time talking to Claude and Adama in the lounge, listening to their encounters and experiences the humans had confronted on an alien world. He checked on Kochanowski's progress from time to time, but otherwise was glued to his distinguished passengers in the lounge.

Chapter Twenty-One

The Camargue

Adama's return trip to Earth was filled with tumultuous emotions. Thoughts of his wife and daughter ran round in his mind. Trepidation at getting nearer to home, closer to Masaka. He was still experiencing flashbacks. Less intense now—at greater intervals, but still as disturbing as ever. He'd wanted to remain at the Embassy, at his post, but Professor Maskalik had urged Claude to insist Adama return home.

As the *Ying Li* emerged from the White Hole into Solar space, Adama's butterflies whipped about inside his stomach. He'd appreciated the Admiral keeping them company in the lounge, listening to their stories. It made the trip seem shorter giving him less time for brooding. Claude on the other hand, was impatient to get down to his wife: he'd missed her terribly throughout the last year. He intended to recommend families be allowed to join the serving diplomats as soon as the Embassy settled.

Kochanowski had done a fair job with the ship's computer, giving the orders, at least the Admiral thought so. For that matter, any of the crew might have done just as good a job. That was the nature of automation. The Space Corps training had a hands-on style, and not being able to handle anything galled Kochanowski. Nevertheless, he was determined to get to grips with the new format.

They approached the Moon, assumed standard orbit, requesting permission to land. The crew and passengers could have teleported but there was still a residual reluctance to use the damned thing. They were finding it difficult to overcome the positive anti teleportation ethos built up over centuries. In the past, only non-biological items were ever teleported, but now they were able to, they still needed to be coerced.

They had teleported on Rakh, and that was simply the alien way. No one made any fuss, but if offered the choice, to a person they would opt for a physical landing. The Rakhians on the other hand, and the rotating Federation diplomats were bemused and puzzled why humans still landed their spacecraft unnecessarily, wasting energy to land a ship. The Federation Diplomats teleported straight to their Embassy in the Gruemberger Township.

The ship came down at the Gruemberger Spaceport. Ryan logged in and reported to Petrusconi on New Caledonia, via the holo link. There were other senior diplomats waiting to greet the homecoming Ambassador and his staff—heroes amongst the diplomatic community.

The returning humans were anxious to get to their families and immediately caught the Earth shuttle. Claude, Adama and his fellow diplomats landed at the Cape York Spaceport, in Queensland. Adama asked for the next available hover shuttle for Uganda. Claude wanted the Hover shuttle for Paris.

'Hover Shuttle?...Hover Shuttle?' spat out the receptionist. 'Where have you been for the last year. There are *no* more Hover Shuttles. *We* have *Hoppers* now.' And that was the first of many surprises they were to encounter.

'Well, then the first available Hopper to Uganda,' responded Adama.

'And the same for Paris,' insisted Claude

'Why not just teleport there? Its much quicker and cheaper,' suggested the smiling woman. 'Hoppers are for sightseeing!'

'Good idea, where's the booth?' they both inquired.

'Over there,' she pointed at a booth marked, "Teleport Booth."

They both thanked her and sauntered over. Its controls were similar to the ones they were familiar with on Rakh. Claude went first, at Adama's insistence. They said their goodbyes; shook hands and Claude stepped into the booth. In a minute, he had disappeared.

Adama entered and asked for the Ugandan co-ordinates, closed the booth, and then tapped the given numbers in. He rematerialised at the old Entebbe Shuttleport, and had to take the Hopper from there to Masaka. The teleport hadn't reached Masaka yet. The changes were being implemented quite speedily, but not *that* rapidly.

*　　*　　*

Claude wanted the numbers for the Champs Elysées, so he could step out into the thick of the French *mêlée* at lunch hour. He'd been dreaming of sitting at one of the kerb side restaurants, ordering a café crème with a couple of hot croissant. His mouth already tasted the coffee. He rematerialised just as he had wanted, in a building containing lots of booths on the corner of the Avenue Montaigne.

He went into the Champs Elysées and said to the air, 'Anne-Marie, where are you?' and she responded into his earpiece 'I'm at Simone's.' He whispered back, 'I'll be with you in five minutes', and set out at a brisk pace.

He arrived breathless at her table; she got up to throw herself into his arms. They kissed intensely, as only those who love, and have been kept apart, can kiss. They patted each other familiarly to reassure themselves this was real, then sat down at a table. He insisted on ordering café crème with a couple of hot croissants.

'The children send their love. Valerie is busy with his underwater laboratory; Marie-Louise's husband is up some mountain, she, on the other hand, waits at the bottom and hopes he doesn't fall. They've promised to come to a homecoming get-together I've organised in two days' time. In the mean time, you'll have to make do with me.'

'I'm sort of glad we're alone. Anne-Marie, I've missed you terribly.'

The deep sincerity in his voice bathed her with a warm glow. She felt his nearness and was immersed in joy to have home this man she was married to.

In due time, after a stroll around Paris, Anne-Marie and Claude returned to their *maison de campagne* they had built just outside Arles, north of the Camargue. From the porch of their reproduction country farmhouse, they could see, standing on a isolated hill, the old Benedictine Abbaye de Montmajour, which looked more like a fortress than an abbey.

Claude sorely missed the stunning sunsets, the smells of the salt marshes drifting from the Camargue. The sight of the *gardians* on their white horses, rounding up the small, fast and agile Camargue bulls for the Provençal *courses a la cocarde,* where the *gardians* try to snatch the red cockade from between the bull's horns, aided by the nimbly evasive *rasetteurs.*

The reunited couple spent many mornings riding in the mists of the Camargue and then stretched out, relaxing in the evening sunsets. One such evening was abruptly interrupted.

'M. Joubert?' The voice was polite in his earpiece, but quite insistent.

'Yes,' he responded cautiously. He was unwilling to return to work just yet, hoping this was a social call.

'My name is Sarranson, Professor Sarranson. I'm anxious to have you give a lecture, to give an account of your experiences, to some of my final year students.'

'Which University, which Faculty?' inquired Claude.

'I'm sorry. It's the new Galactic University near Lake Balaton, in Hungary, and I'm head of the Diplomatic Faculty.'

Reluctantly Claude agreed to give the lecture, frankly he couldn't refuse, not the Diplomatic Faculty of the Galactic University. The following week he teleported over to the University Campus and met a white haired man, who must have been close to two hundred years old. They shook hands and had lunch, over which the Professor explained, although PL and some Holo lectures were the norm with most diplomatic students, his personal presence was a selling point, and a singular great honour for them. The usual PL style of learning had been complemented with real time lectures for the Diplomatic Faculty, mainly to encourage the best students to enlist.

In the afternoon, he sat amongst his audience, thirty young fifty year old doctoral candidates, all ranged in front of their consoles in two semicircular tiers. They faced a raised dais where the lecture holo images were projected. Claude gave an account of how the Embassy on Rakh was set-up, and how it had functioned over its first year of existence.

He explained that in a Galaxy of a hundred billion stars, there were only a thousand plus members of the Federation. This merely implied there were only a thousand plus sentient societies that had reached warp drive technology, not that there was only a thousand plus life forms in the Galaxy. Students should always err on the side of caution when dealing with other races. But then he stopped, struck by a thought.

'Look, I've talked at length regarding off-planet, but the biggest shock I've had is the changes here on Earth whilst I've been gone. I mean, it's only been a year, and I feel like I've been left behind. This new technology has radically changed Earth society.

'Take teleportation. We've had teleportation for inanimate objects for a long time now, but my journey here, what would normally have taken me a couple of hours, took one minute. It's a techno shock for my fellow diplomats to come back to so many transformations.

'We've had control of graviton particle for a while; giving artificial gravity on our spaceships, but the actual antigraviton had eluded us until the alien technology arrived. We now have antigravity on all our new Hoppers.

'We've just begun to work on food replicators with Patanjali's "energy⇒matter" converter, but the aliens had this problem solved long ago and so we bypassed years of research in accepting their version of a food generator. That's now standard on our spaceships, and in large food distribution centres. They've even promised to produce a domestic version.

'Think of it, no more land needed for food production. It's no wonder Rakh is a garden planet. In one short year, their technology had allowed us to stabilise the Venusian crustal plates, quietening the mass of volcanoes punctuating the Venusian surface. We've cleared the poisonous mix of gases on Venus and begun terraforming. Parts of the planet have cooled sufficiently for colonisation to begin.

'Mercury is being terraformed for more colonists, although the surface temperature fluctuates from 350°C at noon to —170°C at night. That's going to be a big problem. It'll be overcome. When I left the Moon a year ago, the moonquakes were a big nuisance, now the

Moon's been stabilised by putting a force field around it. It's stopping the meteor strikes.

'The latest craze I hear, is a massive tree planting programme on Earth. It's a fad created by the Rakhian accounts of their own home world, put out every evening on the Holocasts. What I'm getting at is, if...no—when you graduate, and you're posted off-world, you'll need to get Earth to send you regular holocubes with the latest News of what's happening here on Earth.

'It'll help keep you abreast and help you readjust when you return. Well, that concludes my talk. Has anyone got any questions?'

He'd been at it for a good two hours, and the questions at the end took another half hour. The Professor was delighted by the lecture, by the response from the students. In answer to one student's question, he had promised a momentous new revelation from Rakh, to be unveiled on the occasion of his coming speech to the World Government, at President Li's invitation.

This low-key disclosure ended up in the next day's Holocast News, clearly one of the students had other than a diplomatic career in mind. The Professor asked if Claude could manage to be available for further visits, to be visiting Professor in fact, and again Claude couldn't refuse. The ease with which he could travel, and the speed, simply meant he couldn't refuse.

*   *   *

When he returned to his farmhouse in the Camargue, had made himself comfortable on the porch, his mind mulling over the teleporter business. People would start travelling again. It was going to kill a lot of the Holo image conferencing trade, would finally kill off the virtual reality which had persisted for so long, simply because teleportation was so easy. A person steps into a booth, the next moment rematerialises somewhere else.

The secret lay not only in the power of the new gluon-computers, but in their stability. He had to remind himself—in order to store a human being in a computer, then transmit that information to another location, each atom's position in a molecule must be securely stored. Each molecule's position in a protein must be locked, each protein's position in a cell must be safe and sound, each cell's position in the body secure, and *then* all the neural activity, that is the amplitudes of the electrical charges and direction of the charges must be stored securely—before transmission can proceed.

If memory served him, the average body had a hundred trillion cells in an adult human and each cell had some eighty thousand coils of genes in each cell, to add to that, the average human brain had some hundred billion neurones, that is nerve cells, and around a hundred thousand billion synapses. All needed storing in memory, calling for around ten to the power of twenty-four bytes with almost instant access. To compare, at the end of the second millennium, when the computer was invented, the average super-computer was slow and able to store only around ten billion binary bits of information.

Now, at the beginning of the fourth millennium, the speed and storage capacity had enormously increased with neural circuitry in computers, but the recently invented human bio-storage machines expanded that greatly. It was bio-storage that was able to provide all the capacity for teleportation, unfortunately, the human version suffered from instability. If one atom, or more likely a few atoms, went astray during teleportation, the rematerialised person would not be the same as the one sent.

Then there was the transmission itself. It required a secure and isolated transmission frequency to prevent interference from other frequencies, from the spurious noise, which surrounds us everywhere. One atom out of place, one molecule in the wrong place, would produce catastrophe, and many had taken place before live teleporting was abandoned.

The aliens used a duplex transmission whereby the frequency itself was cocooned within a force field for security. The latter, and the alien computers which went below atomic level, below even quark level, to gluon level, made for stability, enabling this present teleportation breakthrough in travel on Earth.

When Claude was returning from the Moon, they were just about to inaugurate a system where no shuttle landed at either embarkation or destination, Moon or Earth, but went round in space like a carousel, with passengers simply teleporting on and off.

Then there was the liquid metal, or more accurately, programmed metal. The charges on the electrons of the atoms were manipulated to induce a specific behaviour within the atom. An analogy would be of an android, programmed to carry out specific tasks, so each atom was controlled to carry out specific tasks by computer, when liquid metal was being used.

That required the same massive stable computing power needed for teleportation. The principle was similar to the Rakhian water sculptures, where each water molecule was programmed to perform within the constraints of a matrix.

All these thoughts raced round in Claude's mind, the implications of teleportation, the new technology, until he heard Anne-Marie's voice.

'Cher, if you want to get up early to go horse riding, then you'd better turn-in.'

'Yes, I'm coming,' he called.

Just before they retired, she asked, 'When are you going to deal with your backlog of com-traffic? People are beginning to get at me—to prod you into answering them.'

'Tomorrow—I promise—tomorrow!'

In the morning after the riding and breakfast, Claude finally got round to clearing his com-backlog. Adama called, offering to help him at the World Government. There were numerous invitations for him to speak at conferences, symposiums, even down to opening new buildings and laboratories. There were the usual requests to make Holo lecture tours, and even an unusual "invite" to make a lecture tour in person. *There we go*, he thought, *another part of the coming changes*.

* * *

The following week Claude put on his best dress suit and teleported into the lobby of World Government HQ. Ying had invited him to speak to the General Assembly. It was part of Ying's campaign to win over Assembly doubters, and what better way than to have the first Ambassador to the Federation extol the achievements and benefits of Federation. Claude went up to Ying's office and was ushered in.

'What a pleasure to see you again, Claude.'

'President, nice to see you too.'

'Well, how are you settling back in?'

'Its a bit of a techno shock, what with all the changes.'

'Yes, I suppose it must be. We're racing ahead, we've a lot of ground to cover, catching up with the other races.'

'But sir, why *are* we trying to catch up? Surely, we have our own time-line to follow. It might be a mistake running too fast, only to stumble.'

'Claude! You of all people should realise running *is* our time-line. The human race has always run when it could walk. You'll see, once we've integrated the new technology, we'll pause—to assimilate it.'

'I have this feeling we may be pushing ahead, but in the process, our population loses its sense of direction. That could be dangerous—and would create a swell of opposition to the Federation. I think I'd be happier if we explained more of what we are doing.'

'But Claude, you have that opportunity in those lecture tours you've been offered.'

'How did you know about them? Silly of me to ask —I suppose. Did you arrange them?'

'I suggested the idea, yes. Shouldn't I have?'

'I didn't mean that. Look, the other day I was pondering. Take the transformations occurring on Venus, our much-vaunted planet of love. Before humans began changing it, you'll recall, it had a hostile environment with surface pressures ninety times Earth's, and a dense "greenhouse" atmosphere of carbon dioxide and sulphuric acid. All the carbon dioxide had trapped the heat—raising the surface temperature to some five hundred degrees Celsius, even hotter than Mercury.

'Before the alien contact we were moving slowly to transform the planet, with a colonising date maybe a hundred years away. Now the terraforming there means gigantic quantities of lime dust seeded into the atmosphere. With the aid of a large "energy$\Rightarrow$matter" converter aboard a spaceship, using the planet's heat for the source of the energy, we're eliminating the sulphuric acid.

'We're going to seed it with carbon dust to convert the CO_2 into carbon monoxide, and then ignite the remnants of the carbon dust. Pooff! In one week, we'll have got rid of the toxic atmosphere, and then the intention is to speed up the planets rotation, the slow retrograde rotation caused much of the enormous surface pressure. Putting an atmosphere back, and greening the planet is scheduled to take another month and then—? None of that would have been possible without the new technology from the Federation.

'We're talking of another planet we *can* colonise, sitting on our doorstep. Then another major item adds to this techno explosion—I'm told we've been able to extend our life span to something like a thousand years. Is that true?'

'So I'm reliably informed,' answered Ying.

'That means the end of the "two hundred year" termination policy. What with New Mars, and now Venus, we need to increase our birth rate. We really do need to go out and try to calm people's fears, to explain the positive sides of all this new development.'

'Ah! New Mars. I'm glad you brought that up.' Ying neatly sidestepped Claude's main thrust. 'I've had your report on why the Rakhians have caved in, and given us the go ahead to terraform the planet. Any more thoughts on the subject?'

'Well, my strong suspicion is, they'll want to plant a colony of their own down there.'

'What? To live side by side with humans?'

'Yes! Why not? I think looking at us; they've decided they've gone soft. They want us to instil some of the sense of adventure back into the Rakhian psyche. They may have concluded their comfortable garden planet is on the road to decay—in the long run. They *can't* stand still—they need to move forward. Decay is the alternative waiting, unless they do something about it. I think they've decided planting a colony on New

Mars with us, may bring some adventure back into their gloriously mundane lives.'

'Will it work?'

'I think they've identified the problem, and yes, it might work. I mean correcting their lost sense of adventure, *and* being able to live together in harmony with us might revive it. We *need* to let them on-board, not that we could prevent them. Rakh is the nearest inhabited planet to New Mars. We need them as a good neighbour. Humans are a young race; our veneer of civilisation is paper-thin. Our prejudices are just below the surface and I think the more we're exposed to other races, the more likely we are to mature.'

'Claude! That's precisely the reason why I chose you as our first Ambassador to the Federation. I want you to become my personal advisor on Federation matters. What do you say?'

'Thank you for those kind sentiments. With teleportation, yes I think I would like that. Even if I'm on tour, I can still be here in a matter of minutes.' Claude was immensely flattered by the offer.

'And to start with, I want you to call me Ying. I also want you to be forceful and honest with me. If I'm on the wrong track, *I need* to be the first one to know.'

'I'll try my best.'

'I know you will. Now let's go down to the Assembly. It's time for your speech.'

*   *   *

Claude stood on the rostrum before the World government representatives, and told them of Rakh, the garden planet, of the million-year-old civilisation, of the enormous benefits of us having joined the Galactic Federation. Most delegates were already experiencing benefits in their daily lives. He gently remonstrated with them for not putting a more positive spin on their pronouncements, simply letting the technology speak for itself to their populations.

He warned them of a backlash if they failed to explain and consult with the populations they represented, supporting the direction ncw technology was taking the Solar System. He spoke for an hour in the same vein, alternately cajoling, rebuking, and finally praising them for having had the courage to join the Federation in the first place.

He then told them of Theo's unlucky accident, of being marooned on a planet near Rakh, in the neighbouring star system to Rakh—explained the unlucky misadventure might have turned out to be one of the most fortuitous catastrophes ever for the human race.

The desert planet gave all indications of being similar to Mars, hence its newly designated name. It prompted Claude, on Theo's insistence, so Claude explained, to approach the Rakhians to inquire if they had any claims on it, and if they wouldn't mind humans colonising it. Claude said the Rakhians couldn't understand the human penchant for colonising everything in sight, and initially wanted recompense. Now, the latest communiqué from Rakh indicated they had suddenly changed their minds.

Claude wanted the delegates to spell out to all those who lost out when New Earth was quarantined, to re-establish all those prepared plans for New Earth, and switch them to colonise New Mars, if delegates approved? The wizened delegates had heard it all before, but there was a sincerity to his reasoning that touched a raw nerve in them. Maybe they had already begun to experience part of the backlash, sufficiently to elicit a standing ovation at the end of his speech.

Ying was delighted with Claude's performance— especially before such a difficult and fastidious audience, and silently congratulated himself on having inveigled him to join his team.

Later that day, back in the Camargue, Claude let the organisers of the lecture tour know he had decided to accept their offer, but imposed the condition he must have complete control over the programme contents. He was going to explain to all his students what the new technology meant, and give reasons why they should embrace it wholeheartedly.

*   *   *

The following week Claude put on his best dress suit and teleported into the lobby of World Government HQ. Ying had invited him to speak to the General Assembly. It was part of Ying's campaign to win over Assembly doubters, and what better way than to have the first Ambassador to the Federation extol the achievements and benefits of Federation. Claude went up to Ying's office and was ushered in.

'What a pleasure to see you again, Claude.'

'President, nice to see you too.'

'Well, how are you settling back in?'

'Its a bit of a techno shock, what with all the changes.'

'Yes, I suppose it must be. We're racing ahead, we've a lot of ground to cover, catching up with the other races.'

'But sir, why *are* we trying to catch up? Surely, we have our own time-line to follow. It might be a mistake running too fast, only to stumble.'

'Claude! You of all people should realise running *is* our time-line. The human race has always run when it could walk. You'll see, once we've integrated the new technology, we'll pause—to assimilate it.'

'I have this feeling we may be pushing ahead, but in the process, our population loses its sense of direction. That could be dangerous—and would create a swell of opposition to the Federation. I think I'd be happier if we explained more of what we are doing.'

'But Claude, you have that opportunity in those lecture tours you've been offered.'

'How did you know about them? Silly of me to ask —I suppose. Did you arrange them?'

'I suggested the idea, yes. Shouldn't I have?'

'I didn't mean that. Look, the other day I was pondering. Take the transformations occurring on Venus, our much-vaunted planet of love. Before humans began changing it, you'll recall, it had a hostile environment with surface pressures ninety times Earth's, and a dense "greenhouse" atmosphere of carbon dioxide and sulphuric acid. All the carbon dioxide had trapped the heat—raising the surface temperature to some five hundred degrees Celsius, even hotter than Mercury.

'Before the alien contact we were moving slowly to transform the planet, with a colonising date maybe a hundred years away. Now the terraforming there means gigantic quantities of lime dust seeded into the atmosphere. With the aid of a large "energy$\Rightarrow$matter" converter aboard a spaceship, using the planet's heat for the source of the energy, we're eliminating the sulphuric acid.

'We're going to seed it with carbon dust to convert the CO_2 into carbon monoxide, and then ignite the remnants of the carbon dust. Pooff! In one week, we'll have got rid of the toxic atmosphere, and then the intention is to speed up the planets rotation, the slow retrograde rotation caused much of the enormous surface pressure. Putting an atmosphere back, and greening the planet is scheduled to take another month and then—? None of that would have been possible without the new technology from the Federation.

'We're talking of another planet we *can* colonise, sitting on our doorstep. Then another major item adds to this techno explosion—I'm told we've been able to extend our life span to something like a thousand years. Is that true?'

'So I'm reliably informed,' answered Ying.

'That means the end of the "two hundred year" termination policy. What with New Mars, and now Venus, we need to increase our birth rate. We really do need to go out and try to calm people's fears, to explain the positive sides of all this new development.'

'Ah! New Mars. I'm glad you brought that up.' Ying neatly sidestepped Claude's main thrust. 'I've had your report on why the Rakhians have caved in, and given us the go ahead to terraform the planet. Any more thoughts on the subject?'

'Well, my strong suspicion is, they'll want to plant a colony of their own down there.'

'What? To live side by side with humans?'

'Yes! Why not? I think looking at us; they've decided they've gone soft. They want us to instil some of the sense of adventure back into the Rakhian psyche. They may have concluded their comfortable garden planet is on the road to decay—in the long run. They *can't* stand still—they need to move forward. Decay is the alternative waiting, unless they do something about it. I think they've decided planting a colony on New Mars with us, may bring some adventure back into their gloriously mundane lives.'

'Will it work?'

'I think they've identified the problem, and yes, it might work. I mean correcting their lost sense of adventure, *and* being able to live together in harmony with us might revive it. We *need* to let them on-board, not that we could prevent them. Rakh is the nearest inhabited planet to New Mars. We need them as a good neighbour. Humans are a young race; our veneer of civilisation is paper-thin. Our prejudices are just below the surface and I think the more we're exposed to other races, the more likely we are to mature.'

'Claude! That's precisely the reason why I chose you as our first Ambassador to the Federation. I want you to become my personal advisor on Federation matters. What do you say?'

'Thank you for those kind sentiments. With teleportation, yes I think I would like that. Even if I'm on tour, I can still be here in a matter of minutes.' Claude was immensely flattered by the offer.

'And to start with, I want you to call me Ying. I also want you to be forceful and honest with me. If I'm on the wrong track, *I need* to be the first one to know.'

'I'll try my best.'

'I know you will. Now let's go down to the Assembly. It's time for your speech.'

*   *   *

Claude stood on the rostrum before the World government representatives, and told them of Rakh, the garden planet, of the million-year-old civilisation, of the enormous benefits of us having joined the Galactic Federation. Most delegates were already experiencing benefits in their daily lives. He gently remonstrated with them for not putting a more positive spin on their pronouncements, simply letting the technology speak for itself to their populations.

He warned them of a backlash if they failed to explain and consult with the populations they represented, supporting the direction new technology was taking the Solar System. He spoke for an hour in the same vein, alternately cajoling, rebuking, and finally praising them for having had the courage to join the Federation in the first place.

He then told them of Theo's unlucky accident, of being marooned on a planet near Rakh, in the neighbouring star system to Rakh—explained the unlucky misadventure might have turned out to be one of the most fortuitous catastrophes ever for the human race.

The desert planet gave all indications of being similar to Mars, hence its newly designated name. It prompted Claude, on Theo's insistence, so Claude explained, to approach the Rakhians to inquire if they had any claims on it, and if they wouldn't mind humans colonising it. Claude said the Rakhians couldn't understand the human penchant for colonising everything in sight, and initially wanted recompense. Now, the latest communiqué from Rakh indicated they had suddenly changed their minds.

Claude wanted the delegates to spell out to all those who lost out when New Earth was quarantined, to re-establish all those prepared plans for New Earth, and switch them to colonise New Mars, if delegates approved? The wizened delegates had heard it all before, but there was a sincerity to his reasoning that touched a raw nerve in them. Maybe they had already begun to experience part of the backlash, sufficiently to elicit a standing ovation at the end of his speech.

Ying was delighted with Claude's performance—especially before such a difficult and fastidious audience, and silently congratulated himself on having inveigled him to join his team.

Later that day, back in the Camargue, Claude let the organisers of the lecture tour know he had decided to accept their offer, but imposed the condition he must have complete control over the programme contents. He was going to explain to all his students what the new technology meant, and give reasons why they should embrace it wholeheartedly.

Chapter Twenty-Two

New Mars

Standing outside in the Embassy garden, Taras Fisenko gazed at the magnificent tall trees clothed in their yellow foliage. He breathed deeply until he was quite giddy from the rich oxygen atmosphere.

The new replacement Ambassador to the Galactic Federation on Rakh, was taking a short break from his intense consultations with the incumbent Martian Ambassador, Theo Ghali. He was being briefed by Ghali on the ensuing negotiations with the Primearch over New Mars.

'Breathe this in! The freshness reminds me of the Carpathian Mountains back in the Ukraine. It's the crispness of the air, the peculiar tang to it.' He was talking to Chandragupta, his Chief of Staff.

'Me—*I* miss the heat of Calcutta, sir. This climate reminds *me* of Simla, in the Mountains of Himachal Pradesh, and it is much too cold for my liking.'

'Gupta, how are you getting along with Faisal?'

'Quite well. He's good at looking after Ambassador Ghali. Almost clairvoyant in many of his anticipations.'

'We should go back in. We've a meeting with the Primearch in the afternoon, we'd better be ready for him.'

The meeting with Primearch Reithur went particularly well. He was giving way on sovereignty, on trade with the new colony, on its re-supply, and in general was falling over backwards to be nice. Taras had the feeling there was a hidden agenda somewhere, as if all the negotiations of the past few weeks, had been played out beforehand on a model in a computer.

The Rakhian negotiating side had even agreed for the following day, on a ritual signing to hand over New Mars. They wanted to place New Mars legally under Solar jurisdiction, as if they had the paperwork all prepared. Later that day when Taras and Theo got back to their Embassy, they held urgent discussions to try and fathom the change that had come over the Rakhian side.

'My impression is they want something—from us, and I'm puzzled as to what,' said Taras, scratching his head.

'I have a contact in the Rakhian government, who let it slip they're in a tizz about preparing to set up their first colony. Is that why they're being so coy? As I understand it, they've never tried colonisation, not for a long time, and it could be they want to colonise part of New Mars.' Theo was ambivalent on the prospect.

'We could speculate until the stars stopped shining, but the simplest way is to come right out and ask them point blank. Are we agreed?'

'Agreed!'

At the following days meeting with the Rakhian negotiators, Theo demanded to know if the rumour was true, the Rakhians were preparing to colonise New Mars. Put that way; they had to admit they were. They were going to ask permission from the humans if they could found a colony.

They had concluded their society was stagnating, only revealed when they observed human attitudes to life. The Rakhians conceded it wasn't a precondition to the Solar System taking over New Mars as a new colony. Humans would be in charge on New Mars; they would supply the Governor. The Rakhians simply wished to join the humans in the venture. Being the nearest supply planet—it would be good for both.

That was the message Taras had communicated back to Earth, which Claude then took to the World Government in his speech. Taras' recommendation was: they ought to welcome the proposal, which would allow the Solar colonists to get used to living side by side with another alien race. It would teach the human race a lot more in this encounter, than they could learn from a legion of Rakhian advisors on Earth, and diminish prejudice in the process. It was an opportunity to be wholeheartedly embraced, rather than be treated with customary human suspicion.

The diplomatic communications from Earth was, they should agree to the Rakhian proposal, and ask for a liaison office to be set up. Immediately. So they could co-ordinate their efforts. The Rakhians enthusiastically agreed, and suggested a special office be established with its own staff.

After consulting with Taras, who wanted a joint administration, Theo delegated Faisal to head the Solar side, with five members of the Embassy moved into the new office, joining four Rakhians.

The Rakhians chose Thaner to lead their side, which heartened Theo, a fellow traveller on the space lanes of life, but insisted the overall head of the Bureau be Faisal. The name of the office was agreed: "The New Mars Co-ordinating Bureau," or NeMCoB. All contracts and problems would go through the Bureau.

In the next few weeks, the Bureau rolled up its metaphorical sleeves and ploughed ahead with its first mandate. It offered the contract to terraform the planet to a Rakhian Corporation, on the simple basis that it had made a low bid, which would merely cover its costs. It was also close at hand, and had the technology to do the job. A million year old technology.

To be even-handed, the contract was well advertised in the Solar System, and only one corporation made any sort of a bid, Hopkins Technology Inc. Its tender was prohibitively over the top, unclear on its completion date, unable to exhibit the technology required to do the work. To its debit, it could show no successful examples of a previously similar completed contract. Hopkins pointed out neither could the Rakhian Corporation, but he was told their costs matched their inexperience, whereas his was almost three times the Rakhians'.

It was a "no contest" contract and the Rakhians went to work. The close proximity of New Mars to Rakh, only two light years away, made the work relatively simple. Faisal was astonished to realise the Rakhian Government gave use of their SpaceCruisers *gratis* to the Rakhian Corporation.

The primary difficulties in terraforming New Mars were firstly to reduce its spin. Secondly to strengthen the weak Van Allen belt, the two doughnut-shaped regions of radiation trapped by New Mars' magnetic field around the planet. Thirdly, to stabilise the atmosphere. This required a vast quantity of water being injected into the gaseous envelope. Fourthly, to make optimum use of the massive quantities of ice at the poles.

The enterprise was much like the one carried out on Mars over its long period of colonisation. The difference was, that it be completed within three Earth months.

Computer models indicated everything would go according to schedule. The rotation of the planet needed slowing from sixteen hours to around twenty-three. Reducing the spin on New Mars would lower the height of the exosphere, and dampen the raging sand storms a little. It was a matter of reducing the gravitational pull.

A powerful pressure shaft, created by reversing the polarity of a gigantic traction engine, was aimed in the opposite direction of rotation, and maintained until projections indicated sufficient reduction had been induced. The existing weak ionosphere would be strengthened by infusing the outer belt with more electrons. The inner belt needed more protons, so the conducting layers were better able to deflect the solar winds and the harmful cosmic rays.

A fleet of huge spaceships landed on various designated spots of the planet and pumped water vapour from the onboard "energy⇒matter" converter, into the atmosphere, forcing the dynamics of the stratosphere and troposphere to change rapidly.

Rain fell on the arid desert; rivers began to flow, and in the lowest depressions on the planet's surface—emergent seas formed. The only real problem was the profusion of carbonic acid in the water from the carbon dioxide saturated atmosphere; this had to be neutralised. The analogous problem had been present back on Venus, and was solved by injecting large quantities of carbon dust, and igniting the atmosphere.

The Rakhians, however, preferred a less drastic solution flowing more in line with their gentle ethos. They were happier using cold beam converters from space ships to strip off the extra hydrogen from the carbonic acid molecule, mini-burning off the hydrogen and CO as it was released, leaving relatively neutral water. It exhibited a different approach to a problem. The Rakhians tended to go for refinement, whereas the human approach was not so much Occam's razor, as brash mixed with brusque.

The energy for the operation came directly from the local sun, via the far more efficient Federation version of Patanjali's "energy⇒matter" converter. At the end of three months, the Rakhian engineers had performed well. The contract had been completed according to schedule.

The water vapour was injected at ground level and the atmosphere left to achieve equilibrium. A shift occurred in momentum of moisture and heat from the lower latitudes to the higher latitudes, where the heat then escaped into outer space. The anticipated storms raged, but gradually settled into a manifestation of a seasonal cycle. Clockwise in the northern hemisphere and anti-clockwise in the southern.

The atmospheric equilibrium would settle within the next ten years, according to forecasts, but there was no reason why colonisation should not proceed immediately, taking proper precautions. Advance parties of human habitation specialists with their android workforce, employed by R-Tech, were sent from the Solar System, to install force-field-protected quick-erect buildings. The force fields would be removed once the storms abated.

Although Hopkins lost out on the terraforming contract, he combined with R-Tech in picking up the contract to ship new colonists. Hopkins was to supply the technical tools required; R-Tech was to supply the quick-erect buildings and the androids.

Hopkins had secured the plans for the new Federation style ships; R-Tech would build the components prior to shipping them to the Moon, where Hopkins would have them assembled. The business of "business" was in full swing behind the rush to colonise a new world, and no one questioned the wisdom of humans rushing out to seed the Galaxy with their own kind.

Chapter Twenty-Three

Inselberg Palace

Theo Ghali finally received the invitation from Ying to become first Governor of New Mars. He had settled in comfortably on Rakh, pondering on whether to accept the honour.

'I don't know if I'm cut out for this "Governor" thing. I'm a scientist first, but I suppose I'm also impelled to follow my father's footsteps.' Theo was expounding, comfortably ensconced in an armchair in the main lounge adjoining the Embassy dining room.

'It's your fault they're colonising the planet,' Taras interrupted from the next armchair.

'I assume that's why Ying chose me. But it wasn't *my* fault our ship crashed on New Mars.'

'You did suggest colonising the planet, sir,' Gupta interjected enthusiastically from a third armchair. 'Anyway, your Excellency would make a splendid President.'

'Now hold it there Gupta; you'll have me deified at this rate. Being *appointed* Governor is a long way from being *elected* President.'

'But your the natural choice sir,' Gupta insisted.

'To paraphrase Hamlet, Act III, "methinks thou doth protest too much," Taras quoted at him. 'In any case I agree with Gupta!'

Theo said, 'Let's take it one step at a time. I may, or may not, accept the post of Governor to New Mars,' adding with a grin, 'assuming the weather there permits.'

Moving the conversation on, Taras wanted to know, 'What does Faisal say about the atmosphere?'

Theo was suddenly defensive. 'He's been doing a splendid job running his Bureau.'

'I know!' Taras said quickly. 'Nobody is criticising him. I just wanted to know what the weather predictions were. That's *all*!'

'Sorry! I'm really getting deranged trying to decide if this is a good move to make. I know my old man will be over Phobos if I decide to take the job.'

'The Rakhians are enthusiastic. They *know*, you're accepting the position.' Taras was being encouraging.

'How in the name of all..., how did they find out?'

'I think Faisal may have let it slip to Thaner,' Gupta said.

'I'm not sure I like that. It looks like they're pushing me into it. I think I'm going to say yes, before more bricks are piled on.'

'Congratulations!' Taras was the first to jump in, followed quickly by Gupta.

The news spread rapidly amongst the Embassy staff. In half an hour, there was a small celebration under way in the main hall. Faisal teleported in and ardently greeted the *new* Governor. As the party got under way, others began to teleport in. Soon, the whole place was ringing to the sound of Rakhian and human music, congratulatory drinks flowing freely.

Via the thousand-light-year-com-relay, Theo regretfully informed his father, President Ghali of Mars, they would have to send a new Martian Ambassador for the Rakhian Embassy. On the same com-link, he informed Ying he would be pleased to accept the post as the first Governor of New Mars.

*   *   *

Within three months, Theo was established in his new gubernatorial residence. The palace was built in the same inselberg earlier cleaved by their plunging ship, the one that sheltered them from the vicious sand storm. It was a beautiful sop to nostalgia.

The wedge shaped wind eroded rock, eight hundred meters long, and a hundred meters high, consisted of tabular masses of resistant hard rock. It had been hollowed out and turned into many beautifully decorated rooms inlaid with marble, fine reception rooms, a glittering banqueting hall, plush offices, and ornate private apartments.

The inselberg itself was surrounded by a high wind-breaking wall. It now looked more like a bizarre shaped palace thanks to Rakhian builders. However, Theo had insisted the facade be left as nature constructed it, so all the alterations were internal. It was transformed for him, on the explicit instruction of the Rakhian government, as a present and memorial to his and Thaner's encounter with adversity.

Near the sharp end of the inselberg palace, a small memorial was erected to commemorate the passengers who had not survived the journey to their vacation planet. At an early stage, a Space Control Centre was set up, and a spaceport built twenty kilometres downwind from the inselberg.

The thought and grandeur that went into the internals of the inselberg building were appreciated, but the eight hundred meter wedge was far too large for Theo alone. Solely because of its size, he called it the Inselberg Palace. He suspected at a later date, it was designed to function as the Presidential Palace.

Faisal moved NeMCoB to offices in the Palace and began to arrange the contract for the orbiting solar power grid. Other infrastructures were needed for the colony to survive. From that point, Faisal's office was in fact acting as the *de facto* government of the planet.

Heavy teleportation equipment was brought in from Rakh; gluon-computers, Hoppers, and food generators were supplied. More quick-erect buildings were going up. The furious pace was making the planet completely unrecognisable as the bleak desert planet on which Theo had been marooned.

At the outset, the atmosphere had been seeded with a sturdy Rakhian grass, allowed to float and settle where the wind blew it. The air had been enriched with oxygen to reproduce a compromise between rich Rakh and Earth, and the content now stood at twenty-five per cent.

Having created the oxygen, it was vital they assemble an ozone layer at about thirty kilometres above the planet to ward off the ultraviolet radiation from the system's sun. It would have formed naturally but would have taken hundreds of years for the radiation to break down the oxygen (O_2) molecules into oxygen atoms (O), which could recombine to form sufficient ozone (O_3) to produce an effective barrier.

The ecology could not sustain the oxygen as constructed, and a mass of Rakhian gardeners began converting the soil, furiously planting forests and all sorts of shrubs and greenery. The carbon dioxide content had been left at one tenth to encourage the growth of the planted flora, which would then stabilise at much less than that.

The desert had virtually disappeared. The sand had been replaced by a barren rocky ground that was being pulverised and then fertilised by androids to produce a soil in which trees and shrubs would grow. The whole process had an unreal quality that Theo found mildly offensive.

A false dampness permeated everywhere, false because no sooner was it felt, than it oscillated with the dry original air of the desert. Huge patches were covered with quick growing yellow grass; shrubs everywhere. It would take a number of decades for it all to settle. Yet— the transformation had been breathtaking in its speed and completeness.

The enclosed area of the Palace grounds had been turned into a simulacrum of Rakh, making Theo long for the desert. When he mentioned it to anyone, other than Faisal, they were astonished anyone could *miss* a desert. Theo's home planet Mars, had far more desert even after nine hundred years of human habitation, than New Mars was after six months of terraforming.

The first Rakhian colonists arrived and settled into the quick-erect buildings. They were determined to revive their individual sense of adventure. They settled into an area a thousand kilometres due east of the administrative bastion, in a valley below one of the highest mountains.

In the ensuing months, large numbers of human colonists arrived and settled into the quick-erect buildings constructed into an arc around the gubernatorial Citadel. Back on Earth the impulse for human migration was given a boost when the new alien technology promoted people's longevity well beyond the three hundred years previously established as the norm.

People were able to be kept alive up to a thousand years; at least those were the projections from the bio-medical personnel. It was the "over two hundreds" who tended to be the colonisers. With the extended life spans on the horizon, the World Government readily admitted it would have to speed up the terraforming on Venus, and encourage the colonisation of New Mars. They could then encourage new births instead of finding ways of restricting the population growth. The colonisation programme was a massive economic investment in the future for the humans. For Rakh, which had offered to fund much of the initial terraforming, and had acted as the logistics base for the enterprise, New Mars was a leap into the unknown.

It was natural the Rakhians wanted to know why humans felt the need to colonise the Galaxy? There was no simple answer. Humanity was in its infancy, mostly at the mercy of its genetic makeup. Insatiably curious, forever on the move, and insisting on seeking out new frontiers to explore. Coupled with its population pressures, or as one lunatic long ago called it, *lebensraum,* it made exploration an imperative. Rather than a luxury.

A stable population tended towards complacency and stagnation, and the Rakhians had finally discovered this. So the dynamic rationale was the primitive human urge to procreate, which dove tailed perfectly with what evolution had in mind. Now with longevity, even technology fitted in with the evolutionary imperative.

*   *   *

People were settling in on New Mars and dropping in to see Theo on all sorts of pretexts, just to hear the story behind the construction of the Inselberg Palace. Theo began holding open days, when a party atmosphere was flamboyantly created. Theo had an ulterior motive for having open days; it made the rest of the days *not* open, giving Theo a semblance of peace.

This peace was a double-edged sword, for Theo enjoyed listening to classical music, also using the holo-gym, relaxing with Faisal in a game of *ihra*, taught to him by Taras. His mind kept nagging him, reminding him he was essentially alone, and without a partner. He was soon to celebrate his a hundredth year of survival, and although he was relatively young, it was time to begin to look for a partner to share in his life.

He began to contemplate his options. He could ask his old man to find him a soul mate from Mars. He could look up the copious Connective Databases containing all those seeking Solar available partners, categorised and cross-matched. The alternative was to take a vacation back to Mars and do it the hard way. He was looking for a woman with a similar background, someone who would lubricate his compatibility, permitting friendship and love to emerge into the sunlight. It might sound like mush, but that's what Theo wanted.

On Mars and on Earth, Holo dates were the first point of contact, after accessing and connecting with the Database, but at this distance from the Solar System, simply out of the question. He would have to assign this delicate matter to his father or someone, or go back home to Mars and see the Coptic matchmaker. He had already imprinted New Mars in his mind as his permanent home. He had to seek out an adventurous spouse—that was clear. How would that go down with a future partner?

Every spare moment was now occupied on that line of thought, and was getting him nowhere. It would be best to send a note and let the Coptic matchmaker know his intentions, then leave the brooding alone.

Switching thoughts, he wondered how his replacement was working out. He took a break from talking to his journal and wandered round to where Faisal was ploughing away with the administrative work of developing the new government.

'Faisal! Have you heard anything of Basil Dukas,' Theo strolled in interrupting Faisal. 'Is he settling in?'

'As far as I'm able to gauge Governor,' Faisal kept on working.

'What does Taras say in the communiqués?'

'He mostly sticks to business.'

'Any news from your Rakhian contacts?'

'Not much sir. They sometimes slip and refer to you as Primearch of New Mars.'

'What...me? You sure you have that right? They probably mean the Primearch wants to see me,' Theo was a little exasperated.

'No sir. They let it slip, and mean you Governor.'

'So what's it all about? Next time you talk to them, find out.'

'I'll make inquiries sir,' Faisal went on whispering to his workstation. 'You have an invitation from the Rakhian township here to attend their festival of Latha. It's a spring festival of some sorts, probably to do with the planet's equinox. Shall I say you will attend?'

'Yes, of course. I'd love to see how they've preserved this sort of festival over a million years. You make the arrangements, and let me know.' He saw Faisal was up to his eyeballs with work, and desperately trying to get on with it. 'I'm sorry Faisal. You continue, and I'll see you later for a chat.'

'I'll try and have some news for you,' Faisal scratched at his ear, 'regarding that Primearch thing.'

*   *   *

Life back on Rakh was one hectic round of diplomatic receptions designed to introduce the newly arrived replacement for Theo to the rest of the diplomatic community. Ambassador Basil Dukas was as rugged as Theo had been refined. He was an older man of a hundred and seventy-seven; more at home in a desert than in a garden, was enthusiastic and seemingly had lots of energy to spare. Although twenty-two years separated the two men, Taras was finding it difficult to keep up with the older man's plans for this and that.

Basil had been instructed by his boss, Simeon Boutros Ghali, the President of Mars, to get invited to the Galactic Federation HQ on Kaikon, home planet of the Grand Custodian. He was instructed to put in a detailed report on the turbulent volcanic surroundings and its floating aerial cities. The instruction contained the seed of insatiable curiosity as to how a civilisation had managed to get off the ground, both metaphorically and physically, in such a hostile environment. President Ghali could always view the Holo-Vid histories of Kaikon, but that was inevitably an edited version. He wanted the unexpurgated version.

The Rakhian Mehir *demanded* Taras bring the new Martian Ambassador to call on him and introduce Basil to him personally, over a meal, accompanied by music. A Rakhian dance would follow, and then an exhibition of the ancient Rakhian art of *thowering* from the back of a *thergoard*.

When Taras had first arrived, Claude warned him of the Mehir's predilection for human company, and Taras had in turn prepared for him a "meditative" present. This would be an appropriate moment to give the Mehir his gift.

The two Ambassadors arrived at the Palace and were ushered into Mehir Nathur's presence.

'Taras, it is good of you to come.' The Mehir stretched out his hand in the human manner.

'As always, it is a pleasure to see you Sire,' Taras took the proffered hand; surprised the Mehir had adopted the human form of greeting. 'May I introduce Ambassador Basil Dukas from Mars.'

'I'm enchanted to meet you. I hope you will be able to call me Nathur. That is my request, and I shall call you Basil?' The Mehir held out his hand.

'It is an honour to meet you Mehir,' Basil ignored the proffered hand and extended both his palms face upward, in the Rakhian manner of greeting.

'I must say, you look as fit as ever,' Taras quickly jumped in, breaking the awkward moment. Basil will need watching, he thought, he shows signs of being a little headstrong. 'Nathur! I have a small but special present for you,' and he handed him a real book bound in leather.

'It works best if you have the contents read into a datacube, then close your eyes and have the cube read it back to you aloud. You can visualise the descriptive images in your mind's eye, and travel with the voice to the places mentioned, through forests, listening to birds, crossing mountains. These are some of the best poets the human race ever produced. I find in reading these poems I manage to achieve an inner calm wherever I am. I hope you enjoy them as much as I have.'

'Why Taras! That is most generous of you,' the Mehir responded, accepting the book.

He undid the green silk ribbon holding the covers and opened it, gazing at the unfamiliar words. In an unusual piece of anticipation, an aid handed the Mehir a small rod scanner, which he ran over the alien human language on the first page. The translator gave him the Rakhian version on a screen, which materialised in front of his eyes. For a few minutes, there was silence whilst the Mehir read the translation.

'Taras, this is so Rakhian. The trees, the flowers, the mountains. The sentiment is so familiar to me.' The Mehir handed the book to a servitor and ordered the contents read into a cube. Then they all sauntered onto the veranda for the promised meal.

Chapter Twenty-Four

Aerial Cities

Taras seemed to feel pressured both from inside and from outside the Embassy. There was Basil angling for an invitation from the Grand Custodian to visit Kaikon, and urging Taras to do his utmost to support him. There was the Primearch of Rakh gently nudging Taras each time they met, for Earth to invite Theo to hold elections for the Presidency of New Mars.

To cap it, President Ying made his intentions known he was resolved to accept the Quadrant Custodians standing invitation to visit Rakh at his earliest convenience. He pledged to head a high-powered delegation as soon as he was able to get away from World Government. The latter kept Taras on edge in expectation of Ying's impending arrival.

Finally the invitation for Basil to visit Kaikon arrived and it had Basil all excited. Alexius arranged for Basil and himself to attend the Rakhian Medical Centre to be inoculated and pumped full of suppressants to prevent them catching or passing on any contaminating viruses, bacteria, or phages.

Kaikon was the talk of the whole Embassy, a turbulent volcanic planet with its wondrous aerial cities. So, it was with indecent haste Basil delegated all his responsibilities to Taras with the promise of shouldering a similar burden if Taras should want to take a vacation. He ordered his deputy Alexius Balbus to pack for the trip.

Kaikon was over seventy-two thousand light years away from Rakh, on the other side of the Galaxy, and would need two days and two black hole jumps to reach it. The journey could not be accomplished in a single jump because of the massive Black Hole at the centre of the Milky Way, around which the Galaxy rotated.

It was impermissible for wormhole tunnels to come into each other's proximity. That might take the tunnel they were travelling along, out of the control of the ship, leading to a horrendous catastrophe. The huge Black Hole made it impossible to take a straight line through the Galaxy centre, forcing any ship to make two jumps.

A couple of years ago, sane people would have scoffed at the notion anybody could take only two days to travel to the other side of the Galaxy. Now, they were to visit the home planet of the Grand Custodian, where the overall HQ of the Federation currently resided.

Alexius booked seats on the Kaikon Express, a large spaceliner by Rakhian standards. Basil, in all the excitement, was only slightly awed by the Express' size and determined inwardly nothing would faze him.

He and Alexius teleported aboard and settled into the oxygen lounge, one of the many lounges with varied atmospheres available to the numerous life forms travelling. Taras made them promise to note everything, the tiniest aspect, and of course Basil detailed a diary be kept by his Chief of Staff.

The huge spaceliner departed on schedule, soon positioning itself outside normal Rakhian space, establishing their first Black Hole. They came out in the next Quadrant to the left from Rakh; a place called Zyneer, in a solar system that was the HQ for that Quadrant.

The Zyneerians were sentient insectoids related to the insectoids of Murangi, the home world of Adama's kidnappers. They remained in Zyneer's orbit for a complete rotation of the planet, some twenty-earth hours, during which both Basil and Alexius sojourned in the oxygen lounge.

They had read reports of Adama's kidnapping lodged in the Embassy library. The reading of the report was *de rigueur* for all new incoming diplomats. As a result, Basil resisted the curiosity of exploring this new species and its home world. It was a pity the behaviour of a few should have negatively influenced their reactions to the insectoid species as a whole, but human nature was fickle in that manner.

While they were on board their vessel, they were surprised to find the food generators were programmed with recognisably human type food. That pointed at real efficiency by whoever was in charge of the ship. Having reasonable food to eat made the journey a lot easier.

When the time again arrived for departure, they belatedly regretted not having followed the other passengers down to the planet's surface for a look around.

'The next time we're here—and that'll be on the return journey, I'm going to correct this omission,' Basil vowed to his Chief of Staff.

During the next rotation of Zyneer, the ship departed and entered the final Black Hole, going through the wormhole tunnel, coming out in near Kaikonian space. As they travelled further into the Kaikonian solar system, scanners revealed an astonishing view, a reddish planet seemingly ready to combust—a vision of ancient hell.

From datacube stories of the planet, the view could only be of Kaikon, the hyperactive volcanic planet. They entered standard orbit and waited for the all clear to teleport to the city of Kotka, the floating capital of Kaikon.

On their earpieces, their names were called and they were asked if they were ready to teleport. Having given consent, they were relayed down to Kotka. A group of Kaikonians were in a semicircle, smiling a greeting as Basil and Alexius rematerialised.

The humans observed the tallest was one and a half meters short, and he stood a head above the others. The other three were small individuals a meter high; they had huge barrel chests, small heads with large foreheads, dark skins, and large imposing black eyes.

The atmosphere was scarcely breathable, containing only sixteen per cent oxygen. The tall leader motioned to the one on his right, who held out a couple of flimsy masks. In his turn, the leader gazed at Basil, a tall thin balding human with a dark complexion. Alexius also had the swarthy complexion of a Copt, only he was a bit shorter than Basil, but just as thin.

'These are oxygen supplement masks. If my information is correct I believe you'll need them,' said the mask carrier holding them out.

Basil and Alexius took the masks gratefully and gulped a little fresh oxygen. 'Thank you,' Basil managed through the mask.

'My name is K'Gar, and these are my colleagues, K'Asva, K'Pieni, and K'Karhu.'

Basil felt a bit awkward looking down on these diminutive individuals. 'We're pleased to meet you.'

'You must be Ambassador Dukas of Mars.'

'Yes, and this is my deputy Alexius Balbus.'

'If you come this way, I'll show you to your quarters,' said K'Gar.

'Are we standing on a floating city?' Alexius' curiosity was already bubbling over.

'Yes we are. We are currently floating two kilometres up.' Both sides were speaking their own language and the universal translator took care of the muddle.

'And all this is being held up by anti-gravitons; right?' Alexius continued.

'Yes, that's right,' responded K'Gar.

'Once you've settled in, and freshened up from your journey, we'll be pleased to give you a guided tour.'

'I'm looking forward to it,' Basil put in.

They were escorted to a low domed building acting as an official residency for visitors. There, they were allocated adjoining apartments suitable for a visiting Ambassador and left to rest for an hour. After they had rested, K'Gar called on them and asked if they wanted to embark on official diplomatic business, or go sight seeing for the evening. Both eagerly opted for sight seeing.

K'Gar took them along the moving covered walkway towards the edge of the city, out to the red sky. There, on a small viewing platform, there were some seats on a transparent floor. They seated themselves and K'Gar explained the extensive foundations the city was built on was made of the same liquid metal they had already encountered, purely for lightness and tensile strength.

The city itself was two kilometre square, and floated from the ground at between one and two kilometres, depending on the time of day. The weight of the city was around eight hundred thousand metric tonnes with some forty thousand domed buildings and four large covered parks.

The energy required to generate the anti-gravitons and maintain the city floating in the air was gathered from the sun. Each city had its own anti-graviton generator out in space, on a synchronous orbit thirty thousand kilometres above the city, which beamed down the anti-gravitons into a reservoir beneath the city. When the density of the anti-gravitons was increased in the reservoir, the city rose, a decrease in density lowered the city. Small photon drives placed strategically around the perimeter of the city allowed the controllers to move it around laterally.

The city's buildings were constructed as perfect hemispheres without decorations, to cut down wind resistance. There were mobile covered walkways and the city was encased by a huge force field to keep the air in, and to protect it against unusual climatic changes.

'May I ask, why you haven't stabilised the planet?' Basil was almost rude in his inquisitiveness.

'I'll explain some of the thinking behind our history. Maybe you'll appreciate then the philosophy of our life style. You've probably heard this before from your datacubes, but if I bore you, stop me.'

K'Gar began to recount a short history of his civilisation, 'You know our civilisation is well over two million years old. After a million years, we had a well-developed warp-stage civilisation on a beautiful green planet—this one. Then an outer planet in our solar system was hit by a large comet wrenching it out of orbit. It collided with another outer planet, a smaller one, sending two gigantic meteors towards Kaikon. At enormous effort, my ancestors deflected the path of one, but made a catastrophic error in deflecting the other. They only had one week to save Kaikon.'

'My goodness,' exclaimed Basil. 'It's like a cliff-hanger, this.'

Startled by the interruption, K'Gar continued, 'My ancestors swiftly gathered their population and sent them into space, with all the civilisation's records. If things went wrong, and they did, they would be able to colonise other worlds. What they couldn't move they hid underground. For those who wouldn't move, they built underground shelters and strengthened buildings with force fields. When the remaining meteor struck, it created an impact that sent a concatenation through the core of the planet. The impact of the meteor, and the near pass of the deflected meteor, pulled Kaikon out of a normally central elliptic orbit, to the present elongated orbit.

'The cosmic tidal pressures on the tectonics of Kaikon caused the crustal plates to fracture into many smaller plates. That ruptured the rigid lithosphere into many faults creating many thousands of volcanoes on the surface. Enormous fissure eruptions triggered huge "flood basalt" plateaus which in turn were covered with other successive eruptions of basaltic lava, flowing great distances before solidifying. It formed vast areas of hexagonal columns.'

'That's the sign of basalt....sorry,' interrupted Alexius, and immediately apologised.

Unfazed, K'Gar pressed on, 'When the initial impact waves settled, there followed a minor ice age, a short period of cold lasting two hundred and fifty years. The initial clouds of dust and ash began to settle after only fifty years. However, within a further two hundred years all the ash and gases produced by the erupting volcanoes warmed the planet beyond endurance.

'Most of the population moved on to other planets, but those remaining migrated to the colder polar regions of Kaikon and built the tools needed for survival in the changing circumstances. Most of the luscious green biomass of Kaikon was destroyed by the cataclysm and a priority was to bulk produce enough oxygen for the remaining inhabitants to survive. After the atmosphere stabilised somewhat, my ancestors were able to use this period of adversity to push ahead with the development of liquid metal and anti-gravitons. They were almost at that stage when the meteor hit.'

'So we have you to thank for that funny metal, do we?' Basil broke in.

K'Gar's brow knitted, then he understood, 'Well yes—it was us. Anyway, out of a population of three billion,' he was going to finish come what may, 'only a few million died in the meteor impact, considered extremely fortunate, mostly because of their precautionary measures. The tenacious remnants settled in the Polar Regions in domes with an artificial biosphere; there they lived to manufacture the tools such as the gluon-computers. Offers of help from other races had been selectively accepted, but mostly rejected: my ancestors were both stubborn and a proud race. Their recovery and further developments were only made possible because of the already advanced stage of our civilisation. The encounter with the meteor was an impulse of adversity pushing them to build and launch their first aerial village.

'My ancestors concluded, if they intended to stay on their over-heated planet, then they would have to get above the dust and volcanoes. Over time, they turned the aerial villages into cities. At the outset, they had the necessary terraforming tools to put the planet back on a circular elliptic orbit—but they decided to leave nature's handiwork as a monument to their triumph over the adversity they had faced—and conquered.

Alexius intervened, 'You mean they could put things back as they were—and didn't? But...but...' he couldn't finish, trying to hide his outrage.

K'Gar ignored the outburst. 'It was obvious they *had* the tools to reform the vanished Kaikon of old, but that was to *miss the lesson* of *nature*. Yes, they could have put it back, and they missed the vanished green Kaikon, but they *also* loved the fiery new red Kaikon. So they determined to live with the memory *and* enjoy nature's rude imposition.'

K'Gar turned to Basil, 'Your green Earth now looks like our old vanished version of Kaikon; at least that's what I saw in the Holo-Vids of your home-world.'

'I'm sorry K'Gar, but my home is Mars not Earth. Yes, my race is of Earth, but I consider Mars my true home now,' Basil corrected him.

'I'm sorry, yes of course...Mars.' K'Gar looked away. 'Anyway, *our* colonial kin on the other planets wonder why we stubborn Kaikonians still live in the skies on this planet, when we could be living with them, on the ground. Our same kin can't understand why we Kaikonians wouldn't want to live anywhere else. You see Ambassador,' K'Gar was concluding the story, 'the answer to your question is yes we could stabilise the planet, but then it wouldn't be Kaikon. We're used to this atmosphere, this colour, this fiery planet. We have a few biosphere research stations on Kaikon's surface, but we mostly live in our protected aerial cities. The atmosphere down there is quiet unbreathable.'

'I value the time you've taken to recount your history, and it was considerably better *told* than in the datacubes.' Basil hoped a little flattery would pour some balm on K'Gar's obvious sensitivity over the earlier gaffe regarding his home planet. 'Is there any way we can look around near the surface of the planet?'

'But of course. We can use a bubble-hover to take you to the surface, but that will have to wait until *after* your meeting with the Grand Custodian, scheduled for tomorrow morning. Tomorrow afternoon we can go for a ride in the bubble-hover down to the surface, and I assure you it is an experience you'll never forget. Our bubble-hovers are transparent but insulated by a force field, keeping you safe but giving a panoramic view. It will show you why we don't change the planet's surface.'

'We look forward to tomorrow's trip, don't we Alexius?'

'Yes indeed,' responded Alexius.

They sat on the viewing platform and watched the unusual deep red twilight descending in the distance. It became dark, but there was a continued red glow in the sky, and an inferno could be seen through the transparent floor, far down below on the planet surface.

K'Gar asked, 'Would you like some refreshments?'

'Yes, that would be welcome,' Basil responded.

K'Gar called for some, and out of recesses in the far wall of the platform there appeared a small tray bearing their chosen beverages, included were a few snacks. The tray floated over to them and they helped themselves.

Basil described to K'Gar life on Mars—as opposed to Earth, and filled in a little of human history. They sipped drinks and ate on the platform, gazing at the fiery show going on below. Other nearby platforms were similarly filled with Kaikonians out for the evening air.

Basil and Alexius used their oxygen masks from time to time, to replenish their cravings for the gas of life. All three whiled away the evening chatting amiably until time to retire. It had been a long day for the two humans, and they were the first humans to sit chatting on the other side of the Galaxy—even that thought made them tired.

In the morning, after the luxury of a cold-water shower, Basil and Alexius were collected by K'Gar in a bubble-hover. Basil was itching to ask how they managed to have cold piped water, instead of the usual ultrasonics, but felt to embarrassed to ask. After a brief journey the bubble-hover deposited them at the Grand Custodian's Dome. They went through a series of smaller outer domes until they reached a large circular reception hall where the Grand Custodian sat at the far end on a raised dais.

This was the ceremonial part of an Ambassador's duties and Basil wanted to get it over with as soon as possible. His mind was in turmoil since the previous evening, mesmerised by the scenes on the planet's surface. Before he could take a serious look around Kotka for the "report" part of his mission, he felt he *had* to visit the volcanoes, he was being tugged to the planet's surface.

Basil was one of those people drawn by danger and catastrophes, feasting on the adrenaline rush. On Mars, he'd chased tornadoes and survived in the midst of vicious sandstorms. It had been the explosive nature of the volcanic planet that pulled him to Kaikon in the first place.

Basil presented himself to the Grand Custodian, bowed from the waist and offered the customary greetings from his President, Simeon Boutros Ghali of the Planetary Republic of Mars. Formalities over, they sat round a table and briefly discussed items of technology and trade. Basil thanked the Grand Custodian who was forced to other duties, and, wished him longevity, and accepted the customary gift for both his President and himself. After a couple of hours of serious discussions with senior members of the Kaikonian government, Basil took his leave.

Out of the domes and in the open, Basil asked K'Gar, 'Can you first take us to our abode so I can drop off the gifts, and then can we go to the surface?'

The gifts dropped off, the Kaikonian driver at the helm of the bubble-hover was ordered by K'Gar to take the bubble-hover on a tour of the planet.

They flittered over the side of the aerial city and began a two-kilometre descent, spiralling downwards towards a kilometre wide crater of a Caldera volcano.

The main vent had a large plug forcing a couple of new smaller cones to push through on the inside of the steep-walled basin. Although this wasn't a particularly active example, they hovered near the crater for a short time watching gaseous expulsions from small vents.

Witnessing an eruption in the far distance from another cone, hot gas shot kilometres high into the air containing tephra, closely pursued by a lateral pyroclastic flow rushing down the flank making it prudent to move the bubble-hover in the opposite direction.

The lethal superheated shock wave from that blast pushed a pressure front away from the volcano surging at around seven hundred kilometres an hour. It contained a dense fluid mass of large sized rocks, lapilli, ash, and hot gases, and would annihilate anything in its path. The beginnings of a mushroom cloud already shaped above the volcano, fed by heat energy released from the newly-formed supper heated pyroclasts.

K'Gar ordered the driver to speedily swing the bubble-hover many hundreds of kilometres in the opposite direction towards a comparatively quiescent Stratovolcano in full flow. The central vent heaved whilst many secondary vents were fashioned from the enormous pent-up pressures unable to freely escape from below, causing sporadic minor explosions in the main aperture.

The passengers eagerly gazed at the large quantities of lava running down the slopes amongst the ash of the steep overflowing conical shape. Not far from the flattened base a number of solfatara holes exuded sulphurous gases through fissures to the surface.

The driver aimed the bubble-hover towards the terrain right of the Stratovolcano. A vast plateau stretching out as far as their eyes could see. Dotted across it were many hundreds of low profile shield volcanoes with solitary main vents. This suggested numerous fractures in the turbulent crust. Over time most of those volcanoes had developed gentle outward slopes from the lava flows.

A thousand kilometres further, a number of extended elongated fissures were erupting. The tectonic plate movements were throwing out volcanic material along the extended fractures. Fluid magma spread widely below them, building up flat basaltic plateaus surrounding the fissures hundreds of kilometres across.

Seasonal variations of the elongated elliptic orbit continued to cause extreme tidal confluences. This pulled the small tectonic plates in every which way, generating more volcanoes. The Kaikonic mantle was heaving and pushing, then heaving and wrenching the small tectonic plates, releasing the pent-up energy of the core to the exterior. The temperature, K'Gar informed them, was around three hundred and twenty centigrade at the equatorial surface.

Nearer the polar region, thick swiftly cooling lava caused the volcanoes to become dome like. Concentrated in the polar region, a small sea two kilometres across was the only water on the planet surface: more a lake than a sea.

Close by the domed volcanoes, hot water geysers were bursting through the hot rocks spouting jets of water mixed with steam. The jets reached two hundred meters upwards into the open air, releasing built up steam pressure like a safety valve.

In other areas, hot waters were being thrust to the surface, mixing with the soft deposits to form thick bubbling pools of mud. Basil noticed standing incongruously by one of the pools, a solitary dome, but said nothing at the time. The bubble-hover moved over near to some fumaroles, and hung suspended, while the occupants watched the superheated waters form a small pond emitting gushes of steam from the surface. Basil was in what he considered his version of heaven.

Chapter Twenty-Five

Fiery Kaikon

Kaikon's planetary rotation was thirty-six hours making a Kaikonian year equivalent to three Earth years. When the long ellipsoid orbit brought it closer to its sun, the polar region became more volcanically active, as did the whole planet.

This forced the few Kaikonians on the surface to abandon the area for six Earth months: until the planet travelled further along its path, far enough from its sun for the burst of surface activity to subside.

'Tell me,' Basil asked K'Gar, 'what's that dome doing near that mud pool we passed a while ago?'

'It's a mud reservoir,' K'Gar told him longingly. 'When the planet's orbit allows us, we enjoy the mud. We rebuild the domes around the mud-hole each year and relax.'

It seemed to Basil, K'Gar wouldn't mind being in the mud right now, instead of nursing these Martian aliens all over the place.

Basil nodded. He asked K'Gar, 'Is the planet's orbit stable at the moment?'

'For another four months.'

Next Basil asked, 'I wonder if I may be allowed to take a mud bath? I think we have the time, don't we?'

Alexius sat quietly in astonishment.

K'Gar was under strict orders to *safely* care for this human Ambassador. He began to resist the idea of landing on the surface. Basil, on the other hand, when he learnt there were bathers there, insisted.

Finally persuaded, the bubble-hover landed near the effervescent mud, close to a number of other bubble-hovers. The party disembarked with oxygen masks into the heated atmosphere. When they entered the dome, only the two humans required the masks. The inside of the dome was spacious, clean, even luxurious, with a number of Kaikonians relaxing in solid looking plastic tubs of mud.

Mud bespattered, they stared at the unusual sight of two aliens invading their cherished wallowing sessions. Above in the city, none had stared; taking it for granted some aliens would wish to visit their beautiful fiery planet. But down on the surface in their mud pools, this alien intrusion was seen as an invasion.

K'Gar explained to the superintendent who these alien humans were and that one wanted to try their mud bath. That made the Kaikonians less hostile. No alien could be bad if they were willing to join them in their mud.

Basil was shown a cubicle where he disrobed and climbed into his shallow tub of mud, supervised by two Kaikonian attendants who made sure the human Ambassador was well smeared. All over!

He lay in the mud for a good half hour; his pores of skin being sucked clean of grease and other gunk, cleansing his thoughts as well as his dermis layer. Alexius didn't voice what he thought of these goings on and was having none of it—he sat talking to K'Gar, drinking refreshments near a swimming pool, away from the *dirty* mud.

When they left the dome, Basil felt thoroughly relaxed. K'Gar suggested it was time to head back up to Kotka. He had the driver point the bubble-hover upwards.

With no warning, a bleeping sound emanated from the vehicle console, followed by a cackle of Kaikonian speech. Basil's earpiece translated this as "eruption warning—eruption warning" and "please strap in, evasive manoeuvres following." So they braced themselves just in time for a number of sharp evasive manoeuvres initiated by their hover.

No sooner had the "evasive gymnastics" begun, then an almighty detonation threw up a column of lava to the rear of the bubble-hover. It was only their burst of speed that allowed them to evade the blast, pushing them deep into their seats. Even so, their vehicle experienced severe buffeting. Looking behind, the passengers observed a thick large plume rising kilometres into the reddish sky, spreading into a vast dust cloud.

'I'm sorry Ambassador, that was inconveniently close,' apologised K'Gar.

'Yes, it was,' responded Basil, 'but you can hardly be held responsible for the forces of nature.'

'That's most gracious of you, Ambassador. The planet may well be telling us we've overstayed our welcome on its surface. That blow-out was an encouragement to say farewell for the present,' K'Gar teased the humans.

'I'm inclined to regard that as a *serious* encouragement,' Basil joined in the banter.

Alexius had grown pale with the hover's aerobatics. 'Are we all right?' he inquired, 'I mean is the vehicle intact?'

'Yes, everything's fine,' K'Gar reassured. 'We'll be in Kotka in twenty minutes. If you look up to your right, you'll see Kansa, the second city of Kaikon, another one of our beautiful floating cities. Don't you think our aerial homes attractive Ambassador?' K'Gar was fishing. They all looked up at the large levitating assembly hanging above.

'I've never seen anything comparable in my life, and *yes*, I think they're exquisite,' offered Basil. 'I'm astounded I'm looking at thousands, maybe even millions of tonnes suspended in mid air whilst gravity does its damnedest to pull it down. A magnificent achievement.'

'I'm deeply gratified,' said K'Gar, and he really sounded as if he were.

Approaching Kotka; they made a beeline for the side they'd departed from earlier, aiming to land near Basil's Ambassadorial apartment. K'Gar dropped his passengers and promised to call them to give them the promised tour of the city. Even after the mud purge, Basil was still overly stimulated by his encounter with all those volcanoes.

He had all the various types of volcano whirring in his head, barring three, for which K'Gar had only Kaikonian names, and his earpiece-translator couldn't put a human equivalent to it. He spent time inputting to his computer jacket, managing his diary, filing voice reports, housekeeping his system. He noted down the day's happenings in case Alexius missed something, especially the close call they'd on the way back. He hadn't had such a buzz, so much fun in a long time, not since he was forced to become a diplomat and abandon his solar research, with their spectacular solar explosions..

True to his promise, K'Gar later called on them to show them Kotka. Basil, from what he had so far seen, wasn't expecting to be comparably stimulated. You can't compare a city with a volcano, even if it *is* an aerial city. A dome is a dome is a dome; that was his expectation. However, Basil and Alexius were taken on foot, to what looked like a subway entrance, where they descended the escalator to an under-city Shopping Mall. This amazed the humans, to find themselves *below* the surface of an aerial city. It was a contradiction in terms.

It had sidewalk cafés, trees growing everywhere, gardens, and a piazza atmosphere with pedestrians milling around, going about their leisurely business. The ceiling exuded a sun-like luminescence giving the impression they were out in the sunlight. This was also the source of the flora's energy. There were shops for absolutely everything. In a society where replicators were common household items, it was clear the caprice of strolling about, browsing in shops, was considered a pleasurable pastime.

People met and chin wagged in the piazzas; sat around in the cafés and socialised, or simply strolled around chatting to each other, grazing in the shops. It was a picture of a civilised society. Wandering around were various alien species, some in atmospheric suits, some with oxygen masks, and others simply with pleasure on their faces. Basil and Alexius were among those that had to resort to oxygen masks from time to time.

'Would you like to see anything in particular?' asked their host.

'What would you care to show off?' Basil quipped back.

'We could visit one of our colonies,' K'Gar suggested.

'Are you serious?'

'Do you see those seats over there…with those translucent helmets above them; the five rows?'

Basil looked into the direction K'Gar was pointing. 'Yes,' he said.

'They are mostly for family using the Holo Reality cubes to visit relatives on our colonies. The HR's can't really go off planet, but a variety of HR cubes are available for visits to almost anywhere. The Barogians call this a Pragmacast; they invented the system. I think we even have one for your Solar System. Your Solar HR cubes would have been produced by the Rakhian advisors you now have with you on Earth.

'I suggest we have some refreshments at a café I frequent; then we can try the HR cube for one of our colonies, if it meets with your approval? It will also give them a little time to adjust the HR to the human brain.' K'Gar spoke into his communicator in Kaikonian.

Basil turned to his aide, 'Sounds like a good itinerary, what do you think Alexius?'

'Works for me,' said Alexius.

They walked to K'Gar's café, a couple of blocks away and sat at tables out in the open. K'Gar ordered suitable drinks for them, ones their differing metabolic systems found safe. For half an hour they watched Kaikonian society leisurely pass by. After resting and satiating themselves, they sauntered back the few blocks to the Holo Reality seats and Basil allowed K'Gar to seat him under one of the helmets.

The height needed to be lifted for Basil because of his tall stature, whereas it would normally be lowered to twenty centimetres above the Kaikonians heads. Alexius insisted on watching protectively over Basil, declining to use a helmet himself.

K'Gar picked through some cubes on a tray, choosing one, and inserting it in a slot. Within a few moments, an entirely new world appeared before Basil's senses. The first Basil saw was a big sign saying 'Welcome to Kanava'. A differently dressed Kaikonian individual with a big grin introduced himself as his personal tour guide. The guide explained what Basil was about to see was the diametric opposite to Kaikon, Kanava being a green land with many canals.

All the cities on Kanava were criss-crossed by waterways and set in a grid pattern of canals. It was similar to...then the HR extracted a simile from Basil's brain...similar to Motecuhzoma's capital of Tenochtitlán before the arrival of Cortez and his conquistadors in Mexico circa 1519 Earth time.

In due course the guide wished him well and hoped he would visit again. An hour had gone by, but it seemed to Basil he'd spent the day touring Kanava, and now the guide took his leave. Basil blinked—opened his eyes; well he tried to open his eyes, but they were already open. He was sitting in the HR enclave on Kaikon with K'Gar gently shaking him.

He was saying, 'The first time can be overwhelming,'

'*That was astounding*,' Basil expelled. 'What a world! What about the other worlds—are they as real?' Basil enthused. 'Alexius! Why don't you try this Kanava world?'

'Thank you sir, but not just at the moment,' his deputy responded cautiously. Alexius was being the good Deputy by looking after the interests of his Ambassador before his own.

'Ambassador! The other planet cubes that are available are for Tehda, a mainly manufacturing planet, Svatek, a holiday planet, and Rohdos, a chemical R&D and production planet. If you wish, we can let you have a helmet and cubes to take back with you to Rakh?' offered K'Gar.

'If it is allowed, we would be...well, I would be most grateful.'

'Consider it a gift from Kaikon.'

Cautiously Basil said without enthusiasm. 'Well, I think it's time to call it a day.'

'If that is your wish.' K'Gar said. He seemed to be showing fatigue; at least Basil thought so, though it was difficult to tell.

Loath to cut it short, they headed back to the Ambassadorial residency where K'Gar stood for a moment, then said to Basil, 'It has been interesting meeting with you.'

Basil understood that to mean "your species."

K'Gar continued, 'I hope you enjoyed yourself. May you sleep well and I will collect in the morning.'

Early the following morning K'Gar turned up and took them to the platform they'd previously visited. From there they were to teleport up to the ship taking them back to Rakh. K'Gar hoped the Martian Ambassador had a good visit and wished them a safe journey back.

Aboard the large spaceliner they made their way to the oxygen lounge, where they settled in for the two day voyage. The trip was uneventful as far as Zyneer. There they received an invitation to come down to the planet.

Although Basil wasn't eager to meet the insectoids, they were apparently eager to meet him. Diplomacy and inquisitiveness got the better of him, and he agreed to teleport down.

The planet had a noxious atmosphere and they had to wear pressure suits. On landing they were met by three insectoids who stood erect and resembled large upright cockroaches with faceted eyes. Through their translator, Basil understood they wanted him to convey a message to Taras from the Murangi, inviting him to visit their planet and restart their diplomatic relations anew. This was after the disastrous earlier kidnapping saga perpetrated by their kith and kin.

The Zyneerians were merely passing on this request on behalf of their Murangi relatives. Basil promised he would deliver the message to Taras as soon as he reached Rakh, and he was certain this personal approach would be well received.

The rest of the journey back to Rakh was spent on finishing and polishing the report for President Ghali. When he arrived back at the Embassy on Rakh, he handed Taras the message from the Murangi. In the evening, they sat down to discuss the implications of the invitation and the timing of his possible journey to Murangi.

Chapter Twenty-Six

Security Bureaux

On a fine sunny mid-summer day, a figure materialised on the steps of the Earth-Mars Embassy on Rakh. No foreknowledge of the figure's arrival had leaked, and the person slipped lithely through the front door like a burglar.

The individual looked around inside the hall, realised no one was about, then spied several discreetly concealed monitors. Only a surveillance expert would have noticed. The person quickly headed down the stairs towards the Earth Ambassador's office, seemingly knowing the location.

Stopping to listen at the door, the figure knocked gently and entered. Taras looked away from the screen where he'd been following the figure's progress, alerted by the security system. He scrutinised the figure. Her features were chiselled, expressing fierce determination and her bearing said military. She had blue eyes, was of medium height, slim but firmly built, dressed in a dark green tight fitting suit. The figures most stunning feature was her blonde shoulder length hair.

'That was quiet an entrance,' he observed with a smile.

'My orders—were to be discreet.'

'You should have used a cloaking device,' he chided.

'I've got a small portable, but I didn't think it wise, not arriving at the Embassy.'

'Well, sit down.' He pointed at an armchair near his desk. 'Tell me what's all the secrecy. I was warned of your imminent arrival.'

'I suppose it's safe to talk—here?' she looked around the room.

'Yes, it's safe,' his curiosity rose a notch.

'First, let me give you my credentials,' she said.

She took out a small flat data card and handed it to Taras, which he promptly inserted into a slot in his desk. Her details popped up on the screen and gave her name as Heidi Frisch, a Colonel from World Government Security. There was some background information, a DNA string, a retinal scan, and a picture.

Taras rose from his chair and went round to the back of her chair, put his hand on her blonde hair and jerked out a healthy follicle by its roots. He fed the strand into a small DNA analyser built into his desk near the credential slot. She hadn't blinked at this invasive manoeuvre, as if she was completely used to it.

'Sorry about the hair. It all checks out. Well, Fräulein, what's all this leading to?'

'I hate to be the bearer of bad tidings, but you have a sleeper in your Embassy. An "anti." terrorist.' She lowered her voice, 'We believe him—or her—to be extremely dangerous.' She had a hard appearance, yet a soft underlying quality to her voice.

'Are you *serious*?' Taras glared into her eyes for confirmation.

'Ambassador, this *is* serious. The Bureaux has uncovered a nest of saboteurs on the Titan biosphere whose sole aim was to wreck this connection with the Galactic Federation. Your Embassy.' She swept her arm around the room 'The problem for those we caught, resolved itself quickly. They had poison implants which they activated when we took them into custody,' a look of distaste flashed across her face.

She continued, 'Amongst their possessions were a number of data cubes. One contained a sketch, an unfinished plan of action, including a reference to their agent in the Embassy on Rakh. No name. No revealing reference simply that the agent existed. Apparently, they used a double with bootleg memories and switched him/her at the last moment on the Moon, implying they had help from sympathisers there. Those same sympathisers have been rooted out with aid of the *new* PL machines. They went through PL thinking they were safe, only when they knew they were uncovered did they activate *their* poison implants.'

'But these "antis" sound far more serious than a little group of backward resistants, as we were first led to believe. More like a full-blown conspiracy by a determined group,' Taras was beginning to feel worried.

'There's more! We've now vetted all the diplomats in training, and we found one more. Each time we find a potential source of information, they activate poison implants. Remember trainee diplomats were chosen from an elite group, and we're horrified they managed to infiltrate someone into that group.'

'How can you be certain we've got a sleeper *here*? Couldn't it have been a ruse of some sort?'

'Are you willing to take the risk?' and this time *she* penetratingly stared at Taras.

'No, I suppose not,' *just as things were settling down nicely here*, he thought.

'We wanted to bring one of our *new* PL machines to Rakh, but we're getting resistance to the idea from the Galactic Embassy on the Moon. With this *new* version, we could put the staff through it and clear the matter in one day. We could've put it in a diplomatic pouch and simply brought it here, but we thought we'd be polite— and it turned out to be a mistake.'

'Diplomacy between humans and diplomacy between species are somewhat different,' he sighed. 'Let me find out what the difficulty is,' he offered. 'In the mean time, can I get you a drink?'

'Well, a cool *Sierra* would be nice.' She lost the severe look on her face and smiled. 'One of the reasons I'm here is to determine why the Rakhians have such a reluctance to have PL on Rakh. The other reason is to warn you, and maybe help you root out this sleeper by any means you care to mention.' She sank deeper into the armchair, drink in her hand, feeling more relaxed.

'What have in mind?' He didn't want the place turned upside down.

'First, we *must* determine who we can trust.'

'I have to bring Ambassador Dukas into this. It beggars belief he's an "anti." What's your instructions?'

'To work with you. As far as I'm concerned, you're in charge. I'm to work for you and advise you on this matter, if you ask me to.'

'Good! Let me see if Basil's available,' and he spoke into the air. His earpiece responded with Basil's voice. A couple of minutes later Basil knocked gently and came into Taras' office.

'What a pleasure,' as he noticed the occupant of the armchair.

'May I introduce Colonel Heidi Frisch. Ambassador Basil Dukas.'

'As you requested, I'm here,' Basil parked in an empty armchair.

'Heidi, can you fill the Ambassador in, while I try and locate Gupta. I think my Chief of Staff needs to hear this.'

'We're not too *sure* of him,' Heidi put in quickly. 'The Bengali bootleggers have a sophisticated PL— extremely good.'

'You *cannot* be serious. Why he's my Deputy. He must be *above* suspicion!' Taras was adamant.

'Be it on you own head Ambassador,' Heidi retorted.

Guardedly Basil said, 'And what about *my* Deputy, Alexius Balbus? Can I let him in on whatever this is?'

'We're more certain of him.' She looked at Basil and nodded.

She explained the whole story to Basil, about the sleeper and the unknown danger this posed. Both Ambassadors insisted on having their deputies present at further discussions and forthwith called them in. Heidi suggested the rooms of all the hundred and ninety-seven staff of the Embassy be searched as soon as possible, to see if anything incriminating turned up.

The Embassy recently introduced a computer driven notification system to keep track of all their staffs' whereabouts after Theo returned from being marooned on New Mars. Knowing who was in and who out allowed a search of rooms to progress. Heidi acted as an undercover chambermaid. The job lasted a full two days and at the end, Heidi was tired and fed up, although the rich oxygen in the air seemed to give her added verve.

On the third day of Heidi's arrival, the five in the know gathered again in Taras' office. Taras sat at his desk and the rest made themselves comfortable in the armchairs.

'We're no nearer discovering the sleeper than we were when you first arrived,' Basil muttered in disgust to Heidi.

Heidi had a grim look on her face. 'I've a gut feeling whatever this sleeper was intended for, has been brought forward. Don't ask me why, call it intuition.'

'Why don't we use our heads, and try again to work this out,' Taras sat with his chin in the cup of his hands, his elbows resting on the desk. 'Gupta! Are there any special events occurring on Rakh in the immediate future.'

'Nothing of importance your Excellency,' Gupta responded.

'What about the Festival of Melith?' pointed out Alexius. 'It's almost on us. It's a rededication of the environmental principles the Rakhians live by. I mean it only happens once every fifty years.'

'Who's to be present? Where and when is it held?' asked Basil of Alexius.

'It's in a week's time in the Grand old Amphitheatre of Rakh, their eight hundred thousand year old Holy of Holies,' said Alexius.

'I'm sorry Ambassador,' Gupta looked guiltily at Taras, 'it slipped my mind.'

'I seem to remember Primearch Reithur mentioning it last week,' said Taras looking at Gupta

'We all have an invitation, of course, and even the Grand Custodian is expected to attend,' Alexius added.

'I'm going to suggest this sleeper may be activated for this ceremony,' proposed Heidi. 'I suspect my presence has been noted, and whoever it is who's running this operation, may fear being exposed. I mean, we can run this through a computer model and check my intuition, but you'll find I'm right.'

'For my peace of mind, run it through a model and let me know the answer,' Taras ordered. 'I'm going to include it in my report to Earth. I'm inclined to go with your hunch, Colonel; set things in motion as if it were the case. Who's this person going to go after? Isn't that the real question?'

'It's got to be a big wig. No point going after small fry if they want to get us thrown out of the Federation. On the other hand, the person could outrage all of Rakh and blow up the Great Amphitheatre, or try to. This lunatic could even go after both targets,' Heidi suggested.

'I want to involve the Rakhian authorities,' Taras declared, 'unless you have any objections—Colonel?'

'No! I concur, but discreetly. I've never dealt with another specie's security branch,' she said uneasily.

Taras rose from his chair. 'They're much like ours, from the report left by my predecessor, Claude Joubert.' He slowly began to pace the room. 'Claude dealt with them when Adama was kidnapped.'

'However, I turned up something of concern to *you,* Ambassador Fisenko,' she stood up, a smile on her face.

'A minor Turkish clerk in the Consular section called Mesut Demirel seems to have become infatuated with a high ranking Rakhian woman. This I suspect may require the attention of Professor Maskalik, our resident Clinical Psychologist.' She began pacing the opposite side of the room to Taras.

'Is it reciprocated; do you know?' asked Taras.

'As far as I could discern, it's a one sided affair. The Rakhian woman seems outraged.'

'Damn fool! He must have the PL information inside his head. He knows the biology is wholly incompatible. Inter-specie's relationships are simply not feasible, and never can be. The proteins are different; the hormones and genetics have taken a completely different evolutionary path. We have drummed this in to *all* our staff. It's like a giraffe and an elephant wanting to set up home together; even their DNA is closer than Human and Rakhian. It's okay in sci-fi HoloVids or cartoons, but totally impossible in real life. The sooner we get our families out here with us on Rakh, the better.'

'I'll get Maskalik on to Demirel,' promised Gupta.

'So where do we go from here? Heidi! Any ideas?' Taras stood and looked at the pacing figure of his security expert.

'The next step is the Rakhian authorities. If anything goes wrong, we must spread the load..., and the blame.' She stopped pacing and sat down.

'I'll get right on it,' said Taras, 'but in the mean time, all of you, keep your eyes open and your ears peeled. We'll meet here same time tomorrow.'

With this parting remark, the meeting dispersed to their respective duties. Taras got through to the Rakhian Foreign Ministry and gave them a nebulous outline of his problem. They in turn put him in touch with another Department, which immediately suggested a meeting. Permission to teleport to the Embassy was asked for, and granted.

A figure materialised in Taras' office. 'My name is Lithgar of the Rakhian Securitat,' the tallish Rakhian introduced himself.

Taras proceeded to recapitulate the situation in all its details to this Rakhian dressed in dark brown.

The Rakhian listened patiently until Taras finished, then asked, 'Have you a suspect in mind?'

Embarrassed a fellow human was the terrorist, Taras admitted, 'I'm afraid not.'

Lithgar asked, 'Are you running the investigation?'

Taras called Heidi in.

The two security experts excused themselves and left Taras to his job, whilst they got on with theirs. They headed for an empty office and sat at a table opposite each other. After a few moments, Heidi decided she liked Lithgar—as someone whose mind worked similarly.

The question was how to flush out the sleeper? The nature of a sleeper, she mused, was they perform their assigned duties normally without arousing undue attention. Only when they were activated by a code word, implant, or some other manner, did the sleeper begin to carry out their allotted task.

'Why won't you allow us to bring in a PL machine?' Heidi suddenly asked of Lithgar.

Without blinking Lithgar responded, 'We're unhappy having a mind probe loose on our planet.'

'But it wouldn't be loose. We'd be controlling it. Anyway, we couldn't use it without hooking it up to your computers. The Embassy computer isn't nearly powerful enough.'

'We have a little time, so I'm going to explain something *important* to you. Meddling with people's minds is no different than meddling with their genetic coding. Take a simple example; you could produce a race of tall people by manipulating the genes, but then an unforeseen circumstance might arise where only short people were able to survive. If you hadn't tampered with the gene pool and you had the normal diversity of tall, medium and short people, the race would survive, but the race of *only* tall people would perish.

'We went through a phase of tampering with the Rakhian psyche, and concluded good environmental practice was to allow the psyche to develop naturally, without stuffing it artificially full of useful extras. It seems profitable in the short term, savings on teaching and producing instant geniuses, but the mind is a delicate instrument, and all the extra pressures end up generating mutations.

'The emotions suffer, motivational over activity burns minds out; creativity becomes mechanical. In the long run, it pays for nature to take its course, and bear in mind our civilisation has been going for nigh on a million years. We've had experience with your PL, and decided to avoid it like the plague. Some a hundred thousand years ago, it *was* nearly a plague for us.'

She listened to the monologue in silence, dismayed. 'We had no idea you'd used PL. So you're saying we should abandon PL?' A small flutter of fear brushed her thoughts.

'Go back to the way you did things before PL, before it's too late,' he sounded sincere, even passionate.

'This argument would need to go to the highest authorities, and would need unequivocal documentary support. Can you provide that?'

'Let me check with my supervisor. I'll make a strong argument for giving you humans' access to our disastrous experience with PL. After that, it's up to your leaders. *Now* you know why we don't want your PL machine here on Rakh.'

'Yes, *now* I know,' she acknowledged his intensity. 'Since you've made it clear, we ought to get back to the other problem at hand. We've made a frantic background search of all our staff at the Embassy, and there's a short-list of twenty-one. That's our suspect list. I'm staking my reputation he's amongst them.'

Lithgar thought for a moment. 'The simplest solution would be to recall these twenty-one individuals and deal with them on Earth.'

'Yes. We could then put them through the *new* PLC and get definitive answers,' she was enthusiastic again.

'However, I'm going to counsel against. You need to start solving problems without resorting to PL, and you might as well start here and now,' a didactic tone had crept into his voice.

There came a knock at the door, and Heidi called out, '*Enter.*'

A clerk came in carrying a written message. 'Mr. Vivekananda asked me to give you this. He told me to tell you; he found it on the dining table.' The clerk handed the printed message to Heidi, and then went out.

Lithgar looked puzzled.

'It's from Gupta, or rather, he says he found it,' she stared at it a while.

'I'm not sure what to make of it. It's machine written in Cyrillic. There's a translation attached; the note accuses Mesut Demirel of being the saboteur, written in Ukrainian.'

'It's a hoax,' Lithgar stated emphatically.

'Computer!' Heidi spoke into the air. 'Is there a record of a machine printout of a short note referring to Mesut Demirel?'

'Yes Colonel,' came the response from her earpiece.

'Which station was it printed out at?' she demanded.

'The one in the hall,' her earpiece told her.

'*Damn!*' her face turned grim. 'Whoever it is, is toying with us,' she said darkly. 'My list of twenty-one doesn't include Demirel. He's just home sick.'

'We can't go further without a lead, and that printout is *no* lead,' Lithgar stated the obvious. 'I have other work to do. If anything else develops, please let me know at once. In the mean time, I'll try to get our PL data for you. It's been nice dealing with you,' and he teleported out.

Being forced to leave it there galled Heidi, but since nothing could be taken further, at least she reported the PL conversation with Lithgar to Taras. He was flabbergasted by the news PL might be damaging the human psyche. Moreover, he was disgusted by the Ukrainian note. He called in Basil as it concerned him, and together they decided to have a meeting with all their senior staff.

Until the Rakhian PL data arrived from Lithgar, they couldn't send anything back to the Solar System, not without hard evidence. In the mean time, they began to outline a skeleton report to their Moon HQ back in the Solar System. It suggested the wide usage of PL *might* not have been such a good idea after all.

Chapter Twenty-Seven

The Terrorist

The following days went by for Taras, with only one further development, a message from Moonbase HQ. They had narrowed the suspects down to six possible saboteurs. The pressing dilemma for him; the Festival of Melith was now only two days away.

Lithgar was as good as his word, bringing over the datacube containing the Rakhian experiences of PL. After the senior Embassy staff viewed it, and discussed the implications, it was decided to send Basil back to the Solar System with the damning datacube as a matter of urgency.

Everyone was aghast at the anatomical changes in the Rakhian brain that had occurred over the first thousand years of using their version of PL. There was no arguing with the evidence placed before them.

If there was ever a benefit in joining the Federation, this was it. They might yet avoid this horrendous pitfall. This information came from an alien species that had previously dabbled in the use of humanities most useful tools to date, and found it severely wanting.

Heidi asked Lithgar for a quiet word, and told him the suspect list was down to six. She handed him the printout.

'Thank you, but you must know I can't read your language. However, all these people will have to submit to DNA checks and their files will have to be examined with precision,' he suggested.

She was beginning to show tiredness. 'Are you up to it?' she asked.

'Let me just make a quick call, then I'm ready,' he responded.

It was pointless trying to conceal from the Embassy staff now, that Colonel Heidi Frisch was there in pursuit of someone. The staff grapevine managed to produce some bizarre reasons why the Security Bureaux was at the Embassy. Some of it was misinformation put out by Heidi. She waited till Lithgar had finished his call, and then sent for Vitold Teresiak, the first person on the list.

*　　*　　*

The tall dark clerk from the commercial section knocked—then entered the room. Heidi asked Teresiak to sit at the chair facing the desk. She then asked his consent to pluck a hair follicle from his head, and put it through the DNA analyser, and waited. The DNA results agreed with who he said he was.

Vitold Teresiak was 87 years old, came from Odessa on the Ukrainian coast, highly recommended by the Ukrainian Diplomatic Corps as being one of their high-flyers. Heidi took a retinal scan with a portable scanner, just to be on the safe side, and again it merely confirmed his identity.

Without a brain probe, this was as far as she could physically go. She thanked him for his patience and asked him to keep what happened in the room to himself.

'What's your gut feeling about him?' she asked Lithgar.

'I'm not the best judge, with my limited experience of humans.' Anyway he offered, 'Instinct tells me he's straight.'

'I'll note that. Ready for the next one?' She called for Fiona Tizard.

A hesitant knock on the door, and a medium tall New Zealander asked if it was all right to come in. When told it was, she walked to the proffered chair and sat down.

She behaved nervously—fidgeting. Her dossier told Heidi, Fiona worked for the Commercial Attaché. She sat staring at Lithgar, wringing her hands delicately, occasionally flicking her hair out of her eyes, and the latter fluttered excessively.

'Do you know why you've been called here?' asked Heidi.

'No...ma'am,' was her hesitant reply.

'I would like your permission to take a hair follicle for DNA analysis, and then I want to do a retinal scan. Do you agree?'

'Yes...ma'am,' more nervously.

Her eyes fluttered and she slowly wrung her hands, trying to be discreet, failing.

Heidi went round, removed the follicle, and put it through the analyser. No problem there. Her DNA matched the file DNA. Heidi was checking all the DNA against fresh files she had brought with her. She didn't use the Embassy files just in case they'd been doctored.

The retinal scan became an ordeal because Tizard's eyelid kept nervously fluttering. Eventually Heidi had to prop it open. It showed Tizard was who she claimed to be.

The rest of the dossier was just some material on her background. She was 124 years old, came from Dunedin in the South Island, another diplomatic high-flyer. Lithgar's impression of Fiona Tizard was, she was hiding something, and they ought to call her in again and put her through the mill. Heidi had come to the same conclusion.

Yoshi Tanaka was next; a self assured financial controller for the Embassy's expenses. Heidi went through the same ritual of the DNA analysis and retinal scan, and his composure was verging on the arrogant, but it was probably the anti-rational nature of Zen coming through, rather than insolence.

From his file, he was 139 years old, had spent a year studying Zen at the Shokoku Temple in Kyoto, a cadet with the *ninjas* in the local military defence force. He'd intended to eventually enter the Space Corps. For a capricious reason of his own, he'd switched to the Foreign Office and became one of Japan's offerings to the Galactic University Diplomatic School. On his course, he was known as a hard working diligent aspirant.

Lithgar thought Tanaka would make a good saboteur because of his self-composure and discipline. Definitely worth a second talk, but he'd be a tough nut to crack.

The next on the list was Said Mehmet, an amiable Eritrean clerk in the Consular section in charge of issuing visas. He knocked and entered diffidently, sitting on the edge of the offered chair.

Mehmet was diametrically opposite to Tanaka, but equally self assured; his retiring manner made him a private person. His demeanour could be mistaken for servility, but in fact, it was common politeness, a scarce commodity in the modern world.

Heidi took an instant liking to this polite mirage of a bygone age, which would have been an especially useful attribute in a sleeper. People expect saboteurs to be forceful and pretentious, which is why Tanaka seemed too obvious. Aware of the subtlety, Heidi would have chosen Mehmet for the role of an "anti," precisely because he would pass unnoticed in that role. She went through the DNA routine and he was most co-operative.

He was 144 years old, came from the port city of Mesewa on the Red Sea, put forward by the African nations to join the Galactic University Diplomatic School. Nobody had a bad word to say about him. As far as she could determine from the file on him, he was impeccable. He checked out as being Said Mehmet. Lithgar wanted another word with him, just to see if he could unruffle this human.

The next DNA sample was taken from Xiang Yu, whose character was unquestionably similar to Mehmet's, yet the two were separated by nine and a half thousand kilometres, and emanated from two different cultures.

Xiang was 165 years old, and came from the ancient Zhou capital of Xian, on the southern bank of the Wei River, in northwest China, founded in 1066 BC. He was proposed by Asia for the Galactic Diplomatic School, and as with Mehmet, everybody spoke well of him.

He was calm, cool and efficient, and worked in the financial section with Tanaka. His DNA and scan checked out, and little else could be said of him. He gave little away in terms of his private life—or his emotions. Lithgar made the same comment of him as he had of Mehmet.

Finally, there was Chuan Kraprayoon, the Embassy Chef, with the hot temperament of his vocation. He was 89 years old, and came from Chiengmai, in the mountainous region of northern Thailand, close to the Burmese border.

His culinary skills were legendary, producing dishes that took the staff's minds off the long distance from home. He was able to create any of the dishes on Earth, capable of producing meals no replicator could replicate.

Heidi was gentle with him, but firm, since he carried with him a reputation for tantrums, and could flare up at the least provocation. His DNA and scan checked, whilst Lithgar thought him the unlikeliest suspect of all those he'd seen.

Having interviewed and checked all the suspects; Heidi and Lithgar now decided to short-list Fiona Tizard, Yoshi Tanaka, Said Mehmet, and Xiang Yu, purely on the basis of their behaviour during these initial interviews. Since they weren't going to use PL, they had to revert to professional instinct and good sleuthing. Heidi thought Fiona was probably innocent; but then what was troubling her—to make her so nervous. She decided to have Fiona in first.

'Please sit,' she said sternly when Fiona entered. 'We called you back to find out what the hell is troubling you; and I want the truth.' She fixed an intimidating stare at the swarthy woman.

'I'm having an affair with someone in the Embassy, and I know it's against the rules,' she sobbed into her hands. 'Please don't send me back. It's not my fault, he's the boss and I just went along with what he wanted.'

She was pouring out her heart, wringing her hands, and seemed relieved she could finally tell someone.

'There, there,' Heidi came and put her arms around Fiona's shoulders to steady the sobbing woman. 'Tell me; did you agree to his advances?' Heidi wanted to know if there was any coercion on the Commercial Attaché's part.

'Well, sort of. I mean I really wasn't looking for an affair, but he kept pestering me, and one evening at a reception I'd had a few drinks. One thing led to another, and I ended up in his bed. I mean; I wouldn't have, had I been sober. Then, so he wouldn't make a fuss, I kept seeing him at odd times. When you called me in, I thought we'd been caught.'

'Is there anything *else* at all, other than this affair?'

'No ma'am, I swear. Please don't send me back. It would be the end of my career.'

'If anyone is going back, it will be the Commercial Attaché.' She was going to have a word with Taras.

Clearly, the attaché had abused his position, and needed to be dealt with. That was Taras' province and all she could do was advise him of the situation. Anyhow, Fiona was off the suspect list, and as far as Heidi and Lithgar were concerned, she simply hadn't been assertive enough.

That left three other suspects to be dealt with—the next day. Time was getting late and Heidi said goodbye to Lithgar, who teleported out. There was one more day before the Rakhian Melith Festival of renewal. The last day left to catch the sleeper.

The next day Heidi and Lithgar questioned Tanaka again. Then Mehmet and Xiang. But they had little with which to accuse them. In fact, Tanaka was quiet blunt. He had work to do, and if they couldn't get to the point, then he'd be blowed if he was going to waste his time answering any more questions. With that, he walked out, leaving them open mouthed and annoyed. The day ended in frustration with the festival looming the next day.

In the morning, the Embassy roll-call showed neither Tanaka nor Xiang had returned from an evening out. Taras was informed immediately, as was Rakhian Security. Lithgar said he had Xiang in custody after Tanaka and Xiang had argued with a Rakhian. Tanaka had urged Xiang the previous night to strike the luckless Rakhian. Xiang claimed "honour" was involved.

He was about to inform Heidi, when he'd received the Embassy call. That probably meant Tanaka was *the* culprit. Taras ordered Heidi to get Tanaka—at all cost. She asked Lithgar what precautions they were taking at the Amphitheatre.

Lithgar suggested they move operations there since their computer model predicted Tanaka would head to the Amphitheatre. There, she saw a large number of Rakhian Security, all dressed in shimmering black, and the shimmering played with her eyesight, which was the garbs intention.

The Amphitheatre itself contained many tunnels below the seating area, passageways through which the crowds reached their seats. The walls were covered with a dynamic green ceramic coating, which cycled through the spectrum.

She was assured all the tunnels were monitored closely, as were all the seats. At the gates, sensors, peepers, body scanners searched for lethal weaponry or explosives, ID scanners, and much more. Lithgar felt confident Tanaka would not, could not get past their systems.

Unbeknown, Tanaka had been supplied with a small cloaking device, similar to the one in Heidi's possession. He'd already entered the Amphitheatre the night previous, kicking of a few minor sensors, but nothing was found, and the Rakhians assumed it was a false alarm.

It wasn't till Lithgar mentioned the minor security panic of the previous night that Heidi intuitively knew it was Tanaka who'd provoked the Rakhian sensors. But to do that and not set off the others could only mean one thing to Heidi, Tanaka had somehow got hold of a cloaking device. She was hoping to keep the device a secret, but she couldn't if Tanaka possessed one.

'Look Lithgar. I have to tell you something. I possess a cloaking device that renders me invisible. I think Tanaka may have a similar device,' she felt embarrassed at revealing this.

'So you think Tanaka precipitated the sensor malfunctions of last night?' the elfin face looked more quizzical than annoyed.

'I'd bet on it.'

'Have you got the device with you?'

'Yes.'

'Will you activate it for me,' he became concentrated.

'Okay,' and she spoke some numbers into her chest. Immediately she disappeared from Lithgar's view. He looked around to see if there were any telltale signs of her presence, but could see none.

'*Damn*,' was the translator's rendition of the Rakhian comment.

'Sorry,' Heidi remarked when she reappeared. 'Don't you have similar devices?' she was fishing for information.

'Yes, of course we do. But we didn't expect *you* to have them. How long can he stay cloaked?'

'Roughly ten hours,' she said. Lithgar had given nothing away.

He alerted his people to the likelihood of Tanaka's presence in the Amphitheatre. Tanaka hadn't stood a chance of doing any sabotage without the cloaking device. Now, there was just a slim possibility he might succeed.

The main event was to occur at noon, symbolically when the sun was exactly overhead. The Mehir was to act as high priest conducting the ceremony from the rostrum. There were dignitaries from numerous foreign species, including the guest of honour, the Grand Custodian.

As the time neared for the ceremony to start, Lithgar became agitated. Tanaka hadn't been found. The small Earth Embassy delegation arrived. Taras, Gupta, and Alexius were shown to their places. What if Tanaka succeeded in whatever he had in mind? This was torturing Heidi. They'd been in the Federation for less than two years. Already there was a threat from a fellow human.

She got permission to activate her cloaking device —from Lithgar. He tagged her and incorporated her into the electronic sweeps his people were making using the tag. The sweeper adjusted to her cloaking device. Heidi tried to think like Tanaka. Where would she hide if the roles were reversed? Either amongst people, or in the remotest spot of the Amphitheatre.

She began to make her way to the uppermost tiers of the Amphitheatre, when her earpiece told her the Rakhians had cornered Tanaka—at the back of the uppermost tier. She got there just as they were leading him to Lithgar.

He was a sorry sight, caught and held in some sort of force field net. A Rakhian Security held Tanaka's cloaking device in his right hand, and led the would be saboteur with his left. His shimmering outfit reminded Heidi of the *ninjas* Tanaka had tried so hard to emulate.

'Thank the Infinite we've stopped him in time,' Lithgar remarked as he approached the captive.

'I must inform the Ambassador of the good news.' Heidi spoke to Taras on her communicator.

For Taras, the good outcome lifted the gloomy mood he'd brought with him. As soon as Gupta heard the news, he jumped up with a start and ran off, leaving Taras with a puzzled expression on his face. *Now what on Earth has got into him?* Then a scowl appeared, followed by an oath of disgust.

'Heidi! *Heidi! Can you hear this?*' Taras shouted into his communicator.

'Yes Ambassador,' came the response.

'Listen carefully. Tell Lithgar to pick up Gupta *urgently*. Did you *get* that? Gupta just vanished when he heard Tanaka'd been taken. I think he's trying to reach whatever Tanaka was going to do. At all costs, you *must catch Gupta*.'

'Understood Ambassador,' and she hurriedly turned to Lithgar passing on the message.

Lithgar alerted his *"ninjas"* and a frantic search began for Taras' deputy. They picked up Gupta on the security monitors heading straight for the second tier toilets, presumably where Tanaka hid whatever it was.

As Heidi watched, a screen appeared out of nowhere. She saw a group of Rakhian Security close off one tunnel after another, causing chaos to the locals, who were unaware of the drama taking place.

Gupta was trapped at the beginning of the long tunnel leading to the toilets. It became imperative they stop him entering the lavatory. Out of thin air, suddenly four *"ninjas"* materialised between Gupta and the toilet entrance.

'*Well done!*' exclaimed Heidi.

Lithgar shouted something into his communicator, and one of the four *"ninjas"* aimed a gadget at Gupta, catching him in a force field, similar to the one holding Tanaka.

'That's that,' Lithgar announced. 'Could you ask Ambassador Fisenko if he's prepared to waive diplomatic immunity for these two.'

'We waive diplomatic immunity with the greatest of pleasure,' came back the reply from Heidi. 'We decided in advance we would.'

Taras and Heidi had talked this over and determined it would be a good idea if the culprits were left in limbo for a while. 'Let them sweat it out in an alien prison—or whatever they do with their prisoners,' was Taras' comment.

'Consider it a gesture of good will from Earth,' she added to Lithgar. Taras also wanted feedback on the Rakhian penal system, which he'd get, once *their* penal system had finished with the two.

'That's most acceptable,' Lithgar smiled. 'Now can we go and see *why* your Gupta was so eager to go to the toilet.'

The device his Security people found was wrapped in light-curving material hidden in a corner. After scanning, they said it was a small fusion device, but capable of destroying the Amphitheatre. Lithgar took the parcel handed to him by his Security colleague, examined it, and became relieved and angry.

'This primitive device would have *devastated* the whole Amphitheatre,' said Lithgar, handing the device back to his colleague.

'I'm glad it didn't,' said Heidi.

'Yes, I really think you are,' he said poignantly.

'I want to congratulate your people on a job well done. The Ambassador asked me to thank you. And a big thanks from *me*. It was interesting working with you,' she took his hand and shook it.

'Yes it was *interesting*,' he parodied her, shaking her hand vigorously. 'I hope to meet you again.'

'Now I must join our party.'

With that parting shot, Heidi joined Taras to witness the ceremony rededicating the Rakhians to their environment.

It was later that day, back at the Embassy; she learnt from her Bureaux communications that the Bengali Section of Interpol had found the body of the real Gupta. He was up in the Himalayas, frozen to death in a cave high in the mountains. The news shook Taras, mainly because he'd come to trust the false Gupta, and now found his trust was misplaced.

Chapter Twenty-Eight

Klitka Conspiracy

On Murangi, a group of insectoids from the Klitka Hive huddled over a table, hatching a plot to take revenge on humans who had the impudence to visit to their home planet.

Ten sterile females of the warrior caste, in their distinctive yellow and green Klitka colouring, shuffled around the table, antennae bulbs flashing. The heated discussion was over *what* to do, and the timing.

Rogue members of the Klitka Hive were responsible for the kidnapping of Adama Ubongo, and now they wanted revenge for the capture and incarceration of the same kidnappers, their fellow hive members.

Small luminous bulbs on the tips of their antennae flashed furiously: *clicks* followed *clacks*, with frenzied rubbing of their raptorial forelegs giving prominence to their lack of harmony. Chemical pheromones added weight to the altercations, thickening the already dense atmosphere. The group was divided between using a smart bomb, a laser sniper, or the more traditional approach—poison.

*   *   *

The ship carrying Taras and Sandy Gable arrived in standard orbit round Murangi, the system inhabited by the sentient insectoids. The spaceship's Captain asked ground control for permission to disembark his passengers. This was granted, allowing Taras and Sandy to teleport down to the surface.

Both materialised on a vast green common, filled with a profusion of exotic flowers. The long common was surrounded by some of the tallest buildings the humans had seen in a long time. It vaguely reminded them of Central Park in New York. The planet's gravity was less than they were used to, half of earth's. The atmosphere was dense but breathable, thick with scents and a heady rich ambience.

A group of insectoids waited.

'I am called Furzz, the Queen's Chamberlain,' Taras' ear mike translated the blinking lights of their antennae whilst the insectoid's composite eyes looked him up and down. He stared down, somewhat mesmerised by the emitted simulacrum of Morse code from the bulbs.

Shaking his head, he enunciated, 'I'm Ambassador Fisenko representing the Solar System, and this is Sandy Gable, my Chief of Staff.'

'We are pleased to welcome you to Murangi,' articulated his translator. 'We hope we can improve and cement the relationship between our two species,' the Chamberlain twinkled. 'The Palace is only a short distance,' he swung his foreleg right at a huge building looming at the head of the garden, 'Would you like transport; or maybe take a short walk after your long journey?'

'I think it would be pleasant to stretch our legs,' Taras suggested.

Sandy blinked her hazel green eyes in agreement and brushed back her hair from her brow. Her athletic build ached for exercise after their long journey.

The Chamberlain and his staff led the way along a broad pathway towards the huge building, which he'd called a Palace. On the way, they passed numerous insectoids, busying themselves around tall flowers.

'We've modified some of the best pollen producing flowers to maximise yield,' Furzz was explaining. 'But here in the Royal Gardens, we still like to use the traditional gathering method.' He pointed to a row of docile dog size aphid-like insects standing patiently, whilst a group of workers gathered pollen from huge anthers. They were using large combs and brushes, and placing the pollen in long baskets, strapped to the backs of the aphid-like creatures.

'The flowers are most impressive,' said Taras. 'The scent overpowering.'

'Naturally, the large scale production and gathering is mechanised, out in the immense plantations, where we grow our main food.'

Sandy gently mimicked Furzz in her mid-west US accent. 'Naturally.'

'*Tais toi!*' hissed Taras at Sandy.

'Sorry Ambassador,' Sandy murmured back.

As a career diplomat, Taras expected Sandy to live up to her four science doctorates, and act her 96 years.

The procession reached the Palace, and begun ascending the short flight of stairs to the lofty entrance. The building seemed to be of a brown resin like substance, striking gaudy rococo like motifs on its facade.

Guards in blue thorax and grey blue abdomen stood on either side of the entrance, holding a kind of laser rifle. The moving walkway took them to another tall Romanesque arch, through an entrance leading to a high domed hall, where the Queen awaited. Even from afar, it was clear the Queen was at least twice the size of Furzz. From memory, Taras knew she was one point seven meters tall.

The party sombrely traversed towards the impending Queen, which brought home to Taras how alien life had become for him in recent years. As a scientist, he'd studied entomology, familiar with the *hymenoptera,* but the large size of these insectoids left him astounded. The denser atmosphere, a stronger material for the exoskeleton and gills instead of breathing tubes.

It should not have been surprising the Queen was so much larger; still, it elicited trepidation from him as they drew closer to the regal presence. The Chamberlain bowed low on approaching the royal frame, and Taras followed protocol by imitating the bow, as did Sandy. The Chamberlain displayed the Ambassadorial credentials, introducing both humans to the sovereign.

Her bulbs began a leisurely blinking, which came through his translator as; 'We are pleased you answered our request to visit us Ambassador. We hope this will allow both our species to make a fresh start.' She unexpectedly rose and walked down the steps towards him, on her four legs.

'It is our fervent hope we can establish mutually beneficial relations,' responded Taras.

'I think we need to dispense with the formalities,' she flashed at Taras.

'I am called Zarag. Let us retire to an antechamber and get to know one another.'

'I am entirely at your disposal, ma'am,' said Taras.

The Queen led the way to the left, trailing a retinue of servants behind her. Guards opened the way into a spacious chamber, and Taras noticed chairs and a table had been provided, next to a long flat couch. 'Please, make yourselves comfortable,' the Queen indicated, pointing at the chairs. 'I hope they are suitable for your human form?'

'Most suitable,' responded Taras, waiting until Zarag had reclined on the couch, before seating in the chair next to her. His Chief of Staff took the remaining chair. A bowl of nectar and a basket of pollen was brought in, and placed on a low table near Zarag. Another insectoid servant brought a variety of drinks, and placed them on the table around which the humans sat.

'I won't keep you long,' the Queen's bulbs blinked. 'I'm sure you're tired from your journey, and would probably like to freshen up. Your quarters are ready and waiting, on the fiftieth floor. They're the diplomatic apartments for our visiting guests.'

'Your kind ma'am,' said Taras.

'We had intended the Klitka Hive brood queen be in attendance, to offer her *own* apology for the unfortunate behaviour of her hive members, in kidnapping one of you humans, but she has refused to travel. She has a perfectly good anti-grav platform, but claims it's out of order. This matter *will* be pursued. In the mean time, *I* offer you our sincerest apologies, yet again.'

'We unreservedly accept your apology,' answered Taras.

'There is a question I am most curious to ask concerning my fellow species on your planet. I'm informed seventy-eight percent of the animals on your planet are similar to our species. Am I informed correctly?' *Was it a benign question?* Taras wondered. There was no way of ascertaining this from her features.

'Yes ma'am, correct, but you have an advantage—in being somewhat different. Only a small percentage are like yourselves, producing miniature adults at birth. The vast majority, produce a larva stage, then pupate before emerging as an adult,' he stopped to see if she was following.

'Please, go on. I am most fascinated.'

'I must point out ma'am, our planet has a far greater gravity, and most of *our* insects are small and short-lived, that is, compared to the human species. An insect on our planet my size, wouldn't be able to stand because the exoskeleton would break.

It would seem here the lower gravity gave a boost during your early evolution. Your exoskeleton is supported by silicon tubules giving load-bearing capacity unknown to our insects—and you have lungs instead of a simple tubular respiratory system. If *our* insects were your size, they would collapse.' He had to go careful not to upset the sovereign, or the visit would fail.

She interjected on a new course, 'We know of your larval species, but cannot find a reason why they evolved. I'm sure *our* scientists understand the technicalities, but have *you* a simpler explanation?'

He had the impression she was teasing. 'Yes ma'am. The larva stage is almost another species, with a different feeding niche. If all the adult forms were starving, or became extinct, then the larva form *might* survive. The diversification was a survival strategy. It would seem since the latter form now dominate, the strategy may have vindicated itself.' *She must surely know all this*, thought Taras.

'Yes...I see. Hmm—now it's a little clearer than when *my* experts tried to explain the process,' and again he had no way to judge her sincerity. 'Have you any questions you would like to put to me?' She shifted her enormous bulk on the couch: was it impatience?

'Nothing that can't wait till later discussions,' responded Taras. All this time, Sandy listened carefully, but made no comment. At one point, Taras had the distinct impression she was dozing with her eyes open.

'We will talk again, but for now, the Chamberlain will escort you to your rooms. I fear you are somewhat tired,' and the humans were dismissed. The time was early evening. On Earth, they would have been invited for an official dinner reception. On Murangi, protocol was dictated by insect feeding habits and not nearly so formal.

Maybe Zarag had noticed Sandy wasn't paying much attention. *I can't read the insectoids expressions, or emotions, but maybe they can read ours?* Taras was mulling this over in his mind, worrying, as Furzz ascended in a turbo lift with them to the 50th Floor—to the diplomatic apartments. He *was* tired, and needed some real human food.

To his utter relief, their hosts had installed a food generator into their apartment, programmed with Earth food. Taras freshened and then called next door, on Sandy. Normally he would have summoned her, but this time he wanted to talk to her socially; as one human to another.

'Were you asleep earlier, when I was talking to Zarag?' he hadn't meant to start with a rebuke.

'You noticed? I'm sorry sir, it won't happen again,'

'I didn't intend it as a reprimand. I was simply surprised you could just nod off like that, with your eyes open,' he was trying to understand his new Chief of Staff. 'Were you so bored, or simply so tired?'

'When the Queen spoke, I kept looking at the flashing bulbs on the tip of her antenna, and I think the combination of tiredness, and those flashes, almost mesmerised me. Ambassador, I know you rely on me to keep up, even stay ahead of what's happening, so I promise, it won't happen again.'

'Okay. Enough of that! I know you're new, but I do trust you. Have you eaten yet?'

'I was just about to, when you knocked.'

He consciously softened his demeanour. 'Good! Then we'll have dinner together. I want to hear if you have any ideas on how we can turn this visit to our advantage. They do owe us for Adama's kidnapping, and I think they want to make amends. We must try to turn it to our gain. The people back home, would expect nothing less.'

After a lengthy dinner amid much planning, they finally turned in for the night.

Some time later, Taras heard noises erupt in the corridor—well into the night. There was a loud *thwack*, followed by another. Many running footsteps, more *thwacks*, and what sounded like the *sizzle* of a laser weapon discharging. Sandy came running in, without knocking—through the adjoining doorway—weapon at the ready in her hand.

'Are you all right Ambassador?' she hissed.

He was crouching by his bed with his weapon out.

She squatted beside him. 'All *hell* seems to have broken loose in the corridor.'

'Safest move, is to stay put, and leave them to it. Unless something comes through the door that threatens us, I propose we keep well out of it,' he pointed with his weapon to the door leading out into the corridor.

After twenty minutes, during more *crunching* and more feet running along the corridor, the ruckus eventually subsided. Now the silence began to get at them. It was not knowing what had occurred that unsettled them. When the quiet seemed permanent, Taras ordered Sandy back to her room and bed, and then followed back to his bed. They would find out in the morning.

At breakfast, Sandy was making speculative comments about the previous night's ruckus, when Furzz sent a request asking to see them. The Chief Officer of the Queen's Household arrived and was made comfortable on a couch, at Taras' invitation.

'You may have been woken, in the middle of the night, by a series of noises in your corridor,' he began. 'We profoundly apologise. Let me assure you, we have fully dealt with the matter.'

'And what matter are you referring to?' Taras inquired.

'In the past, we tended to prevaricate if an unpleasant situation occurred. We now find, when dealing with humans, it is best to be forthright and honest.'

'That's most refreshing, *and* reassuring,' Taras said.

'Last night, members of the Klitka Hive penetrated our security, and attempted to cause you harm. The palace security forces beat off the attack, and arrested those responsible. Our Security Council is currently in session, deciding what to do about the Klitka Hive. If the rogues emanate from the top, then the whole Hive may be terminated. If it is only a disgruntled few, then they must be caught and dealt with. The Klitka brood Queen, and her advisors, have been summoned to the Supreme Sovereign this day. We invite you to attend, and witness our judicial system.' After this lengthy speech, the chamberlain's antennae ceased flashing.

'I believe, we will take up your invitation to attend,' Taras quickly accepted.

'Good! That's settled then. First, we offer you a tour of Murangi, and then in the evening, we will hold the Klitka Inquiry. Will that suit you?'

'Yes, indeed it will. You're most kind.'

The Chamberlain then proceeded to leave; telling them the tour would commence in half an hour.

Sandy turned to Taras with a quizzical expression, 'Why are you so keen to attend their judicial process?'

'The binding force of any civilisation is the strength and determination of its legal system. It is the legal system that enforces commercial contracts, and allows trade to proceed in an orderly manner. If the legal system is weak, or fails to protect the members of society, then banditry and piracy becomes the order of the day,' Taras paused for emphasis. 'That is what I wish us to witness,' he continued. 'The determination of Murangi's legal system to prevail. Today, we shall see if we can safely trade with these insectoids.' He led the way to the door. 'They are masters of chemistry and genetics, and humans will encounter them a lot more, especially since they need to swarm and find new planets to colonise.'

They went into the corridor, which looked freshly sanitised. Not a sign anything had taken place the previous night. They'd heard laser firing, but there were no scorch marks. They took the turbo lift to the ground floor—Furzz awaited them.

'This way. We have a flitter waiting for your tour. It's been strengthened and enlarged to take your weight. It's in the plaza.'

They went through the main entrance, to the plaza. In front of the palace, they found a flitter with a delicate dragonfly array, shimmering in the morning dew.

'That is one of the most beautiful and delicate flying machines I've ever seen,' commented Taras.

Sandy just stared in amazement—the elegant lines took her breath away. It seemed such a flimsy contrivance. The pilot stood with open doors, waiting for them to climb aboard. They settled serially, behind one another. The doors closed, and they heard the gentle flapping of the iridescent wings. Then a rapid high pitch buzz took over as the beating of the wings increased, and the flitter became airborne.

They climbed, the engine barely audible. The panoramic vista of a flower filled planet lay spread out like a giant garden. From somewhere in the cockpit, a voice—probably the pilot—began a set speech—it might have come from any guided tour.

'Our society is made up of social hives,' it intoned, 'and the large structures you will see, reaching into the heavens, are the hives themselves.'

In the distance, they glimpsed a number of the tall structures mentioned, spaced apart by hundreds of kilometres. Everywhere, there were fields of flowers being worked with mechanised pollen gathering equipment.

'Each Hive is controlled by a brood queen,' the disembodied voice continued, 'and all the hives on Murangi elect a supreme Queen to govern the planet, for an eight year period. You met our current supreme queen yesterday.'

Throughout the day, the droning voice and the tour —continued. But even beauty could become monotonous, with field after field of flowers. For a low gravity planet, there weren't many mountains; in fact, there weren't any mountains to speak of. The oceans were equally distributed with regard to the landmass, and after the first few thousand kilometres, a sort of sameness set in, which the humans couldn't dispel.

Around noon, Sandy spied three other flitters heading their way, from below. A burst of green light passed her cock-pit window and she yelled, '*Someone's shooting at us.*'

Taras was banging on the pilot's partition with his fists, gesticulating in the direction of the oncoming flitters. The pilot was nodding, and rolled the flitter to avoid the laser bursts.

'*Dive...dive....,*'Taras shouted at the pilot.

Sandy had her hand over her mouth to prevent herself from screaming. The flitter went into a steep climb, trying to outmanoeuvre the attacking flight. A number of times, the flitter rolled out of the way of the laser beam at the last moment. Then more flitters appeared—out of nowhere, attacking the attackers. The aerial dogfight lasted a matter of minutes. Sandy and Taras watched as the three attackers were blown out of the skies.

Their flitter landed at the nearest hive, and they got out trembling, terrified.

'Are you all right?' Taras walked to Sandy, putting his arms around his quivering Chief of Staff.

'I do-do-don't know,' she stuttered.

The Squadron Leader of their rescuers landed, and came towards them.

What Taras heard in his translator was, 'I'm not a diplomat so I'll put this bluntly: you had a narrow escape!'

'That's understating it,' Taras growled. Then he remembered he was talking to his saviour, 'We are grateful for your intervention; thank you!'

'It was our duty to protect you,' the insectoid Squadron Leader replied.

'Who were they?' Taras asked.

'There were no markings on the flitters and the pilots are all blown to pieces, so we can't see their hive colours. There will be an inquiry. *We will find out who they were, you may be sure. A simple genetic test.*' The latter was translated with malice.

They had landed at the Zind Hive, and all the hive members were distinguished by a green thorax and a blue abdomen. They came running to the field where the flitters were parked, a little distance way from the Hive itself. Servants were setting up a table, two human type chairs were brought out of the flitter, and a number of insectoid couches placed in a semicircle.

The brood queen, Queen Myzor, appeared on her anti-grav platform, followed by her entourage. She rested the platform in a vacant niche in the semicircle. Around 6.8 meters in circumference, she was twice the size of the administrative queen they'd met earlier. Food was brought out—for the queen, followed by human food and drink. Clearly, all had been prepared in advance.

Sandy, a little more composed now, seemed to have struck up a nervous conversation with one of

Myzor's many aides. Taras talked of their ordeal with the Queen, who was most apologetic such a horrendous thing had occurred to their invited guests—in *her* Hive precinct.

Near the end of the visit, she cautioned, 'It would be unwise for you to go on alone. The squadron will accompany you for the rest of your journey, unless you wish to return to the capital?'

'No! I insist this journey be completed. I will not bow to a bunch of terrorists,' Taras was adamant.

'What about your assistant?'

'Why don't you ask her?'

'I go where the Ambassador goes!' Sandy replied.

'It is common knowledge in the Zind Hive—the Klitka Hive is out to get you humans,' Myzor told them.

Taras wanted to know, 'Is that the Hive, or just some rogue members. I mean is Katana involved?'

'The Klitka brood queen has always been a bit xenophobic to all other species, but I don't think a *brood queen* would be involved in any attempt to harm *guests*.' Myzor could not bring herself to believe such a thing was possible.

They thanked her, and went on with the tour for the rest of the day—the presence of the accompanying squadron giving then a feeling of safety.

Any previous twinges of monotony had completely vanished. By late afternoon, they found themselves approaching the plaza they'd left from. They weren't conscious of having turned back, yet here they were at their starting point.

Returning to their apartment on the 50th floor, Sandy looked furtive and whispered in Taras' ear. 'Back at the noontime meal, I got talking to one of Myzor's aides. She told me, some of the hives smuggle drugs to other species, and she had the strong impression the Klitka Hive was one of the ring-leaders in this trade.'

'Why are you whispering to me?' Taras wanted to know.

'Because I think our apartment is probably under surveillance,' she looked around again.

'That as may be, but *we* have nothing to hide,' he said loudly.

She shrugged her shoulders, 'In that case we have to assume the Klitka brood queen *is* involved, at least tacitly, if not explicitly, in the attempts on us.'

'Let's see what transpires at the judicial inquiry,' suggested Taras. 'We'll know where we stand with Murangi, when we see how they conduct this inquiry.'

A note arrived from Zarag, apologising profusely for the *unfortunate incident* they had been put through that afternoon.

'Is that supposed to make it okay,' Sandy said loudly.

*   *   *

After they'd eaten and rested, a call from below informed them they should descend to the great hall. They would be escorted into the legal chamber for the Klitka Inquiry. They were ushered through a series of large rooms, until they reached one with four of the Queen's Life Guards, armed to the teeth, barring their way. The escort flashed something at the guards, and they quickly opened the door.

Inside, Furzz was waiting. There was a large circular room with a sunken area in the middle. Four tiers of couches surrounded the sunken section, permitting those on the couches to look down in a superior manner.

As the humans settled next to Furzz, on specially provided human chairs, another great door retracted into the ceiling. A large brood queen entered, riding an anti-grav platform. From her complexion, yellow thorax and green abdomen, they immediately recognised the Klitka colours. The platform manoeuvred itself into the central chamber, and only then did Zarag enter with her retinue. It seems she was to be the presiding judge. She settled on a large couch, raised on a dais, with two immense red flowers on either side of her, holding large reservoirs of nectar. It looked like she was going to be there for some time.

The large circular room began filling with various insectoids. It seemed each hive on the planet had sent observers. A special discreet audio translation had been provided for the humans, enabling them to follow the proceedings.

The only audible sounds in the room were the rubbing of raptorial forelegs, substituting for arms, and the occasional movement of a couch. The proceedings were accompanied by a series of furious flashes of the luminous bulbs on their antennas by one party, and return flashes by the responding party.

The clerk of the inquiry flashed out the accusations. The Murangi Government accused the Klitka Hive, represented here by the brood queen, that on the previous night, they attempted to assassinate guests of the Murangi Government. That during this afternoon, they had attacked the flitter carrying the humans, in an attempt to kill the same guests.

Was Queen Katana aware of her hives plot? Did she encourage the plot in any way? Was she informed of what was happening in her hive? Were her advisors involved in the plot? Did her advisors know of the plot? Did her advisors know what transpired in their own hive? Was the hive *ruled* by the brood queen or *not*? Was she aware other hives considered the Klitka hive leader in a conspiracy to usurp law and order on Murangi? Why did she refuse to meet with the human visitors? Why did she refuse to apologise for her hives kidnapping? The questions went on and on...relentlessly for well over four hours.

Zarag was relentless, and the massive Katana shifted her weight more than once in discomfiture. All of Katana's answers pointed the finger at her advisors, on whom she *relied* to govern the hive, and centred on her advisors not doing their jobs properly.

So that's how it's going to be. Thought Taras. *The queen's advisors are going to be the fall guys. They're being sacrificed to save her.* He felt revolted by Queen Katana's obvious cowardice. It seemed rulers were the same all over the Galaxy.

Evidently, Zarag was equally disgusted by the brood queen's answers. She called a halt to the proceedings, announcing they had sufficient evidence from the brood queen, and she could return to her hive— for the moment. If she was required the next day, she would be summoned. Zarag would retire to consider whether or not to prolong the inquiry, or bring in a verdict, coupled with the incriminating evidence gathered by the Security Services.

When the humans were back in their apartment, Taras sat Sandy down.

'Tell me, what was your impression of how the court was conducted?' he asked.

'Well...I can't say I would want to be accused by it,' she said hesitantly.

'Bearing in mind what I said earlier, is their legal system strong? *Can* we do business with them?'

'*Strong?* I think it may be a little *too* strong,' she answered. 'It seems to be somewhat autocratic.'

'Never mind. Before we had a unified legal system on Earth, there were many fragmented systems of law; some were even based on religious revelations. The religions even refused to accept a clear distinction between secular and religious law, because they claimed the religious laws were revelations from their god. Then there were ethnic traditions, and *their* legal codes. All that changed. Out in the Galaxy we are going to come across some esoteric legal systems, and frankly, they are not to be condemned by our notions of legality. It's none of our business whether they're fair or not, but we must be able to determine whether we can do contractual business with them. We do have the Galactic Court to fall back on, with arbitration, but we ought to be canny enough to avoid getting tangled with the Galactic Court. Do you understand what I'm getting at Sandy?'

'Yes sir. I'm beginning to see *why* you were so keen to attend this inquiry.'

'My recommendation to Earth, will be—we can do business with Murangi, but only if the findings go as I expect. If they don't, I'll have to think again.'

The next day Zarag announced she had enough evidence to come to a verdict, to *terminate* the Klitka Hive. Not only was it deemed to be out of control, but the criminal activities of the hive were a source of friction with the Grand Custodian, and the other members of the Galactic Federation.

This attack on the humans, in Zarag's own palace, had been last straw. They had been warned a number of times, but chose to ignore the warning, and now they must *all* pay the price. The known culprits would be reprogrammed; Katana would be sterilised and retired; her advisors would be made docile, and join Katana; the rest of the hive would be genetically re-coloured; reprogrammed, and spread to other hives. That was Queen Zarag's decree.

The totality of the judgement took Taras' breath away. Nobody was actually going to be put to death, although that's what he'd expected, but everything had been thoroughly disposed of, and tidied up.

Later that day, Taras had another chat with Queen Zarag. They agreed to investigate the possibility of a number of treaties between the Solar System and Murangi, and to set up a working party to thrash out differences. Taras officially invited Zarag to visit the Solar System, and the Queen in turn invited the head of the World Government, and the President of Mars, to make a State visit to Murangi.

'So that's the end of the Klitka conspiracy, *and* the Klitka Hive,' he said to Sandy. 'I must say, they've been fair—and ruthless.'

Chapter Twenty-Nine

Grand Convention

The time had arrived, so the ancient Federation protocols ordained, for the Galactic Federation members to gather in a conclave, and elect the next Grand Custodian.

The fifty-year term of the venerable K'Rel of Kaikon had run its duration, and the time had come to begin the consultations to replace him. Many said it would be a tough performance to emulate. Throughout his term of office, he'd brought stability, prosperity, and above all, maintained the long peace among the fellow members of the Federation.

* * *

Holding the gathering on Klosh was a bold move, and a strange experience for most of the delegates. Klosh was a planet with one gigantic sea, a sea floating in space. It was eighty-seven per cent ocean, and only thirteen per cent land. It made the many land dwellers nervous; most were unaccustomed to so much water. What land there was, protruded as mountainous peaks from the imposing body of water as though seeking to escape.

During this particular cycle of "orbital eccentricity" in the planet's journey around the two suns, Klosh's polar ice caps had melted. This was coupled with the worst stage of its "axial tilt" and "axial procession," causing a catastrophic inundation every ninety thousand years, lasting for around twenty thousand years. The land was flooded and the magnificent cities inundated.

Yet, Kileni's home planet had been chosen to hold the exalted Grand Convention. One of the protruding mountain tops had been flattened and the ensuing plateau now held the bustling thriving skyscraper city of Maresh, whose buildings rose a kilometre into the clouds. This acted as the relatively new capital of Klosh.

Ambassadors Taras Fisenko and Basil Dukas found the view from their apartment stunning. They were half a kilometre above the blue-green ocean, with the occasional cloud rolling by their windows. Magnificent! They stood on the terrace overlooking the city, agreeing they'd never seen anything as imposing, or as breathtaking as this panoramic spectacle they beheld.

The door retracted into the ceiling—Kileni ambled in on his tentacles into their apartment through the half-moon entrance. He was remarkably agile on those muscular appendages. The door slid silently down behind him.

'Gentlemen, how are you settling in?' He moved to one of the couches suited to his form, and reclined.

'The air's too rich—but invigorating,' Taras responded.

'But outside.....,' Basil swept his hand across the sea.

'Damp?' Kileni offered.

'*Really* damp, almost suffocatingly so,' Basil said, half serious, but with a smile.

'It's an interesting contrast—the rich oxygen almost compensating for the high humidity,' suggested Taras.

Taras asked, 'Kileni! If there's little or no biomass, how on Klosh do you have...?'

'Such rich oxygen content...?' Kileni finished for him. 'Technology, my dear sir. We have underwater fusion powered fractionating columns breaking down the water into oxygen and hydrogen. The oxygen...well—you're breathing it—the hydrogen we use as fuel.'

Later Taras swore; Kileni seemed smug.

'So why do you put up with the flooding, when there's all that technology available to prevent it?' Basil wanted to know.

'Sooner or later everybody gets round to asking the same question. Ambassador Dukas! I was informed you'd been to Kaikon. Is that correct?'

'Why yes! News travels,' Basil had a momentary twinkle in his eye.

'Kaikon is a volcanically active planet; they are able to transform that, yet they prefer to live in their aerial cities. Did they tell you why?' Kileni turned his large yellow eyes on the Martian Ambassador.

'Yes *indeed*. There was a well-informed guide, K'Gar was his name, who related the story, and I quote..."They both missed the vanished green Kaikon, and loved the fiery new red Kaikon." They could have terraformed the planet, put it back on a more circular elliptic orbit, but they chose to leave it as an example of the Universe's handiwork; as..."A monument to the triumph of spirit over adversity."' Basil was lost in his memories for a moment.

Kileni continued, 'In a sense, we too are loath to interfere, even though it causes this periodic chaos. We are an old civilisation, prone to introspection. We did stabilise the ice caps for one cycle, half a million years ago, but lost more than we gained. We gained a warp drive, and began to lose the planet's humidity, which in turn produced changes in our skin porosity. We became more rigid, less flexible, both physically and mentally.

'Our evolution has produced a species *able* to live on land, but delights in the aquatic environment. We need both, and our planet supplies both, as long as we adapt to the planet, and not the other way round. Following each inundation, we go through a period of renewal, rejuvenation, and emerge as a stronger and reinvigorated civilisation.' After this lengthy speech, Kileni turned to Basil. 'Does that explanation give you any comfort?'

'Hmm! It sort of makes sense—as it did on Kaikon. Even on Mars, my home planet, we have stabilised the atmosphere at a little less oxygen than on Earth, and the population has adapted by developing larger lungs. We could have got rid of the desert, but we haven't. Turning each planet we come across into another version of Earth may not be the solution. It may be more environmentally friendly to adapt, to go with what the other planet has to offer, rather than go with a mentality that forcibly terraforms everything.'

'Well, I never,' Taras exclaimed. 'This is a side of you I've never heard before. You sound like an old fashioned environmental warrior. Everyone is environmentally conscious now, but you sound like a campaigner, a fighter for universal environmentalism.'

Kileni watched—listening to this side of the human character. Then said, 'My sentiments are with Ambassador Dukas. He seems to understand our inundation philosophy. That's most comforting for our future relations.'

Basil explained with conviction, 'In the last year I've been thinking: the human race joined the other races in a fully developed galactic civilisation, and I think our tendency for adapting the universe to suit ourselves ought to be reversed. If we're to fit in, *we* must adapt. I'd like to believe New Mars was our *last* huge terraforming project.' Basil was serious.

Taras stood stunned. He'd just heard Basil criticise his predecessor, now Governor of New Mars. Was this a personal squabble, or a different philosophical approach? Did Basil resent Theo Ghali, the *son* of the Martian President? Taras would have to look into this in more depth—it might affect Basil's decisions; maybe even have a knock-on effect on Earth's policies. Inherent bias in human reasoning was taught at Diplomatic school. If the budding diplomats were conscious of bias, then objectivity might have a chance.

Basil will need watching.

Firmly Taras changed the subject, 'How long is the selection of the new Grand Custodian going to take?' He looked at Kileni.

'The previous convocation was reasonably quick and took around two of your weeks,' Kileni answered. 'The one before, that lasted nigh on seven of your months. It all depends on the candidates put forward. Have you anyone in mind?' That surprised both Ambassadors.

Was he really expecting them to divulge, whom they were going to vote for, Taras thought. 'I hope it's quick this time. We intend to keep an open mind, and as the newest member, we will need to carefully listen before coming to a decision,' Taras looked conspiratorially at Basil.

Their round of intense discussions with their respective Governments before they came to Klosh, now made them wary of outside influences. Apparently, a number of Planetary Ambassadors had been in touch with the President of the World Government, and the President of Mars. They were endeavouring to influence the choice. Offers were made—rejected—promises ventured and declined. All accomplished diplomatically and with the greatest of tact, so as not to aggrieve any of the proposing parties.

Moreover, Ying Li and Simeon Ghali had decided to assert an independent streak in their relations with the Galactic Federation. They wished to exhibit themselves as a vigorous independent species that could not be bought. This time round, they didn't have sufficient information as to how the Galactic Council power structures aligned themselves. Waiting another fifty years would simply be prudent.

'We have an old saying. "Showing all your tentacles leaves nothing in reserve." You're wise to be cautious on who you support to exercise supreme power,' Kileni conceded.

'I'm sure your right,' Taras agreed. 'I'm reminded of an ancient British politician who remarked ". . . that all power is a trust—that we are accountable for its exercise—that from the people, and for the people, all springs, and all must exist." We are merely Ambassadors *of* our Government *and* our people, instructed by them, and accountable to them. We will try to do what's in their best interest.'

It was Basil's turn to stare at Taras. 'I wish I'd said that. In any case, I support those sentiments,' and he made a small bow in Taras' direction. 'On a different note—tell me Kileni; isn't it time we made an appearance down in the Convention Hall?'

'That's apt. Shall we...' Kileni made a move towards the half-moon door, which retracted into the ceiling.

They proceeded towards the free-fall shaft and floated down an exhilarating eighty floors on a cushion of air. When they reached the ground floor, they headed for the enormous Convention Hall. It had been organised into two tiers; the top tier for the one thousand, one hundred and thirty-four delegation chiefs, which comprised the Electoral College. The latter were voting chairs. The ground tier was for their supporting staff. The 1,134 votes were encoded with electronic passkeys to prevent blocking and double voting.

The Hall was called to order and the opening ceremony began. Primus Kolen of Klosh welcomed the delegates—then handed over to his number two, Vice Primus Roleni, presiding over the convention. Grand Custodian K'Rel then gave a farewell speech as the outgoing incumbent, wishing his successor all the best. The opening ceremony lasted for a good hour, short by any standard.

On adjacent screens in front of Taras and Basil, appeared the nominees for the vacant Grand Custodianship. There were forty-seven names followed by their seconders. By Potong's name there appeared the names of Earth and Mars, Potong being the Primus of Barog. Primearch Reithur of Rakh was the natural quadrant candidate, but he was getting on in years, and thus instead put his weight behind Barog.

Only then could Kileni see whom the Solar System delegation favoured. Amongst the list of names was that of Ying Li, seconded by Barog. The two newest members had agreed to support each other's candidates in the first round of voting.

The Solar-Barog coalition was designed to flush out the various alignments. To start the ball rolling, Chair Roleni suggested an immediate vote. This revealed Potong had twenty-two per cent of the votes, putting him into the second round. Ying Li only managed two per cent, and was duly eliminated.

That only four candidates went forward into the second round looked promising to Taras and Basil. In one sweep, forty-three names had been eliminated from the contest. Both thought the convention could turn out to be a short.

Chair Roleni decreed a recess till the next day, to allow the Electoral College to assess the implications of the last vote, and to allow for further consultations amongst the delegates. At this point Taras noticed the delegates who voted for Primus Potong gathering near himself and Basil, waiting for a joint meeting. They got up and joined the group, and were surprised to find Kileni in the group.

'You're a welcome sight,' opened Taras, and walked over to him.

'I think you'll find most of our quadrant in this gathering,' Kileni said. 'We have a room available to us over there in that recess,' he pointed to the wall at the back of the tier.

Kileni led the way, and the assemblage followed him into the spacious room. The door descended, cutting of the noise from the Hall. It looked as if the room had been well prepared, and Kileni swept a tendril at two seats clearly meant for the human physique. The seating arrangements were circular, everyone facing each other across an old fashioned round marble table.

Kileni squatted on a couch on his four flexible feet, looking comfortable, if somewhat bulky. He was like a beige beanbag with feet and two pairs of manipulative tendrils extending from shoulder height. His beaked mouth invited his fellow delegates to their resting poses, and then trained his two enormous bulbous yellow eyes on Portuk, the Ambassador for Barog.

'It's clearly no accident there are only four nominees left for the post. The four quadrants of the galaxy have been in intense consultation with their constituents, and have each agreed to support one of their number. That is evident from our gathering here.' He looked around at the differing ocular styles. 'I suppose the first order of the day is to elect a chair amongst us.'

Kileni was unanimously to chair the mini-convocation, despite his protestations.

'I must say I'm uncomfortable with this degree of polarisation. Blocs always tend to come to discord when they're thwarted,' he intertwined his tentacles on the tabletop. 'I'd have been happier if we had some cross quadrant activity. If there's little cross quadrant lobbying, then we may be in for a long election. At this point I think we need to hear if we can pull one of the other quadrants over to our cause?' He looked carefully at each delegate in turn. 'We have 269 planets in our quadrant, and the only hope we have of electing our candidate is to swing one of the other quadrant meetings behind ours,' Kileni now leaned back expectantly.

'We have been in touch with the Zyneer quadrant members,' the Falkiti delegate offered. 'Some of their planets are sympathetic to us.' The Falkiti was a delicate boned vertebrate with spindly appendages, and clearly from a light gravity planet, here supported by a structural brace-frame. Although the Falkiti was on the other side of the huge table, Basil heard him clearly thanks to acoustic technology and interpreting devices.

'That's also the Murangi quadrant, isn't it?' asked Basil, looking sideways at Taras. 'Didn't you establish cordial relationships with Queen Zarag of that planet?' Basil pressed Taras.

'I'm not sure it was enough to ask her to support us in this election. She has to be supporting her fellow species from Zyneer?' insisted Taras. 'After all, Zyneer is their quadrant HQ.'

'Well, if you think it'll do any good?' Taras left it hanging.

The humans had been conversing like this, oblivious of the rest of the room, which sat there quietly listening to them.

'Why not meet with the Murangi Ambassador and see what he has to say,' asked Kileni.

Other delegates also had contacts with various members of the Zyneer Quadrant. On Kileni's suggestion, the meeting decided to put their energies into swinging the various members of the Zyneer Quadrant onto their side. They didn't have nearly the same contacts with the other quadrants. The meeting broke up to put the plan into effect.

Basil disappeared until the evening. Taras went with Kileni and Portuk, taking twenty or so of the delegates with them. The group retired to a quiet holo-computer console to run some models on speculative alliances using parameters such as trade, personal friendships, private inside knowledge, and some other more sinister information. The rest of the delegates were dispatched to gather information as they could. They were to put various pressures on, and glean inside information on how the other three meetings were progressing.

Chapter Thirty

Below Klosh

The mini-convocations. The voting, the plotting. Then the voting again. Went on without let for a couple of weeks. The voting figures stubbornly remained roughly the same, with the Electoral College deadlocked. Proposals met with counter proposals. Quadrant allied with quadrant, only to renege on the deal at the last moment. Planets changed allegiances— then changed back, using it as a ploy to discover the strategies of the other side. Niccolò Machiavelli, had they heard of him, would have been quietly satisfied with their princely antics.

In the second week, some of the haggling became extremely acrimonious, with delegations walking out on each other. For the first time in a thousand years, there were even threats mooted to break up the Federation and set up a separate coalition. The humid ill-natured atmosphere in the Convention Hall could be cut with a laser.

Yet this, Kileni claimed, was merely posturing. An attempt to gain the ultimate prize of having the Grand Custodianship in their quadrant. His psephologists had predicted Primus Potong would eventually win because he was the only acceptable candidate to all the GF. The caustic arguments, the affectations; the heated altercations, were part of a vast ritual pantomime engaged in with much relish by the participants. Kileni claimed to have seen it all before. Taras and Basil found that hard to credit.

Both took the in-fighting seriously, and after two weeks, were openly exhausted. They spent their spare time in exercise exploring the flat land surrounding the city; the cramped raised tract of land standing above the adjacent sea. It was their way of escaping the stress of the endless negotiations. They had their immunisation shots for Klosh before they left Rakh, and felt safe sun bathing in the rays of the two suns of the binary system. To escape the humidity, they swam in the large filtered pool of their hotel.

The binaries caused the huge climactic changes— an inundation when the two suns were at their maximum distance, and a dry climate when they were close. The sea encircling them was full of dangerous life forms, strictly off limits to all except the Kloshi. The Kloshi had chutes going from the city, half a kilometre into the sea, and frolicked in the sea at every occasion, making the humans envious. At each opportunity Portuk joined the humans, and noticed their fatigue, despite the high oxygen content. He took Kileni aside and had a word with him. Kileni then suggested a small party join him in his submarine, to visit the inundated cities and maybe explore the beautiful bountiful sea.

On a day on which Chair Roleni proclaimed a day of recess, Kileni, Taras, Basil, and Portuk took the Convention Hall free-fall chute down to the basement. There, connected by a series of gigantic caverns, the humans discovered an immense underground port full of variously shaped submarines. When they'd boarded Kileni's small but spacious, and extremely luxurious submersible, Basil was bubbling with excitement.

'So this is how the cities stay in touch with each other,' exclaimed Basil.

'The complete lack of surface vessels puzzled the hell out of me, until now,' added Taras. 'I could see little aerial traffic, yet the cities clearly conducted large volumes of trade.'

'All you had to do was ask,' offered Kileni.

'These stubborn negotiations kept me too busy,' responded Taras. 'By the way. Your submarine shape reminds me of a dolphin back on Earth.'

'Really? A dolphin?' Kileni mused. 'Is that good? Must look it up. Anyway, Portuk noticed you were getting tired. I can't distinguish those nuances in humans yet, so I asked him to tell me if you were becoming stressed. This short trip will take all of our minds off the election.'

Basil turned to Portuk, 'Thanks Portuk.'

'And from me,' added Taras.

'I wanted to show you how we lived when the polar caps were in place,' Kileni said, as he gave orders to the on board computer. 'We'll run through the exit caverns out to sea within a short time,' he swept a tentacle in the direction of a portal, 'then we'll go through to the observation lounge at the bow.'

The sub got under way and moved through the caverns at a steady rate, following green pointers indicating their allotted outward route. They went downwards, and in fifteen minutes were out into the open sea.

They had to pass through the force field a kilometre out in the sea, surrounding the mountain city of Maresh. It was there to protect any Kloshi swimmers from the more ferocious sea creatures. In the bow, the group found themselves in a clear reinforced transparent bubble, with a panoramic view facing forward.

The sub began to run straight, at around twenty fathoms. Kileni joined the group, who were staring out into the blue-green waters. They saw a shadow appear just hanging out of sight, then a huge creature like a cuttlefish advanced, moving elegantly through the water by a series of undulations in its lateral fins, coming into view.

It came to the bubble and looked at the staring creatures inside . Then another appeared, joining its cousin looking into the sub. The large gazing yellow eyes reminded them of Kileni's eyes, although they were too polite to mention it. They stayed with the sub for a while, then swam off to join their unseen companions.

The submarine glided effortlessly through the darkness, going ever deeper. As the light faded, they came across a school of globefish lighting up a sizeable area of the ocean, attracting a variety of prey, which they then enveloped. Looking closely, the whole of the globefish seemed translucent, but managed to emit a powerful blue-white light. Near the sea bed there were monster spiny lobster-like creatures scurrying about, and predatory hide fish sitting in the silt on the bottom, waiting for a passing meal.

Kileni explained; they were on a vast plateau that before the inundation a thousand years ago used to be green pastures. Some two hundred kilometres further on there used to be the old shoreline, where the old sea had been. They were now some two hundred fathoms below the surface. Soon they made out non-natural shapes resolving themselves into some low-lying buildings. As they moved closer, more crumbling buildings become visible beneath. It turned out to be the decomposing silhouettes of a small town with large low bungalow style housing.

'A thousand yeas ago, before the inundation, we lived close to the ocean in low rise housing, never more than three or four floors. Now we live in skyscrapers,' clarified Kileni. 'This place used to be called Valiti and my whole family originally came from here.'

'So you brought us to visit your ancestors?' marvelled Portuk.

Along former streets now crawled giant sea slugs, large sea snails, with and without shells. There were a great variety of molluscs of every shape and colour. Some bore small shells, others were as large as any one of the onlookers.

Kileni aimed the sub upwards, away from his nostalgia. They neared a mountain situated on the plateau; Valiti stood at the base of that mountain. As the mountain loomed, they observed flower-like sea anemones stuck to boulders and huge starfish with powerful adhesive tube-feet clinging to rocks.

Unexpectedly from round the mountainside a gigantic shoal of small red fish emerged, millions of darting crimson flashes. It took the shoal a good half hour to go by, but whilst they were passing, the onlookers could only see cerise fish wallpaper. Immediately following were hungry predators, chasing the shoal.

There were sleek medium sized needlefish spearing the small red fish, scooping them in with small appendages. Razor fish with scythe like snouts swiped through the water cutting the small red fish in half, feeding on the bits. Great armoured fish with huge maws scooped up fish in large numbers. Finally, sea alligators with ravenous mouths and razor sharp teeth chased the feeding predators, especially the scythe fish.

The sub rose and came to waters containing a rich opaque thick green layer of phytoplankton suspended in the first few hundred meters below the surface. They noticed bizarre arrays of widely spaced tentacles, dangling a hundred meters below the surface.

'What on earth...*Sorry!* I mean what on Klosh is that?' Basil called out.

Kileni was giving commands to the on-board computer, and now turned towards what Basil was shouting about, barely visible outside the bubble. He discerned a forest of tentacles obscuring their vision.

'It's all right! It's only a colony of hydrozoans. Probably fifty meters wide, wind driven—living at the surface. Those are their tentacles suspended underneath. They're harmless!'

'It must be getting towards evening,' Taras changed the subject.

'We must get through to the Convention Hall,' suggested Basil, reading Taras' mind. 'Get an update on how the alignments are progressing. Who's meeting with whom? Maybe we need to start back?'

'Relax,' Kileni insisted. 'We have full com-link to the voting computer. We're on-line to the bulletin board. Nothing can happen behind our backs. Our staff at the Convention Hall has immediate access to us. So again I say; relax.'

'How long do you intend this trip to last?' Portuk asked.

'I had contemplated taking a couple of days to circumnavigate Klosh. Remember, the point of the excursion was to relieve the stress of the Convention Hall. If you're going to worry about the journey, maybe we should conclude the trip right now?' Kileni seemed a little offended.

'We appreciate your taking time to offer this tour,' Portuk jumped in quickly. He looked at Basil and Taras for support.

'Yes, of course,' Taras joined in, looking sternly at Basil.

'I'm sorry if I've offended by harping on the voting. Promise not to mention it again—swear,' Basil came over and stood by Kileni.

It had the desired effect.

Basil didn't notice Kileni wink at Portuk.

Whilst the interchange took place, the sub broke the surface. The bow observation bubble had a visual arc of some 270°, yet all they could see was lots of sky and the setting suns. No protruding mountains. The humans had expected the mountain they'd passed to be rearing out the water; they'd expected to dock on dry land for the night. They seemed momentarily confused. Then they noticed a huge bulbous object, inflated like a balloon, drifting into view. It was twice the height of the submarine, and Basil gave a little yelp.

Kileni looked in his direction. 'It's only a blowfish,' he said casually. 'They inflate and sit on the water dangling their long tentacles below the surface. They're feeding.'

'I must say! You have some extraordinary life forms in this sea,' Basil said awkwardly.

'And that?' Taras was looking in the other direction.

'Ah! That's a bit more serious. That's a giant sea snake. I mean it's more serious for the blow fish.' Kileni ordered the sub to back off.

The huge sea snake had its jaws wide open, set on a collision course with the blowfish. They were on the surface and Kileni expected some turbulence as the two outsized creatures joined in a death struggle.

'I think it might be prudent to retreat back under,' Kileni suggested.

He proceeded to give orders to that effect. The sub dipped below the surface, moving away from the colossal struggle in progress. Half a kilometre further, they entered a great forest of seaweed growing a hundred meters from the seabed, reaching for the light. It was a mass of various green, yellow, blue coloured algae, thick as trees, with a variety of other life forms living amongst the underwater forest. The sub had slowed to a crawl, trying to avoid hitting any of the sturdy trunks.

After a while, they were through the forest and out into clear sea. As they again reached the two hundred fathom line, the fauna change to more sinister silhouettes. Kileni pointed out large flat stun fish discharging colossal voltages at their prey. Three even had a go at the sub, which absorbed the charge and stored it in its energy banks. Nearer the bottom, they encountered large sea scorpions with immense claws. For some reason they seemed to have congregated at this spot on the ocean floor. Kileni implied they might be in the middle of their mating season, searching for partners.

The sub continued through the night, whilst the on-board party retired to their spacious cabins. The humans found comfortable beds in their quarters, and presumed Portuk was equally well taken care of. By morning, they reached another large inundated city; the former capital also named Maresh, much larger than the previous Valiti.

There was a mass of multi shaped and multi coloured coral growing along the wide boulevards. According to Kileni, this had been their planetary capital a thousand years ago. Now the sea floor contained an immense congregation of coral polyps forming rock-like ridges along the abandoned thorough ways. These were marine polyp invertebrates, hollow cylindrical bodies with a ring of tentacles round the mouth secreting chalky or horny skeletal material. They normally occurred with united branchings, encrusted into solid colonies. This proliferation suggested the sea was in a healthy vibrant shape.

After the former capital, the party observed schools of giant squid, and later on, came across some giant nautiloids with attractive long spiral shells. The excursion enchanted and calmed all those on board. The kaleidoscope of flora and fauna under the waters of Klosh had an uplifting effect on Taras and Basil. They encountered creatures similar to sea-urchins, sea-cucumbers, sea-lilies, all with locomotery tube-feet and calcareous exoskeletons.

Floating in the depths were large paramecium-like single-celled animals with elongated bodies rounded at the front, and oblique funnel-shaped grooves bearing the mouth at the tip. Closer to the surface were what looked like powerful jelly fish, similar to feeding sea hydra, trailing extended poisonous tentacles in search of prey.

By the time they'd circumnavigated Klosh, an atmosphere of ease and relaxation overcome everybody on board. The humans almost felt like humans again; less agitated, sharper and eager to get back into the fray.

Watching this, Kileni felt well satisfied with his philanthropic work, and thanked Portuk for suggesting it.

* * *

Back in the Convention Hall, Basil managed to inveigle Queen Zarag's Ambassador into promising his support to Primus Potong. The latter would happen only in the final ballot, however, and no one knew when that was going to take place. How on Klosh did he know when the final balloting was to occur?

While they had been at sea, enjoying the visual spectacle of underwater Klosh, ponderous shifts had occurred within the Quadrant meetings. Swathes of votes had shifted sides, and Chair Roleni had the distinct impression they were reaching a decisive point in the elections.

The Electoral College reconvened. Another vote was held. Primus Potong now commanded thirty-eight per cent of the vote; by far the largest bloc to date. A majority from the Zyneer Quadrant had thrown in their lot with the Rakhian Quadrant. Some of the Kaikonian Quadrant were in league with the Grafhi Quadrant, but some Kaikonian allegiance also crumbled—the latter came over to Potong.

The Zyneer Quadrant withdrew their candidate as hopeless, leaving only three candidates. Primus Potong of Barog with 38%, Primus Rhelo of Grafhi, 34%, and Primus K'Lor of Kaikon had 28%. If the Rakhian Quadrant gained more of the Kaikonian planets, the election would be over; but that equally could be said for Grafhi.

Two hectic days of bargaining, of horse-trading, of promises, finally produced the expected breakthrough. Most of the Kaikonian Quadrant threw their weight behind Potong, giving him the magical 51%. The election suggested many planets were unhappy. Taras heard Potong being called an "upstart, only in the Federation a mere two hundred years, and already with pretensions of guiding the destiny of over a thousand planets."

At the closing ceremony, Primus Potong gave a stirring speech of reconciliation, promising to work on behalf of all the planets of the Federation. He would bring with him justice and harmony, following in the footsteps laid down by his predecessor, K'Rel.

In Potong's speech he told them, 'I intended to consult—and to listen—to all advice without favour.'

That went down well, and seemed to heal some of the bruised egos.

Potong boomed, 'I call on Grand Custodian K'Rel to come up and share the platform with me. More—I invite him to be my Deputy for the next five years.'

That clinched it; a co-regency in the manner of the old Egyptian Pharaohs, Basil thought. Martians were always on about Pharaohs.

It was as predicted, a short election. The new Grand Custodian exuded a breadth of vision promising to bring continued stability, prosperity, and above all, to maintain the eternal peace among the fellow members of the Galactic Federation.

Chapter Thirty-One

Sneak Attack

The Earth-Mars Embassy on Rakh settled to its normal routine on the return of the two Ambassadors from Klosh. The after dinner conversation continued to revolve around the underwater journey.

Basil enthused, 'I loved Kaikon, but Klosh has stuck most memorably in my mind. Water and fire—eh?'

All of the Embassy staff was eager to hear of the watery planet.

A couple of days later, at breakfast, the outside world intruded. Taras waved a flexible A4 screen at Basil.

'Listen to this,' Taras motioned urgently to Basil, 'it's just been translated from the Rakhian Foreign Ministry.' He held the screen in his hand, reading from it. '"On Thursday September 3rd 3007, that's our time, a small fleet of renegade space ships attacked a Tofali outpost on Karn, the second moon of their outermost planet. Tofali, a member of the Kaikonian Quadrant, immediately lodged a protest with the Grand Council on Barog. They called for an emergency session of the Security Council, claiming they were attacked by Susina, a member of the Grafhian Quadrant."'

'Wasn't it the Tofali Ambassador who spoke on behalf of the breakaway group, when we were trying to get the Kaikonian Quadrant to join us in voting for Potong on Klosh? You remember, during the elections for the Grand Custodian,' Basil interrupted.

'Yes, I believe you're right,' answered Taras. 'Do you know; I think those witless hot-heads are still arguing over that damned election.'

'Are you suggesting they'd be stupid enough to start a brawl over a pedestrian ballot?' Basil was incredulous.

'According to this report, the Susini are blaming the Tofali for besmirching their honour. They claim the Tofali betrayed their pledge to stick with the Grafhi alliance. The Susini accuse the Tofali of being a bunch of deceitful dishonest scuzzbags,' Taras looked shocked at the undiplomatic language used. 'The whole report then continues in that vein. This could get serious if they don't moderate their language.'

'This is the one time when we need reports from somebody on the spot,' suggested Basil.

'Basil! I would send Sandy over to Portuk's, but I fear she'll overlook something. Be a sport and pop over to the Barog Embassy on both our behalves. Find out what's afoot, and how serious it *really* is.'

'Good idea! But if you don't mind, I'll take Sandy with me for company,' he winked.

Taras nodded and thought; *he's incorrigible.*

After Basil had gone, Taras rose from the breakfast table and went down to his office. He called Heidi Frisch in for a chat. She'd been seconded to the Embassy at his request, as permanent Security Officer, following the embarrassing episode with Yoshi Tanaka and the false Gupta.

'Colonel!' he acknowledged.

'Ambassador,' she responded.

'Please sit. I don't know if you're up to speed on the budding conflict between Tofali and Susina?' He gave her a chance to answer.

'No more than what you've heard. Three small spacecraft attacked the Tofali outpost on Karn. The

Tofali are livid, and have put their military on alert. They've lodged their grievance with the final arbiter, the Galactic Court on Barog, the Grand Custodian's home world. That move prompted the Susini to put their military on alert. That was the last I heard,' she sat back and looked attentive.

'You seem to be right on top of this. So, it was only three ships, not a fleet? Okay! So how do *you* assess the situation?' He looked at her with increased respect.

'It's probably only a border skirmish to restore injured pride; on the other hand it could blow into a full-scale conflict. It all depends on what restraints the politicians are exerting. Was the Susini attack supported by their military? More to the point; did the military mount it in disguise, or was it a private expedition of a few hot-heads?' She stopped to give Taras a chance to comment.

'Yes, those are the precise questions I want answered. We need to be well informed if we're not to get sucked in, or end up giving unintentional offence. Heidi!' he switched to a confidential tone, 'I want you to catch the next vessel to Kaikon, and if possible, to go on to Tofali. I want on the spot reports. We must have precise information to make rational decisions.'

'For what it's worth, I think the Security Council will send in a couple of StarCarriers, interposing them between the belligerents—pending the Galactic Court's decision on Barog.'

'If they do, see if you can get on board one of the StarCarriers. I'll give you my backing,' he rose from his chair.

Heidi got up and left the room, going up to her apartment to pack. She briefed her deputy on her mission, and handed over all her Embassy duties to him. Then she picked two of her best operatives, Leo de Vito and Marcus Reynolds, to accompany her. They were to back her up if it became necessary, and act as couriers if the need arose. They equipped themselves with the latest technics, communications, cloaking devices, and weaponry.

The little party left on the next regular spaceliner flight for Zyneer and Kaikon, hoping to connect to Tofali.

Transport in the galaxy was organised with Quadrants as hubs, so the flare-up shouldn't have interrupted the Kaikon to Tofali connection, both being in the same quadrant.

The journey to Kaikon was over seventy-two thousand light years from Rakh, on the other side of the Galaxy, and would need two days and two black hole jumps. The group settled in the oxygen lounge of the huge spaceliner and were soon glued to the Holo-Vid screens. They surfed news channels, looking for updates on the skirmish. They gleaned, things weren't looking good.

* * *

Whilst the GF Security Council was in session, with the belligerents in attendance, their military took the opportunity to up the stakes. The Tofali retaliated for the Susini attack on Karn, by occupying Macska, a Susini mining colony on their mutual border. They also deployed all their military spaceships, in a show of force, along their side of the boundary with neighbouring Susina.

Prior to both planetary systems joining GF, there'd been a history of numerous squabbles and acrimonious disputes. This led to a tradition of hostility between the two systems. For the two species, the present crisis was merely a continuation of ancestral enmity.

The show of force along the Tofali border activated old alliances, dormant since the coming of the GF. It was again energised by the perceived threat from their old enemies, fuelled by the presumed betrayals and illusory insults. Furthermore, the GF recognised the Susini were an exceptionally sensitive species, quick to take offence. This made implementation of the standing mechanism for conflict resolution doubly delicate.

The real problem in the whole morass was Grafhi. It was pushing all the buttons; it was the real instigator of the calamity simply using Susina as its *agent provocateur*. Primus Rhelo of Grafhi, the Grafhi Quadrant Custodian had set his two hearts on being the next Grand Custodian, and he didn't take kindly to being thwarted.

His anger was directed at Primus K'Lor of Kaikon, but being a realist, he knew he couldn't get at K'Lor directly. However, if he could cause a lot of trouble for Tofali, who were nominally under Kaikonian guardianship, then Rhelo could make K'Lor lose face, make Kaikon seem weak and unworthy of being the Quadrant HQ.

Thus Rhelo was hoping to stir K'Lor's Quadrant into revolt, and into choosing a different Quadrant leader. That was the overall strategy; the skirmishes were merely the tactics. When Tofali grabbed the mining colony, it precipitated the allies of the Susini, the planetary systems of Lakas, Meglep, and Nyugat to join the affray.

Instead of fomenting the desired revolt in the Kaikonian Quadrant, the addition of the three Susini allies expanded the conflict, and exacerbating the GF Security Council meeting on Barog. It cemented cohesion amongst the other members of the Kaikonian Quadrant, who all now felt threatened by the escalation.

All the Grafhi Quadrant space going traffic was quarantined. At that point, the GF Security Council sent in the three StarCarriers, *Ynar, K'Mar*, and *Thorap*, with their attendant battle formations.

The force of two hundred and twenty ships placed themselves between the two Quadrants. The StarCarriers were the largest spacecraft at GF's command, each carrying a complement of just over five thousand. It had the latest sophisticated technology equipped with an immense destructive firepower. It would be a foolhardy enemy that took on such a Battle Group.

But then again, the Battle Group had been constructed with just such a mission in mind, and if need be, it could be doubled in no time. Both protagonists ceased all warlike preparations when this Battle Group interposed itself between them.

*   *   *

When Heidi and her two companions arrived after the two-day journey at Kaikon, the GF Battle Group was just taking position between the two Quadrants. Whilst they teleported down to Kotka, the aerial capital of Kaikon, an uneasy peace had returned. The speed at which the GF Security Council moved took Heidi by surprise. It was as if they'd predicted the whole scenario; and in truth, they probably had.

Running vast conflict prediction models on the gigantic gluon-computers tended to place the GF one step ahead of any conflict. Always. In a sense, they should have nipped this one in the bud, but they hadn't foreseen such a violent reaction to a simple election issue. They made up for their lapse by placing the Battle Group on manoeuvres in the Kaikonian Quadrant, at the area needed.

Heidi requested to board the lead StarCarrier, but the permission had to go through channels; firstly to Earth and then to Barog. In Kotka, in the mean time, she took her group down what looked like a subterranean entrance. They descended by escalator to an underground Shopping Mall below and began the search for transport to Tofali. Theoretically, there was a daily vessel leaving for the planetary system, but in practice; travel had been suspended for the time being. The main booking office for the normal Spacelines told them to wait for a couple of days until services were restored.

She led her company to a café in the Mall, and ordered some food and drinks. There were trees growing everywhere, beautiful gardens, and a piazza atmosphere. A great deal of pedestrians milled around going about their business. The ceiling exuded a gentle sun-like radiance giving the impression they were out in the sunlight. This was also the source of the flora's dynamism. Around them were a profusion of shops doing a roaring trade. There seemed to be a frenzied atmosphere and Heidi put it down to an undertone of fear for the shopper's future.

'Hum! Excuse me!' a small Kaikonian stood by their table. 'My name is K'Gar. Can I be of assistance to you?'

Heidi looked at him, 'If you can tell me how to get to Tofali, you can help me. Won't you sit down?'

'Thank you. Why would you want to go there,' he inquired, taking a seat.

'Let's say, I have business there.' She hoped he wouldn't press her.

'I may be able to help, but I must know the nature of your business,' K'Gar turned his dark sharp eyes on her.

'We are on a reporting mission for the Solar Embassy on Rakh. It's an official mission for our Government.'

'If it's for your Government, then I might be able to help,' he smiled at her. 'The simplest way, is to hire a shuttle.'

She tried to look astonished, 'Why didn't I think of that!' She looked to the ceiling. Before the Kaikonian appeared, that was to be her next move.

'Would you like me to arrange it for you?' He seemed to have a permanent smile on his face.

'That would be kind. Are you sure you don't mind?' She seemed to be rummaging in her memory. 'You're the guide Basil Dukas mentions, aren't you?'

'Yes. I had the pleasure of showing Ambassador Dukas and his aide, Alexius Balbus, around Kaikon. The Ambassador seemed to enjoy Kaikon almost as much as we do.'

'Basil talks often of Kaikon, *and* of you. He has fond memories of this planet, but most especially of the volcanoes down below.'

'When you next see the Ambassador, give him my regards. If you please wait here, I will go and arrange the shuttle.'

With that, he hurried off down one of the walkways. Half an hour passed before he returned. This time, his smile was even broader, if possible.

He sat down and began, 'I have arranged a four seater shuttlecraft for your party. It's fuelled and waiting below. It belongs to the Kaikonian Government, but is discretely registered. You may use it as much as you need. When you've finished with it, press the "Return" button. It will find its own way home.'

'This is good of you. I have the distinct impression we're in the same business. I'm expecting a communication from our Embassy on Rakh. If it somehow gets routed through to you, will you be so kind as to forward it to me?' She looked closer at this Kaikonian operative.

'If I receive such a message for you, I will pass it on. Now, let me take you down to the shuttle. I presume you want to get on your way immediately?' He got up from the table.

Heidi moved briskly, with assurance and firmness of purpose, accompanied by de Vito and Reynolds. All followed K'Gar down another moving walkway on a descending escalator. On the floor below the Mall, there was a large landing bay for shuttles and a yawning exit leading out into the fiery red sky. K'Gar led the way to one of the shuttles. Standing before it, he fiddled with a small hand held gadget, opening the entry hatch. He then handed the gadget to Heidi and bade them all a safe journey. Turning from the humans, K'Gar retraced his steps back to the Mall.

'That was a real stroke of luck, him turning up like that,' de Vito exclaimed as they climbed aboard.

'*Luck*, was it?' Heidi questioned. 'I'd say we were monitored as soon as we teleported down; maybe even earlier.'

Reynolds busied with the shuttle controls, trying to look silent and efficient. He had a rough sombre appearance, trying to bring some of the Oregon Mountain man toughness to the fore. In contrast, de Vito had the charm and looks of a Neapolitan, a silky tongue and a ready wit. He was forever playing up to the woman in Heidi, but without much success. It wasn't a conscious attempt to woo her, but came from the natural makeup of the macho Latin inside him.

'Ready for lift-off, Colonel,' Reynolds reported.

Heidi got into the left control seat of the shuttle and took charge of the console. She asked Kotka flight control for permission to lift-off; this was given and she aimed the shuttle out of the bay, into the yawning exit, out into the fiery red sky. As the shuttle rose from Kotka into the blue-darkness of space, she thought; *Traffic Control didn't even ask me for my flight plan or my destination.* She felt uneasy; with so many people knowing she might be on a clandestine mission.

The course for Tofali was laid in, and the shuttle was put onto *automatic*. Heidi then sat down with her two agents for a discussion, but first, she swept the shuttle for any listening devices; it was clean. In the earlier two-day journey to Kaikon, she had not been certain who might be listening. Now she had decided was a good time for her operatives to be fully briefed on their mission, since she was assured they were completely alone out here.

'I couldn't tell you what our assignment was, because we were never alone. So now, listen carefully. We're going to Tofali, as you've already gathered. Essentially we're the on-the-spot reporters for Ambassador Fisenko. He needs to know how serious this conflict really is. In itself, it's a simple job. The down side, and implicit in our brief, is that if we get a chance we ought to sabotage the Susini alliance.' She knew this type of work was right up their alley.

Eagerness shone in their eyes. They could be in for a bit of action, and they liked the idea. That the action came much sooner than expected, was a big surprise to those on the shuttle.

*   *   *

The shuttle had completed three-quarters of the journey, when a small vessel hailed them from an asteroid, claiming a medical emergency. Cautiously Heidi responded, thinking it might be a trap. What caught her somewhat off guard was they were still in the

Kaikonian Quadrant, well away from the Susini border, and as such were not expecting any hostile behaviour.

The distressed vessel sent some horrendous pictures of carnage from their ship. It looked bad, and it would have been inhuman to have ignored the call for help. The Holo-Vid transmission indicated there had been a fire on-board the distressed vessel and a number of crew were shown as badly burned. "Could Heidi's shuttle transport the worst to Tofali? And then ask them to send a rescue vessel to the stranded ship." That was the request.

The pictures sent were phoney, and when Heidi landed on the asteroid, she encountered two more camouflaged vessels. Once Heidi had landed, one of the ambushing vessels lifted off and hovered over Heidi, to prevent any escape. A boarding party of six teleported unexpectedly onto their shuttle, and quickly immobilised the humans. Heidi was furious for falling for such a simple ambush. Reynolds tried to fight—was stunned by a weapon.

The humans were quickly put into a stasis field chamber, and were only released from it on Meglep.

Chapter Thirty-Two

K'San's Philosophy

On Meglep the humans regained consciousness, finding themselves in a nondescript room. A senior Meglep officer came and apologised to Heidi for the abduction. He explained the raiding party had panicked when they thought they had been discovered, and went into a pre-programmed evasion routine, which included removing any witnesses.

They had sneaked deep into the Kaikonian Quadrant, past the border patrols, cloaked and under orders to cause a little mayhem. They'd managed to cross the border just before the StarCarriers were placed in position. Heidi's shuttle had come as a useful gift in order to provide them with a diversion so they could return to their own side of the border. The shuttlecraft had been used to create chaos in one sector of space, whilst the raiding party sneaked back over the border, some distance from the chaos.

'We are sorry you had to be involved,' the officer was saying. 'You are the first humans I've come across,' he added quizzically.

'You're telling me your military was involved?' Heidi stared at the officer.

The officer ignored her quip, shifting on three flexible stumps, alternating from one to the other two. A ball like protrusion emanated above a uniform of impeccable finesse in deep scarlet, but to the humans, it seemed to hang badly on a shapeless upright stump. The outer skin of what passed for its head, the ball, seemed to be of a grey bark texture, all crinkled and indeterminate. Heidi could see no mouth or eyes, yet she clearly understood what it was saying. There were no visible appendages protruding from the uniform, barring those it was standing on, but the garment had Galactic Federation insignia on it, defining its rank as a senior officer, comparable in rank to Heidi.

The surreal nature of this alien both shocked and tickled Heidi. It was a child-like caricature of a robot, yet clearly sentient. It appeared to have a biological make-up, and was unquestionably in charge.

'Whilst we're being held captive; I'm sorry, but I can't accept your apology,' she said stiffly. 'Whom am I talking to?' she demanded.

'I'm called Tavolsag. Rakot Tavolsag. I think Rakot is equivalent to Colonel in human terms.'

'Well, Rakot Tavolsag, how long do you intend to keep us captive?'

'We are moving you to Grafhi, immediately,' Tavolsag responded. 'It will be up to them to decide what to do with you.' He swivelled on his stumps and left the room.

Heidi insisted on berating herself for the foolish mess she'd got her party into. She was in command, and that laid the responsibility squarely on her shoulders. She should have double-checked the distress call. But how was she to determine if a distress call was genuine or not? Well, then she should have been more cautious; maybe even ignored the request for help. That didn't sit easily in her mind. She was military, she was a hard bitch sometimes, when needed; but deep down she was also a humanitarian, and the distress call was a sucker's punch.

In the stasis chamber the journey to Grafhi was uneventful. They were back in suspended animation.

They could dream, but that was the limit of their sensory perception.

On Grafhi they were incarcerated in the general Confinement Hub, three humans amongst a variety of imprisoned hostiles. The current conflict had prompted the Grafhi to round up all non-Grafhi Quadrant aliens, and the detention centres were overflowing with the growing number of detainees.

The holding pens had room for around twenty prisoners, but now contained more than fifty. Heidi got her group to push their way into a corner, with Reynolds leading and de Vito bringing up the rear. She had instinctively associated with the Kaikonians; the corner being exclusively occupied by Kaikonians.

She looked at the group around her. Most were a meter high, had large chests, dark skins, with small heads but large foreheads, and striking large black eyes. The trio of humans settled on the floor, space being at a premium, and dared anyone to move them. The jovial de Vito got chatting to a Kaikonian sitting next to him.

'My name is de Vito,' he introduced himself.

'I am named K'San,' the fellow seemed quiet cheerful.

'Doesn't it bother you we're locked up like chickens in a coop?' asked de Vito.

'What is a chicken?' asked K'San innocently.

'It's an Earth bird. What I meant to ask is, how long have you been here?'

'Only two days. This is my fate; I accept it,' he said calmly.

'So if they come to execute you, will you accept that as calmly?' Below the joviality, de Vito sounded on edge.

'If it is my fate.' K'San sounded as if he meant it.

'On my planet we believe in survival, and we'll fight to support that belief,' de Vito said through clenched teeth.

'Oh please, don't misunderstand me. I too will fight for survival, but not right *now*. Now I stay calm and think of ways to escape.'

'Now *that* I like the sound of,' said the Italian.

'Have you been on Kaikon?' K'San switched the subject. The small Kaikonian shuffled on his bottom cheeks, trying to get more comfortable.

'Yes, we came through there. Do you know K'Gar?'

'Oh yes! He's high in our Security Service. How is it you know him?'

At that point enthusiastically, de Vito related in some detail his short stay in Kotka. Mostly it was his nerves talking, trying to relieve some of the stress of the situation.

'I'm not from Kotka myself,' K'San said, 'but everyone on Kaikon knows who K'Gar is. I'm from Kansa, which is our second largest city.'

Heidi and Reynolds had their eyes closed, and were trying to calm themselves in preparation for interrogation, or even escape activity if the chance presented itself. From time to time, Heidi opened an eye in de Vito's direction. She was half listening, just in case de Vito disclosed too much. So far, he hadn't mentioned they might be on a mission, and she intended it to stay that way.

'You mentioned fate just a moment back,' de Vito was persisting.

'Yes. I'm of the opinion there are events that may have a profound effect on me, but are completely outside my control, and this I term *my fate.*'

'Okay. But in terms of life, and its meaning: how do you react to this fate. Passively or actively?' de Vito now seemed to have got his teeth into a subject he hoped would completely distract him from his predicament.

'Wait one moment! I said nothing of the *meaning of life*,' objected K'San. 'That is a different subject altogether. Fate is accepting there are matters outside one's control. What life *is*, and whether it has a meaning, is a much larger, or smaller topic, depending on the philosophical approach adopted.'

'We have some time,' de Vito nodded all around the cell. 'I would like to hear your attitude to life, I mean as a Kaikonian.'

'You really mean, as another species of life form. But you're right; it will pass the time. So, to ask such a fundamental question as, "What is the meaning of life?" we must look at what we *use* to define the question.'

At that, de Vito began to look puzzled.

'I'm referring to language of course. Would you agree language is composed of words, strung together to make a sentence?' K'San looked at de Vito for confirmation.

'Yes, I agree so far.' He was beginning to enjoy this.

'And long ago, when we began to use words, each word was carefully chosen and had an urgent concrete meaning; a meaning most likely associated with food or danger?'

'Yes,' de Vito said cautiously. He recognised the style and wondered where the trap would lead.

'If someone pointed at "fire" and said, "What is that?" it was a concrete question, and if someone answered "fire!" then it was a concrete answer.'

He'll get to the point, thought de Vito, and so he nodded.

'If on the other hand someone had answered "water" when they meant "fire", any listener would have known the answer to be false. Where the thought-word-action association begins to fail, is when the subject matter becomes more complicated. When people were beginning to ask abstract questions, or questions which sought the meaning behind the weather.'

Again, de Vito nodded to encourage K'San.

'The wise man or woman of the tribe, not wishing to seem ignorant constructed gods, spirits, or demons to explain catastrophes, sicknesses, or nature in general. They discovered, as in astrology, this gave them extraordinary power over others. And *there* began the hidden agenda, so much so, in many instances the priests accumulated almost as much power and wealth as the ruler, without having to take any of the associated risks.'

'I can't fault any of your reasoning so far,' de Vito said. *It sounds like a Socratic monologue,* he thought admiringly.

'Later on, people noticed the accumulation of wealth, and questioned why priests needed such wealth; and questioned their role. Why should they be able to insist, "such and such was the case," but offer no concrete proof whatsoever? The rational activists insisted that without concrete proof, any listener had a duty to disbelieve the priests,' K'San looked intently at de Vito to see if this human was following his reasoning.

'I'm listening,' is all de Vito could say.

'They say "this exists" or "that is the case" looking fanatical with bigotry in their eyes, daring you to call them a liar. The transition from subjective to objective is a painful process, requiring an empirical approach. Simply insisting and repeating "this exists" or "that is the case" is naive and childlike. Quoting books written long ago as substantiating evidence is no better than having the long dead writer standing in front of you and saying the same,' and again K'San paused.

'I'm still listening,' de Vito assured him.

369

'We are an old race, and much of our early history was endowed with a rich mythology, but what was constructed out of the imagination was *not* concrete. Let me give you an example. On Kaikon, we have retained the festivals of the seasons, to remind us of our vanished green Kaikon. We have a "Spring Maiden," a "Protector of Crops," "The Harvesting Life-Giver," and finally a festival of "Death and Rebirth" represented by a skeleton holding a child. "Father Bones," we fondly call the skeleton.'

'On Earth we have someone similar for that season. Only we call him "Father Christmas,"' interrupted de Vito.

'All planets have seasons, so there is always someone *similar*. Our children believe "Father Bones" is real, until the age of eight, then they realise he is someone dressed as "Father Bones". They are disappointed at first, but then someone explains the symbolism, and they feel smug at being just a little bit older, and in the know.'

'I'm not at all certain I know were your leading me,' de Vito complained.

'I'm illustrating the transition from a conviction, a firm belief, to the realisation of symbolism, in the form of a construct. I'm talking of the use of words to create an idea; to construct a mythology; but clearly distinguishing the construct from concrete reality. Your "Father Christmas" is a construct, a symbol of a seasonal change, but there is no such real entity as "Father Bones" or "Father Christmas." Our children ask, "Where does Father Bones live?" and we tell them, "deep in the planet".'

De Vito was nodding in agreement, as the trail of K'San's thought began to dawn on the Italian.

'So it is, with the question of, "What is the meaning of life?" It is essentially a nonsense fruitless question. Just *because* you can phrase and *ask* a question, it doesn't mean there is a sensible answer. Life-forms using words, distinguish between the subjective and the objective, realising simply juxtaposing words at random may produce nonsense sentences, even when those sentences are then interpreted as having a mystical meaning to the less discerning. Your existence, my existence, doesn't require a meaning. We live, we survive, we procreate, and we die. That is the meaning of life. No animal *needs* to ask, "Why am I here?" and yet it fulfils its bounteous purpose by merely being.'

'But we're not animals, we're reasoning people,' protested de Vito.

'You are still an animal: you may be able to *think* you are somehow above an animal, and their lies the confusion, but you are merely a thinking animal. It is not the gods that have placed you *above* the other animals, it is you who have placed yourself above the other animals *using* gods.'

'Hmm! Okay, but how does this fit in with *the meaning of life*?' de Vito asked.

'Let me finish my train of thought,' K'San insisted. 'Only the unhappy, the unsatisfied *need* a grander meaning to life. They excuse the question by saying, "that civilised species have brains and *need* to ask these questions." They ask, "Why me?", "Why was I born?", and "Why did this have to happen to me?" Asking the question is not really the problem; that's natural. But these questions infer a painful dissatisfaction with their surroundings. It's the cause of the dissatisfaction that needs to be addressed. The parents of these children have been *careless*.' Again, K'San stopped to allow his listener to digest the reasoning.

De Vito nodded encouragement.

'When there isn't sufficient nurturing to console the dissatisfactions, then the problems fester, and the rejections begin. Worse still, the questions *in themselves* are rhetorical and meaningless.

'The people who've had an authoritative upbringing, who were properly nurtured, are comfortable inside their skins and brains. They get on with their lives, their careers; they marry and procreate, bring up their children, without asking fundamental questions. That is because they have no need to ask unsettling questions,' K'San paused for breath.

De Vito was fiddling with his fingers but nodding in agreement. 'You sound a little bitter.' De Vito had noticed both Heidi and Reynolds had been listening to the tail end of K'San's reasoning.

'A sister of mine is dabbling in some irrational nonsense, and no matter what I say, she ignores me,' K'San said a little sadly.

'What do you think of this so far?' de Vito asked Heidi.

'Sounds like common sense to me,' she answered. 'Ask him about Rhelo,' she brought the subject back to their objective.

De Vito took that as a direct order, rather than a request. 'I think your reasoning has actually strengthened me, and for that I thank you,' he looked at the Kaikonian with a little more respect. 'Err...K'San! What can you tell us of this Primus of theirs? This Rhelo.'

'He's a queer individual. He's supposed to be elected, but the Grafhi legislature fears him for his vindictiveness, and has let him rule without any further elections. It's unconstitutional, and is the subject of talk amongst the Grand Council of the GF. They talk of taking action against Grafhi, but are hesitating; which only strengthens Rhelo's hand.

'It's the thwarted megalomaniac in him that has taken us to the brink of war. He hoped to be elected to the position of Grand Custodian, and then use his position to make himself Emperor. The Kaikonian Quadrant had decided before going to Klosh, to side and vote with the Rakhian Quadrant, but we had to go through the motions of haggling. Kaikon could not be seen as supporting Rakh too quickly, otherwise the indignation and outrage of Grafhi, of Rhelo, would have been even greater than at present. That he thought he could get away with his scheme, means he's divorced from reality. Personally, I think he's psychotic.'

Heidi listened to this with deep concentration. She'd heard rumours to this effect, before they had left Rakh, but she hoped they were just malicious propaganda. It made the situation much more dangerous. It probably meant a reasoned solution was futile against this budding demagogue. He would have to be toppled, probably by force.

How had things got to this impasse? Surely, the computer models had predicted the rise of this lunatic? Maybe the Grand Council sought to test its military, and its weaponry in a real-time scenario? No! That was too cynical. Well, it was no use speculating on the overall strategy of the Grand Council; all this went through Heidi's mind. *What they had to do right now, was get out of here.*

She addressed K'San directly, 'I'm Heidi! You mentioned you were looking for ways to escape from this hole: before the philosophical monologue. Have you found a way?'

'Maybe...,' he stared at the humans.

They could see him wondering if he could trust them. What did he know about them? With bioengineering, they could make anyone look like another species. They could be spies infiltrated into the prison to report back to the Grafhi authorities. K'San looked at the other Kaikonians around him, said something to them the universal translator couldn't interpret, and suddenly the Kaikonians near them closed in on the corner were the humans were sitting.

The three looked around nervously, hoping they hadn't made a mistake throwing in their lot with the Kaikonians. From K'San's face, they could see he had come to a conclusion. His big black eyes stared at the humans. To their relief, he began to explain his plan, implying he now included the humans as allies.

'This Confinement Hub,' began K'San, 'is located on the outskirts of Ge'patra, their capital. Because of the overload in prisoners, their manpower is being stretched to the limit. There's a lot of grumbling going on. On top of that, the general mobilisation and their war preparations have taken most of the population into training camps. This venture may be dangerous; are you willing to risk your lives?' K'San looked at Heidi.

'I'd rather take the risk than stay here indefinitely,' she spoke for all three humans.

'Good! A totalitarian regime breeds discontent and corruption, and our prison guards are grumbling incessantly. We've begun negotiations with our immediate warder, to bribe him to help us escape. We could be walking into a trap; but we must risk it. We're due to be fed in an hour: that's when we'll get confirmation he's willing to help, or not, as the case may be. Are you with us?' and again K'San looked for confirmation from Heidi.

'If it's any good to you, we have gold secreted in the heels of our boots. Reynolds and I have the gold, and I have a distress transponder in one of my heels. They've been a bit sloppy in searching us. De Vito should have a small stun gun in two parts, in his heels.' She stopped because of the looks she was getting.

K'San said something to the other Kaikonians, and they all seemed to smirk. 'I'm not going to ask why you are so prepared,' the little Kaikonian said, 'but it clearly no accident. The gold is primitive, but I think it will greatly help. The stun gun is a piece of luck, and will probably make the difference between failure and success. I'm now glad to have you with us.' He seemed genuine in expressing that.

'That's welcome news to us. If there is any combat, I hope you will allow us to take the lead.' She was thinking of size; the humans were at least half a meter taller than any of the Kaikonians, and far heavier.

'If you wish it; so be it. We will do the talking, and you may do the fighting, if there is any to do.'

The following hour went by quickly. The cells were finally opened, and all the prisoners were escorted, in strict rotation, to a canteen where the appropriate food for the species had been pre-programmed into a series of food dispensers. The numerous prisoners sat, crouched, or did what they normally did when they ate, in their groups. The Kaikonians sat with their human allies at tables so thoughtfully provided. Heidi noticed a Grafhi guard had positioned himself near K'San, who sat at the head of the table near the aisle.

The Grafhi guard had bird like spindly legs, a portly rotund body, and spindly arms. His face has two forward facing eyes, and a vestigial beak; there would have been feathers all over once, but now there were only a small tuft on the top of the head. To the humans, they looked faintly ridiculous. But there was nothing ridiculous about the sinister weapon the guard carried.

K'San was having a sly conversation with the Guard, out of the side of his mouth. If anybody were watching, they would have seen the guard was simply guarding: there was no sign of any conversation taking place. Back in the corner, after the food, K'San gave them the good news.

'We're set for tonight,' he said in a hushed whisper. 'There will be a diversion from our Murangi friends in the next block. That should set the alarms going.' K'San turned to Heidi and said, 'The reason *we're* making this effort, is so the outside galaxy is told what's going on in here; all these detainees must be heard.'

Heidi just nodded. She *had* to get out; there was no question of her group staying captive. She'd consciously made up her mind, *if there was any way of assassinating Rhelo, she'd have a go.* It was the frustration of confinement talking. Deep in her subconscious, she knew Earth's Security Bureaux would never sanction an assassination. The time for clear thought would be when they were safely on Tofali.

When the time came to put the escape into effect, everyone was geared up and ready to go. The Kaikonians divided into three groups; each would head in different directions on the outside. The other two groups were to ensure they diverted all the attempts to recapture them, onto themselves. This would give the main group, including the humans and K'San, a better chance.

Heidi had reassembled de Vito's stun gun, and led the way. They halted at the cell door, waiting until the promised diversion had set the alarms howling. The cell door had been unlocked, and it should have shown on the monitors; *maybe* they were busy with the next block.

There wasn't a guard anywhere in sight, and that made Heidi feel ill at ease. It could still be a trap. They went down the corridor and found the next door unlocked. She found an electronic pad discretely hidden near a junction box, and the party moved on quickly to the next door. She placed the pad against the electronic lock, and the lock slipped open.

Instead of going down the wide corridor leading to the exercise yard, they took a right into the guards' quarters. Through a recreation room, past some offices, empty at that time of night. Then along a small corridor and to a door only the guards used. The pad opened that door as well.

Heidi peered out into the night. The two diversionary groups went out in short intervals; one left, the other right. Out in front, there was an air-car waiting with room enough for seven, the three humans and four Kaikonians.

K'San climbed in and took the controls. So far so good, thought Heidi. *I hope the hell he knows how to pilot this thing.* With everyone on board, the air-car took off and headed away from the City.

'The Grafhi guard promised to arrange a small space shuttle ten clicks from here. The onboard computer is set to guide us to it,' K'San informed the group.

'This isn't the kind of spontaneous escape I expected,' Heidi commented out loud. 'Air-cars? Shuttles?'

'We have a network of sympathisers here in Ge'patra,' K'San tried to explain. 'We didn't have one before Rhelo took on dictatorial powers. Now the discontent is widespread. Our guard wasn't a sympathiser; but neither was he for the Government. He took our credits, and passed on our intentions to our network. The car and shuttle are from the network.'

In ten minutes they came to the shuttle; landed, and took off again in the shuttle. They cloaked as they lifted into the dark reaches of space. They put the shuttle into maximum speed for a dash to Tofali, whilst Reynolds activated the transponder. At the border, the

Grafhi defences spotted the cloaking signature of the shuttle and demanded they surrender.

That would have been that, but the sector StarCarrier intervened, and told the Grafhi to back off, or else. *Bless the Space Corps*, went through Heidi's mind. The Grafhi blustered and acted outraged at the "flagrant interference in their internal affairs," but faced with the StarCarrier's overwhelming firepower, they backed off and allowed the shuttle to proceed. K'San aimed the shuttle at the StarCarrier, and allowed its tractor beams to pull it aboard.

Chapter Thirty-Three

Battle of Kaikon

Taras had settled into his comfortable hotel room, with Sandy in the adjoining suite. The Hotel was a large sprawling complex of interconnecting walkways and spiralling blocks, eminently suited to the tall thin Tofali. He had been co-opted onto Portuk's moderating Commission, sent to mediate between Kaikon and Grafhi, as Earth's impartial observer. The Commission was to be based on Tofali, and that ruffled some feathers on Grafhi (sic); some questioning its impartiality, being based on one side only.

Portuk's voice came through on Taras' earpiece. 'I've just received word from the *Ynar;* you'll be pleased to know, they've just tractored Heidi and her group aboard. There's been some kind of chase, and the StarCarriers intervened.'

'That is the *best* news I've had in a while,' the relief spread on Taras' face. 'Portuk! *Where are you?* I'd like to speak with you in person,' Taras' face was one big grin. '*Sandy!*' he shouted towards the next room. 'I'm sorry Portuk! Did I boom into your ear? I was trying to get my aide Sandy.'

'I'm in my room, nursing my eardrum,' responded Portuk amiably.

'*Sorry* again! May I come down?' Taras asked.

'I'll be waiting,' Portuk replied.

It took Taras a few moments to descend to Portuk's apartment; he was practically running, and Sandy had the devil of a time trying to keep up.

The news Heidi had been found safe and well made him overflow with joy. When they had been reported missing, he blamed himself for sending them on the *unnecessary* jaunt. It was Basil who had to remind him it was indeed *necessary*, and it wasn't a jaunt. Heidi's job was in fact the one she was trying to carry out; she was regarded as being good at it. If anything had happened to her and the group, then it was in the line of duty, and they ought to be supporting them in carrying it out.

For that salutary pep talk, Taras was somewhat grateful. It brought him back to his senses, and resulted in him sending a coded message to the StarCarrier Battle Group on the border, to keep a weary eye out for the three humans.

As he burst into Portuk's apartment, he became calm and serious. 'Portuk! I've had an idea—I want your opinion on it.'

'Please! Catch your breath and sit down.'

'Thank you! You mentioned to Heidi, back on Rakh, our cloaking devices were somewhat primitive. What did you mean by that?'

'Only, we could probably penetrate them, and distinguish their residual signature. It's not a cloaking device if it doesn't completely cloak.' Portuk had a quizzical expression on his face, wondering what the human was up to.

'Bear with me. So what's the best you can do?'

'Our latest product has subterfuge features which deceives the trace instrument. It's a *real* cloaking apparatus. Why? What do you have in mind?'

'I want to take Heidi's group back into Grafhi again.'

Portuk looked astonished. 'But you haven't even heard their report yet.'

Taras quickly threw back, 'I thought you said we needed to get rid of Rhelo?'

'So we do! If we don't, he's likely to try and make himself Grand Custodian by force. I told you in confidence regarding the fixed elections on Klosh. How we couldn't afford to have Rhelo as Grand Custodian. Don't you think he knows the elections were fixed? It was Grafhi Quadrant's turn to host the GF HQ, but we couldn't allow that lunatic to be elected. That's the real reason he's so angry.'

'If the elections are always fixed, then why hold them at all? Why not just hold Quadrant elections in the rotated Quadrant?' quizzed Taras.

'Because if we did it automatically, we wouldn't have the leeway to manoeuvre. We couldn't have legitimately bypassed Rhelo. He would have automatically become the Grand Custodian this time round. This way, we had an election and Rhelo didn't get elected. All quiet legal and above board. You could say holding the fixed elections is an in-built safeguard,' Portuk explained as if to a child.

'We still need to get rid of Rhelo; right?'

'Right!' Portuk began to look puzzled again.

'We're going to Grafhi tomorrow to talk to Rhelo. I would like that mission to fail! I want us to engineer a pullback of the Battle Group; I mean he's going to demand that anyway. So we pull back, giving him the room to attack somewhere; then we pounce with the Battle Group, and bloody the Grafhi military nose.

'When the news of the defeat reaches Grafhi, it gives their military a chance to act. That's why I want Heidi there, so she can liaise with the people who will carry out the inevitable *coup d'état*. At the right moment, we need to reassure the Grafhi Military if they depose Rhelo, *and* reinstate the democratic process, that they will be embraced again by Galactic Federation and things would return to normal. Do you see what I'm getting at?' Taras stopped to see if Portuk was looking as if he might agree.

'With a few minor adjustments, that *was* substantially the plan proposed by the our military modelling department. It has the benefit of being simple and blunt. If you think sending Heidi in would add anything to the plan's success, then by all means send Heidi in. You have my blessing. Oh! And we'll supply the upgraded cloaking devices your so eager to acquire.'

At that last innuendo, Taras felt a little exposed. Portuk seemed to have seen through his ploy of gaining the improved cloaking gadget. 'I'm convinced Heidi can be of great help, and thanks,' Taras said. He excused himself and went back to his room, still with the silent Sandy in tow.

* * *

The next morning, Taras managed to get Heidi discharged from the *Ynar*, whose security had insisted on questioning the humans. They were trying to extract the smallest details of what was happening on Grafhi. Heidi understood the necessity, but she and the others were exhausted. She had insisted on saying goodbye to K'San and his plucky Kaikonians. She thanked him for including them in their escape plan, and wishing him well. K'San had elected to continue co-operating with the *Ynar* intelligence and security people.

* * *

'I am glad to have you back in one piece,' Taras told Heidi when they were alone in his apartment. 'You've no idea how worried I was when they told me you'd disappeared. Really pleased to have you back Colonel.' He stopped lest he overstep his enthusiasm.

'They pulled a dirty trick to catch us: false distress call, leading us into an ambush. It's all in that report in your hands. We were lucky to have been put into the same cell as the Kaikonians. I've developed a great respect for those little people. Without them, we might still be rotting in that Confinement Hub on Grafhi.' She had begun to feel her old confident self again.

He wasn't certain how she would receive his next suggestion. 'I don't know how this is going to go down with you, but I want you to go back to Grafhi.' He was expecting her to register surprise, maybe even protest, but instead she simply sat and waited for him to finish. *A true professional,* he thought.

He continued, 'We're going to supply you with a new type of cloaking device, one that is undetectable. Tomorrow, and I'm sorry for the short notice, you'll accompany the Commission to Grafhi, cloaked, and the rest is in this data cube. Any questions?'

She took the proffered data cube and said, 'Let me have a look at the mission profile first; then I may have some comments.'

'How are the other two, what are their names, Reynolds and de Vito?' He switched to small talk.

'They're up to the mark. They held up well. We're just a little tired; it's the nervous energy drain. We'll be ready tomorrow. I might as well take them along—keep the team together.' She rose, and Taras saw her to the door.

He told her as they neared the door, 'We've adapted a z-boson pulsed frequency to act as a communicator channel. This is such an unusual frequency, and one fitting in well with the background space emissions. We think you ought to be able to use it in an emergency without being detected. It's all on the data cube. Oh! By the way...it's good to have you back.'

Heidi acknowledged his last remark with a parting nod and then returned to her rooms, settling down with a drink and engaging the data cube Taras had given her.

*   *   *

The following morning, Heidi's group boarded the space vessel taking the ten members of the Commission to Grafhi. Only being cloaked, they were never seen to board the vessel. The spacecraft had Portuk on board leading the Commission, and Taras as the so-called impartial observer.

When they reached the border between the Kaikonian Quadrant and the Grafhi Quadrant, they reported in to the flagship of the Battle Group, the StarCarriers *Ynar*. Once over the border, they were escorted by two Grafhi heavy SpaceCruisers, all the way to Grafhi.

The Commission was taken to the conference venue, immediately on landing. Grafhi Security swept the Commission's vessel for any unusual bugs, or concealed spying contraptions. Heidi's group would have been discovered there and then, if they hadn't had the new cloaking devices.

Surreptitiously, Heidi's group disembarked and headed for the civilian spaceport, next to the military spaceport on which they had landed. The Grafhi military were putting on a big show for the benefit of the Commission, trying to convince the Commission members they were quiet ready to resolve the dispute by force if it came to an armed conflict.

Kaikonian intelligence had arranged with the dissident group on Grafhi, for Heidi's group to be picked up at the civilian spaceport and taken into hiding.

The pick-up occurred on time and without incidence. A hover with the markings of a seed merchant named Fheltha arrived, stopped long enough for Heidi's group to climb in, and then shot off erratically, climbing faster than usual. Somebody yelled something in Grafhi, and the hover slowed to the usual traffic speed.

The hover next stopped in what looked like a run down business district, at a seed warehouse on the outskirts of Ge'patra, the Grafhi capital. Heidi and her two companions were taken into a concealed room in the basement, where they were to meet the head of the Grafhi resistance to Rhelo's regime some time later.

*   *   *

Back at the conference table, Portuk demanded the Grafhi military cease all military actions against the Kaikonese Quadrant. It was an essential requirement of the Galactic Federation's Charter to allow GF Security Council peace procedures to be implemented. Portuk reminded Rhelo, when Grafhi joined the GF, they signed a protocol preventing them from ever taking up arms against a fellow member of the GF.

Equally, Rhelo reminded the GF Commission, although it was not enshrined or encoded in the protocols, each Quadrant was to take its turn as Grand Custodian as decreed by precedence and custom. This had always been the case. For Grafhi to have been ignored and snubbed the way it had been on Klosh, was justification enough for its military to take action against the perpetrator of the snub if Grafhi was not to loose face.

Accusation from one side was met by a counter accusation from the other side; yet, neither side became unduly acrimonious, each side desiring to provoke the other into that state.

Although Rhelo had demanded at the outset, it was only at the conclusion of the exasperating conference he again called for the withdrawal of the Battle Group from their border. This time they were visibly surprised when Portuk acquiesced, claiming it was a good will gesture from the GF.

Since there seemed to be no further movements in their negotiations for the moment, the Commission requested an adjournment of a week, and decided to return to Tofali.

According to a previously arranged plan, as the Commission's space vessel passed the flagship *Ynar,* the force of two hundred and twenty ships, led by the three StarCarriers, moved into open space, opened Black Hole jump gates, and were gone. The Commission's space vessel continued onto Tofali.

What occurred next, although expected and planned for, happened far sooner than anticipated. The Grafhi military quickly launched a lightening all-out attack on Kaikon. Their full armada had been stationed some light years away. When Portuk agreed to remove the GF Battle Group, a message had been sent to the armada to open a Black Hole and jump to Kaikon. Had Kaikon not been ready and waiting for such a move, the losses would have been catastrophic.

As it turned out, only a few of the Grafhi SpaceCruisers managed to penetrate the Kaikonian defences. That in itself was a disaster. Two aerial cities were damaged to such an extent it destroyed their ability to stay afloat. Katlasa had the geo-stationary anti-graviton generator damaged, the one sitting out in space, on a synchronous orbit thirty thousand kilometres above the city. It caused the city to tumble out of the sky, onto the volcanic planet. A number of minutes elapsed between the generators failed, giving the inhabitants time to get out. The loss of life was minimal as the rescue services teleported most of the citizens off in time. Others used the innumerable bubble-hovers to escape to the other aerial cities.

One Grafhi SpaceCruiser managed to be shot down into the Kaikonian planetary atmosphere, and as it went down into the lava below, it passed Kuva, a small aerial city. The Grafhi gunners on board took a final desperate shot at Kuva and crippled the anti-graviton reservoir slung beneath the city.

Here the loss of life was a little more serious because the rescue teleporters were already busy with Katlasa. A couple of thousand Kuva citizens lost their lives, but over fifty thousand were saved, some by using the bubble-hovers; the rest being teleported out.

What turned the battle of Kaikon into a rout for the Grafhi military was the sudden appearance of the GF Battle Group in the middle of the fight. They were supposed to be there at the beginning of the confrontation but the speed of the Grafhi move caught them in transit. When the Battle Group showed up and demonstrated its firepower, within minutes the Grafhi were suing for peace.

They were ordered to surrender unconditionally or they would be blown apart in space. The humiliation was completed by installing new Captains on all the Grafhi military vessels, and interning all of the old Commanders. The Grafhi armada was brought under GF command and the second in command of the Battle Group installed as the Grafhi fleet Commander.

That fleet was taken deep into Kaikonian space, well away from the Grafhi Quadrant, well away from Rhelo's influence. The old Commander of the Grafhi armada, Admiral Hurfiol, was given a small space vessel. Together with his immediate senior planning staff, he was sent back to Grafhi with orders to remove Rhelo and reinstate democracy on the planet.

When Heidi got wind that the Grafhi had suffered a humiliating defeat in a great space battle, she assumed quite rightly this was the time she had been waiting for. She asked to see the resistance commander again. Fhiale came as soon as he could get away from Ge'Hub.

Fhiale rushed into the basement and immediately said, 'We have to get you out of here! I don't know how, but GrafSec knows you here and are on their way right now.'

'There's a traitor in your organisation. That's how!' Heidi responded icily.

'That as may be, but you still have to move. Are those cloaking devices as effective as you claim?'

'We're here aren't we? Sorry! Yes they are effective,' she forced herself to calm down a bit.

'Right! I'm taking you were they wont' think of looking. I'm going to stash you under their noses,' and he led the way out.

In an alley next to the warehouse, a hover waited for them. The hover markings seemed to relate to security, but it wasn't GrafSec or the local police. It lifted off with the three humans inside, and Fhiale at the controls.

'Nice to see your keeping well,' Fhiale said to Heidi as he set the course. 'All hell's broken loose at Ge'Hub. There must be at least a dozen conspiracies hatching since the military defeat.'

'What's Rhelo doing?' Heidi wanted to know.

'He's shouting and ranting at everybody. He blames the military for being hasty; for being sloppy; for not winning. His enforcers are rounding up everybody he can think of as traitors and malcontents. Unless the top brass move quickly, there may not be enough resistance at Ge'Hub to topple him.'

Heidi felt Reynolds sitting immobile in the back, a grim look on his face. De Vito was relaxed and quietly reading some screen novel he'd started in the basement.

She turned her attention back to Fhiale, 'You told me you ran the enterprise providing security at the military HQ; at this Ge'Hub of yours. I hope this hover is part of your set up,' Heidi regarded the rotund form of this Grafhi, whose beaked face was concentrating on a small gadget lying on the dashboard.

'This thing is monitoring GrafSec traffic,' he pointed at the gadget. 'Yes, I own SecCorp if that's what you mean. Why do you ask?' He returned her stare with one of his own.

'Can you get me close to the Chief of Staff in Ge'Hub? That's Admiral Fahilo, isn't it?'

'Yes, that would be Admiral Fahilo,' Fhiale agreed.

'Admiral Hurfiol arrived back earlier today; head hung low, and in a foul temper,' Fhiale volunteered. 'The top brass in Ge'Hub are holding an emergency conference. They've been at it all day. It seems they've lost the whole Grafhi armada; and then some.' Fhiale seemed pleased.

'Nothing travels faster than bad news,' and here Heidi went carefully. 'The GF have confiscated the captured armada until Rhelo is deposed.' She noticed Fhiale wince at the word "confiscated," at least that's what she interpreted on the bird-like face. *He reminds me a little of a Golden Eagle; especially the forward facing eyes with their ferocious unblinking stare,* she mused.

'Serves them right,' Fhiale underlined forcefully. 'We've had peace for over a thousand years until this lunatic Rhelo pushed his way into power,' Fhiale spat out Rhelo's name. 'I can't say I'm happy we've been defeated, after all I'm Grafhi. But if it teaches the military a lesson in democracy, it will all have been worthwhile.'

'The Grafhi could do worse than elect you as their next leader,' Heidi suggested.

Fhiale looked startled for a moment. It was either because it was the first time such an idea had been mooted, or it could have been because his innermost desire had suddenly been exposed to daylight.

'If the people wish that, then it is their wish. I have been wondering whether I should offer myself when the time came. I think you've just made my mind up. I *will* stand, if they'll have me. If elected, I will *serve*.'

The humans cloaked as Fhiale spoke.

Fhiale continued, 'We have to strengthen the democratic procedures, and revise our safeguards so another Rhelo can't grab power and usurp the office of Primus for his own ends.' It sounded as if the humans were privy to the beginnings of a political electioneering speech.

The hover arrived at Ge'Hub, a tall aerodynamically thin kilometre high building, putting down on the eyrie, the roof landing pad. To the casual observer, a lone Grafhi got out and swiftly moved to the tube; the hover being automatically moved aside to a parking bay by the building computer. Fhiale, accompanied by the cloaked humans, dropped down to his office, that of Chief of Security. To his computer secretary, Fhiale ordered he was not to be disturbed on any account.

*   *   *

It was late in the afternoon, the day after the Grafhi armada had been defeated, and still the Armed Forces Chiefs were closeted in their day long meeting. Admiral Hurfiol sat inside with his head bowed quietly, shame pouring out of each pore in his ornithoid body. Admiral Fahilo was holding forth.

'Gentlemen, for the last time,' he was saying in a rasping hoarse clacking voice, the result of hours spent talking, 'we've absolutely no choice but to go with the proposed course of action. We must make a move, otherwise we'll have civil war thrust on us.' Again, uproar enveloped the room; as many voices tried to make themselves heard.

Fahilo banged a gavel on the table, 'We're as much to blame for this defeat as is our benighted leader. We went along with his crazy plans, either from fear, or maybe just sycophantically hopping for merit, promotion and profit.

'Now it's turned sour we must salvage what we can. We've already lost all our military space vessels. We're completely vulnerable,' he paused for emphasis, 'from the military point of view. Anybody could simply appear in our skies, swoop down on us, and take our planet from us.'

He shouted all this as best as he could, to his grumbling audience, exaggerating a little for emphasis. The latter point on being defenceless seemed to have got their attention.

Fahilo now played his trump card, having had Hurfoil's agreement to this ploy beforehand. 'I'd like us now to hear from Admiral Hurfoil. It was *he* who risked all, whilst we sat in our comfortable nests, safe in the knowledge we had sent our best space warrior to do battle on our behalf. He's sat silent all this day, feeling humiliated he couldn't supply the victory we demanded of him. What does he propose we do to salvage our military honour?'

Hurfoil rose from his seat, and now for the first time looked like the proud soldier he was. Clear penetrating yellow eyes surveyed the room where his fellow officers sat.

'You already know the deep shame I carry as a result of having lost all our military space vessels. It was foolish of us to have underestimated the will of the GF. At no time in all of our history have we been so thoroughly vanquished as we've been this day. I agree with Admiral Fahilo; we are defenceless. I also agree with him in what needs to be done.' At the last statement, further uproar ensued.

The uproar came from the same hot heads who were the first to demand the beginning of the disastrous military campaign. They refused to accept they had been comprehensively defeated. Their answer was to propose an initiation of punitive guerrilla actions throughout the Grafhi Quadrant.

'*I repeat*,' Hurfiol continued above the noise, 'we have been given *no choice* but to arrest Primus Rhelo if we're to prevent the internecine strife into which we're descending. It may be the case Rhelo will try to move first, and have *us* arrested. Should we wait for that to happen?' he looked at the taut faces staring at him.

'*No!*' came back the firm response from the majority.

'Then it is agreed; we move first.'

The dissenters remained quiet for the first time that day, whilst the proponents of this course of action called out clearly, '*Yes!*'

'Good!' said Fahilo getting to his feet, Hurfiol in his turn sat down. 'We really have little choice in the matter,' Fahilo continued. 'I've just initiated a little device in my pocket, which will send a Military Police battalion to arrest Rhelo. They were standing by in case we needed them.

'Furthermore, to illustrate the inevitability of our failure; of the pure folly of having let this thing get so far out of hand; we have been monitored by the GF as we speak in this gathering.' At that, a deadly hush descended on the room. 'Please Colonel, would you decloak now,' Fahilo called out, and then stood waiting.

In a corner of the room, Heidi, Reynolds, and de Vito suddenly appeared out of nowhere. 'I must offer my apologies for this covert intrusion,' Heidi said quickly.

Fahilo lifted his hand to stop her from further speech. 'May I introduce Colonel Heidi Frisch, and her two companions from the GF intelligence section.' The room was full of open beaks, astonished and somewhat outraged at the turn of events. Their security had been so thoroughly compromised.

'We most heartily agree with Admiral Fahilo's proposed course of action,' Heidi quickly added, 'and I'm empowered to offer its adherents the support of the Galactic Federation.'

Fahilo held up his hands, asking for silence. 'I am receiving news over my communicator Rhelo's bodyguards have just been defeated...Rhelo is under arrest...and...is being brought here.'

Admiral Hurfoil got up from his seat, 'Admiral Fahilo, sir. I'm being a bit impertinent, but events are moving rapidly now.' He spoke clearly and with confidence. 'It would be most opportune if we asked the Speaker to recall the suspended Congress for tomorrow. If we send military messengers to all the Congress members advising them of Rhelo's arrest, with visual proof, or they may think it's a hoax to bring their loyalty out into the open. We could then swiftly try to get back on the road to democracy.' He stopped to see if he was getting a positive response. He was gratified to see a sea of nodding faces.

*   *   *

The Grafhi Congress met at the request of the Coup Council, and overwhelmingly voted to impeach Rhelo for abuse of power. Rhelo had to be sedated because of his constant interruptions of the proceedings. He continually screamed at the Congress members he would deal with all the traitors present. That he would sack or imprison them all; he would send them to the outermost asteroid incarceration facility; he would have their brains fried. Sedation was the simplest solution.

There could be only one verdict. Rhelo was sentenced to be reprogrammed. To have the megalomaniacal streak removed from his mental makeup. The Speaker of Congress was unanimously appointed temporary Primus.

The following week elections were held and to nobodies surprise; Fhiale was elected as the new Primus of Grafhi. He moved swiftly to restore credibility by re-establishing the pre-Rhelo democratic order. Potong was invited, and came for the inauguration of the new Primus, confirming to the whole Grafhi Quadrant Rhelo's lunatic reign was over. He emphasised the GF had indeed restored good relations with the errant Quadrant. It was this sense of magnanimity, this gesture of good will vindicated Potong's election as the Grand Custodian.

* * *

On the short journey back to Rakh, de Vito commented to no one in general, 'So much for advanced civilised societies. Instead of the "meaning of life," I should have got K'San to explain to me, "the peaceful nature" of "an advanced civilised society."'

'Your joking, of course!' Reynolds shot at him.

'I think we can safely say he is,' Heidi assured them all. Then added, 'I must say, I had thought we'd seen the last of armed conflicts between nations or races when we joined the Federation.' A little dance of anger flitted across her face. 'Let's hope this is the last bit of lunacy on that score.'

Everyone sat quietly in concord with her last sentiment. There had been peace for over a thousand years in the Federation and they looked forward to the same in the next thousand years now Rhelo was out of the way.

*   *   *

With a great sigh of collective relief, peace returned to all the members of the Galactic Federation. Peace and healing missions were sent to all the Grafhi Quadrant planets, trade and travel was re-established, and hopefully for another thousand years the Galactic Federation would prosper in amity and concord.

Chapter Thirty-Four

Barog

The Ambassador for Barog invited Claude Joubert, then Ambassador of the Solar System on Rakh, to visit his home planet as a personal guest of his after Ubongo's kidnapping.

The proposed visit was on, then off, then on again, and so it went for a while. Claude's duties as the personal advisor to President Ying of the World Government, had increased his workload enormously. He also lectured at the Galactic University, being in great demand on the speaking circuit. Only the use of the teleporter made his schedule at all possible.

Finally, Claude took the bull by the horns and demanded a vacation of himself. The prime agitator for this move was Anne-Marie, his wife, seeing him overworked all the time.

To Claude's astonishment, Ying was only too delighted to have Claude visit Barog, but then Ying had his own agenda. Claude put his affairs in order, and with a little help from Anne-Marie, delegated the University work. He loaded his assistant with his World Government duties. When he'd cleared his desk he booked passage for Barog and asked Anne-Marie to join him, since Claude insisted he couldn't relax without her company.

Barog had joined the Galactic Federation just two hundred years before the Solar System, and as the two most recent members, they felt a growing mutual bond. It helped that His Excellency Portuk, the tall muscular dinosauroid

Ambassador to the GF, and Claude, had hit it off on a personal basis.

Late one afternoon, Portuk was waiting outside his mansion when Claude and Anne-Marie teleported down with their luggage.

'Your most welcome to Barog and to my humble country estate,' Portuk opened, addressing the humans. 'I believe one of your human sayings coincides with one of ours. "My house is your house."'

'That is gracious of you. From space, we saw Barog as a picturesque green-blue planet. On behalf of myself and my wife Anne-Marie, may we thank you for inviting us to visit your beautiful planet, and your home,' responded Claude.

'Now, may I introduce my mate Manka to you,' Portuk turned to his right.

Manka had all the features of Portuk; the similar yellow eyes, the rounded hairless head, the green skin, yet her stance and bearing was a little smaller and unmistakably suggested femininity. She was dressed in a flowing shimmering silvery-green dress down to her ankles, which definitely enhanced her grace. Portuk was smartly dressed in a suit made of the similar material.

Anne-Marie proffered her outstretched hand, and Manka gripped it gently in her three-fingered hand. Like Claude, Anne-Marie had dressed in a casual light-green jump suit for travel, and both now felt distinctly underdressed. Manka took Anne-Marie to their rooms and called for an android to lug the luggage. When Anne-Marie made a favourable comment regarding Manka's dress, she immediately offered Anne-Marie a dress of a similar style.

The two males were left alone on the veranda, whilst the females became more closely acquainted upstairs. Out of the blue suddenly, in front of Claude appeared a small black screen with what seemed writing in a number of different alphabets. Portuk said something angrily to the screen, and the screen vanished.

397

'What the devil was that?' asked Claude.

'A curse of our free enterprise civilisation,' Portuk explained. 'Your DNA is unregistered on this planet, and the commercial sweeper didn't recognise it, so the screen was asking you which language you wanted your adverts in.'

'Are you telling me your commercials here, are DNA targeted, *and* they check the DNA of everyone on the planet?' asked Claude somewhat flabbergasted.

'That *is* an astute appraisal of our ad-blasts,' Portuk seemed delighted at Claude's quick grasp.

'And you put *up* with it?'

'That's free enterprise for you,' Portuk seemed resigned.

'What did you say to the screen for it to vanish?' Claude was intrigued.

'I told it; you were a visitor from Earth. It vanished because it probably doesn't yet know where Earth is. It's gone to find out some data, before trying to sell you something.'

'Am I going to be visited again?' Claude said dubiously.

'Not if you don't want to be. I'll get through to Central Ads and ask them to leave you alone. Is that what you want?'

'Yes please, and the same for Anne-Marie.'

'I'll arrange it. Now come inside so I can offer you some refreshments.'

They went into the Mansion, through rooms with holographic portraits projected onto the walls. Other rooms had scenic scenes. It seemed all the internal decorations on the walls were holo projections.

'Those were a few of my ancestors, and the scenes were of various parts of the estate,' Portuk elaborated. He took Claude into a large room with a high ceiling, and sat him on a soft leather couch. 'Now what can I entice you with...a soft drink, or something with ethyl alcohol in it. I believe humans are quiet partial to that?'

'In moderation. But right now, a cool fresh lemonade would be nice,' Claude was thirsty after the trip.

'Lemonade? Hmm! Let's see...if the replicator has this "lemonade" programmed into it.'

When they had both settled down with drinks in their hands, Portuk continued, 'Whilst the women chat upstairs, let's relax and make small talk. I'll start with a gentle question, if I may? There are parts of your planet's history that still intrigue me.'

'But of course. Fire away.'

'I've been looking at a period of your history, which you call the Cretaceous,' Portuk began cautiously.

Aah, here it comes. Thought Claude, *I've been expecting this.*

'Sixty-five million years ago, your planet seems to have been dominated by relations of mine, based on the theory of convergent history, the dinosaurs. If I understand it rightly, a meteor then hit a part of Earth called the Yucatan Peninsular, in a region you call Mexico, and in the ensuing artificial winter, all the dinosaurs died off.'

Portuk stopped to see if he might be offending with such questions. When he saw he wasn't, he continued. 'The impact of the meteor allowed the mammals to become the dominant species on your planet. Because we also have small mammal like rodents on Barog, and we have hunted them for food since time immemorial, I find it hard to imagine these rodents could evolve into humans like yourselves.'

'I'm no expert in this so bear with me,' Claude responded, 'but it would seem had the meteor not crashed into Earth those many years ago, our planet would probably now be dominated by the descendants of a turkey sized big-brained dinosaur called *Troodon* or more likely a theropod called the *Velociraptor* from the Late Cretaceous.

'Either might well have evolved into the intelligent species of our planet, much as in the manner of evolution on Barog. Without the meteor, the small mammals of the time, would most likely not have stood a chance against *Velociraptor* or *Troodon,* both preyed heavily on the little rodents.

'But on Earth, those 65 million years ago, it is thought the dinosaurs were wiped out by the harsh weather conditions after the meteor hit. The dinosaurs were caught by two extreme weather related factors at the same time,' Claude stopped to take in breath, and felt a little like he was still giving lectures.

'Firstly,' he continued, 'the meteor threw up a lot of dust which cut off the sunlight and produced a long winter. This killed off much of the vegetation sustaining the herbivores. When the herbivores died off, so did the carnivores who predate on them. Secondly, the prolonged meteor-winter deprived the dinosaurs of the life giving heat from the sun and many may have simply died of severe cold.

'Whatever the initial cause, it was the severe climatic change that precipitated the extinction of the dinosaur after 150 million years of successfully surviving all else. In fact, nothing larger than a dog survived the catastrophe. Yet, the dinosaur did survive in a way,' and Portuk pricked up his ears, 'although in a different form. The direct ancestors of the dinosaurs are the birds, and with 8,700 kinds of birds on the earth, they are a robust example of tenacity under adversity,' and Claude hoped that was that.

'The matter of cold bloodedness had bothered me, since all my species are warm blooded. But the dying of the vegetation in the meteor-winter is really the key, isn't it?' Portuk was gently scratching his bald head with one of his left clawed fingers. 'It's fate. One species extinguished; another survives. I suppose it could have happened on this planet, had there been a meteor with our name on it, heading in this direction in our history.'

'Fate is an interesting notion, comparable to its companions, destiny and luck,' Claude was in the realm of probabilities, a favourite subject of his. 'What is outside of our control, is deemed to be fate and destiny. Surely, *no one* can argue a meteor was *within* our control, not at that stage in our history. But at present, there isn't a meteor that would be able to get through the Solar defences. One could argue *timing* is *all,* probably with a shade of luck thrown in for good measure.'

'Another drink?' Portuk sent a serving android over to refill Claude's tumbler.

'I wonder where the women have got to,' Claude said.

'Probably getting to know one another,' suggested Portuk.

'We'll probably talk of this later in more detail, but switching the subject; I've been authorised by President Ying to acknowledge your request to buy Earth's history and some emotiograms. I assume you're still interested?'

'The commercial interests I represent on Barog are most definitely interested,' Portuk's attention level seemed to rise.

'However, I've been instructed to evaluate the Pragmacast system personally.'

'That is most welcome news. I have a hood set up over there, above the corner chair. What about trying it out now?' Portuk pointed enthusiastically to Claude's right.

Claude went over to the chair in question, and looked at the transparent hood above it. 'I'm to sit below this hood, and it will access all the relevant sensory parts of my brain, such as the visual cortex, auditory, olfactory, tactile, and even gustatory.' Claude was stalling. He was running through a list of what he had read on the subject. 'Integrated into this hood,' he continued, 'are emotional probes so if the Pragmacast is showing an angry talker, then I'll feel the anger as if I were standing next to the talker.'

'Precisely,' Portuk said, beginning to adjust some controls on a console at the back of the chair. 'I thought you might like to try a session, so in anticipation; I've had this one calibrated to the human brain.

'Do you remember the rescue of Adama? Of course you do...you were there. Well, one of the élite forces was recording the battle using a Pragmacast recorder. It will be used in future training within his unit. I want you to experience the battle for yourself. You remember watching the screen? This recording will put you right into the thick of it. Then *you* can decide the difference between what you saw, and this Pragmacast. Are you game?'

'Put like that, how can I refuse.'

Claude sat in the chair beneath the hood. Portuk lowered the hood onto Claude's head, just as the women returned from upstairs.

'This should be fun,' Manka remarked.

'Is it safe?' Anne-Marie asked.

'Perfectly safe,' Manka reassured her.

'Are you ready?' Portuk asked Claude.

'Ready when you are,' Claude replied.

'If you want this to stop, just raise your hand, and I'll switch it off,' Portuk said reassuringly.

Portuk pressed a button, and Claude found himself back in the cavern, *fighting for his life.* Insectoids were scoring hits on his force shield, lighting it up. There was firing from his side behind him, at the insectoids presumably, and a hail of returning laser fire from the defending insectoids. He was in the midst of dust, obscuring his line of fire; *only he had no weapon.* The shock of the realism was frightening, exhilarating, the latter because part of his mind reminded him this was a Pragmacast. His senses kept insisting this was real. He *was* in a battle deep below the planet's surface. He raised his hand, and found himself sitting in an armchair, beginning to sweat.

Anne-Marie was gently wiping his brow, saying, 'Claude, *Claude! Are you all right?*'

'Yes mon chéri, ca va bien,' he automatically reverted to French with his wife.

'What's your verdict,' asked Portuk, once Claude had recovered from the shock of the realism.

'I felt like I was right *in* the battle. Whoever has the patent on this, will be hearing from our commercial people on Earth. I can't see how we can avoid this. I'm told Basil Dukas brought something like this back from Kaikon, as a present. However, we're talking commercial use.' Claude was bubbling over with enthusiasm. 'But where do the emotiograms come in, as far as Earth's history goes?' Claude wanted to know.

'If we could purchase say, a million or more varied emotiograms from your Programmed Learning centres, then we can add emotions to the events in your history, bringing them to life. It's like adding a sound track to a Holocast recording.'

'Because we think it will be good advertising for us humans to become more familiar *to* other species, I'm instructed to inform you we support this deal. It ought to be good PR, but this data could easily be distorted, and used for nefarious purposes. I'm trusting you not to let that happen. With that proviso, you have a deal, subject to a legal contract, of course.

'The only part needs to be tidied, is the purchase price for the emotiograms. We could settle it right now.' Claude straightened his face. 'In return for the emotiograms, we would like the commercial patent for the Pragmacast system for the Solar System.' He looked straight at Portuk.

'Off the top of my head, I would think we have a deal, subject to legal contract, *of course,* but let me check it with the appropriate people,' Portuk seemed delighted. 'Now, as it is the evening, are you both ready for dinner?'

'We certainly are,' Claude looked at Anne-Marie, and she nodded. 'I'm going to go upstairs, freshen up, and change out of this jump-suit. With your permission?' Claude glanced at Portuk.

'I did mean it. Please treat this house as your home.'

Chapter Thirty-Five

Andromeda

For the next morning, Portuk promised them an experience of a lifetime. When Claude and Anne-Marie came down for their surprise, they found Portuk had arranged a morning ride before breakfast, on what he called a *Zetter*.

From Claude's perspective, it had similarities to an extinct *Anatosaurus* from Earth's prehistory. A bipedal herbivore with a long tail for balance, standing three meters tall, smaller arms at the front, a medium long neck, what looked like a bill shaped snout and seemingly intelligent eyes.

It had a saddle on its back, and an android was holding the reins.

'I've brought out the most gentle of my *Zetters* for you to ride,' Portuk was already in the saddle of his *Zetter*, as was Manka.

When Claude and Anne-Marie were securely mounted, the party set off at a steady pace away from the mansion. Portuk was leading, followed by Claude and Anne-Marie, with Manka bringing up the rear.

Once the humans had got the hang of their mounts, their hosts put on some pace, heading out into the vastness of Portuk's estates. They rode through a conifer like forest, then through open meadows covered with sparse patches of small shrubs. Further on they came across something that looked like ferns and horsetails. A little beyond, there were palm-like cycadales, intermixed with a profusion of seemingly tall fern trees.

They rode for a good half hour at a brisk pace through the amazing flora, which eventually brought the party to the edge of a wide ravine. A river flowed down the middle. They dismounted at Manka's urging and stared at the beauty of it all.

'This is lovely,' Anne-Marie said trying to control her *Zetter,* which kept pulling her off the ground with its tall neck.

Manka sighed and explained, 'It's one of my favourite spots on the estate; this and the waterfall. I try and insist Portuk brings me here at least two or three times a week.' Manka stood looking at the enchantment.

Claude was staring into the sky, squinting and scrutinising a tiny dark red spot that had appeared. 'Portuk, what the blazes is that,' Claude pointed at the dark red spot.

'I don't recognise it,' Portuk answered, looking puzzled. 'Our Space Centre must have put something large into orbit around Barog,' he concluded. The dark red spot had grown somewhat, and now could be clearly seen. It looked menacing.

'I'm not sure I like the look of that,' Portuk said, and remounted his *Zetter.* 'I have a feeling of foreboding. Can we please remount and head back to the house,' he wheeled his mount around and set off slowly, waiting for the others to follow.

Once the rest were on their mounts, Portuk set off at a cracking pace. His two-legged beast loped along with strong strides, leaping over ditches and hedges, opening up a distance between him and the rest. Claude felt something serious was afoot, and urged his mount to greater speed, but always with one eye on the whereabouts of his wife's mount. The pursuing party reached sight of the house just as Portuk's figure disappeared through the doors.

They found him inside looking astonished, staring at a screen suspended in mid air. The screen seemed to show a close-up picture of some bullet like red monstrosity out in space.

'For us to see that,' he pointed at the screen, 'from the ground, it would have to be enormous.'

'What are they saying?' inquired Claude, as he reached Portuk.

'That it suddenly appeared out of nowhere. It's nothing like we've ever seen before, I mean it's not a GF vessel.'

'Are they sure it's a vessel?' Manka added.

'They're calling it a vessel. Our attempts at probing it are being blocked, so we don't know if there is anyone on board. There's no response from the communication attempts. It's simply sitting there.'

'How big is it?' Claude asked.

'They say it's two kilometres long and a kilometre wide. Frankly, it doesn't look like a space going vessel. The red glow might be due to heat,' Portuk told him.

'Are you sure it's not GF?

'I know the profile of all the GF vessels. Take it from me...that's not GF,' Portuk insisted.

'Wherever it came from, it went through some pretty fierce friction, to end up glowing like that, I mean for its size,' Claude was speculating.

'Wait! The reporter on the screen is saying our long range detector array has it as entering *our galaxy* some time earlier from the direction of...*Andromeda!*' Portuk's mouth was open.

'Portuk! Are quiet *sure*?' Claude was staring at the screen, eyes wide.

'That's what they're saying.'

'Over two million light years away. *That monster has travelled more than two million light years*...no, that can't be right.' Claude looked aghast. Then as an afterthought he asked, 'I wonder how long they took?' Claude was gently scratching his head.

'The Galactic Federation has been trying for a number of centuries to make contact with our neighbouring Galaxy, Andromeda, but with no success. *Now* they've turned up on our doorstep? Why now? Why here? Why Barog?' Portuk was talking more to himself, than to his guests. Then he tried answering his own questions, 'How could they know we're the new HQ for the whole GF? It can't be an accident they chose Barog!'

'What kind of signature did this long-range detector array receive? How sure are we this ship, if it is one, is actually from Andromeda?' Claude was having a hard time with another *first contact,* but this time from another galaxy. Clearly, Claude was trying to find another more mundane explanation for the alien ship around Barog, and failing abysmally.

'If this really is from Andromeda, then all hell's going to break loose in this part of space. I must go to Radag, find out exactly what is going on,' Portuk looked at Claude.

'Radag is the capital of Barog,' Manka added by way of explanation.

'Yes, of course,' Claude agreed. 'When are you going?'

'Immediately. I'll teleport from here; stay at least a few hours, and be back by the evening. I'll fill you in when I get back.'

Portuk went over to Manka to say goodbye, and to reassure her. 'Claude, if you need to get in touch with your planet, Manka will show you where our communication equipment is. Help yourself.' Portuk then went out into the hall, and vanished.

'Manka, can I get through to Earth from here. I must find out how aware they are of what's happening here.' He turned to Anne-Marie, 'This event, if it is another first contact, will probably change our galaxy as much as Earth society was changed by the human first contact with the GF. I need to know what Earth knows, so I can then fill in the gaps from here.'

'This way,' Manka was saying. 'I'll take you to our communications room.'

Manka led Claude through three large rooms before they arrived at a door. She stopped and said something in Barogian. The door retracted into the ceiling. Inside, Claude found a pristine medium sized room filled with all sorts of elegant electronic equipment. There were a couple of seats facing a round console.

'Here, I'll show you how to activate the com-link to our deep space satellite, and if you know your Earth prefix codes, it will automatically connect you with Earth's Central Com System. It's all voice activated. I'll get our satellite to connect with Earth, then leave you to it if I may.' She uttered a string of sentences in Barogian to the console, waited a couple of minutes, then a human woman's face appeared on a screen. It was that simple. The human was saying, 'How can I help you.'

'This is Claude Joubert, Personal Assistant to President Ying. This is *urgent*. Patch me through to the President immediately. Interrupt everything; I'll take responsibility.'

'Yes sir,' and the face disappeared for a second, then was replaced by Ying. He was in his office, saying something to someone out of the line of sight.

'Claude, what's up? I'm in a meeting at the moment. What's so urgent?'

'Have you heard the news yet?' Claude began.

'What news?' Ying was polite but brusque.

'Then you don't know? I'm still on Barog...and all hell's broken loose here. A huge spaceship has arrived from Andromeda. I unequivocally suggest you personally make provisions to come here as soon as possible. Bring the President of Mars with you. Don't take long...within the next day or so,' Claude said a little excitedly.

'Did you say *Andromeda*? *Are you sure?* When did it arrive?' Ying looked flabbergasted.

'Sometime this morning I think, local time. Now it's just sitting there, orbiting the planet. I think it's cooling off. The Barog authorities have tried to communicate with it, but to no avail. The probes are being deflected.'

'Claude, I want you to stay there and report back....' and the line went dead. *Damn this.* Claude called for Manka, who arrived after a little while with Anne-Marie in tow.

'This line has just gone dead and I can't read the message on the screen,' he said with frustration in his voice.

'It says there is a com-overload, and they're trying to fix it. Please wait, normal services will be resumed shortly,' Manka translated.

'The whole galaxy is probably trying to get through to Barog right now,' Claude mumbled. He turned to Manka, 'Any word from Portuk?'

'Not yet! Shall we go and have a little breakfast. What with all this fuss, I haven't eaten yet,' and she led the way out of the com-room.

After they had eaten, Claude tried the com-room again. He got through to Ying, who guessed the lines were full. His office was now full of people.

Ying told Claude, 'Stay close to the com-link, you're being given top priority on the line.'

A technical com-expert interrupted and told him how to patch this link to his personal earpiece.

Claude had left his earpiece in the bedroom, still in his luggage, hoping to get a rest from it. Now he hurriedly sent Anne-Marie to get both his and hers.

'Look Claude,' Ying was saying, 'Once the permanent voice link with Earth has been established, you're to report on the situation every hour, or sooner if anything breaks.'

'Yes, good idea,' agreed Claude.

'Either myself or my deputy will arrive on Barog as soon as we can manage it,' Ying told him. 'We'll bring Mars with us. In the mean time, maybe you could visit the capital city...Radag isn't it? See if there's anything developing. If possible get in to see Grand Custodian Potong.'

Ying would get through to Barog and Rakh from their end; see what the official line was.

For two whole days the massive vessel hung in Barogian space, neither contacting, nor allowing contact. Portuk came back more perplexed than ever. 'Why won't they talk to us? How can they just sit there having come all this way?'

Life in the mansion continued, but always with one thought on everybody's mind. When will the ship break silence? They went out each morning on the *Zetters*. Manka showed them the waterfall she was so fond of. The problem was, the intrusive red spot just hung there in the sky, dominating any conversation. It could not be avoided.

In the evenings, the foursome had long discussions on the implications of the visit, the possible effects on their lives from this first contact. Claude told them of the impact on human civilisation from *their* first contact. Barog had only been in the GF for some two hundred years, and their experiences were still fresh.

But Barog's experiences were also a window into Earth's future, a future that seemed to be quiet bright if

Barog's example was anything to go by. After all, they had just had their Primus elected as the new Grand Custodian and Barog was now the HQ for the whole of the GF.

Ying kept in constant touch with Claude, his man on the spot, demanding news, and getting equally bewildered by the lack of it. He was enroute to Barog, after being delayed by the aftershock. It seems the whole galaxy was converging on Barog. The previous Grand Custodian K'Rel was on his way, as was Quadrant Custodian Thesor, together with the other two Quadrant Custodians from Zyneer and Grafhi.

Portuk informed Claude a couple of military StarCarriers were expected. They would be kept discreetly out of sight, so the enormous carriers didn't appear threatening, but were there if needed. The problem was the enormous StarCarriers were small compared to the visiting vessel.

Then on the third day, there appeared magnificent gigantic laser hologram pictures transmitted across the Barogian sky. Pictures of the evolution of life on a number of planets in the Andromeda system, from microbes to aquatic life forms, to land reptiles, to a type of dinosaurs, then to a dinosauroid civilisation, suggesting convergent evolution was universal. Then through its industrial revolution, through flight, electronics, space flight, through to a galaxy wide civilisation of advanced stage. Various exotic species were shown gathering to form a galaxy wide government, and their version of the Grand Custodian was a tall spindly ethereal creature.

Then came unmistakable pictures of the Milky Way Galaxy, and the neighbouring Andromeda Galaxy. More pictures of a ship, the immense bullet shaped ship, leaving Andromeda and arriving here in the Milky Way, at Barog. What had baffled the authorities and all the onlookers was, there didn't seem to be any type of engine on the immense ship. The stern end was smooth and flat, and looked like any other part of the ship, made of what seemed like dark grey metal, or something.

Whilst the picture show was in progress, hundreds of spaceships were gathering in Barogian space. Dignitaries from all ends of the galaxy arrived, and beamed down to Radag, a cosmopolitan city filled with every type of species.

Claude had gone with Portuk on a visit, and they found themselves in a bustling metropolis, to Portuk's utter disgust.

'It's like a galactic market place,' he commented disparagingly.

Ying arrived with a small retinue, on Ryan's ship and all were invited to stay at Portuk's mansion. Apparently, the World Government had decided not to disclose the emerging news to the human population of the Solar System, after consultation with Mars of course. The news leaked out anyway, and everyone stayed calm. The humans were maturing rapidly. Earth's population was behaving more like the adults they aspired to be.

The picture show lasted until the third day, and then ceased. It ended with scenes of five beings rematerialising in the main plaza in Radag, just outside the Barogian Congress building. Grand Custodian Potong, flanked by the other three Quadrant Custodians gathered in the cordoned off plaza on the afternoon of the third day, in anticipation of the arrival of the Andromeda delegation.

At around the middle of the afternoon, five figures rematerialised in a pentagonal formation facing outwards. Those that had appendages, were extended showing they had nothing in them. There was a tall yellow dinosauroid who stood a good meter above his green skinned cousin, and seemed more fragile in appearance, with an aura of yellow energy seemingly surrounding it.

There was a meter wide ball of greenish energy hanging a meter off the ground at the second point of the pentagon. On the third point of the pentagon stood a figure almost human in appearance, two meters tall, looking somewhat purplish in colour. The fourth corner was occupied by squat brown ball of something, with short tentacles extending from every part of it; it had four black eyes on stalks rising twenty centimetres, reaching towards the sky. Finally, there was a two-meter tall spindly ethereal creature who behaved as their leader. They were oblivious of the Barogian atmosphere, and maybe the light being emitted from all five was some form of protective energy shield.

Greetings were presented by the Grand Custodian to the travellers from our neighbouring galaxy. The tall spindly ethereal creature responded in kind. Seats, couches and other form of furniture had been carefully arranged in the plaza, to accommodate the gathered delegates. A holo picture of the Milky Way galaxy was displayed side by side with a holo picture of the larger Andromeda spiral galaxy.

Amongst the mass of welcoming delegates, Portuk, Manka, Claude and Anne-Marie stood in one tight group. Close by stood Ying with Simeon Boutros Ghali and his son Theodore next to him. Basil Dukas stood behind his President, arriving with Alexius in tow. A small entourage stood discreetly behind Ying. On the other side of Ying was Taras Fisenko who had brought Sandy with him. Ryan had Kochanowski by his side and stood talking with Heidi.

Green carpeting was everywhere. Portuk whispered they must have resolved the communication problem, since both visitor and host seemed to be understanding each other, probably through some form of discreet interpreting device. The ceremony had got under way and would no doubt last some time.

For a moment as he turned his attention from Heidi to the visitors, Ryan's thoughts were on something other than ceremonies. He had in mind the huge recent changes that had transformed him from a mere Captain to an Admiral, the enormous upheavals the human race had only just undergone. He felt a great responsibility had landed on his shoulders and he would have to live up to them.

Now, there was this intergalactic vessel orbiting above them. Ryan wondered what it would be like to be the Captain of such a ship, make the first human voyage to another galaxy. The human thirst for the unknown, for exploration, had firmly reasserted itself in the spacefarer's imagination. He would have to talk to Ying Li about getting n board such a ship.

Epilogue

Thus it was, as the fourth millennium got under way, the human race was brought face to face with its long anticipated *first contact* with an alien species. It forced the previously isolated humans to grow up as a civilisation, requiring it to make a mental shift in their paradigm of what constituted intelligent life.

The human race had only *just* acclimatised to *their* first contact of a few years ago. Now, it seemed; the adjustments would have to start all over again. More unfamiliar transformations, more exotic encounters, although they had not fully yet assimilated their own first contact. They would want to comfort themselves in hoping it would be somehow easier the second time round. It never was.

Now the whole Galactic Federation would have to join in re-appraising and readjusting to the idea of a first contact. No longer could the Galactic Federation control the destiny of their domain in isolation. They would have to share its future with its neighbouring galaxy Andromeda. Did Andromeda have contacts with other galaxies? Life could never be the same again for anyone, but change spices life up like no other drug.

End

Murder in Hattusas

Sasha Garrydeb

This is the first volume of the Hittite Trilogy. At the close of the Old Kingdom in 1420 BC, the realm of the ancient Hittite Empire is in chaos. Muwatallis, the king has been assassinated in the capital, Hattusas, by the feared Kaska Assassin's Guild. Muwas, the dead king's brother blames the two sons of the previous king, Huzziyas, and he insists he be the one to succeed his brother. The two sons of Huzziyas, Kantuzzili and Himuili, insist the next king be Tudhaliyas, son of Himuili, since rewarding Muwatallis' previous assassination of Huzziyas, is unthinkable. Neither side is prepared to give way, and the scene is set for civil war. Tagrama, the High Priest of the temple of the Storm God Taru, tries to broker a peace, but is up against outright stubbornness.

Muwas then hires Harep, of the same Assassin's Guild, to kill Tudhaliyas. Only Mokhat, the former spiritual adviser to the Assassin's Guild, knows what Harep looks like, and he is determined to stop all the damnable assassinations. He's had enough of the Guild's murdering ways.

Muwas calls upon his Mittani allies, the Mittani King Saustatar, who sends his son Artatama with an army to Muwas' aid. The Kizzuwatna King Shunashura changes allegiance and abandons the Mittani in favour of Kantuzzili's faction, sending an army to help Tudhaliyas. The Pharaoh Amenhotep II threatens to invade Mittani unless they pull their army out of Hatti. Saustatar refuses.

When Tudhaliyas meets Nikal, he falls for this daughter of the Kizzuwatna king. They announce their engagement. Harep, the hired assassin, makes a number of attempts on Tudhaliyas' life, but is foiled. The major Battle of the Wide Plateau settles the civil war but in the mean time, Harap manages to kidnap Nikal.

The protagonist, Mokhat, is in search of himself after his sordid ministrations to a bunch of murderers. It is a bronze-age thriller, which includes a romp through the Hittite landscape, a civil war, and chariots in battle. This is a tale of love and adventure set in the most fascinating recently discovered culture of the ancient world. 2nd Volume of this trilogy is due out Easter 2011.

A must for all fans of the Hittite civilisation. Volume 3 is scheduled to be published in 2012.

Madduwatta's Rebellion

Sasha Garrydeb

This is the 2nd Volume of the Hittite trilogy. It is now three years since the Battle of the Plateau (Vol 1—Murder in Hattusas) put Tudhaliyas on the throne in the realm of the ancient Hittite Empire, yet instead of feeling secure, he feels menaced. His chief spy, Satipilli, has vanished, and trouble is brewing in the west, possibly from Ahhiyawa. The Mittani are threatening Ishuwa in the east. All this needs reliable intelligence reports. Tudhaliyas turns to the unknown faces of Mokhat and Palaiyas and asks them to go to Millawanda and discover the truth.

At the close of the Old Kingdom in 1417 BC Madduwatta, the Governor of Lukka, a nominal vassal of Tudhaliyas, has plans of his own. He wants to be a King in his own right and will use any means to achieve that. He has his eyes on Arzawa. He badly needs friends, and will ally himself with anyone prepared to help him achieve his goal. But who has stirred him up? Who has gone to these lengths to create a rebellion for the Hittites?

Meanwhile, Ahhiyawa is in the grip of Civil War, with two brothers fighting it out for the throne in Millawanda. The outcome of the war will impact on their neighbours, Arzawa, the Hittites, *and* Lukka.

From Milllawanda, Palaiyas, a Prince of Tiryns, decides to cross the water and go home to make peace with his father, the king. While in Tiryns, he's arrested by his uncle, the Mycenaean Wanax (king), taken to Mycenae to account for his desertion, and then forced to complete his tour of duty on Keftiu (Crete). Mokhat follows to rescue him and they end up in Khemet (Egypt), then Ugarit, then Lukka and back to Ivalanda, all in an effort to stay alive and search for Satipilli. Someone keeps trying to kill them, and with each failure, their attempts become more desperate. Somebody doesn't want them to complete their mission.

Volume 3 is scheduled to be published in 2012. A must for all fans of the Hittite civilisation.

ᘓһe Wizard of Kalar

Sasha Garrydeb

On the distant planet of Kalár the two hundred year old life cycle of the Schánda once again menace the idyllic lives of the Boláni, a small tribal village of forest dwellers living in their hollowed Lándo trees.

The schánda stand half a cubit high, have a two hundred year life-cycle and normally live up on the northern edges of the tundra of the planet of Kálar. They are an insect, something like a cross between a spider and a scorpion. The adult form has no poisonous stinger and isn't carnivorous. Then the mating urge mutates the schánda into a massive swarm of ferocious carnivores. It doubles in size, grows the stinger and large claws in its fourth and final moult, then begins its long march from its home-ground in the North of Kálar, south to its mating grounds on the shores of the Golden Sea.

In its path live the small peaceful Bólani tribe who make their homes in living Lándo trees in the forest. Around the same time as the schánda begin their journey, the Bólani's collective unconscious, an imbedded memory of these carnivorous insects, triggers nightmares. They dream of an unstoppable carnivorous procession intent on eating their way to their mating grounds, heading their way.

The Bólani must gather their possessions and flee ahead of the encroaching swarm. They escape south to the shores of the Golden Sea just ahead of the voracious insects. Their long march to the shores of the Golden Sea takes them through a series of adventures with small blood sucking insects, vicious storms, predatory birds, unfriendly villages, lakes of volcanic lava, and desert worms. Only the skill of their apprentice wizard, Morác, saves them from disaster—transforming his powers in the process. Even when they reach the Golden Sea their problems are not at an end. Imprisoned by a coastal tribe and then buffeted by storms on their flimsy rafts the dynamics of the tribe are changed forever before they finally manage to return to their small forest village back up in the far North.

This is an eco-fantasy tale stretching the imagination beyond the solar system.